THE GREAT ESCAPE

Fiona Gibson is an author and journalist who has written for many UK publications including the *Observer*, the *Guardian, Red* and *Marie Claire*. She also writes a monthly column for Sainsbury's magazine.

Fiona lives in Scotland with her husband, their twin sons and daughter. She likes to run, draw, walk the dog, play her sax, watch cheesy movies and lie in a bubble bath with the door firmly locked. To find out more, visit www.fionagibson.com.

By the same author:

Babyface
Wonderboy
Lucky Girl
Mummy Said the F-word
Mum On The Run

FIONA GIBSON

The Great Escape

AVON

This novel is entirely a work of fiction.
The names, characters and incidents portrayed in it are
the work of the author's imagination. Any resemblance to
actual persons, living or dead, events or localities is
entirely coincidental.

AVON
A division of HarperCollins*Publishers*
1 London Bridge Street
London SE1 9GF

www.harpercollins.co.uk

A Paperback Original 2012
14
First published in Great Britain by
HarperCollins*Publishers* 2012

A catalogue record for this book is
available from the British Library

ISBN-13: 978-1-84756-260-9

Set in Sabon by Palimpsest Book Production Ltd,
Falkirk, Stirlingshire

Printed and bound by
CPI Group (UK) Ltd, Croydon CR0 4YY

MIX
Paper from
responsible sources
FSC™ C007454

Enormous thanks to Caroline Sheldon and Bryony Woods, and to Sammia Rafique and the super-talented team at Avon. Thanks to Margery and Keith for unfailing support, and to my lovely friends Jen, Kath, Cathy, Michelle, Marie, Cheryl, Carolann and Fliss for always being there. Every two weeks, I get together with Tania, Vicki, Amanda, Sam and Hilary – I'm lucky to belong to such a brilliant, boosting writing group. Above all, a million thanks to my wonderful family. Jimmy, Sam, Dex and Erin – I love you more than words can say.

For the fabulous Dolphinton writers

ONE

Garnet Street, Glasgow, 1998

'*Tadaaa*! All hail the party buffet . . .' With a flourish, despite the fact that she's alone in the kitchen, Hannah sets out three bowls on the worktop. She's wearing an outsized white T-shirt, sipping beer from a bottle and pretending to be hosting a TV cookery show. 'Here on the left, we have sumptuous tortilla chips, chilli flavour, the ones with red dust on . . . moving along, we have dry-roasted peanuts and this, the *pièce de résistance*, is my very own dip, which you can whip together in just a few minutes with some beans, garlic and, er . . .' She swigs her beer, and detecting a garlicky whiff on her fingers, tries to remember what the other stuff was.

'Ugh, has someone been sick?'

Hannah's flatmate, Lou, has appeared at her shoulder, her freshly washed hair dripping rivulets down her cheeks.

'It's our buffet,' Hannah explains with exaggerated patience. 'Come on, you're supposed to be impressed. I've finally managed to cook something before I leave. You should be in *awe*.'

'I don't think that counts as cooking.' Lou winces as if Hannah might have scraped the stuff in the bowl off the pavement.

'Well, I was going to make hummus but we didn't have chickpeas, so I mashed up those butter beans instead.'

'It looks ill. Kind of . . . beige.'

'It'll be fine once everyone's had a few drinks,' Hannah insists, mopping up a smear from the worktop.

Lou smirks. 'Han, those butter beans have been in the cupboard since we moved in. Three years they've been sitting there. Your parents brought them in your emergency rations box, remember?'

'Isn't that the whole point of canning? They find tins at the bottom of the sea that have rolled out of shipwrecks, and when they open them they're perfectly fine. These things just don't go off.'

Now Sadie appears, swathed in a silky robe, dark hair pinned up with an assortment of clips. She peers at the dip from a safe distance. 'Is that all we've got to eat?'

'Well,' Hannah says, 'I was thinking of knocking up a banquet, wild boar on a spit, ice sculptures and all that, but . . .' She checks her watch. 'I kind of ran out of time.'

'How late is it?' Sadie asks.

'Just gone seven . . .'

'Hell . . .' In a flash of red silk, Sadie flies out of the kitchen to the bathroom where she turns on the juddering tap (the tank only holds a bath-and-a-half's worth of hot water, so the three girls are accustomed to a water-sharing system that requires a frequently flaunted no-clipping-of-toenails rule). Hannah glances down at the dip. Oh well, she thinks as Lou drifts back to her room, it'll do for filling in that crack in the bathroom wall. It can be her parting gift to the flat.

Hannah doesn't want to think of tonight as an end-of-era party. It's a celebration, that's what it is: of four years at art school, three spent living with Sadie and Lou on the first floor of a red sandstone tenement block perched on a perilously steep hill around the corner from college. *Funny*, she reflects, how a place so distinctly unlovely, with its mould-speckled bathroom and grumbling pipes, can feel like the most palatial abode when you're about to leave it. It's like getting a haircut. You can hate your hair, absolutely despise it to the point of wearing a hat at all times. Then, as you trot off to the salon, you glimpse your reflection in a shop window and think, actually, it looks great.

She wanders into the living room. It's oppressively orange, thanks to the embossed patterned wallpaper which the girls' landlord had said they were welcome to remove – as if three art students would be likely to get around to stripping it off and redecorating. Anyway, orange isn't ugly, Hannah thinks now – it's warm and cosy. Her beanbag, too, looks strangely lovely, even though it has long lost its squishiness and now resembles a large cowpat in brown corduroy. There were two beanbags originally; the other burst mysteriously at a previous party, disgorging its beany contents all over the floor. Johnny from the upstairs flat had accompanied Hannah to buy them from a closing-down sale. He'd insisted on carrying both beanbags – unwrapped, clutched in front of his body – with the sole purpose of pretending they were unfeasibly large testicles.

Hannah looks around the room, taking in the dog-eared magazines on the shelves, the film and exhibition posters fraying at the edges on the walls. A rush of panic engulfs her as she tries to imagine no Sadie, no Lou, no Johnny; no orangey living room to hang out in late into the night, no kitchen table to congregate around over breakfast. *Don't be maudlin*, she tells herself firmly. *This was never supposed to be forever. You've got a new job, a new life and it'll be fantastic* . . . At the sound of running water, Hannah makes for the bathroom and raps on the door. 'Sadie, you nearly finished in there?'

'Yeah, won't be a minute . . .'

'Hurry up, it's nearly half seven . . .'

3

'God, sorry, didn't realise . . .' There's a squeak as Sadie's wet feet hit the glittery lino. She emerges from the bathroom, damp dark hair tumbling around the shoulders of her robe. Her toenails are painted fuchsia, her dark brows arched dramatically against her creamy skin. Sexy Sadie, the boys call her, although Sadie is blasé about her allure, a combination of Italian colouring and sensational curves. Catching Hannah's eye, she pauses in the hallway.

'You okay, Han? Feeling a bit wobbly about tonight?'

Hannah shakes her head firmly. 'I'm fine, honestly.'

'Just wondered,' Sadie adds gently, 'with this being our last party, end of an era and all that . . .'

Hannah musters a wide smile. 'Yeah. Don't remind me.' Her eyes moisten, but she quickly blinks away the tears. 'Anyway, better make myself look presentable. We've still got to sort out the music *and* I've got to get this garlicky stink off my hands . . .'

'I'll do the music. You go and beautify yourself.'

'Okay. And look, I know you might find it hard to control yourself, but keep your fingers out of that butter bean dip, okay?' With that, Hannah strides into the bathroom, dropping her T-shirt and underwear onto the floor where they lie next to Lou and Sadie's discarded clothing. Sadie's red fluffy mules have been kicked off by the washbasin; Lou's beaded Indian slippers are neatly paired up by the door. Hannah sinks into the lukewarm water, detecting a prickle of toenail at the base of her spine. Shifting up onto her knees, she fits the pink plastic hose over the taps and lets the water pour over her wavy fair hair. It's shudderingly cold at first, then come the gurgles as the last dregs of hot water splutter through.

She can hear Lou singing through the thin bathroom wall. Hannah knows she's probably trying on dress after dress in those weeny vintage sizes that only someone with her doll-sized proportions could ever hope to squeeze into.

4

Hannah is more athletically built, with taut, defined calves from cycling furiously around Glasgow's hilly streets. Will London be like that? Will it be possible to cycle to work without getting flattened under a bus? She hasn't even figured out her work route yet. Archway to Islington isn't that far, apparently, but how will she get from one page of the *A-Z* to another whilst riding her bike? Hannah doesn't want to look like a tourist, peering at maps. She wants to be a proper, breezy London girl who *belongs*.

Her stomach whirls as she turns off the hose. She's always anxious before a party and this one matters more than most. Drying herself with a towel that has all the softness of a road surface, she can hardly believe she's leaving. She'll miss those hungover breakfasts of bendy white toast and Philadelphia cheese. She'll miss all of them piling into Johnny's battered pillarbox-red Beetle and planning numerous jaunts to Loch Lomond, but never quite making it because there was always some party to go to instead. She'll miss whiling away entire afternoons in Puccini's, the best Italian café in Glasgow. The thought of those ordinary things no longer being part of her life triggers an ache in her gut. Hannah can't cry, though. Not now.

Glimpsing her wide blue eyes in the tarnished bathroom mirror, she wills herself not to lose it tonight. She's a grown-up now – no longer a student, but a real woman with a job waiting for her, *and* a flat, albeit with the dimensions of a Shreddies box. And she's not planning to ruin her last night here by being a blubbering wreck.

TWO

'Lighten up, Lou-Lou. Hannah's not dying, she's only going to London.' Spike, Lou's boyfriend, rolls his eyes and looks up at the multicoloured plastic chandelier in mock exasperation.

'You don't understand,' Lou retorts. 'It's a *huge* deal actually.'

Hannah moves away and grabs her glass from the top of a speaker. For the past five hours she's been as bright and bouncy as it's possible to be, and now she's flagging a little. London, she keeps thinking. By this time tomorrow, I'll be tucked up in bed in *London*. Hannah has only been there twice – the first time was on a mini-break with her parents when she was ten years old. All she can remember are monkeys hurling themselves around in their zoo enclosure, and her parents taking zillions of pictures of Big Ben while she tried to understand what was so thrilling about an enormous clock. You don't get that in a tiny Fife fishing village, she'd concluded.

On her second London trip, six weeks ago now, Hannah had travelled down alone on an overnight coach to meet her new colleagues (the very word thrills her) at Catfish, the small design company that offered her a job as an in-house illustrator after her final degree show. Her new boss, Michael, put her in touch with a property-letting agency, where a Japanese girl who looked about fifteen took her to see a studio flat in Archway. 'See, it's all freshly decorated, perfect for someone like you who's starting out,' the girl enthused.

Starting out. That's it, Hannah decides. It's a new chapter, waiting for her to dive right in. Right now, though, of more immediate concern is the fact that there doesn't appear to be a drop of alcohol left in the flat. Someone hands Spike a drink, and he's appalled to discover it's plain lemonade.

'What's *this*?' he cries, in a voice that suggests they're trying to poison him.

'He's such an arse sometimes,' Lou mutters, sidling up to Hannah.

'You love him really,' Hannah teases.

'Do I? Sometimes I don't know. Sometimes, and I know this sounds awful and I really shouldn't say it, but . . .'

'What?'

'I wish I was you. God, Han, I do love him, he's great, but it feels so scary now, having no lectures to go to, no structure, no nothing. It's just me. Me and Spike.'

'Hey, you.' Hannah pulls in Lou for a hug. 'You'll be fine. We all will. Anyway, as soon as I'm sorted, you and Sadie are coming down to visit and maybe you'll move too . . .'

'*He* won't,' Lou says dryly.

'Well, maybe he will.' Hannah hesitates, then takes Lou by the hand and leads her to the beanbag where they both flop down. 'Anyway,' she adds, 'it's really about what *you* want, isn't it?'

Lou nods mutely. Sadie is dancing in front of them, her outrageous curves encased in a black Lycra dress. It's gone 3 am and around twenty people are still here, mostly dancing, some kissing in corners. It's a warm June night, and Hannah hasn't kissed anyone – at least not properly – since their New Year party, which Lou and Sadie regard as a serious snog drought. It's better this way, Hannah decides now, spotting Johnny locked in conversation with his new girlfriend Rona. Being ensconced in a relationship, like Lou is with Spike, would just be too complicated.

'Dancing, Han?' Having managed to detach himself from Rona, Johnny has appeared in front of her, all gangly limbs and dark Irish eyes and clothes that always look a shade too big for him.

Hannah laughs and shakes her head. 'I'm knackered, Johnny. Completely done in. I'm having a little sabbatical here.'

'Oh c'mon, lightweight.' He bobs down and grabs her hand.

'I've been dancing for hours!' she protests.

He cocks his head to one side. 'Come on, Han. Last chance.'

Grinning, she allows him to pull her up to her feet. She dances, conscious of Rona watching her intently, as if she might be planning to kidnap Johnny, stuff him into one of her crates and whisk him off to her studio flat in Archway. 'I'm dying of thirst,' she announces as the song finishes.

'There's definitely nothing left to drink,' announces Sadie, glossy red lipstick somewhat smeared.

'We must have *something*,' Hannah declares, heading for the kitchen as Rona reclaims Johnny with a sharp tug of his arm.

'Spike saves the day!' Spike announces, brandishing a bottle of red wine like a trophy.

'Where d'you find that?' Hannah asks.

'Ah, well . . .' He taps the side of his nose. 'It was hiding at the back of your cupboard behind Lou's bird food cereal.'

'Spike, you can't drink that!' Lou shrieks from the doorway.

'Why not?' He grips the bottle to his chest as if someone might try to wrestle it from him.

'My parents gave it to me the day I left home. It's to stay unopened for fifteen years – that's why it was hidden – and then it'll be worth a *fortune*.'

'Fifteen years?' Spike looks bereft. 'How can anyone be expected to wait that long for a drink?'

'Mum and Dad'll go crazy,' Lou laments. 'God, Spike, you'll have to jam the cork back in. Quick, before air gets in and ruins it . . .'

'Jeez . . .' Spike rakes a hand through his hair. 'Sorry, Lou-Lou. I just thought, seeing as it's still early . . .'

Lou pauses, then her small, dainty face erupts into a grin. 'You honestly think my parents would trust me to keep a bottle of wine for fifteen years? It's just ordinary stuff we must have forgotten about. Come on, get it open.' Obediently, and clearly relieved, Spike pours a glass.

'You're not actually planning to drink that, are you?' Rona has wandered into the kitchen, and is gripping Johnny's hand firmly.

Spike raises his glass unsteadily. 'Yeah. Why not?'

'Because it's disgusting. It's got *bits* in it. Look.' Rona steps forward – she's all bones and sharp edges, Hannah decides – and prods his glass with a burgundy fingernail.

Spike peers at it. 'Right. Well, they're probably just bits of grape, and fruit's good for you, isn't it . . .'

'. . . says Glasgow's top wine connoisseur,' someone quips.

'No one would drink that unless they had some kind of problem,' Rona retorts, glaring at Johnny as if expecting him to agree.

'The only problem Spike's got,' he chuckles, 'is how to strain out the bits.'

Spike frowns as if faced with a tough mathematical equation. 'Yeah, you're right. What can we use?'

'A colander?' someone suggests.

'I know.' Spike brightens. 'Get me some tights, Lou. Clean ones, not fishnet, and not grubby old things out of your linen basket either . . .'

'What for?'

'Straining. Rona's right – there are bits floating about in it. God knows, you girls keep a terrible wine cellar.'

Giggling, Lou rushes off to her room, returning with a pair of black tights, which Spike carefully stretches over a stripey milk jug so a leg dangles down at each side. He pours out the contents of his glass, and then the rest of the wine from the bottle into the gusset. Filtration complete, he removes Lou's wine-sodden hosiery from the jug and shares out the wine. A disgusted Rona clip-clops back to the living room.

Someone has turned the music down, and a sense of quiet – or, perhaps, hushed respect for Spike's ingenuity – settles over the group. 'Where did you learn to do that, Spike?' asks Sadie.

'Boy scouts,' he sniggers, 'although there wasn't a badge for it, sadly.'

With a smile, Hannah sips from her glass and lets her gaze skim over her favourite people in the whole world:

Lou, a talented jeweller, who, despite the odd flash of exasperation, is bonkers in love with the most flirtatious man in Glasgow (even now, with Lou in the room, Spike is sneaking quick glances at some friend of a friend with a long blonde plait coiled ingeniously on top of her head).

Sadie, the half-Italian beauty, who's already had orders for her sensational hand-printed corsets, and on whom pretty much every boy in their year has nurtured an ill-disguised crush.

Johnny from upstairs, a catering student, virtually their fourth flatmate and provider of emergency rations ever since, one bleak winter's night, he popped down to find the girls stony broke, trying to pretend that Weetabix and lime marmalade constituted a perfectly well-balanced meal. Johnny, whose new girlfriend is, although icily beautiful, a most *unsuitable* choice.

Hannah knows, too, that Johnny's love life is none of her business, especially now, when she's leaving. Feeling her stomach tighten, she glances again at Sadie and Lou who catch the look on her face, and who at once wrap their arms tightly around her. 'Don't forget us, will you?' Sadie murmurs.

'Are you mad? Of course I won't . . .' Then, as Rona comes in search of her fake alligator bag which someone must have 'stolen' – she finds it wedged behind the kitchen door – Johnny grabs Hannah by the arm and says, 'Great party, Han. The best.'

'Thanks, Johnny.' She blinks, not knowing what else to say.

He meets her gaze, and she's surprised by the flicker of sadness she sees in his eyes. 'A new start, isn't it?' he adds.

'Guess so. It's bloody terrifying, though . . .'

'Yeah, I know what you mean,' he mutters.

Hannah frowns. 'What, London?'

He glances around the girls' devastated kitchen. 'Um . . . yeah. Sort of.'

'Johnny?' says Rona sharply. 'You ready to go now? I've got a pounding headache.'

'Yep, just coming.' He smiles stoically. 'So you're off tomorrow?'

Hannah nods. 'Mum and Dad are coming with the van at eleven. The way Dad drives, it should only take us about three weeks to get to London.'

Johnny laughs. 'Bye, then, Han.'

'Bye, Johnny.' They pause, and he hugs her before Rona takes his hand and leads him to the door.

The final stragglers leave amidst drunken good-lucks,

and Spike totters unsteadily towards Lou's bedroom, a smear of pink, which doesn't match Lou's lipstick, on his cheek. 'My God,' Lou breathes, taking in the nuts and tortilla chips crunched into the cork-tiled floor, the gigantic pub ashtray piled high with butts and the table crammed with smeared glasses and empty bottles. 'We really should make a start on this.'

Hannah nods wearily. 'Yeah, let's do it now.'

'No,' Sadie declares, 'not on your last night. Me and Lou will do it tomorrow after you've gone.'

'But I can't leave you with this!'

''Course you can,' Lou cuts in. 'It'll keep us busy – stop us pining for you, sobbing into your beanbag.'

'Well, if you insist . . .' Suddenly, Hannah's attention is caught by a tissue-wrapped bottle nestling between the bread bin and the microwave. 'Look, someone's left this.' Frowning, she examines the gift tag attached to its neck and rips off the wrapping. 'It's from Johnny. Oh, that's sweet of him. Look, there's something else too.' As Sadie wrestles out the cork, and Lou grabs three plastic cups, Hannah peels the lid from a faded Tupperware box. GIRLS – FOR YOUR LAST BREAKFAST TOGETHER MAYBE? J x is written neatly across it in felt-tip. It's an apple tart, the segments fanning out in circles beneath a golden glaze. Hannah smiles, snaps off a fragment of pastry and lets it dissolve on her tongue.

There's a card, too, propped up against the bread bin. She studies Johnny's old-fashioned forward-sloping writing on the envelope and rips it open. The card depicts a wobbly line drawing of Glasgow, with the famous buildings all jammed in together, jostling for space. *Dear Han*, it reads, *So you're off! We're all going to miss you like mad, you know. What's going to become of us? Who knows? And we'll definitely miss your cooking! Haha. But we'll be okay as long as you remember us and wear a bloody bike helmet in London. That's an absolute order, and I've alerted the police to keep an eye on you too. Love, J.*

'Oh, Johnny,' Hannah murmurs as Sadie fills the cups with tepid champagne. Raising hers to her lips, she wipes away the hot tears that have sprung to her eyes. 'I'd like to make a speech,' she says.

'Speech! Speech!' cry Sadie and Lou.

Hannah takes a deep breath. 'I just want to say . . . I love both of you and we're never going to lose touch, okay?' She pauses as her friends murmur their agreement, then adds, 'And there's another thing.'

'What?' Sadie asks.

'Johnny's apple tart. I don't think I can wait till breakfast, can you?'

THREE

The morning after

As Hannah and her parents trundle down the M6 in a hired van, Lou heads back upstairs, breathless and grubby from lugging a third black sack to the wheelie bin outside. 'Oh, hi,' she exclaims. Johnny is sitting at the kitchen table, studying Hannah's butter bean dip into which someone has extinguished a cigarette.

'That's horrible, that.' He looks up and smiles. 'It's an absolute crime against humanity. It looked so tempting as well.'

'Ha. Yeah, disgusting. God knows who did that. Spike, probably. How old is he again?' Johnny looks at her blankly. 'Thirty-five,' Lou reminds him. 'I'm going out with a thirty-five-year-old man who still can't use an ashtray because so many other things will do instead.'

Johnny smirks. 'Where is he anyway?'

'Went back to bed for more beauty sleep.' Lou pulls a wry smile. 'So has Sadie, lazy sods.' She laughs, suddenly conscious of her limp, hungover hair and shiny face flecked with the remnants of last night's mascara. She's still in her pyjamas too – embarrassing ancient fleecy ones, not like the posh silk ensemble Sadie wears. Thank God she's flung a sweater over her top. 'Thanks for the apple tart,' she adds. 'That was very sweet of you. I'd have saved you some but we scarfed it all down last night.'

'No problem. It was my first attempt, thought you could give me your verdict. So, left you with all the clearing up, have they?'

Lou grins. 'Oh, Spike managed to pick up a beer bottle and rinse out my wine-strainer tights.' She perches on the opposite chair. 'Are you okay? Feeling a bit fragile?'

'Er, guess so.' He looks it, Lou thinks; not mildly poisoned, as Spike currently is, flat on his back in her bed with a saucer-cum-ashtray perched beside it, fag ends piled up like a mini Mount Etna. Johnny's is a different kind of malaise altogether.

He looks up at Lou, and it fazes her, the way he regards her so intently. She gets up and rinses out the Tupperware box. No one knows – not even Hannah or Sadie – how she really feels about Johnny. She hasn't said anything because he's a friend to *all* of them, a flatmate really, separated only by one floor. Admitting that she's nurtured a crush on him this past year, since Spike's less endearing qualities came to the fore, would upset the balance and change everything. Anyway, she has Spike and Johnny has Rona. Spike might be annoying but he's lived a life that Lou still finds fascinating, *and* he adores her. Lou has never been so completely adored by a boy – well, a *man*, Spike is thirteen years older than her. She looks forward to the moment when her Johnny-crush suddenly clicks off, as if by a switch.

'D'you want an Alka-Seltzer?' she asks to break the awkward hush. 'Or something to eat? I might be able to rustle up a bagel if you're lucky . . .'

He exhales. 'No thanks. I'm not hung over, Lou. I hardly had anything to drink last night.' There's another pause, broken by Spike launching into a coughing fit in Lou's bedroom. 'Listen,' Johnny adds. 'I'm . . . I'm not supposed

15

to tell anyone this. Rona'll kill me if she finds out because she's not ready to—'

'What?' Lou murmurs, frowning.

'She . . . Rona's pregnant.'

'Oh God, Johnny.' No, that's not right. He might be delighted – perhaps they even planned it – and he's just a bit shell-shocked and hasn't quite taken it in. Lou sits on the chair beside him and tries to settle her face into a neutral expression. Johnny doesn't look delighted, though. He looks like someone whose life has spun out of control.

'We found out a few days ago,' he adds dully.

'So it's still early?'

Johnny nods.

'Um . . . what d'you think you'll do?' There are soft footsteps in the hall, then extravagant splashing as Spike pees into the loo, followed by a clanking flush as the flat's prehistoric plumbing system kicks into action. Lou wills Spike to go back to bed.

'I don't know, Lou. Fuck . . .' He shakes his head. 'It's a mess . . .'

Lou stares at her friend, a twenty-four-year-old student who loves staying up all night watching Steve McQueen films, and who'll suddenly be propelled down that mysterious supermarket aisle that she's only ever found herself in by mistake – the one with gigantic packs of disposable nappies and row upon row of little jars of food, every product bearing a baby's face.

'Oh, Johnny. I'm sure it'll be okay . . .'

'Will it, Lou? I just don't know.'

What he does next shocks her. Capable Johnny, creator of proper meals, incorporating vegetables – obscure vegetables sometimes, like yams and butternut squash – has his head in his hands. Then he turns to her and cries into her grubby old sweater as she holds him and says that whatever happens, he'll be okay, she'll help him, she'll do anything she can. Lou's eyes are wet too. He pulls away and looks at her, then he's kissing her on the lips, and her head spins and she knows she should pull away, but just can't. It's Johnny who stops, looks at her and pulls her into an embrace. They are holding each other now, not moving or speaking and not seeing Spike who's happened to glance into the kitchen, hoping to find a cigarette or even a decent-sized butt in the ashtray. Instead, he sees his beautiful girlfriend wrapped up with that tosser from upstairs, who has always had a thing for Lou, he bloody knew it.

Spike turns slowly and pads back to Lou's room where he'll rummage through her chest of drawers in case she has a stray packet of cigarettes lying around. Then, once his nicotine levels have returned to an acceptable level, he'll crawl back into her unmade bed and plot the slow, painful death of Johnny Lynch.

FOUR

Thirteen years later

Hannah steps into her wedding dress and studies herself in the mirror. She'd liked the simple cream shift when she'd tried it on at the department store, or at least she'd believed the persuasive salesgirl who'd said she looked 'elegant, sort of Grace Kelly-esque.' Heels were picked out too, plus a matching cream-coloured clutch. 'It's an elegant look,' the girl reassured her, 'but still lovely and young and fresh.' Now, though, at 7.35 am in the chilly upper reaches of Ryan's townhouse, Hannah doesn't feel young, fresh or remotely Grace Kelly-esque.

She looks like a fat nurse. As if the perfect accessory isn't the seed-pearl tiara Lou has already made for her, but one of those blood pressure devices that clamps around your arm. Instead of neatly skimming Hannah's body, as it had in the changing room, the dress now clings a little too tightly to her breasts and hips and bunches up like a carrier bag around her middle.

Either she, or the dress, must have changed shape in the two days since she bought it. Even its *shade* seems to have altered. The shop girl had called it oyster, but Hannah is now thinking over-boiled cauliflower. She is a fat nurse in a cauliflower dress. You hear of people bolting from the

18

church or registry office in blind panic just before they're due to exchange vows. She can just picture Ryan glimpsing her in that dress – it's already become *that* dress, and not in a good way – and hurtling out of the building.

It's not, Hannah decides as she tugs it off over her head and throws it onto the bed, the best start to a grey Monday morning.

*

'He stole my iPod to look at my photos and now he won't give it back!' wails Daisy, Ryan's ten-year-old daughter.

'Who cares about your stupid sleepover photos?' Josh, her big brother, shoots back. 'I've got better stuff to do than look at your dumb friends.'

'Why were you looking then?'

''Cause I wanted to see what you had on it.'

'Dad. DAAAD!' There's a screech, and as Hannah pulls on her black vest top and faded jeans, she detects the soothing tones of Ryan, her future husband, possessor of infinite patience and soon-to-be-witness of the cauliflower nurse dress.

'Hey,' he says, 'come on, you two . . . isn't this a stupid thing to argue about? Yes, I hear what you're saying, Daisy, I *know* they're your private pictures, but Josh . . .' Hannah pulls her fair hair back into a ponytail and waits at the top of the stairs.

'Little shit,' Josh barks. 'You're *so* spoilt.' Ah, Ryan's firstborn, just turned fourteen, liberal sprayer of Lynx (preferred fragrance 'Excite' – 'A rare gourmand-oriental mixture of fresh green accords and woody base notes,' Hannah had read while perusing the can with interest in the bathroom). Although she's been living here for six months, it still strikes her as completely bizarre that Ryan is responsible for half the genetic make-up of the most life-sapping kids she's ever met. Occasionally, Hannah wonders if she's really doing the right thing by marrying him – but then, why should his offspring sabotage her future with the man she loves? This is the sweet, funny, sexy man with whom she exchanged life stories on the night they met. The man who turned up unannounced at her flat one sunny Sunday morning with a picnic for two. The man with whom she's travelled to Barcelona, lain kissing on a Cornish beach and joked that, if they spent any more time in bed together, they might have to arrange for a delivery man to slide a pizza under the door.

'Arsewipe,' Daisy shoots back.

'That's *enough*,' snaps Ryan as Hannah heads downstairs, gritting her teeth, a vein pulsating in her jaw as she tries to mentally transform herself into a vision of smiles and perkiness.

'But Dad, all I did was—' Josh starts.

'You should respect your sister's things,' Ryan barks as Hannah steps over a lone, grubby-soled football sock in the hallway. 'She doesn't fiddle about with your stuff.'

'She nicked my headphones,' Josh counters. 'She broke 'em and peeled the spongy bits off.'

'I did not,' Daisy snarls. 'They were broke anyway. They were crap.'

'Daisy,' says Ryan firmly, 'I don't want to listen to this and I'm sure Hannah doesn't either.'

'Huh,' Josh snorts, clearly meaning, *Who cares what your stupid girlfriend thinks?*

Pausing before entering the conflict zone, Hannah sees flashes of Ryan through the half-open door as he darts back and forth across the kitchen. Busy Dad, rattling through the morning routine before hurrying off to work. Hannah can't help feeling irritated on his behalf and, rather than sauntering straight in, she takes a moment to consider what she should do next.

She could face the horrible truth that, despite her fantasies of being a friendly elder sister type to Daisy and Josh – watching movies together, perhaps even *advising* them occasionally in those rare moments when Ryan runs out of steam – it won't happen. In their eyes, she will never rise above the status of an apple core they've found rotting on the floor of the car. This means she should probably tiptoe to the front door and let herself out, leaving Ryan, his kids and that disgusting nurse dress, and never see any of them again.

Or she could stride into that kitchen, mature and confident like the grown-up woman she is, and seize control of the day.

FIVE

A muffled beeping noise is coming from somewhere in the depths of Sadie's bag. The bag is enormous and bulging and looks more like a vast quilted navy-blue pillow than anything you'd willingly lug around. It makes Sadie feel unbalanced, although she's started to feel that way when she's *not* carrying the bag, so perhaps it's her natural state now.

The beeping noise is Sadie's mobile, gasping for breath beneath the nappies, bottles, hats, wipes, bibs, extra sweaters (lovingly knitted in pale lemon yarn by Barney's mum), bendy rubbery spoons and jars of baby food. It might as well be in Tasmania for all she can reach it. She stops with the buggy on the damp path in the park and frantically searches for it. Typical. Just as she manages to locate the phone, it stops ringing.

Missed call from Hannah. It's 8.07 am. Why is she calling so early? Is something wrong? More to the point, what's Sadie doing, marching around Hissingham Park on a blustery morning when normal people are having break-fast, drinking coffee in their cosy homes and browsing the newspapers? Yet she *had* to get out. Barney leaves at seven am every weekday, catching the train for his London-bound commute. Dylan and Milo took exception to Daddy leaving today, swiftly working themselves up to inconsolable on the baby mood-scale. Sadie tried feeding them, then carrying them both, one plonked on each hip, through every room in the house. She tried singing and even dancing in their small, cave-like kitchen, then gathered them onto her lap and read *Peepo!* twice. Nothing worked. She sees her imaginary parenting test paper covered in angry red scrawlings with FAIL written across it in huge capitals. *Must try harder, Sadie Vella. Eight months into this course and we're still seeing little improvement.* Now, as a cool wind stirs the branches of a sycamore above her, scattering rain droplets onto Sadie's pillow-flattened hair, Dylan starts to cry again. This means that returning Hannah's call will have to wait.

Sadie strides on, hoping that the buggy's steady motion will soothe her son, and also that Hannah is okay. Of course she is. Her life seems to be going spectacularly well at the moment. She has a great job, having risen through the ranks at Catfish to become head of the entire creative department. She has a gorgeous, caring and enviably grown-up man who loves her to pieces and writes adverts for – actually, Sadie can't remember who Ryan writes ads for. Hannah has told her several times but it whooshed in through one ear and out the other, as most things do these days. Sadie wonders what's now occupying the space in her head where her brain used to be. Teddy bear stuffing, or stale air, like the inside of a neglected fridge? Only this morning it took her fifteen minutes to locate her keys before she could leave the house. She couldn't find the boys' soft leather baby shoes either, so they're each wearing two pairs of thick baby socks. Supposedly simple tasks have become virtually insurmountable. Sadie can't fathom how women manage to hold down paid jobs as well as look after their children, bake cakes *and* fashion 'amusing' toddler meals where the cannelloni look like little people sleeping under a blanket.

'It's okay, sweetie,' she murmurs, parking the buggy next to the café that hasn't even opened yet, and bobbing down to try and soothe Dylan. A young girl is in the café – Sadie thinks she's Polish – placing small vases of flowers on each table. Milo, apparently unconcerned by his brother's anguish, is studying the spindly weathervane on the café's roof. Sadie unclips Dylan's buggy restraints, picks him up and cradles him close to her chest.

Rocking him gently, she absent-mindedly jiggles the buggy with her free hand. A ruddy-faced woman, her round cheeks accentuated by a short, choppy hairstyle, is striding along the path towards her. Hannah knows without doubt that this woman will stop and talk to her; it's what people in Little Hissingham do. As well as motherhood, Sadie is also trying to get to grips with village life where everyone seems to know her as 'the one with the twins', even though she hasn't the foggiest idea who most of these people are.

'Oooh, you're the one with the twins,' the woman exclaims unnecessarily, cocking her head to one side as she fixes her gaze on Dylan's tear-blotched face.

'That's right,' Sadie says, pulling her lips into a smile.

'What've you got again? Boy and a girl?'

'No. Two boys.'

'Aw, shame! Were you awfully disappointed?'

No, of course I bloody wasn't, Sadie thinks angrily. 'No, not at all,' she says firmly. That's better. She's managed to wrestle her thoughts under control instead of having to restrain herself from slapping the woman.

'Well, you got more than you bargained for there,' the woman chuckles.

Sadie places Dylan, who's calmed down a little now, back into the buggy. 'Well, yes, it is pretty busy. Keeps me out of trouble, you know.'

'IVF?'

'Sorry?' Sadie laughs involuntarily.

'I mean, are they IVF babies?'

'Er . . . no . . . why d'you say that?' Sadie feels her heart quickening as, for a split second, she wishes Barney were here to tell the woman to mind her own damn business. Even if they had had fertility treatment – which they hadn't – why would she wish to discuss it with a stranger in the park?

''Cause my sister,' the woman continues, scratching her chin, 'she and her fella tried for years, the old ovulation kit with the menstrual cycle and all that. Nothing happened. Took all the romance out of it, you know? Became, like . . . *mechanical*. Not romantic at all.' Sadie is jamming her molars together so hard, she fears they might start to crumble. When did she start needing Barney to protect her in situations like this?

'So it was twins they had,' the woman rants on, 'and God, they're hard work, aren't they? Not a second to yourself. You'll know all about that, haha!' She peers down at the buggy. 'Don't they have any shoes?'

'Er, yes, but I couldn't find . . .'

'It's a cold day,' the woman scolds her. 'Their little tootsies'll be freezing. . . .'

Phone bloody social services then, Sadie wants to scream. *Or make a sodding citizen's arrest.* 'Sorry, I'm in a hurry,' she blurts out, charging off with the buggy, and wondering where she can go that's not the inside of her soul-crushing house – sorry, *cottage* – but also where that woman won't find her and start interrogating her on her sex life.

Both the children are crying now, signalling that feeding time is upon them. Sadie is still breastfeeding the babies, although they do, mercifully, also have bottles of formula, jars of food and her home-made concoctions. Determined to up her parenting grade – she's awarded herself a D-minus

25

so far – she bought a vast array of vegetables yesterday which she chopped at midnight and simmered until 1 am when Barney (and probably the entire Western hemisphere) was sleeping soundly, only to realise that the damn stuff couldn't be frozen in ice cube trays until it had cooled properly. She found herself blowing on the vatful of steamy mush, then worried that she was breathing stinky adult germs on it and would infect her children with gastro-enteritis. It was too smooth as well – she'd overdone the mushing. By eight months her children should be managing lumps, finger food, great saddles of lamb, probably. Sadie finally staggered to bed at 2.30 am, cursing Barney for the sole reason that he had the audacity to be asleep, precisely ninety minutes before the babies woke up, eyes pinging open to full alertness, ready for their first feed of the day.

Is Sadie feeding them too much, too little or too often? She has no idea. She's read so many baby manuals that they've all merged into one fat, hectoring tome. When she presented her hastily defrosted home-made baby food this morning – realising she needn't have frozen it after all – Milo and Dylan spat it all out onto their white towelling Monday bibs.

Who could blame them? she thinks now, pushing the double buggy at a determined speed. What's wrong with shop-bought baby food anyway? It's made by experts – people whose *lives* are dedicated to formulating stuff packed with nutrients that babies will actually enjoy and not spit out. Sadie can't compete with that.

Catching her breath, she heads for the rose garden where she knows there are benches, and which is shielded from the rest of the park by dense, square-cut hedges. For someone who was once body-confident, pouring her luscious curves into corseted lingerie which she constructed herself, Sadie is incredibly self-conscious about breast-feeding in public. She and Barney pored over soft pencil illustrations of possible feeding positions in *Twins: Your Essential Survival Guide*. It's okay for the women in those drawings, she thinks now. They don't have to sit on damp park benches with a baby clamped to each bosom and spot a teenage boy glancing through a gap in the hedge, looking completely appalled. Plus, the women's breasts in those illustrations don't overproduce milk until it seeps through their breast pads, making their gargantuan nursing bras wet and smelly (no boned, hand-stitched underwear for Sadie these days). She has never felt more aware of being a mammal in her entire life.

She's just sat down, and is lifting an agitated Milo from his buggy, when her mobile trills into life again. Clasping him tightly to her lap, she fishes the phone from her bag, quickly enough to take the call this time.

'Sadie?' comes Hannah's voice. 'Are you okay to talk for a minute?'

'Yes, sort of,' she says, phone in one hand, and wrapping her other arm around her writhing son. 'Just about to feed, though. Boys are a bit unsettled. Oh, hang on a sec . . .' Milo squirms in her lap. 'Are *you* okay?' she asks quickly.

'Er, yeah, I'm fine . . .'

'Where are you?' Sadie asks.

'Outside. Just outside the house.'

'What, *your* house?'

'Um, yes . . . just had to get out for a minute. I know this sounds mad . . .' Sadie hears Hannah blow out a big gust of air.

'What's wrong? Is everything okay with you and Ryan?'

'Yeah, it's fine! I mean it's fine with *us*. It's just, um . . . the kids, Sadie. They're just . . .'

'Has something happened?'

'Oh, not really . . . Look, I'm sorry to load this on you at this time in the morning but they're all in the kitchen right now, bickering, and I just . . . I don't know why, but

27

maybe it's because I've just tried on my wedding dress and it's horrible. Really ugly and plain. What was I thinking? I should've asked you to come into town and we could have had a lovely day and picked something together. *And* I bought a clutch bag. A clutch bag! I've never owned one in my life. Will I have to go around clutching it all day?'

'Well, I'm sure you are allowed to put it down, or someone will look after—'

'It's horrible,' Hannah cuts in. 'Like something Princess Anne would carry. Can you imagine me with a clutch bag? And I got this *fear*, you know? This horrible feeling about . . .' Her voice falters.

'What, about getting married?' Sadie exclaims, unable to work out whether her friend's distress has to do with Ryan's kids, the dress or the Princess Anne bag.

'I don't know,' Hannah says. 'I . . . I just had to talk to you.'

'Maybe it's just the wedding,' Sadie murmurs. 'All the organising and preparations . . . you know what? You should have a hen party. Let your hair down and have a bit of fun.'

Hannah laughs weakly. 'I'd love one, and the girls at work have been on at me to sort something out . . .'

'Well, why don't you?' Somewhere in her distant past, Sadie remembers clubs with music playing, drinks flowing and women moving freely without lugging gigantic quilted bags. She pictures a glass of white wine, and her entire body tingles with longing.

'Oh, I don't know . . .' Hannah tails off. 'What's that noise anyway?'

'It's the boys, they're hungry. Sorry, Han, I'd better go . . .' Sadie clamps her mobile between her shoulder and ear while gently bouncing Milo up and down and rocking the buggy. She eyes the hedge and wonders if anyone would mind if she crawled under it and fell asleep.

'God, they sound upset. I won't keep you a minute. Yes, I've thought about a hen party but you know what? I'd only want you – you and Lou, I mean – and that would be impossible, wouldn't it?'

'Maybe not. I'm only an hour away and York's not *that* far . . . maybe you'd better speak to Lou. I haven't talked to her in ages. Look, Han, I'd really better . . .' Sadie's attention is diverted by a large black dog bounding towards her, pink tongue lolling from its mouth.

'D'you think Lou's okay?' Hannah asks. 'I worry about her and Spike sometimes. He never seems to appreciate . . .'

'Uh-huh,' Sadie mutters, holding Milo tightly as she jumps up and tries to form a human barrier between the buggy and hound.

'I mean, she's working all hours at that horrible soft play place *and* keeping the jewellery thing going . . .' Perhaps it's chronic sleep deprivation, or the fact that becoming a mother has turned Sadie into a lumbering beast incapable of rapid movement. Whatever the reason, the dog shoots past her and proceeds to lash Dylan's terrified face with its tongue.

'No!' Sadie screams with her mobile still clamped to her ear. Dylan squeals loudly.

'I mean, what does Spike do all day?' Hannah wants to know. 'Sits on his arse, strumming a guitar, waiting for a recording contract to drop into his lap . . .'

'Stop that!' Sadie shrieks, shoving herself between the dog and Dylan, whose cries have morphed into hearty wails.

'What's happening?' Hannah asks.

'There's a dog here! It's trying to attack Dylan and there's no bloody owner and—' She drops her phone onto the path and its back pings off. 'Shit,' she mutters, deciding that her baby's immediate wellbeing is more important than a three-year-old Nokia. A tall, scrawny man whistles for the dog at the rose garden's entrance. No apology, no acknowledgement that his slavering beast has nearly devoured her child, or at the very least infected him with some terrible dog-tongue disease, *and* caused Sadie to wreck her phone. As the dog bounds away, Sadie blinks away tears of stress, unleashes Dylan from the buggy and sinks back onto the bench, clutching both of her boys and panting.

She doesn't feed them straight away. She can't, not with her heart banging madly and her children so distressed. Sadie just sits there, conscious of faint drizzle now falling on her hot cheeks, and an empty Bacardi Breezer bottle lying on the ground.

She glances down at her babies, taken aback as she always is by the fierce rush of love that engulfs her. Her sons, all round brown eyes and tufts of dark, fluffy hair, gaze up adoringly at her. The fact that they emerged from her own body still strikes her as nothing short of miraculous. All those years of debauchery as an art student, a lifestyle which continued steadily through her twenties, and she was still capable of incubating these utterly perfect human beings. Dylan is smiling now, and Milo is gazing up at her as if she were the most wondrous creature on earth.

This is what it's all about, Sadie reminds herself. *It doesn't matter that I'm stained and knackered and every little thing Barney does irritates the hell out of me. It doesn't matter because it's all about this – being Milo and Dylan's mum.* Sadie bunches up her T-shirt, frees her breasts from her huge, shiny scaffolding-bra and clamps a child to each nipple. Both babies fall upon her as if they hadn't been fed for weeks. Sadie inhales deeply, kicks the Bacardi Breezer bottle under the bench, then focuses hard on the cracked screen of her mobile which is lying at her feet.

SIX

'Why aren't you and Dad getting married in church?' Daisy fixes Hannah with a cool stare as she enters the kitchen.

Hannah pauses, taken aback by the fact that Daisy's query isn't about why she crept outside to make a call on her mobile. Ryan is muttering about gym kits in the utility room and Josh is chewing slowly and rhythmically, like a bull, whilst staring blankly ahead. 'Well,' Hannah says brightly, 'we're only having a small wedding with the people we're closest to, and it's . . .' She falters, deciding not to utter the unmentionable words: *and it's your dad's second wedding, after all.* 'It just seemed right for us,' she adds. 'We don't want anything too fancy or formal, you know?'

Clearly, Daisy doesn't know. She gnaws on a toast crust and blinks down at Hannah's bare feet. Josh continues to eat in silence, the Lynx Effect engulfing the kitchen as if being pumped in through a pipe. 'Why not?' Daisy asks.

'Well, er,' Hannah starts, deciding yet again that it's ridiculous to feel intimidated by a ten-year-old, 'I'm not really religious so it wouldn't feel right for me to get married in church when I don't go any other time.'

Hannah hears Ryan slamming the washing machine shut and switching it on. Daisy is now gawping at Hannah as

31

if she's just confessed to a liking for torturing kittens. 'You mean you don't believe in *God*?' she gasps.

'Well, not really,' Hannah blusters, her cheeks flaring up. 'I mean, I believe in *something*, I suppose, like we should treat people well and respect each other but, er . . . I'm not really a churchy type.'

Daisy purses her pink lips. '*I* believe in God.'

'Well, that's good, Daisy. It's completely personal and up to you what you believe in.'

'Don't you believe in Heaven either?'

No, because I'm the Antichrist . . . 'Er, not really, I mean . . .'

'Dad doesn't go to church either,' Josh intercepts, pushing back a dark, shaggy fringe from equally dark, foreboding eyes. 'But him and Mum got married in a church and *that* was all right.' He juts out his bottom lip.

'Well, I suppose what I mean, what I should've said,' Hannah explains, feeling her jaw tighten and any semblance of hunger rapidly ebbing away, 'is that I don't really follow a religion.'

'Do you *follow* a religion then?' Josh meets her gaze over the gingham tablecloth.

Hannah frowns. 'What d'you mean, Josh?'

He flares his nostrils at her, like a horse. 'You said you don't *follow* a religion. Like you'd say you *follow* Chelsea but you don't *follow* Spurs. Like religion's a football team.' He sniggers and clamps his mouth shut like a trap.

'Oh, right!' She laughs a little too heartily. 'Well, what I mean is that I don't support – I mean *practise* – any particular religion.' As Josh blinks slowly, waiting for her to dig herself into an even deeper hole, Hannah wonders if this is how it'll be when she's Ryan's wife, and their stepmother. Like being sandwiched between a Gestapo interrogator and a belligerent English teacher who ticks her off

32

for using an ill-chosen verb. Christ-on-a-sodding-bike. She has a sudden urge to shriek, *Okay! We're not getting married in church because your dad was married before, as you both know, a fact I've avoided mentioning because I'm trying to be nice. And actually, while we're on the subject of marriage, why don't we just forget the whole business and carry on living together? It was your dad's idea in the first place, you know. Getting married, I mean. Because he loves me. Yes, I know you might find the idea completely repulsive, and God knows, his feelings might waver a bit when he sets eyes on my cauliflower nurse dress. But still . . .*

'What were you saying, Daisy?' Ryan asks, emerging from the utility room with a bundle of sports kits.

'We were just talking about the wedding, Dad,' Daisy says pleasantly.

'Oh, right.' Ryan smiles at Hannah, his eyes meeting hers, making her stomach flip as it always does when he looks at her like that. 'Well,' he adds, turning to Josh, 'speaking of the wedding, we should all go shopping next weekend and pick you both something to wear.'

'But it's ages away,' Josh replies. 'It's *weeks*.'

'Yes, I know there's still six weeks to go. But you'll be at Mum's the next three, and then we'll be cutting it fine, really, to get things organised . . .'

'Eddie's birthday's on Saturday,' Josh mumbles. 'We're going bowling.'

'Oh,' Ryan says. 'Right. Well, that's nice. Maybe we could do it on Sunday instead.'

'And we're staying over till Sunday,' Josh adds, 'like *all* day.'

'Are you? Oh . . .' Hannah can detect the stress creeping across Ryan's forehead, and longs to ask Josh why he's being so bloody difficult when all his dad wants to do is festoon him with new clothes. However, she suspects that

33

that would be even more outrageous than admitting she doesn't *follow* Christianity. Anyway, perhaps Ryan doesn't mind this rudeness, or has become immune to it over the years. Maybe he thinks Josh and Daisy's behaviour is perfectly fine and it's the wedding that's stressing him out. They've planned it together, with the intention of keeping it low-key and simple. But the guest list has grown, and Ryan's new suit came back from being altered with the trousers so short they flapped pathetically around his ankles. He's been worrying about the food when Hannah would be perfectly content with a pile of sausage rolls dumped on the table if that'd put a smile on his kids' faces. Now, what started as Ryan blurting out, 'I want to marry you, Han, and spend my whole life with you' has morphed into something stressful and dark, like a storm cloud billowing towards them.

'And I've got stuff to wear anyway,' Josh mumbles, looking down at his crumb-strewn plate.

'I know, but I thought you might like something new.' Regaining his composure, Ryan rolls his eyes good-naturedly at Hannah. How he manages to scrabble together these reserves of patience, she has no idea. Perhaps it just happens when you have children. You suddenly develop this bottomless well of kindness and goodwill.

'You're not going to turn down your dad's offer of new clothes, are you, Josh?' Hannah asks lightly.

'Well, I've got plenty of T-shirts and jeans.'

'Right, so which T-shirt were you thinking of?' Ryan asks with a snort.

'Dunno. My dark green one maybe.'

'The one with the rip in the shoulder?' Ryan laughs. 'Sure, that'll look great in the photos, Josh.'

Josh stares at him uncomprehendingly. 'Photos?'

'Yes, *wedding photos*, like people usually have when they get married,' Ryan says with exaggerated patience.

'What's wrong with my T-shirt?'

'Well, apart from the rip, it does tend to whiff a bit even when it's been washed,' his father explains, 'like something's actually embedded in its fibres and will never come out, even if I boil-wash it which I've done on several occasions . . .'

Daisy starts giggling. 'You smell, Josh. That horrible T-shirt stinks of BO and even washing powder can't get it out.'

'*And* it's age nine-to-ten,' Ryan reminds him, 'and you're fourteen, Josh, if I remember rightly. Now, I know you're fond of that T-shirt but we could be radical and buy you something in the right size.'

'Oh, Josh can wear whatever he likes,' Hannah cuts in. 'It's not going to be formal, is it, Ryan?' She smiles at his son. 'It's probably best to wear what you feel happy and comfortable in.'

'He's *not* wearing that T-shirt,' Ryan mutters.

'I just don't think it's worth falling out over . . .' Hannah glances at Josh. Instead of responding, and being grateful to her for not trying to cram him into a suit, he takes a big gulp of orange juice, wipes his lips on his cuff and allows his mouth to hang open, as if airing its interior. Trying to decipher these kids is a bit like learning to drive, Hannah decides as Ryan shoos them upstairs to fetch their schoolbags. In fact it's *harder* than driving because at least she was able to pay for a teacher. As far as Hannah is aware, there's no British School of How to Handle Daisy and Josh.

'I'd better be going,' Hannah tells Ryan, trying to quash the trace of relief from her voice.

'Okay. Have a good day, darling.' He steps forward and pulls her close, smelling freshly showered and delicious.

'What are *you* wearing to the wedding?' Daisy has reappeared in the kitchen doorway.

'Me?' Ryan springs away from Hannah. 'Erm, a suit, Daisy. A new one that's being altered for me.'

'I meant Hannah, Daddy.' Daisy gives them a fake smile.

'Oh, just a simple dress,' says Hannah quickly.

'Aren't you wearing a veil?'

Hannah pauses. 'No, but Lou, one of my best friends from—'

'Why not?'

Because I don't like them! 'Well, veils are lovely but my friend Lou from college is an amazing jeweller and she's made me this beautiful silver tiara with—'

'Mum's wedding dress was pretty, wasn't it, Dad?' Daisy beams at her father.

'Er, yes. It was very nice . . .' Ryan turns away and swills out the washing-up bowl noisily.

'Mum's dress,' Daisy continues, eyes fixed determinedly on Hannah, 'was white and low at the front like this.' She draws an invisible V-shape to indicate a plunging neckline.

'Well, that sounds gorgeous.' Hannah smiles tightly.

'And it was long with millions of sparkly beads sewn on, and the veil was so massive two people had to walk behind and carry it through the church, didn't they, Dad? So it didn't drag on the floor and get dirty. Didn't they, Dad?'

'Er, yes,' Ryan croaks, now scraping the remains of the kids' breakfasts into the bin.

'Wow,' Hannah says hollowly. *Why don't we get out the album,* she thinks darkly, *then we can all gather round and ooh and ahh over Petra's incredible dress before I go to work, and I can show you how crappy and plain I'm going to look in my dumpy little shift that I must have chosen in a fit of madness . . .*

'Mummy looked beautiful,' Daisy breathes.

'I'm sure she did.'

Sorry, Ryan mouths from the sink. Taking a deep breath,

Hannah pauses for a moment, focusing on the area behind Daisy, where the family-sized super-deluxe fridge stands proudly, with its ice maker gadget which once spurted frozen crystals in her face, causing Daisy and Josh to keel over with helpless laughter. It had never done that before, Daisy had informed her when she and her brother had finally managed to compose themselves. Well, of course it hadn't. Petra had chosen it – she'd picked virtually every appliance and piece of furniture – and at times like that, Hannah couldn't help feeling that the whole house was against her. 'D'you want to see a picture of Mummy's dress?' Daisy enquires.

'Daisy!' Ryan barks. 'Could you hurry up and get your shoes on?'

'But, Dad . . .'

'Sometime, maybe,' Hannah says briskly, 'but I'd better get off to work now. I'm running late as it is.'

SEVEN

As Lou pulls on her uniform – a brown nylon tabard bearing the soft play centre's 'Let's Bounce' logo across the chest – it occurs to her that the person who designed it might possibly be a pervert. Lou turns this thought over in her mind almost daily, and as she's been working at Let's Bounce for nearly a year, that makes it – well, at 8.30 am she's incapable of working out the exact figure off the top of her head. But it's something in the region of 230 times, which she fears is verging on obsessional. It can't be normal to allow dark thoughts about play centre uniforms to occupy such a large part of her brain.

Yet that vile piece of clothing really ticks all the boxes, Lou thinks, teasing her curly auburn hair with a long-toothed comb and sweeping on powder and lip gloss at the dressing table mirror. No one, apart from people who go in for medieval jousting contests, wear tabards. Even worse, Dave, her boss, insists that said garment is worn on arrival at work and has even ticked off Lou's friend Steph for not modelling hers on the bus on the way in. 'You're all walking advertisements,' he's fond of reminding the staff during his 'motivational talks'.

In their bed behind her, Spike emits a long *mmmmmm*

sound, and Lou turns to see a faint smile flicker across his lips. His eyes are closed, his dark lashes dusting his lightly-tanned skin like tiny brushes, his strong, defined jaw bearing its customary blur of dark stubble. Looks as if he's having a pleasurable dream, lucky sod. Lou's friends often tease her about living with a man with a super-charged libido, and she knows she should feel flattered that he's so up for it, especially as they've been together for sixteen years. In fact, if anything, Spike's sexual appetite has intensified as he's grown older. Maybe it's the tabard, Lou thinks wryly. 'You up, babe?' Spike has awoken from his reverie.

'Yep. Running a bit late actually.' Lou pads over to the bed and dispenses a speedy kiss on his slightly clammy forehead. 'Gotta go,' she adds, grabbing her bag from the floor, pulling on her tabard-concealing black trenchcoat and hurrying out of the flat, down one flight of dusty wooden stairs and into the hazy April morning.

It feels good to be outside. The flat seems even dingier when Spike isn't working, which happens to be most of the time. It's been six months since he last had a job, and the more time Spike spends in bed, or comatose on the sofa, the staler their surroundings become. Some mornings, like today, Lou is almost *grateful* to be escaping to Let's Bounce. Although she loves Spike, and he's still handsome and ridiculously youthful-looking at forty-eight, Lou can't help worrying that his lethargy might engulf her completely until it's too late to fight her way out.

Is sitting on your arse all day actually contagious? she wonders as she walks briskly to work. Does it become progressively worse, until the sufferer is unable to separate himself from the sofa apart from occasionally staggering to the loo? Spike can't even be bothered to drop used teabags into the kitchen bin. He just lobs them into the sink, and every time she removes them – unwilling to start an argument over something as petty as teabags – Lou is seized by an urge to pelt them in his face.

She marches on, now feeling more annoyed with herself than Spike for allowing yesterday to slip away in a fug of TV and housework instead of making the most of her one day off. She always imagines Sadie and Barney taking their babies to some beautiful spot in the Cambridgeshire countryside for a picnic on Sundays. And Hannah and Ryan probably take his kids on a family walk in some particularly photogenic part of London – Primrose Hill or Hampstead Heath – like characters in a Richard Curtis movie. Lou sees expensive white wine being lifted from a coolbox and Ryan's kids chatting nicely with Hannah, laughing at her jokes and feeling lucky that their dad has found himself such a cool girlfriend. And here's Lou in York – not that she's blaming York for the situation she's found herself in – wearing a synthetic tabard on her way to extract stray nappies heavily laden with pee from the ballpool.

Still, she thinks, approaching the redbrick former factory which houses Let's Bounce, at least there's Hannah and Ryan's wedding to look forward to. Six weeks to go now. A trip to London will shake her up. She's made a pact with herself to get out of this crappy job by then, after which . . . well, she isn't quite sure *what* will come after that. Something to do with Spike, she suspects. Something to change her life and lift her out of the humdrum existence which has somehow sucked her in. Yes, after the wedding she'll do it. She'll be refreshed and energised then. But it's far too big and scary to think about right now.

EIGHT

Hannah cycles like a maniac, legs pumping and heart banging against her ribs. It feels good being out; in fact after the interrogation over breakfast, about weddings and veils and *God*, for Christ's sake, having a toenail ripped off would feel pretty damn fantastic. Even though she's lived in London for thirteen years, Hannah can still taste the traffic fumes on her tongue. It tastes of excitement and life going on all around her. Her childhood in a tiny fishing village made her yearn for a fast-paced city life: first Glasgow, where she'd studied illustration, followed by a succession of insalubrious rented studio flats and shared houses scattered all over north London. Now, as she zips between vehicles, heading for Islington, she feels the stress of her interrogation blowing away in the light breeze.

The trouble is, Hannah has never imagined herself becoming a stepmother. She'd have been no less amazed if someone had announced that she must fly a helicopter or raise a family of baboons. Yet, when you meet a man in his mid-thirties, you can hardly fall over in a dead faint when it transpires that he has children. Ryan became a father relatively young, at twenty-three. Parenthood has occupied a huge portion of his life, making his two years with Hannah a mere dot on the map in comparison. Checking her watch as she turns into Essex Road – she's early for work, as is often the case these days – she replays the Saturday night when Ryan Lennox dropped into her life.

It was a bitterly cold evening and Hannah had recently ended her year-long relationship with Marc-with-a-'c'. Actually, 'relationship' was too grand a term for what had consisted mainly of him showing up infuriatingly late for dates, or not at all – then drunkenly buzzing the bell to her flat at 3.30 am, crying and blurting out declarations of love loud enough to wake everyone in her post code. When he'd mistaken her T-shirt drawer for the loo and peed into it, that had been the final straw. Hannah hadn't been looking to meet anyone that night as she'd waited for her friend Mia. She was enjoying her single, Marc-free life, cycling to Catfish, working hard, knowing that nothing untoward was going to happen to her T-shirts.

She and Mia had arranged to meet in Nell's, a cavernous bar in Frith Street. Ryan was standing at the bar, and although the place was already bustling, Hannah sensed an aura of calm around this tall, slim man in jeans, a pale shirt and fine, wire-rimmed glasses. Squeezing her way through a bunch of loud girls on a hen night, she ordered a beer and looked around for Mia. Hannah was five minutes early and, as she paid for her drink, she had an over-whelming urge to talk to this man standing a couple of metres to her right.

Sipping from her glass, Hannah conjured up possible scenarios. He was a Saturday dad having a restorative pint after showing his children armadillos or Egyptian artefacts in museums before heading home to his new wife. The wife would be astonishingly pretty, obviously (Hannah had already assessed his striking dark eyes, the nicely full mouth, his cute dimple). Or maybe he was single and putting off the miserable business of going home to a chilly flat and a meal for one. Yet neither scenario seemed right. There was no wedding ring, nor did he seem like someone who'd limp off home to peel the foil lid off a shrunken frozen lasagne. *He's probably just waiting for his girlfriend*, she decided, feeling foolish for letting her thoughts run away with her.

The man glanced at Hannah as her mobile rang. 'Han?' Mia croaked. 'I'm really sorry. I set off to meet you but I feel so crap, really sick, that I just had to come home . . .'

'Oh, poor you,' she said. 'Don't worry. Just get well . . .'

'But I've ruined your night,' Mia wailed.

'It doesn't matter, honestly.' Hannah caught the man's eye as she finished the call.

How could she start talking to him? All her life, Hannah had stumbled into relationships with no chatting up required, and now the only thing she could think to mention was how much she hated 'Eye of the Tiger', which was playing rather loudly right now. But what if he liked it? She glanced at him again. He seemed thoughtful, bookish and unpretentious – the kind of man who'd prefer to eat in a casual Italian place than a poncy establishment.

Hannah chewed her lip and tried out possible conversation openers. *Hi. Rotten night out there.* To which he'd reply, 'Yes.' And then there'd be a horrible silence. *I hate this record, don't you?* she'd add with a strained laugh. And he'd say, 'Do you?' Because by this time, 'Eye of the Tiger' would have stopped, and it'd be something like Marvin Gaye singing 'What's Going On?', and she'd have to bluster that it was the *last* one she hated. 'What was the last one?' he'd ask, backing away from her and looking for the quickest exit route.

What on earth was wrong with her? She was single. She was thirty-three years old. Why couldn't she act like a normal woman? It wasn't that she lacked confidence. At work, she'd been recently promoted and was often expected to present to terrifying panels of suits. Whiteboards, PowerPoint, coming up with concepts for new ranges: she was fine with all of that. Yet she couldn't figure out how to talk to a handsome man in a bar, even though he'd glanced at her on several occasions and, crucially, wasn't giving the impression that he thought she was completely hideous.

Then he turned to her and said, 'Hi.'

God, his smile was nice – sweet, warm and genuine.

'Hi,' Hannah said.

'Horrible night out there.'

'Yes, it is.'

Small pause. Hannah took a gulp of her drink.

'Waiting for someone?' the man asked.

'Um, I was, but she's just called to say she can't make it.' Hannah smiled broadly. 'So I guess I'll just finish this drink and go home.'

'Well,' he said, 'it doesn't look like the person I'm meeting is going to show up either.'

'Really? Who's that?'

He grinned and paused, as if wondering how much information to divulge. 'Er . . . I don't really know,' he said, blushing slightly. 'I mean, I've never met her. We've just emailed a couple of times.'

'Blind date?'

The man nodded, raising his eyebrows ominously. '*Guardian* Soulmates. I know it sounds a bit . . .'

'No, not at all, it sounds *fine* . . .' It really did. It meant he was single, read the *Guardian*, and was looking to meet someone. Which immediately made him a more attractive prospect than someone who showed up at 3 am, awash with tears and snot, and peed on her favourite T-shirt.

'I'm not even sure it's the best way to go about things,' he added. 'In fact, *Guardian* Soul-destroyers would be more apt.' He laughed and pushed back his light brown hair self-consciously.

'Had a few bad experiences then?' Hannah asked with a smile.

He shrugged. 'Let's just say it's been a bit of a non-event so far. Anyway, I'm Ryan . . .'

'Hannah . . .' And that was that. They talked, not about whatever godawful song was on the jukebox, but about their lives. By 10.30, in a cosy Italian restaurant, Hannah found herself telling Ryan about the T-shirt drawer incident while he confessed to hiding his eight-year-old daughter's favourite story book after he calculated that he must have read it 150 times. Hannah learnt that, while Ryan's job as an advertising copywriter sounded glamorous, his latest campaigns had been for mould-repelling tile grout and a toilet deodorisering brick that came in six different scents inspired by the wild herbs of the Corsican Maquis. 'Seriously?' She exploded with laughter.

'Unfortunately, yes – we're talking thyme, lavender, sage . . . the range is called "The Scented Isle".'

'So you can have your own Scented Isle in your toilet? I never knew that.'

'Er, yes, if you really want one. They're only a couple of quid . . .'

'Cheaper than a package holiday,' she suggested, noticing how Ryan's eyes crinkled when he laughed.

'You know,' he added, 'we might use that line.'

Thank God your date didn't turn up, Hannah thought a little while later as they stepped out into the wet night and hailed a cab together. She didn't know Ryan – not really. But she knew about his ex-wife and children and more about toilet brick fragrances than she'd ever thought possible. As he dropped her off at her flat, after they'd swapped numbers and he'd kissed her briefly but incredibly sweetly on the lips, she'd decided that she wouldn't bother to pretend she was too busy to see him for at least a week. She'd be calling him the very next day, to hell with it.

What Hannah hadn't realised then was how swiftly and deeply she'd fall in love, and that eighteen months after meeting, Ryan would ask her to move into the house he shared with his children at London Fields, and marry him, and that she'd want to very much.

*

And now, as she chains up her bike in the small courtyard at Catfish, Hannah feels a sharp twinge of guilt. All the stuff about church weddings and veils and their beautiful mother – of course, none of it is their fault. They're just kids, she reminds herself. Even Josh still needs constant reminders from Ryan to clean his teeth and not wear the same boxers three days running.

No, it's up to *her* to make things work. And she will, Hannah decides, greeting Adele at reception and entering the light, airy space of the design studio. She'll start with Daisy, because surely it's easier to befriend a ten-year-old girl than a boy of fourteen. She'll suggest something simple, like a shopping trip. As Hannah says hi to her colleagues, and pours herself a strong black coffee, she feels a surge of optimism. She and Daisy will have a whole day together – a girlie day – to try on clothes and stop off at cafés where they'll giggle and chat. It's a great idea, she realises now. Why didn't she think of it before?

NINE

At Let's Bounce, 'York's Premier Soft Play Experience', Lou plucks a small object from the ballpool and holds it gingerly between her forefinger and thumb. It's dark brown and sticky and it occurs to her that, just a few months ago, she'd have retched if she'd had to pick up such a thing with her bare hands. Now, though, it seems like a normal part of her day.

Lou works six shifts a week at Let's Bounce. Although she was grateful for the job when three shops which stocked her jewellery closed down, she vows that, if she ever has children – and with Spike, it seems increasingly unlikely – she'll insist that they play on grass and in rivers and never in putrid places like this. Lou knows that parents need somewhere to take their children, especially on rainy days, but she never thinks the adults look happy or even faintly relieved to be here. They slump over plastic plates of chips and baked potatoes and horrible yellowy stuff called coronation chicken, whatever the heck that is, looking as if their lives are teetering on the brink of collapse.

Wrapping the brown squidgy thing in a paper napkin, Lou carries it to the ladies' loo. While the main play zone is dimly lit – to conceal the decaying food lurking amongst the equipment, Lou suspects – the fluorescent strip in the ladies' is so unforgiving, she'll be able to get a proper look at the thing. If it's poo, or something equally gross, she plans to present it to Dave, her boss, which will hopefully make him do something about the state of the place.

Lou places the paper parcel on the Formica top beside the washbasins and peels it open.

'Ew, what's that?' Steph, Lou's friend and fellow staff member, has emerged from a cubicle and is eyeing the parcel from a safe distance.

'Don't know,' Lou replies, 'but I think it might be a squashed muffin. It smells kind of sweet . . .'

Realising what she's doing – ie, trying to *analyse* the lump – Lou quickly re-wraps it and flings it into the plastic bin.

'I bloody hate this place, Lou,' Steph mutters, washing her hands and picking a clump of mascara from an eyelash.

'Me too.' Lou checks her watch. 'C'mon, if you hoover and I clear the tables, maybe we'll get out on time for once.'

'Yes, boss.' Steph grins.

Lou smiles back. Thank God for Steph and the rest of the staff here, united in nugget-frying hell. 'Fancy a quick drink when we're done?' she asks.

'Could murder one,' Steph replies. She stands back from the mirror, smoothes her hands over her rounded hips and inhales deeply as if summoning the strength to face the mayhem outside.

And it *is* mayhem. By midday, the blue sky had turned a moody grey, and the onset of rain always brings in the hordes. In her first week here, Lou discovered that things don't gently wind down towards the end of the day as they do in normal workplaces. No, they wind *up*. By 5.30 pm the kids are usually so overwrought and exhausted that at least two-thirds are crying, lashing out at their parents and refusing to leave. Plus by that time, their stomachs are swishing with cheap blackcurrant squash and churning with horrible deep-fried nuggets. So they feel sick as well. Some children actually *are* sick. Compared to mopping up puke, Lou thinks wryly, retrieving a squashed muffin from the ballpool is almost a perk of the job.

'I don't wanna go home!' a little girl wails in the play zone. 'Wanna climb on the big rope again!' The mother throws Lou an apologetic look. Lou smiles back. Although the woman looks young – late-twenties perhaps – her shoulder-length bob bears a thick swathe of wiry grey at the front. Perhaps motherhood has done that to her, or she's just had to endure one too many bleak afternoons at Let's Bounce. Will that happen to Lou if she works here much longer? She noticed a solitary grey hair nestling among her auburn curls this morning – at *thirty-five* – a defiant, silvery wire which she yanked out in disgust.

The girl is now darting between the scuffed, primary-coloured tables. 'Come *on*, Bethany,' the woman cajoles, holding out her hand ineffectually.

'No! I hate you!'

'They're closing in a minute,' the mother adds. 'Look – all the other boys and girls have gone home. This lady' – she indicates Lou, who wonders at what point she became a lady – 'wants to go home and if you don't come right now, you'll be locked in all night.'

'Good!' the girl thunders. 'It'd be fun.'

'Your mum's right,' Lou says lightly, dragging the vacuum cleaner with its 'amusing' cartoon eyes towards them. 'But if you don't mind, I've got to hoover up first.'

'Right. Sorry,' the woman says, stepping away from a scattering of nuggets on the carpet. Lou switches on the hoover while Steph loads a tray with dirty plates.

The child is now refusing to put on her shoes. 'Want to help me hoover?' Lou asks.

The girl eyes her warily. 'Okay.' Lou hands the tube to

her, quickly glancing around to check that Dave isn't lurking around. He'd snap that she was contravening health and safety regulations (although discarded food and nappies in the ballpool area don't seem to bother him one bit).

The girl is hoovering with reasonable efficiency and her mother looks relieved. 'You've done a great job there,' Lou praises the child.

'Thanks.' She grins proudly.

'You know what?' the mother adds, clearly grateful for Lou's intervention, 'you're a natural to work somewhere like this.'

Lou smiles and thanks her, but by the time the mother and daughter have left the building, she's thinking that being a natural at scraping up chips off the carpet was never supposed to be part of the plan.

'Still fancy that drink?' Steph asks as they leave, tearing off their tabards and stuffing them into their bags.

Lou thinks about Spike lying around at home, perhaps strumming a guitar but more likely depositing yet more used teabags into the sink. 'God, yes,' she declares. 'Let's go.'

TEN

'Result,' Spike says, placing his mobile back on the bedside table.

'What's that?' Astrid asks.

'Lou's in the pub, having a drink with her friend from work. Reckon she'll be a couple of hours at least . . .'

Astrid laughs and shakes her head in mock despair. 'You're terrible, giving her all that crap about rehearsing at Charlie's. I don't know how you can live with yourself, Spike.'

'Well, I *could* be rehearsing,' Spike murmurs. 'In fact, we could practise a few things right now.' With a broad smile, he swivels back into Astrid's rumpled bed, pulling her towards him. She's so beautiful, he thinks, like one of those gamine actresses from the sixties. All smooth, golden skin and perky breasts and that curtain of long, straight hair with a fringe hanging over her clear blue eyes.

Astrid, who is entirely naked, coils around Spike like a cat and plants a kiss on his fevered brow. He's not ill, yet that's how he feels when he's with her: hot and feverish, as if the inner workings of his body which control mood and temperature go haywire the minute he arrives at her small terraced house.

'You okay, baby?' she asks in that vaguely posh voice with husky undertones, which always sends tiny sparks zapping up his spinal cord.

'Better than okay,' he replies with a smile. 'Absolutely fantastic.'

She chuckles throatily, swinging her legs out of bed and stretching up to her full six feet before sashaying towards the open bedroom door. Spike stares at her bum, deciding it's so perfectly formed, it looks airbrushed. 'Want a cup of tea?' She glances back with a teasing smile.

Tea? How can he think about tea when he's just copped a long, languorous look at her backside? Yet that's what Spike loves about Astrid Stone. Her casual air, the way nothing seems to ruffle her. The way she can enjoy a full four hours in the sack, then swing out of bed and suggest a hot milky drink, as if prolonged afternoon sex is a completely normal and expected part of a drizzly Monday afternoon.

'Tea would be great,' Spike replies, although it's the last thing he fancies right now. He wants Astrid back in bed with him instead of wasting valuable time waiting for the kettle to boil and, if any beverages are to be consumed, he'd prefer a nice cold beer.

He can hear her now, padding lightly downstairs and pottering about in the kitchen. As she hums a lilting, unrecognisable tune, he sinks back into her plump white pillows and congratulates himself on his stupendous luck.

He really is a fortunate bastard. Astrid made all the moves, from the moment they met at the Red Lion, six months ago now, one wet October night. She'd come along with Charlie, a friend of Spike's with whom he has vague intentions of starting a band. It had felt like an ordinary night until Astrid strode in – a blonde, blue-eyed goddess.

'Spike,' Charlie said grandly, 'meet my dear friend Astrid.'

Astrid beamed at him. 'Uh, hello,' Spike croaked, taking

in the cute peasant top and slender hips and legs that went on for about seventy miles in dark skinny jeans. Her ankle boots were scuffed, and she wasn't wearing make-up which, to Spike, suggested a self-assuredness he found incredibly loin-stirring. 'Hi, Spike,' Astrid said breezily, kissing his cheek and nearly sending him staggering back into a table laden with drinks.

When Spike tries to replay that night, he can't remember all of it. If someone were to ask, 'What did you and Astrid talk about? What did she drink?' he wouldn't be able to answer. All he remembers is Charlie melting into the crowd, and some godawful Dire Straits tribute band playing on a tiny stage, and he and Astrid escaping to flirt in a dark corner until last drinks were called and they ventured out into the night.

Somehow, they found themselves falling into a damp alley where they kissed against a wet wheelie bin. Spike found his hands accidentally falling into Astrid's top, getting pulled up there by some kind of strange magnetic force, at which point he realised she wasn't wearing a bra. She laughed and disentangled herself, and they swapped numbers before going their separate ways. Spike watched her swish off down the street (she wasn't wearing a jacket – Astrid seemed impervious to the cold) and realised that something incredible had just happened to him.

Spike had just met a woman who knew how to *live*.

'Here you go, baby.' Astrid has reappeared at her bedroom doorway with two mugs of tea.

'Thanks, honey.' She's no longer naked, disappointingly, but at least she's only wearing a short, silky slip thing. It's nothing like the floor-length pink dressing gown that Lou bundles herself up in, constructed from two-inch-thick fabric with all the sexual allure of a gigantic marshmallow. No, the thing Astrid is wearing definitely isn't a dressing gown.

It's, um . . . Spike sips his tea and tries to think of the word. 'What's that called?' he asks.

She glances down and frowns quizzically. 'What's *what* called?'

'That . . . that thing you're wearing.'

'What, my chemise?'

Ah, *chemise*. He might have known it'd have a sexy French name, like something you could happily drown in. 'Yeah,' he says, pushing dishevelled dark hair out of his eyes. 'I knew it was something like that.'

'You're funny,' she says, 'but listen, much as I'd like to discuss my chemise at great length, I need to get moving so you'll have to get out of here I'm afraid.'

'What?' Spike groans. 'Already?'

Disappointment wells in his stomach. He'd envisaged another couple of hours here at least; it's only half-six, and he's already constructed the Charlie alibi. He'd even planned to call Lou a little later to say the rehearsal was going so well, they'd be carrying on late and she needn't wait up for him.

'I'm booked to do a voiceover at half-seven,' Astrid adds briskly, 'and I still need to get showered and sorted.'

'What, in the evening? Who works at that time?' Spike tries to erase the hint of possessiveness in his voice.

'Loads of people do,' she laughs, 'especially at radio stations. It's for some programme trailers and I need to do it with the guy who does the evening show.'

Despite his irritation, Astrid's job as a voiceover artist actually increases her attractiveness. Spike can imagine happily buying incontinence pads if it were her voice purring away in the ad.

She marches over, grabs the duvet and pulls it away with a laugh, exposing Spike's naked form. 'Hey!' he cries in protest.

'Oh, don't be shy, baby.' Then, just as things are looking

hopeful again, she fixes him with a steady gaze. 'So, does Lou have any idea about us, d'you reckon?'

'Um, no, I don't think so . . .'

She tuts loudly. 'Ah, so you keep telling me it's all over between you two, that you're just flatmates really, blah-di-blah, yet you still act as if you're terrified about her finding out.'

'I'd just rather pick the right time,' he says, feeling hurt.

'Oh, I'm not saying you *should* tell her,' Astrid adds brusquely. 'That's up to you. It's your life, Spike, but I hope you're not kidding me, yourself or Lou by pretending your relationship's dead in the water when your girlfriend obviously doesn't think it is.'

'Actually,' Spike mumbles, 'I probably will say something soon. Maybe it's for the best . . .'

'She might be pleased,' Astrid says with a shrug. 'Maybe she's been trying to pluck up the courage to tell *you*.'

'To tell me what?' he asks, aghast.

'That she wants to break up. Face it, Spike – the only reason why you're round here four times a week is because you're both in such a rut, which is hardly surprising, is it, after how many years together?'

'Um, about thirteen,' Spike says dully.

'Hey.' Astrid's face softens. 'I'm just being realistic, honey. I mean, you were both so young – well, *she* was young when you first got together . . .'

Spike nods, marvelling at how Astrid manages to drop in casual references to his age. She, like Lou, is younger than him; in fact at twenty-nine, she's even younger than Lou. Is it *his* fault, though, if he attracts younger girls? What's he supposed to do – go out hunting for forty-eight-year-old women?

Spike clambers out of Astrid's bed, gathers up the clothes he threw off in haste and reluctantly puts them on.

'You make me sound like a real shit,' he huffs.

'I didn't mean that, babe. You're not shitty to me. You're quite lovely, in fact. Apart from that time when you didn't tell me Lou was going to show up at that gig . . .'

'What, the Christmas one? I had no idea! She said she was going to her work party.'

'Yeah,' Astrid says sternly, 'and she snuck off early so she could see you play, devoted girlfriend that she is.'

Spike's face droops. 'Yeah. Well, I'm sorry. That must've been uncomfortable for you.'

Astrid smiles, takes hold of his shoulders and kisses him firmly on the mouth. 'I've had better nights, but never mind. Now move it, you. I need to get ready.'

'Okay, *okay* . . .' He follows her downstairs to the front door which she opens with a flourish, mouthing bye-bye, apparently not caring that anyone could walk by and see her clad only in a chemise.

'Bye,' he says, stepping out onto her path. He knows he's sulking, and he turns to give her a big smile, but Astrid has already shut her front door.

*

Spike doesn't feel guilty, he decides as he leaves her street of tidy redbrick terraces. It's not thirteen years he and Lou have been together, he realises now, but *sixteen*. God, that makes him feel old. Spike is two years off fifty, a fact he rarely dwells on, but which now causes a flutter of panic in his chest.

He met Lou at the end of her foundation year at art school: a beautiful, fresh-faced doll of a girl who'd gone on to study jewellery, scooping prizes galore, while he'd scraped a living with the odd short-lived job – van driver, kitchen porter, postman – whilst trying to revive his music career. At twenty-one, Spike had had a hit with a plaintive, acoustic love song based on the *Black Beauty* TV theme tune, imaginatively entitled 'My Beauty' which had, for one summer, been the slow-dance song of choice. He'd moved from Glasgow to London, hoping to follow it up with another release to showcase his talents, but his second single had flopped, as had his third, and then his record label had dropped him and the horse telly thing had become a bit of a joke. There'd been a brief frisson of hope three years later, when his manager had called him, suggesting continuing the horse theme with 'an ironic, tongue-in-cheek version of Follyfoot or maybe even White Horses, you remember that one . . .'

'I don't want to be seventies-horse-telly-man,' Spike had snapped. Broke and desolate, he'd drifted back to Glasgow and into the arms of a cute art student called Lou. Is he passionate about her, after all this time? Not really, he reflects, striding past Sound Shack, his favourite music shop in York and giving Rick, the owner, a nod through the window before marching purposely home. Oh, she's pretty all right. She's barely aged at all, with that cheeky little face and smattering of freckles that he finds so sweet and endearing. Yet spending sixteen years with the same woman, no matter how lovely, is hardly sexy and dynamic, is it?

Spike doesn't know any couple, apart from his own mum and dad (who are old and therefore don't count) who've been together that long. Surely it's not natural to meet one person and stick with them forever, all through your young years when you're meant to be wild and crazy and shagging like mad. And *he's* not old. Forties are the new thirties these days, and he still *feels* young, which is what matters. Spike can proudly say he's never set foot in a Homebase. So here he is, a youngish virile man, and if Lou can't appreciate him and insists on wearing that marshmallow dressing gown instead of a chemise, then who can blame him for having a little dalliance now and again?

It's not as if he's ever brought Astrid home while Lou's

been at work. *That* would be out of order, Spike decides as he strides down their shabbier street and climbs the stairs to their first-floor flat. As he lets himself in and grabs a beer from the fridge, Spike contents himself with the fact that no one can say he doesn't have morals.

ELEVEN

Daisy is cleaning her teeth before bed. Normally, Hannah avoids going into the bathroom if she hears one of the kids in there, even if the door is wide open as it is now. Occasionally, she's made a mistake, and leapt out at the sight of Josh clad in his boxers, dabbing at a chin-spot with a little piece of loo roll. But now, hearing the sound of bristles vigorously scrubbing enamel, she figures that teeth cleaning isn't too personal and that it might be okay to tiptoe in.

'Hi,' she says casually. Daisy turns to her from the wash-basin with a mouth oozing pink froth. 'Er, I was thinking,' she starts, 'that maybe me and you could go shopping in the West End on Saturday, just the two of us?' Daisy blinks slowly as if anticipating a cruel punchline: *Because I'd like to buy you an embarrassing coat.* 'I know your dad suggested all of us going,' Hannah ploughs on, 'but Josh is going to Eddie's and I thought, well . . . wouldn't it be nice, just me and you? Would you like that?'

Daisy wipes some toothpaste from her chin, then turns back to the washbasin where she spits noisily. 'I dunno,' she says.

Hannah wonders if this means she's unsure of her

availability, or whether or not it would in fact be 'nice'. 'Well, I thought maybe we could choose you a dress,' Hannah offers, starting to sweat a little now. 'I mean, you are our bridesmaid, Daisy.'

She spits again – more for effect than out of necessity, Hannah suspects – then fills her cupped palms with water from the cold tap and slurps it noisily.

'Or, if that's too girlie for you,' Hannah soldiers on, 'maybe you'd like a skirt and a nice top, and a little cardi in case it's cold. It doesn't matter really. We don't even have to look at clothes. We could, er . . .' She tails off, stuck for words, as if faced with a particularly hostile interviewer. Why is she doing this anyway? Hannah doesn't care what anyone wears to the wedding. Yet it's not about shopping, not really. Hannah and Daisy have never done anything on their own together, because Hannah has always assumed Daisy would either come up with an excuse, like she was planning to stay home and count the woolly tufts on her bedroom rug, or reply with a curt 'No, thank you.' But now, with the wedding thundering towards them, she's decided to stop assuming anything.

Daisy sucks on a tendril of hair and looks at Hannah as if she's just suggested a trip to the chiropodist.

'Just me and you, d'you mean?' she asks cautiously.

'Yes. Wouldn't that be fun?'

Daisy pulls her lips into a thin line and nods.

'Great, then,' Hannah says, turning to leave the bathroom.

'Hannah?' Daisy has followed her out to the landing.

'Yes?' Hannah says eagerly.

'Wanna see something in my room?'

'Er, sure.'

She follows Daisy into her pale turquoise bedroom, carefully treading between the books, clothes and sweet wrappers that litter the floor. Hovering uncertainly, Hannah watches as Daisy crouches down to rummage at the bottom of her wardrobe. Finally, she pulls out a small, black, leather-bound book.

'What's that?' Hannah asks.

'Mum and Dad's wedding album.' She clutches it in front of her, as if about to present it to Hannah as a prize.

'Oh! That's nice. Did they, um . . . give it to you?'

Daisy perches on the edge of her bed. Hell, Hannah thinks, she's going to make me look through it. She's going to make me examine her mother in that billion-sparkles dress. Hannah feels vaguely queasy, and can feel beads of sweat on her upper lip.

'She made me and Josh one each,' Daisy explains, tossing back her long dark hair. 'I don't think he looks at his though.'

'Oh. Well, I guess boys aren't really into that kind of thing.'

'What, weddings?'

'No, um . . . looking at wedding *photos*. You know.' Hannah's entire body is now prickling with unease as she tries to conjure up a fictitious emergency downstairs – the smell of burning or gas – that will give her an excuse to charge out of Daisy's room. She doesn't want to scare the child by making her think her home is about to explode, but nor does she wish to peruse the album, which Daisy has now opened on her lap to reveal a full-page close-up of Petra's radiant smiling face.

Petra doesn't look like a fat nurse. There's nothing medical about her whatsoever. She's so lovely and elegant with her jet-black hair piled up that Hannah's breath catches in her throat. For an instant, she thinks Daisy must have found a copy of *Brides* magazine, snipped out a picture and stuck it in the album to trick her. But no, it's her mother all right – those are Petra's steely grey eyes, sharp cheekbones and perfectly painted red lips. 'This is Mummy arriving at church,' Daisy murmurs, stroking the side of Petra's face.

'That's nice.' Hannah swallows hard.

'And that's Grandma Esther standing next to Mum,' Daisy adds, turning the page.

Hannah feels ridiculous, perching gingerly on Daisy's bed, and sneakily checks out roughly how many pages the album might have. A dozen or so and she'll probably be able to hold it together, but this is a chunky album that could conceivably go on forever. 'Maybe you'd better get your PJs on now,' she says gently. 'It's gone half-eight . . .'

'Yeah, in a minute. Anyway, look – that's Daddy in his wedding suit. Is he gonna wear the same one at *your* wedding?'

'No, he's having a new one altered, remember?' Hannah says, willing Ryan to come upstairs, witness the cosy tableau and chivvy Daisy into bed.

'Oh yeah. Look! That's the dress I was telling you about.'

Hannah tries to focus on the stunning woman before her. But her head is swimming and she can no longer make proper words come out of her mouth. How can Ryan not still be in love with this woman? Hannah has met Petra numerous times, when she's picked up or dropped off the children, and has always thought, yes, she's striking, but somehow her chilliness cancels out her beauty. But she's never seen Petra look like this – like a woman in love, who'd go on to bear Ryan two children whom they'd raise together until her shock announcement three years ago that she must 'put myself first'. Heartbroken and stunned, Ryan simply hadn't seen it coming. As far as he was concerned, Petra's career as a concert cellist *had* come before everything else.

Maybe that's it, Hannah thinks, a sense of dread washing over her. Ryan asked her to marry him simply in an attempt to get over Petra. He is trying to *force* himself not to love her anymore.

Daisy is still going on about her mother's billowing veil. Hannah tries to show appreciation, but her tongue feels like a dry thing flapping around in her mouth. *They're only wedding photos,* she tells herself sternly. *She's just showing them off because she likes to look at them. It's nothing more sinister than that.*

'Don't you like it?' Daisy swivels round to face her.

'Oh, yes,' Hannah croaks. 'It's beautiful. A really amazing veil.' *Turn the page,* she thinks desperately, *so we can look at pictures of the bridesmaids or cake.* Daisy turns the page. There's a group picture with everyone neatly arranged in two rows in front of the church, squinting in the sunshine. So many people. Hannah wonders who they all are. There's also a close-up of Ryan standing next to his new bride, two beautiful people setting out on a life together. 'So you're up for this shopping trip at the weekend?' she says faintly as Daisy flicks through the final pages.

'Yeah, okay,' Daisy mutters.

They sit side by side for a moment, with Daisy now resting the closed album on her knees as if reluctant to put it away. Hannah isn't sure if she's imagined it, but Daisy might possibly have shuffled a millimetre closer to her on the bed. 'Thanks for showing me the album,' Hannah says gently. 'It obviously means a lot to you.'

Daisy nods mutely and bites her lip.

'I'm looking forward to our day out, are you?'

She nods again.

'I, er . . . I hope you're looking forward to our wedding too,' Hannah ventures, wondering if it would be okay to put an arm around Daisy's shoulders, or if she'd flinch, or leap up and run out of the room. No, better not.

'Yeah,' Daisy replies, her gaze fixed firmly on the album. 'But I still can't understand why it's not in a church.'

*

'I can't believe she did that,' Ryan whispers in bed that night. After half a year of living here, Hannah still finds the nocturnal whispering bizarre. It's not even as if they're up to anything. Ryan is wearing pyjamas, for God's sake. With Josh's bedroom next door, and Daisy's the one after that, the only time it feels remotely okay to have sex is if the kids aren't home, or if she or Ryan happen to wake up at some ungodly hour, like 4.30 am, when they'll grab the opportunity. It gives their sex life during the week an urgent quality, and makes the three out of four weekends when Daisy and Josh are at their mother's feel like a bit of a treat.

Lately, Hannah has started to hanker for a baby of her own; yet, as she's never had the faintest yearning before, she worries that this might be some desperate attempt to redress the balance. 'It doesn't matter,' she tells Ryan, snuggling closer. 'Daisy wasn't doing it to be mean or anything. And I bet every girl's entranced by her mum on her wedding day.'

There's a beat's silence and she breathes in the scent of Ryan's skin. There's something almost *edibly* warm about him: sweet and moreish, like a croissant. Hannah's paranoia about Petra has ebbed away, and she plants a soft kiss on his chest.

'I know they don't make it easy for you,' he says.

'Well . . .' She hesitates. 'It's not easy but, you know, I'm an adult. We'll get there. It'll just take some time.'

'I'm sure you're right,' he says, kissing her. *I am*, she reflects. *I just need to keep believing that*. Anyway, what kind of person of Ryan's age doesn't come with a little baggage? In fact, she likes the fact that he knows what days gym kits are needed and never forgets to pay the deposit for a school trip. So much information to store, and he manages it so admirably. She doesn't even think of Ryan's children as baggage; after all, they *belong* here, while she feels like an awkward guest at a fancy boutique hotel, under the watchful eye of two stern concierges. 'Anyway,' she adds, 'I've got some good news. I've been thinking me and Daisy should spend some time together, so I asked her if she'd like to come shopping and she said yes.'

'But you hate shopping,' he exclaims. 'You can't stand it. You don't see the point . . .'

'I know, but I thought she'd enjoy it.' *Because I don't know her, you see. I don't really know anything about your daughter.*

'Well, I think it's a great idea.'

'And hopefully,' Hannah adds, 'it'll get her in the wedding mood.'

Ryan pauses, then asks, 'Are you in the wedding mood, Han?'

Hannah frowns in the darkness. 'What d'you mean?'

He hesitates, and the hand which has been stroking her back and shoulders comes to a halt. 'I . . . just think you seem a bit tense, that's all.'

'Um, just wedding nerves, I guess.'

'Not getting cold feet, are you?' he asks.

'No, of course not. It's just . . . I don't know. Right now, it doesn't seem quite real. I'd never imagined getting married, being a *wife*.'

'But you're glad I put the idea in your head?'

'Yes, of course I am. Actually, no one's ever asked me before.'

'But they all wanted to, I bet,' he says affectionately.

'Hey, less of the *all* . . .'

They lie in silence for a few moments, and Hannah hears Josh padding to the bathroom.

'Maybe you should plan a hen night,' Ryan adds.

'It's funny, but Sadie was saying the same thing.'

'Well, I'm having one.'

'What, a hen night? I didn't think you were the type, darling, for the L-plates and the bunny ears.'

'No, a stag party. Not a *stag* stag party,' Ryan adds quickly. 'Not your gigantic piss-up and being stripped naked and tied to a lamppost . . .'

'Come on, I know you'd *love* that . . .'

'No,' he insists, 'I just mean something to mark the occasion. You should do something too.'

'Ryan,' she says firmly, 'if I was having a hen night, I'd want Sadie and Lou to be there.'

'But that's not impossible, is it?'

'Well, there's the little matter of Sadie having the twins and Lou being in York, plus they're coming to the wedding so I can't really expect them to schlep down to London twice in six weeks . . .'

'How about rounding up some of your other friends?'

Hannah shakes her head. 'I'd only keep wishing those two were there. Anyway,' she adds, realising they're forgetting to whisper, 'I'm really pleased about Saturday. I thought me and Daisy could choose her bridesmaid's outfit, if you don't mind not being there . . .'

'No,' he chuckles. 'You go ahead. I'm happy to leave that to you two.'

You two, thinks Hannah as sleep starts to close in on her, as if they might possibly become a little gang. And somewhere down the line, perhaps there'll be another person in the gang. A baby – a little brother or sister for Daisy and Josh.

Hannah wants to mention it – to say, 'I think I'm ready, Ryan. I can now almost imagine myself being a mother.' But as she turns to him, Josh makes a rather noisy exit from the bathroom, shutting the door unnecessarily firmly behind him.

It's as if he's reminding them that he's there, awake and prowling around on the landing, ensuring that no future babies are made. And by the time she hears Josh's bedroom light click off, Ryan has already fallen asleep.

TWELVE

Sadie isn't used to attending birthday parties at 11 am on a Saturday. In fact she isn't used to attending babies' birthday parties at any time of day, and hopes that her present, tucked into the little wire compartment beneath the buggy, will be deemed acceptable. The whole business of toys seems terribly complex these days. Sadie grew up in Liverpool, playing with the ordinary things little girls played with back then – Barbie, Sindy, a severed doll's head on which you could practise make-up techniques. None of the children she's encountered on the Little Hissingham coffee-morning circuit seem to own such things. The babies have scrunchy bead-filled bags to encourage fine-motor skills, while their older siblings play with tasteful wooden construction kits and Brio train sets. It's good to be invited, though, Sadie reminds herself, as this suggests that she's starting to belong.

'So glad you could come,' says Monica, the hostess, beckoning her in beneath a voluptuous swathe of lilac hanging over the cottage door. 'Isn't Barney with you?'

Although Monica has never met Barney, all the women around here seem adept at remembering not only everyone's children's names, but the names of their partners too. Sadie can't understand how they can store so much information. 'He'd loved to have come but he's working today,' Sadie fibs.

'He works on Saturdays?'

'Sometimes, at home,' Sadie says, which *is* the truth. 'Just to catch up, you know.'

'That's a shame,' Monica says, looking genuinely crestfallen. 'Anyway, come on in. Party's in full swing already.'

It sounds like it, too, with a blend of chattering toddlers, the odd crying baby and a dozen or so women all talking at once in Monica's overwhelmingly floral living room. Actually, Sadie didn't even ask Barney to come. He'd accompanied her to one parent-and-baby get-together in Hissingham church hall a couple of months ago, but it was impossible to even try to mingle when, whichever way Sadie turned, she could still see her husband, pressed to the flaking pale pink wall with terror flashing in his eyes. 'How long does this go on for?' he asked, grabbing her arm while she politely took a biscuit from an offered plate.

'Only about sixteen hours,' she joked, hoping he'd crack a smile and at least try to relax. But his jaw clenched even harder and she detected a faint lick of sweat on his upper lip.

'Oh, your babies are so cute!' a small, neat woman exclaims as Sadie manoeuvres the buggy containing her snoozing children to a far corner of Monica's living room.

'Thanks,' she says with a swell of pride.

'They're just like you, aren't they? Same colouring, face shape and that lovely dark hair . . .' Dylan and Milo wake up simultaneously and Sadie smiles, relieved that she's managed to kit them out to a reasonable standard – not too matchy-matchy, but in a vaguely coordinated selection of blues and greens which, she hopes, gives the impression she's some kind of alpha-mother. She's even managed to find all four soft leather shoes.

'Oh,' Sadie says, as Monica swoops past with the birthday baby in her arms, 'this is a present for Eva.' She snatches the present from beneath the buggy, which Monica accepts with thanks, placing it on an enormous pile on the oak dresser.

Freeing her babies, and lifting them down onto a circular rug littered with various multicoloured wire-and-bead contraptions, Sadie scans the room for somewhere to station herself. She glimpses her reflection in a large gilt-framed mirror. Although her hair is bleating for a cut, at least she's wearing lipstick. It's slightly askew, but it's *on*, and that's the main thing.

'So you're the one with the twins,' says a blonde-bobbed woman, beckoning Sadie to squish onto the rose-patterned sofa beside her.

'Yes, that's right.' She smiles brightly, keeping a close eye to ensure that Milo and Dylan aren't attacked by the other babies on the rug.

'I've seen you around. You moved here a few months ago, didn't you?'

'Yes, that's right, it's been six months now.'

'I'm Polly, and this is Justine,' she says, introducing the redhead next to her, who offers Sadie a dazed smile over the baby clamped to her breast.

'I'm Sadie . . .'

'So you moved with new babies?' Polly says. 'That was brave of you.'

'Well, we didn't plan it that way,' Sadie explains. 'We'd been trying to sell our London flat for ages but it didn't shift, then it finally did, and after having the babies I probably wasn't thinking straight, so . . .'

'You mean you don't like it here?' Justine asks with a small frown.

'No! No, I love it,' Sadie declares. 'It's so, er . . . peaceful and pleasant and everything. And it's safe, much safer than where we lived – in fact we were burgled when I was pregnant and that set us thinking that we should move somewhere small and quiet and er . . .' Hell, she's broken her rule already, babbling on when all these women want is a bit of light chit-chat. Sadie glances at the table laden with chocolate brownies and cupcakes and her stomach rumbles ominously.

'It's much better for children out here,' Justine remarks. 'There's such a strong sense of community.'

'Oh, yes, I can see that . . .'

'Especially if you're planning a big family,' chips in Polly, whom Sadie has realised is mother to three of the children in the room, which seems almost unimaginable. 'It's wonderful how everyone helps each other out.'

'Well, I'm not sure we'll have any more,' Sadie says with a grin.

'Oh!' Polly frowns at her, then a flicker of understanding crosses her face and she adds, 'Of course, if it was difficult for you the first time . . .'

'No, it's lovely, and I'm really happy and everything,' Sadie explains, 'but, you know, managing the two of them is probably enough to be going . . .'

'I mean conceiving,' Polly murmurs. 'If you've been through all that, you probably won't want to again with all the drugs and expense and the stress of it.'

Sadie blinks at her. What is it about having twins that makes everyone assume they were conceived by IVF? Sadie is tempted to have a T-shirt printed saying WE DIDN'T HAVE ANY BOTHER CONCEIVING. IT WAS RIDICULOUSLY SIMPLE – IN FACT IT HAPPENED THE FIRST TIME WE TRIED!

'No, that part was easy,' Sadie says lightly. 'We didn't have IVF.'

'Oh, didn't you? I'm sorry, I just assumed . . .'

'It's okay,' Sadie says, feeling bad now for making Polly

70

uncomfortable. 'What I mean is, we're not in any hurry for another.'

'Don't rely on breastfeeding as contraception then,' Justine remarks. 'That's how we got Benjamin . . .'

'Oh, I'm not,' Sadie says quickly.

'I got a coil after that,' she adds.

'Me too,' Polly says eagerly. 'It's fantastic.'

Sadie falls silent, not sure she has anything to add to this new, startling line of conversation that doesn't feel quite right at a child's first birthday party. Anyway, contraception is hardly an issue at the moment. Since Sadie was around six months pregnant, the very prospect of sex has been as appealing as having a foot amputated – which makes it nearly a year since she and Barney last did it. *God*, she realises, *we're heading for our first no-sex anniversary.*

As Milo starts to cry, Sadie rescues him from the rug and holds him on her lap. 'He thinks it's an ice lolly,' Polly chuckles, indicating her toddler who's sitting nearby, gnawing at a yellow disc.

'What is it?' Sadie asks.

'Frozen banana. It's great for teething, soothes the gums . . .'

'And he really thinks it's a proper lolly from a shop?' Sadie marvels. Out of the corner of her eye, she can see Monica starting to unwrap the presents, showing each one to baby Eva in turn.

'I wouldn't give Alfie an ice lolly from a *shop*,' Polly exclaims, as if Sadie has just suggested feeding him frozen Red Bull. 'I make them at home with fresh juice.'

'Of course, that's what I meant . . .' she says feebly. Monica is opening Sadie's present now, and says a brief 'Ahhh' to the garish giraffe before dumping it on a teetering pile of already opened gifts.

'Have *you* ever frozen a banana?' Polly asks.

71

'Er, no, but I'll definitely try it,' Sadie says, seized by an urge to leave the overheated room and almost grateful when Dylan emits a howl from the rug.

'Oh dear. Your boys are a bit unsettled, aren't they?'

'Yes, I think they're a bit hot . . .' She gathers him up, holding both babies who are now wailing heartily.

'They make quite a racket, the two of them!'

Sadie nods. 'They certainly do. In fact I think we'd better go.'

'Maybe you could just give them a little push back and forth around the garden?'

'No, I really think we should head home.' Trying not to seem too eager, Sadie tries, unsuccessfully, to soothe the boys. Strapping them into the buggy, she says a collective goodbye and makes for the front door, trying to stroll rather than charge towards it, and filling her lungs with crisp spring air once she steps outside. She needs to talk to Hannah or Lou, someone who really knows her and won't start going on about their 'fantastic' coil or imply that she and Barney should get on with the business of baby production.

Sadie tries Hannah first, who thankfully picks up. 'Sadie? How's it going?'

'Good, fine . . . whereabouts are you?'

'Just out shopping in the West End with Daisy,' Hannah replies, and the hubbub of voices and traffic, then a siren wailing, almost makes Sadie faint with desire.

'What are you looking for?'

'We're just trying to find something for Daisy to wear to the wedding . . .'

How cosy, Sadie thinks – reassuring, too, to be reminded that babies grow up, and that at some point it's feasible to take them to the shops. To the West End, even.

'What about you?' Hannah asks.

'I've just been to a party.'

'Really? Like, a lunch party or something?'

'Er, yeah, sort of.'

'That sounds nice . . .'

And you sound distant, Sadie thinks, *as if your mind's on something else – which it is, of course, because you and Daisy are browsing in some chi-chi little shops in* . . . actually, Sadie can't think what part of London has chi-chi shops anymore, and she only left six months ago.

'I'll ring you some other time,' she murmurs.

'Yeah, okay. Sorry, Sadie, it's just . . . *tricky* right now . . .'

'Are you okay? You sound a bit hassled . . .'

'No, look, I'll have to go now, sorry, sorry . . .' And she's gone.

Sadie tries Lou, but both her landline and mobile go to voicemail. She's probably at work. Sadie hasn't got her head around Lou's shift pattern yet, but she seems to virtually live at that soft play centre these days.

Of course, both of her friends are busy right now, as most people are on Saturdays. They're working, shopping, living their lives, and although she can't quite identify what it is she's missing, Sadie suspects that freezing bananas to make pretend ice-lollies probably won't fill the gap. She's been kidding herself that she can pull this off – fit in with these women who bake brownies all day, and be a proper mother to Milo and Dylan. Even Barney is slipping away from her, and who can really blame him when her sense of humour and sex drive seem to have completely disappeared? A lump forms in Sadie's throat as she marches home, knowing she can never tell anyone about the horrible, claustrophobic mess she's found herself in.

THIRTEEN

The day isn't turning out quite the way Hannah had imagined. All the way into the West End, Daisy was stonily quiet, as if mentally preparing herself for extensive dental drilling work. And now, as they hoof along a packed Oxford Street, surrounded by eye-popping stores crammed with everything a ten-year-old girl could possibly desire, she still hasn't perked up. 'See anything you like?' Hannah asks, instantly overwhelmed by a sea of pastel lace and excitable teenagers in New Look.

Daisy shakes her head. 'Nah.' Hannah casts a glance around the vast floor. Perhaps there's just an overabundance of . . . *stuff*. If she's finding it all too much, maybe Daisy is too. It can't be easy picking, say, a top, when there's something like eight thousand to choose from.

Daisy wanders away from Hannah to flick through a rail of sludge-coloured trousers. Like Hannah, Daisy isn't really a dress sort of girl; she prefers a complicated layering system that involves long tops, short tops, leggings, shorts and opaque tights, often with a drapey cardi flung nonchalantly over the top. With her tall, willowy frame, it usually works pretty well. Whenever her mother takes her shopping, Daisy always returns with bagfuls of uninspiring-looking items that look fantastic when she puts them on. Maybe, Hannah wonders, it's *her* that's putting Daisy off. As Ryan reminded her the other night, Hannah doesn't enjoy shopping. She practically exists in jeans and vest tops; practical clothes for cycling or painting, although she hasn't painted much lately. Anyway, she thinks now, picking up trousers Daisy's knocked off the rail, isn't shopping a classic mother-daughter activity? Daisy is probably missing her mum, especially since Hannah doesn't seem to know what to do. While mums and daughters all around her are bonding over sequined tops and asymmetrical dresses, Hannah is loitering awkwardly like an alien whose first, baffling experience of earth involves being dropped into the chaos of New Look on a Saturday afternoon.

'How about this?' she asks, holding up a stripey top with an ostentatious bow on the front.

Daisy cringes. 'No thanks.'

'Or this?' Hannah indicates a denim mini-skirt. Daisy shakes her head and moves swiftly on, as if Hannah's offered her a peach twinset.

In hot pursuit, but trying to appear calm, Hannah begins to feel redundant and foolish. She thinks about Sadie, in the country, nipping off to lunch parties with her babies in tow. *She'd* know how to handle Daisy. She'd have chosen her something – Sadie knows instinctively what goes with what – and by now they'd be giggling away in a café, a cluster of carrier bags at their feet. Someone biffs Hannah in the ribs with a rucksack, sending her staggering sideways into a rack of handbags adorned with gleaming buckles and chains and, in one case, a plastic lizard. She loses sight of Daisy, her heart racing until she pops into view again. Daisy's sour expression suggests that she's being dragged down the poultry aisle of a supermarket, not being given the run of a fashion emporium.

They make for Zara, where Daisy grudgingly tries on a

couple of outfits that don't fit, then they head to the kids' section at Primark, which is even more crowded than New Look. 'I'm gonna try these on,' she announces, having amassed an armful of clothes.

'Great. I'll wait by the changing room, okay? In case you want to come out and show me anything.'

Daisy frowns at her. 'I'll be all right.'

'Yes, I *know* you'll be fine, I just meant if you wanted, um, a second opinion . . .' But Daisy has whipped into the changing room, and all Hannah can do is plonk herself on a small plastic stool and resist the temptation to text Ryan: HAVING TOTALLY CRAP TIME. COMING HOME NOW. She desperately wants to phone Sadie back, but what would she say? Admitting how bleak things really are would mean facing up to the fact that she doesn't have the faintest idea about how she intends to carry off this step-mother lark.

Hannah waits patiently on the stool for what feels like a week. She can actually feel herself ageing, her skin shrivelling and her bones beginning to creak. Nearby, a leggy woman in tight jeans is having an altercation with her teenage daughter. 'You've got trousers just like those at home,' the woman snaps. She's gripping the handles of a buggy containing a screaming toddler.

'Wanna go,' he keeps yelling. 'Wanna go home NOW.' It's a sentiment Hannah can sympathise with entirely.

'They're *different*, Mum,' the girl declares. 'These are a much brighter blue.'

'Yes,' her mum replies, 'because the ones at home have been washed.'

'So they're all faded and *that's* why I need new ones . . .'

'Go on then, try them on . . .'

'Want Daddy!' the toddler wails. With a sigh, the woman parks the buggy beside Hannah and sinks down onto the stool next to her.

'How come we mums end up spending so much of our lives sitting outside changing rooms?' she says with a wry smile.

'I know,' Hannah says. 'I think she must be trying on everything at least twice.' Daisy reappears briefly, grabs a few more items from a nearby rail and struts back into the changing room.

'Pretty, isn't she?' the woman observes. 'Lovely sense of style she's got.'

'Yes, she has.' Hannah manages a smile.

'Takes after you,' the woman says kindly.

'Thanks.' Hannah falls silent, feeling deeply uncomfortable about taking credit for Daisy's fashion sense. 'Actually,' she adds, 'I'm not her mum.'

'Oh?'

'No, I'm her . . .' Hannah tails off, wondering how to put it. Stepmum still doesn't feel accurate; she fears she'll never be remotely qualified to assume such a terrifyingly grown-up job title. 'I'm sort of . . . seeing her dad,' Hannah adds, realising that's completely wrong too. They're getting *married*, for God's sake. They've chosen rings, booked the registry office and bar-cum-restaurant for a small party afterwards, *and* she's bought that fat nurse abomination. They're even planning a honeymoon somewhere down the line, although they have yet to book anything as Petra hasn't come back to Ryan about when it might be 'convenient' to look after her own children. The cello comes first, naturally, taking Petra all over the world to give performances. Hannah imagines it strapped in the aeroplane seat beside her, being asked by a flight attendant whether it wants chicken or fish.

'Oh, hell,' the woman cries as her toddler breaks free from his buggy restraints and her daughter glides out of the changing room. 'Right – we're getting out of here.'

'Can't I have these trousers?' the girl bleats.

'I said you've got some at home. What d'you think I am, made of money?' Manhandling her toddler back into his buggy, and starting to march away, the woman flings a quick glance back towards Hannah. 'Enjoy your day with your, er . . .'

'Thanks. You too.' Hannah checks her watch as Daisy finally ambles towards her. 'Wasn't there anything you liked?' she asks, now feeling horribly hot in the stuffy store.

Daisy shakes her head. 'Nah. But there *is* something . . .'

'Oh, what's that?'

Daisy pushes back her hair and meets Hannah's gaze. 'You know for the wedding, right?'

'Yes?' Hannah says eagerly.

'Well,' Daisy fixes her with a defiant stare, 'I'd like my ears pierced.'

'Really? Well, I guess you'll have to talk that over with your mum and dad.'

'Oh,' Daisy mutters as they make their way down the escalator.

'Anyway, are you hungry yet? I'm starving . . .'

'Yeah. A bit.' They step off the escalator and squeeze their way through the buffeting crowds towards the exit.

'The thing is,' Daisy says, 'I really need to get it done today.'

'Well, I'm sorry,' Hannah replies, 'I can't let you do that without your mum or dad saying it's okay.'

'But it's *my* ears,' Daisy shoots back, 'and the thing is, if I get it done today, it'll be all healed for the wedding and I'll be able to take out the boring plain earrings and put in ones I like. 'Cause you've got to leave them in for six weeks. How long is it till the wedding?'

'Er, six weeks.' Hannah pushes the main door open, steps out of Primark and takes a big gulp of cool air.

'See! I'll *have* to get it done today.'

'I . . . I'm just not sure, Daisy. It's quite a big, significant

78

thing. You might feel sick and queasy and one of your parents should . . .'

'No, I won't. I'm never sick. I have *never actually been sick*.'

'Really?'

Daisy shakes her head. They've stopped on the pavement next to a man who's shouting that he can save everyone from all the greed and nastiness in the world. Hannah is tempted to ask if he can help out with the earring issue.

'And it's not a big thing,' Daisy adds firmly. 'It's just two teeny holes and they use a gun.'

'A gun?' Hannah is trying to maintain a pleasant expression, which is becoming trickier as she recalls her own ears being pierced at sixteen, courtesy of a darning needle and a lump of cold potato held at the back of her lobe.

'Yeah,' Daisy says. 'It's really easy. Why don't you phone Dad and ask him?'

'I, er . . .' Hannah pulls out her mobile. It doesn't feel right, calling Ryan to confirm what she already knows; that he won't allow it and, worse, it'll imply that she's incapable of handling the situation herself. She feels ridiculous now, having pictured the two of them trotting happily along Oxford Street, stopping off for cakes and Daisy realising that Hannah's sole purpose isn't to steal her father and ruin her young life after all.

'Well, are you gonna phone Dad?' she demands.

'Okay. I'll do that.' Bristling with irritation now, Hannah calls Ryan's mobile, which goes to voicemail. He's not at home either, and she doesn't bother leaving a message, because how pathetic would her voice sound, drifting out of the answerphone, wittering about earrings?

'Claire's Accessories,' Daisy announces. 'That's where everybody has it done.' Hannah smiles tensely. Then a brainwave hits her. Of course: Sadie will know what to do.

Capable Sadie, who's managing to live in that teeny village in the middle of nowhere without going mad, while raising not one but two babies *and* going to lunch parties. Hannah feels guilty now, being so distracted when her friend had called earlier. And if Sadie can't offer a snippet of sage advice, then who can?

Damn, she's not picking up either. Probably at another lunch party by now. 'Phone Mum,' Daisy barks. 'Mum'll say it's okay.'

'Fine, but I *have* to get something to eat first, okay?' Boldly, without any debate, she takes Daisy by the hand and whisks her into Prêt à Manger.

Here, none of the sandwiches is deemed acceptable. A plain bread roll is chosen, even though it's really offered to accompany soup (Daisy wrinkles her nose at Hannah's suggestion of soup, as if she's trying to trick her into consuming vomit).

'Dad said I could have my ears done for the wedding,' Daisy mumbles, picking a crumb off her lip.

Hannah has an overwhelming urge to tip a large glass of chardonnay down her throat. 'Well, we'll see,' she murmurs.

'You've got *your* ears done,' Daisy ventures as they leave.

'Yes, Daisy, but I'm thirty-five! And I was sixteen when I had it done and you're only ten. There's a big difference.'

'If you don't let me have it done,' Daisy growls as they head outside, 'I'm not coming to your wedding.'

Hannah stares at her. 'You really mean that? You wouldn't come to your own dad's wedding because of *ears*?'

Daisy shrugs. 'No.'

'But he'd be so upset! Can you imagine how he'd feel if you weren't there?'

Daisy juts out her chin. 'I want to wear earrings at the wedding.'

'What about clip-ons?' Hannah suggests desperately.

'There were loads of nice clip-ons in New Look. Come on, we'll go back and choose you a pair . . .' The thought of braving that store twice in one day is beyond horrific. But Hannah is prepared to spend the whole damn *night* in New Look if it'll settle the earring issue.

'I don't *want* clip-ons.'

Don't wear bloody clip-ons then! Hannah wants to yell. 'Okay,' she snaps, yanking her phone from her pocket, 'I'll call your mum and you can talk it over with her.' A vein pulses urgently in her neck as she scrolls through her contacts.

'Hello? Hannah?' Petra's voice is needle-sharp.

'Hi, Petra, are you busy right now?'

'Yes, just a bit, haha,' Petra says, meaning, *when am I not rushed off my feet*? Hannah wonders if she's interrupted a performance, whether Petra's gripping her bow in one hand, mobile in the other, bony knees thrust apart with her cello between them. This image makes her feel a tiny bit better.

'It's just—'

'Is this urgent, Hannah, or can we talk later?'

Hannah glances down at Daisy who's picking out a bit of bread from between her teeth. 'It is urgent actually. I'm out shopping with Daisy and she's decided she wants to get her ears pierced.'

Silence. No, not quite silence. Hannah can detect the faint whirring of Petra's *incredibly* overworked brain. 'Petra? Are you still there?'

'Yes, Hannah. I'm just . . . digesting it.' Hannah pictures a conductor drumming his fingers impatiently on a little podium thing.

'Oh.' Hannah bites her lip. She assumed Petra would deliver a brisk yes or no, not that she'd need time to mull it over. The silence seems to stretch for an eternity. Daisy squashes a smouldering cigarette butt with the toe of her patent boot. 'Shall I call you back later?' Hannah suggests.

'No, there's no need for that. We can talk now, even though I'm trying to do *fifty* things at once . . .'

'Petra, look, if it's not a good time . . .'

'That's not the issue,' Petra barks. 'It's us, having this conversation about my daughter who you seem to think is perfectly old enough to have her body *disfigured*, her lobes punctured by some teenager wielding a needle . . .'

'Well, I wouldn't call it disfig—'

'She's ten!' Petra exclaims. 'Do you think it's okay for a ten-year-old girl to have something *irreversible* done to her body, with needles?'

'Er, they use a gun these days,' Hannah says dully.

'A gun? Good God!' Petra really is bloody unhinged, Hannah decides. She knows Ryan was devastated when she left – he made no secret of that. If she'd been him, though, she'd have been popping champagne corks and dancing wildly on the scuffed bit of floor in the attic where her cello used to stand. Petra is now babbling on about infections and pus. Daisy has extinguished the cigarette and is kicking it towards a smear of pigeon droppings. 'It's fine, Petra,' Hannah cuts in firmly. 'Actually, I thought you wouldn't be keen. I just called because Daisy asked me to, and as you're not happy, we definitely won't do it.'

'Well, I hope not.' Her voice softens slightly.

'Of course we won't. I'd never do anything like that without asking you or Ryan first. Anyway, as you're obviously in the middle of something . . .'

'Bye then,' Petra says curtly.

What a monstrous mother, Hannah thinks, not even asking how Daisy is, or saying a quick hello to her. Despite the disastrous nature of their day, Hannah has a sudden urge to envelop her in a hug.

'What did Mum say?' Daisy asks quietly.

'Um, she's not keen, sweetheart. But that doesn't mean never. Maybe, when you're a little bit older, you could ask her again.'

Daisy's mouth sets in a scowl as, agreeing that they've run out of shopping steam, they march purposefully towards Oxford Circus tube station. Jesus, Hannah reflects, anyone would think the poor kid had asked for a facial tattoo.

*

Hannah can't sleep. It's unusually hot and stuffy for late April, and she tosses and turns, replaying her day in town. Unable to convey its true awfulness, she made light of it to Ryan and even threw in a few jokes about being trampled underfoot by herds of antelopes in New Look.

Ryan is sleeping soundly, but Hannah just can't get comfortable. She's replaying Daisy announcing, 'Hannah bought me a plain bread roll for lunch!' as they all sat around the dinner table, and Ryan throwing her a quizzical look, as if he imagined for a second that Hannah hadn't given Daisy any choice. Slipping out of bed, she considers going downstairs to make a cup of tea, but is wary of being discovered by one of the kids as she sits bleakly in the kitchen in the middle of the night. She might look as if she's losing it, which would cheer them up no end.

Instead, she heads up to the converted loft – formerly Petra's music room – and now Hannah's very own studio. Sitting down at her desk, she flicks on the wonky Anglepoise lamp she's had since art college, then turns on her ageing computer and waits for it to whir into life. All around the room, canvases are stacked against the plain white walls. Cityscapes, mostly, exploding with colour. Although Hannah studied illustration at college, she still loves to paint. She runs her gaze along the row of canvases leaning against the wall. These were painted before she moved in with Ryan;

he seemed entranced as she unpacked them and helped to peel off their protective bubble wrap layers. But there's no evidence of recent painting activity. No tubes out of their wooden boxes, no brushes in jars or hardened worms of paint stuck to her palette. In fact, she's only started one painting – a portrait of Daisy which she had to abandon because it felt wrong, the two of them up here with Daisy reminding her, in that prim little voice, 'This used to be Mummy's music room, you know. She kept her cello over there. That's what made the scratches on the floor.'

Focusing on the screen now, Hannah begins to type:

Girls, hope all's well. Been missing you loads lately and I've had an idea. I'm planning a hen weekend, just the three of us. How d'you fancy going to Glasgow for old time's sake? Her attention is momentarily diverted by a painting of the Clyde, silvery-green beneath a searing blue sky. *Sadie,* she continues, *I know the babies are still little, but d'you think Barney would be okay with you coming away? And Lou – I know York's hardly on the doorstep but d'you think you could make it, get some time off work? We could go to all our old haunts, try to track down some of the old crowd, maybe even find Johnny, although God knows where he disappeared to. Or maybe it'd be better just the three of us.*

So what d'you think? Shall we talk about dates? I know you'll be at the wedding in just a few weeks, but I honestly think I'll burst if I don't see you before that. No pressure though!!

Lots of love, Han xxx

As she clicks 'send' and turns off her computer, Hannah feels her spirits rise as she pictures the three of them – the Garnet Street Girls – back together again. *Please come,* she murmurs as she pads back down to her and Ryan's bedroom. *Please, please say yes.*

FOURTEEN

Lou feels renewed after seeing Jo, the friend who championed her jewellery, helping to get it stocked in various boutiques and gift shops around York. It's a bright, sunny day and she's glad she's following her new rule to make the most of Sundays. Spike hadn't wanted to come. 'Brunch?' he'd laughed as she was heading out. 'Who has *brunch*? I mean, what's the point of it?'

'The point,' she explained, 'is that there isn't any point – it's just *nice*.' And she'd skipped off, relieved to escape the flat which now felt as if there was no air left in it at all. She's glad, too, that Spike didn't come. He still tends to slip into flirt mode, his default setting with women, which might have been vaguely charming when he was in his mid- or even late-thirties, but is less endearing at forty-eight. In fact, although Lou's wide circle of girlfriends know him well, and aren't averse to bantering lewdly with him, she worries sometimes that he might be starting to come across as a slightly creepy middle-aged man.

On a whim, Lou had two Bloody Marys, which have made her feel pleasantly woozy as she takes the walkway along the river before turning up into the slightly grubbier neighbourhood where she and Spike live. But as she steps into the hallway, before she's even climbed the narrow stairs to their flat, she senses her *joie de vivre* ebbing away. She inhales a vaguely unsettling scent of something germy and festering. The smell leads her into the flat where her boyfriend is curled up on the living room rug, the gas fire flickering its feeble orangey glow. Some old black-and-white sci-fi movie is on the TV with the sound down, and the rug is strewn with crumpled tissues.

'Hi, love.' Lou bobs down to plant a kiss on the top of his head. 'It's a gorgeous spring day out there. D'you really need the fire on?'

'Yeah. I'm feeling kind of shivery.' To demonstrate, he shivers dramatically.

Lou straightens up and observes him. Spike has constructed a sort of nest for himself on the floor with the sofa cushions, plus her fluffy pink dressing gown, which he's bunched up and fashioned into a fat pillow. 'Maybe you should get out, have a walk or something,' she suggests. 'It's really stuffy in here. No wonder you feel awful.'

He looks at her with mournful eyes and dabs his nostrils with a wet tissue. 'I don't really feel well enough for that, Lou-Lou.'

She frowns. 'You seemed okay when I left. Just had a bit of a sniffle, didn't you?'

'Yeah, well, it's more than that now. It's a *lot* worse than that.' He delves under her dressing gown where, much to her consternation, he seems to be storing yet more tissues, like a squirrel secreting away nuts for the winter months. Lou glances around the newly-appointed sick bay. Their flat is shabby, and bits have started to ping off the Ikea shelves. There's a fine layer of dust on the TV screen, and the wicker newspaper rack is overflowing with ageing papers. Clearly deciding that Lou isn't being nearly sympathetic enough, Spike picks up a tatty paperback, finds his page and holds it open at arm's length.

'I don't know why you don't get reading glasses,' Lou offers, carefully sidestepping the collection of abandoned mugs.

'Because I don't need them,' he mutters.

'But you do! If I needed them, I'd just go out and get a pair. What does it matter? No one's going to see, it's not as if you'd have to wear them out if that's what you're worried about . . .'

'I don't need glasses,' he retorts, shutting the book.

'I just mean *reading* glasses. They're really cheap. Poundland have them for . . .'

'A quid. Yeah, I know! You've mentioned it before, many times.'

God, have I? Lou thinks. *Have I turned into the kind of person who goes on about reading glasses in Poundland?*

Several sneezes in succession curtail the discussion, and Lou throws him an exasperated glance. Perhaps she should mop his fevered brow and make him a mug of fresh tea to join the extended family of cold, half-finished teas that are dotted around him. But she picked up the Sunday papers on her way home and, rather than read them here, surrounded by snotty tissues and germs, she fancies perusing them as she takes a bubble bath instead.

'D'you need anything, hon?' she asks.

Spike shakes his head, clearly still smarting over his eyesight being called into question. 'No thanks. I'm *fine*.'

As she runs her bath, relieved to get away from him, Lou mulls over Hannah's email. Lou picked it up before she hurried out to meet Jo, and she has yet to reply. 'Forgot to tell you,' she calls out to Spike over the rush of the water, 'Hannah's planning a hen weekend.'

'Uh?' he croaks from the living room.

'Hannah wants a weekend away, in Glasgow – just me, her and Sadie. She emailed me about it last night.'

'Glasgow?' Spike exclaims, at the bathroom doorway

now, looking oddly perky, considering he was on the verge of death a few moments earlier.

'Yes.' Lou quickly undresses and sinks into the warm, sudsy water. 'It would make sense, wouldn't it, going back there to celebrate? We could relive our misspent youth.' She laughs hollowly, waiting for Spike to protest that it's too far away and too expensive, and what would he do by himself all weekend?

'When's it happening?' he asks.

'Don't know, but pretty soon I'd imagine. She wants me to call her so we can talk about dates.' Lou reaches over the bath to grab one of the Sunday supplements from the floor.

'Dates?' Spike repeats.

It's irritating her now, this echoing thing, as if words like 'Glasgow' and 'dates' are unfamiliar and strange and he needs to practise making the sounds.

'You know,' she says slowly, as if speaking to a small child. '*Dates*. Not the sticky kind that come in a box. The calendar kind – like when we'd go.'

Spike runs a hand through his hair that's pressed in different directions from where he's been lying on it. Dark, bruisy patches lurk under his eyes, and his skin looks starved of daylight. 'You mean like a *whole* weekend away?' he says. 'In Glasgow?'

Lou eyes him steadily over the magazine. 'Yeah. Me, Hannah and Sadie off the leash for two whole days.' She widens her eyes, teasing him. 'God knows what we'd get up to.'

He grins, a faint flush replacing his deathy pallor. 'So are you going then?'

'How can I, Spike?' Lou pokes her toes out of the water and flexes them.

'Well, why not?'

'Um . . . for one thing, there'd be the train fare, the

hotel, meals, drinks and . . .' Lou shrugs. 'I can't afford it. I'm absolutely stony broke.'

'But . . . you just went out for brunch.'

'Yes,' she says, 'and it was Jo's treat. I can't afford a whole weekend away.'

'God, that's a shame.' Spike's forehead crinkles in sympathy. 'I mean, they *are* your best mates, and Hannah will only be getting married once, hopefully.'

Lou inhales the mildewy bathroom air as an image forms in her mind: of Hannah and Sadie perched on bar stools, laughing their heads off like old times. Hannah will be glowing with pre-wedding excitement, and Sadie will be all red lips and curves and tumbling chestnut hair, and men will be falling over themselves to talk to them. Then she sees herself, not in her favourite vintage cocktail dress which she bought when she was a student, and which she loves and still fits her, but in an acrylic brown tabard with Let's Bounce written across the chest. And she's not on a bar stool between her two best friends, but on her hands and knees, using her little purple plastic scraper to remove a blob of congealed coronation chicken off the floor.

Spike is at the bathroom cabinet now, taking out a pair of tiny scissors and tilting his head back in front of its mirrored door, all the better to study his nasal hairs. He didn't have those when she met him. He just had a hairy chest – still does, of course – which Lou had found manly and sexy because, at nineteen, she'd never encountered one in an intimate setting before. Spike was different in other ways too, with his dangerous dark eyes and brief flurry of pop stardom in his youth, which she'd felt certain would burst back into life, if she stood back and waited patiently for long enough.

'Ooooh,' Spike exclaims, snipping a hair. Lou drapes the magazine over the edge of the bath and observes the process with interest. To his right, three pairs of wrinkly boxer shorts are spread out to dry on the radiator. Nasal clipping complete, he turns and looks at her naked body in the bath. Not lustfully, Lou realises, or even approvingly, even though he still seems to fancy her, at least when they're in bed. No, the way Spike is observing Lou now suggests that she's a piece of sculpture he's not sure if he likes or not. She imagines him turning away from her in the gallery and deciding to go to the café instead.

'Well,' he says thoughtfully, 'maybe we could figure something out so you can go.'

'I don't see how,' Lou replies. 'The wedding's coming up, isn't it? I know we're staying at Ryan and Hannah's, but still . . . I might as well be realistic.'

Spike frowns and scans the bathroom, as if seeking inspiration from the cracked blue tiles or his collection of mangled ointment tubes, which he stores in a plastic plant pot on the windowsill. 'Couldn't Hannah or Sadie help you out?'

'I'm not asking them, Spike. God, I'd never ask my friends for money. It would sound so . . . *pathetic*.'

'Why?'

'Well, you know – thirty-five years old and I can't scrape together a train fare to Glasgow . . .' She snorts.

He looks crestfallen. Lou blinks at him, wondering how he manages to appear so much younger than forty-eight. Probably because he doesn't have much to worry about, apart from which bodily part to idly scratch next, or whether it's time to slope to the kitchen for another cup of tea or a beer.

'Lou-Lou, honey . . .' He pauses. 'You know what I think? You've been working too hard at that awful place. And if you go to Glasgow it'll be a change of scene and a laugh, *and* I could spend the whole weekend working on my CV.'

'Your CV?' she splutters. 'What d'you mean, your CV?'

He frowns, looking hurt. 'You know. One of those things people send out when they're applying for jobs.'

'Yes, I know what a CV is, but . . .' She stops herself from saying *what would you put on it?*

'What kind of job would you apply for?' she asks.

'Oh, I dunno, I suppose I'll have to start thinking more . . . laterally.'

The bath water is lukewarm now, but Lou is too dumbstruck by Spike's announcement to reach for the hot tap.

'What about your music?' she adds. 'I mean, are you thinking of getting a full-time job or what?'

'Well,' he shrugs, 'I suppose I'll just see what's out there and keep music going on the side.'

'On the side of what?' she asks, laughing now.

'I've no idea!' he huffs, all symptoms of his sudden illness vanishing. 'But you're right – we need more money. We can't keep going like this. Since I've been ill, I've been doing a lot of thinking . . .' He reddens slightly.

'But you've only been ill for like, a couple of hours, and anyway, *I'm* not stopping you from doing your CV. It's not as if I breathe down your neck putting you off. In fact there's no reason why you can't do it right now, without me being 200 miles away.' She clamps her mouth shut. Here he is, talking about taking a positive step, and she's giving him a lecture.

'Yeah, I know, babe,' he murmurs, 'but it'd just be me, all on my own, and I know I've been a bit, um . . . *relaxed* lately. I feel shit about it, to be honest. And if you went away I'd have nothing to do than focus on applying for jobs.'

'Okay,' she says slowly, 'but I've told you, I don't even have the money to . . .'

'Let's sell something then,' Spike says firmly.

Lou stares at him. He looks so energised now, with his newly-clipped nostrils and glowing cheeks.

'What would we sell?' she asks warily.

'Couldn't you knock up a few necklaces?'

'I don't *knock up* jewellery,' she retorts. 'I know it might not seem much to you, Spike, but it takes me days to make a piece, and I don't even have any silver or stones at the moment . . .' She tails off, prickling with guilt at the sight of his sad, puppy-dog face as he turns and leaves the bathroom. 'Sorry, I know you're only trying to help,' she calls after him.

When he doesn't reply, Lou climbs out of the bath, looks around for her dressing gown, then remembers that Spike's stolen it for a pillow and wraps herself in a towel instead. As she joins him on the rug in front of the gas fire, he turns to her and smiles. 'I've had an idea,' he says, pointing at the guitar propped up against their coffee table. 'See that? Reckon I know someone who'd buy it.'

'What?' She frowns. 'You're not selling that! Don't be crazy.'

'But you said you wanted . . .'

'Of course I want to go, but you're *not* selling the first guitar you ever owned, and even if you did, I wouldn't take the money for it.'

'I just thought Rick at Sound Shack might want . . .'

'No, Spike! Can you imagine how bad I'd feel? It's really sweet of you and I can't believe you even thought of it, but it's not happening. So let's just forget all about it.' With a smile, she snuggles close to his chest, overwhelmed by his generous suggestion. Yet, as they lie together, sharing Spike's nest, she becomes aware of something else mingling with the gas fire's oppressive heat – not sickness or germs but a lighter, fruitier, almost *floral* scent.

No, she's probably imagining it. It must be her age – she's such a lightweight these days. Two Bloody Marys and she loses a grip on her senses.

FIFTEEN

Sadie knows she can't possibly join Hannah and Lou in Glasgow. She's a mother, and proper mothers don't jump on a train, abandoning their eight-month-old babies for a whole weekend. Yet the thought of escaping, and having forty-eight hours in one of her favourite cities with her best friends makes her feel dizzy with yearning. Sadie is picturing herself dressed up, in a dimly-lit bar, perhaps having had her eyebrows threaded. Would a proper mother hanker for such things, in between reading picture books and freezing bananas? No, she would not.

Sadie has yet to respond to Hannah's mail, or mention it to Barney, even though it popped into her inbox in the early hours of this morning, and it's now 1.30 pm. She should reply now, get it over with – like ripping off a plaster. *Sorry, Han, you know I'd love to come, but it's just too difficult.* Yet she can't make herself do it. Becoming a mother has made Sadie, who once taught art and design at a challenging north London secondary school, virtually incapable of making even the smallest decision.

Of course, Barney will say she should go, Sadie reflects as she tries to scrub an orange blot out of a towelling bib. You could hardly find a more decent, caring man than her husband, who's currently tapping away on his laptop at the kitchen table, tweaking his little beard occasionally and rubbing his green eyes. Even the subject of his document reveals his innate goodness: a proposal to raise funds to build a girls' school in Ghana for the charity he works for.

'Still going to your mum and dad's later?' she asks.

'Yeah,' he murmurs, taking a swig from his mug. 'I just need to finish this.'

'Sure you don't mind me not coming?'

There's a quick burst of typing. 'No, it's fine.' Tap-tap-tap. 'You need a break.' Tap-tap.

Sadie bends to kiss the back of his light brown neck. 'I don't want your mum and dad to think I'm being rude,' she adds. It's true, but while her in-laws are lovely – welcoming and non-judgmental – the prospect of an entire afternoon to herself is even lovelier. And it doesn't feel right to tell Barney about Sadie's hen weekend now. To be awarded a few hours off duty, then to demand an entire weekend away would be greedy beyond belief.

Barney sets off with the babies, taking jar food and two bottles of formula, which makes Sadie feel even guiltier (she's trying to keep formula consumption down to a minimum, as a Proper Mother would). Now, all by herself in their small, dark house, she wonders how to fill the baby-free hours ahead. She could leaf through the newspapers, stimulating her mind – these days her reading is pretty much limited to *Peepo!* and *My Little Farm*, which doesn't even have proper sentences. However, there are at least three weeks' worth of papers in an ungainly pile by the sofa, and she doesn't fancy sifting through them to find the most recent. She could sneak off to bed – no, too lazy – or flop out on the sofa in an exhausted stupor (ditto). For one wild moment she considers mashing up an overripe avocado to smear all over her face. There are several avocados in the kitchen – she'd bought them to feed the babies, who'd decided they tasted worse than ear wax. Wasn't that what busy mums were supposed to do? Indulge in a little 'pampering'? But Sadie has already wasted fifteen minutes of her precious afternoon and doesn't want to be pampered. No, she needs to get *out*.

But where to? Barney has driven to his parents' place, so she's temporarily carless, and although Little Hissingham is charmingly pretty with its village green and white-washed pub, there isn't a hell of a lot going on. Everyone raves about the pub, the Black Swan, but Sadie isn't sure she'd feel entirely comfortable wandering in on her own. She'd be bound to spot someone she knows, however vaguely: that woman from the park, who'd want to know if she'd found her babies' shoes yet, or Monica whose baby's party she hurried out of far too eagerly. Plus, drinking in the daytime, all alone, she'd probably be marked as an alcoholic.

If she were Hannah, she'd be out on her bike, every inch of her body taut and fit, with a flush of rude health springing up on her cheeks. However, Sadie's bike now resides in the tiny shed in their back garden, having suffered seemingly irreversible gear damage when one of Barney's mates crushed it under a flat-pack wardrobe when they moved. She could go for a run, if she was lithe and tiny like Lou – but it would probably kill her, and she doesn't relish the idea of Milo and Dylan being motherless. Plus, Sadie doesn't own any trainers. Swim, she thinks. That's more like it: rhythmic, soothing, with no bodily parts thrashing about. And she'll be able to report back to Barney, 'I went swimming' and feel proud and purposeful. Sadie quickly throws her kit together and heads out.

The pool is just over a mile away in the small town of Corlingwood, an unremarkable cluster of new-built homes in virtually identical cul-de-sacs. In the sports centre – a faceless slab of pale grey brick – Sadie changes into her Proper Mother swimsuit (black, sporty, serious bosom support), ties back her chestnut hair and plunges into the deep end.

This is good, she thinks, launching into a breaststroke. She'll do twenty – no, thirty, maybe *fifty* lengths and soon slip easily back into her dark-wash jeans. The pool is pleasingly quiet; there's only an elderly man ploughing steady lengths, and a woman in a flowery swimsuit, her hair trapped beneath a pale blue bathing cap, who dives into the deep end in an elegant curve.

A man strides out of the changing room. Tall, slim, closely-cropped dark hair – something about him reminds Sadie of Johnny, her old friend from Garnet Street who just disappeared when that icy girlfriend of his (Sadie can't remember her name) got pregnant. She'd had a slight crush on him in her second year, then worried that she fancied him just because he was so easy to talk to, someone you could wake up at 2 am for a chat, knowing he'd be pleased to see you. She began to suspect he fancied Lou, or maybe Hannah – surely he found *one* of them attractive – then the years rolled on and what she'd regarded as matey-flirtatiousness with all three of them turned out, disappointingly, to be just plain mateyness.

The man has swum to the shallow end. He stops, propping his elbows on the pool's edge, and smiles at her. Sadie smiles back, alarmed by how unfamiliar it feels these days to be noticed by a man. She realises then that he's not looking at her, but at the woman who's just come out of the changing room, and quickly rearranges her face. 'Hi, Sadie,' the woman says with a big grin, clambering into the pool.

'Hi.' Sadie smiles hazily. The man has lunged off in a splashy crawl, and the woman glides through the water towards her. Hell, Sadie has met her before, and has precisely five seconds to remember not just where and when, but her name, the name of her husband and however many children and pets she might have. Her brain whirs ineffectually.

'Did you try it then?' The woman is beside her now, briskly rubbing her upper arms to try and warm herself.

'Er, I, um don't think . . .'

'You should! You really should. It's one of those things that's so simple but really works.'

Sadie gazes at her. 'Mmm. I will.'

The woman laughs as the man swims past them. 'Frozen bananas! As lollies, remember? My tip when we were chatting at Monica's?'

'Oh, God yes,' Sadie booms, relief surging through her.

'Polly, are you swimming or what?' the man calls out jovially from the other end of the pool. Polly! At least Sadie now knows her name. She feels her shoulders relax and her brain start to function normally once again.

'So, not with your twins today?' Polly remarks as they start to swim steadily together.

'No. Barney's taken them to see his parents. I've got time off for good behaviour.'

'Us too. Left the kids with my sister. It's our regular thing.'

'What, this? Swimming?' Sadie asks, surprised. With no discernible logic, she'd assumed that having the dedication to make bogus lollies also meant you'd have at least one of your children tethered to your bosom at all times.

'Oh yes, every week. It's our regular date.'

Sadie takes this in. She's always assumed dates should involve alcohol and possibly food, maybe a movie, but each to their own. 'Not next weekend though,' Polly adds, 'because I'll be in New York for work.'

'New York?' Sadie blasts out.

Polly chuckles. 'Well, it's not that often. Just every

couple of months. I work for a magazine publishing company and I'm kind of straddling two continents at the moment.'

'Oh,' Sadie murmurs. 'I mean . . . that's great. Wow. Do you, erm . . .' She doesn't know how to put this without sounding disapproving, which she isn't; she's just awestruck. 'I . . . I guess your partner's fine keeping things going at home,' she adds.

'Yes, of course he is. We manage it together, me and Phil' – she casts the man who reminds Sadie of Johnny a fond glance – 'and we have a brilliant nanny. It's good, I think, for children to form bonds with other adults. Makes them independent and sociable and—'

'Oh, I agree,' Sadie says quickly. 'I mean, I'm at home with the babies just now, but only because I couldn't figure out how I'd manage to keep on top of my job with the two of them. I was an art teacher in north London. I'm going back at some point. Just not sure when . . .' They reach the end of the pool, turn and set off again.

'I couldn't be at home full-time,' Polly says. 'I take my hat off to you.'

Sadie laughs. 'Well, to be honest I'd love to go away, just for a couple of days. One of my best friends has invited me on a hen weekend in Glasgow. It's where we studied at art school . . .'

'That sounds fun. You're going, I assume?'

'Er . . . well, I'm not sure. I know this sounds weedy but I've never left Milo and Dylan before.'

'But they'd be with Barney, wouldn't they? I've seen him around the village. Looks calm, capable . . .' Polly chuckles indulgently.

'Oh, yes, I know they'd be fine, it's not that . . .'

'So why not go?'

'I . . .' Sadie hesitates. 'It just feels . . . *alien*.'

'Well, you're going to go away at some point, aren't

98

you? So why not start now? I mean, it's your friend's hen weekend!'

'I know,' Sadie says. 'It's just so soon . . .'

'And you can't *not* go to that. It's a special occasion. It's not as if you're waltzing off just for the hell of it.'

'Well, I'll see,' Sadie says cautiously. She doesn't count lengths for the next hour because she's imagining herself with Hannah and Lou, away from bibs and being woken up at all hours and marching around Hissingham Park.

And by the time she climbs out, she's decided to go. She isn't planning to straddle two continents, for God's sake. It's only *Glasgow*. Saying goodbye to Polly, Sadie strides towards the changing room, focusing on placing one foot after another on the wet tiled floor to stop herself from leaping excitedly into the air.

*

'Are you absolutely sure?' Sadie asks Barney that night. They're in bed, having settled the babies, and she's resting her head on his chest.

'Of course I'm sure, honey. You don't need permission, you know.'

'But it would mean you taking Friday off work.'

'It's not a problem, okay? I've racked up loads of extra hours lately.'

Sadie blinks in the dark. 'But what about feeding? I know we've been using the odd bottle, but I'm not sure I want to give up . . .'

'Maybe you could express some milk?' Barney suggests.

'Yeah.' She smiles, impressed that he's even heard of the term. 'Yes, I could do that.' She stretches up to kiss him, wondering if there's any connection between her impending escape and the return of her libido, which burst back onto the scene tonight with such gusto that Barney seemed, initially at least, a little taken aback. Not for long, though. It had happened – and Sadie's body had responded the way it used to. So everything still works. She's still capable of enjoying herself with the man she loves. Which means, she thinks, kissing him lightly on the lips, she's still Sadie Vella underneath.

SIXTEEN

It's a broody-skied Monday and Spike is absolutely knack-ered. He's had quite a morning, having already been round to Astrid's, ostensibly for a late breakfast – 'brunch' she'd called it, laughing so he'd know she was being ironic. He'd enjoyed watching her, every fibre of his being fizzling with anticipation as she made perfect poached eggs on some strange kind of toast with nuts and dried berries nesting inside (Spike isn't a fan of mysterious shrivelled fruits lurking inside his toast, but pronounced it delicious). He also enjoyed a brief but particularly raunchy encounter with Astrid on her bathroom floor, and after that, legged it back to the flat to pick up the first acoustic guitar he'd ever owned. Now he's heading to Sound Shack, the tiny music shop sandwiched between a bookmaker's and a launderette in a beleaguered side street.

'Hey, Spike,' Rick drawls from behind the counter. 'Haven't seen you around. Been hibernating?'

'Just had a lot on my plate,' Spike fibs, aware of being eyed by Rick's straggly grey dog of no discernible pedigree who's lounging in a hair-strewn wicker basket. The dog opens its mouth wide in a yawn, exposing black gums, then flops its head back down on its cushion.

'Yeah? What kind of stuff?' Rick wants to know.

'Just this and that.'

'Any gigs coming up?'

'Got a few irons in the fire,' Spike says blithely.

'So . . . anything you're looking for?' Rick asks.

'Er, maybe. There might be something . . .'

'Yeah?' Rick says hopefully.

Spike pauses, overcome by a wave of regret as he looks down at the guitar case he's clutching. His parents had bought it when he was fourteen, despite the fact that they knew less than nothing about music. A couple of albums of terrible church music had been the sum total of their record collection, yet they'd saved up the princely sum of £180 because it had meant so much to their son. 'Er . . . I'm thinking of selling his. Thought you might be interested.' Something catches in Spike's throat, and he busies himself with removing the guitar from its case.

'Right,' Rick says with interest, scratching his small salt-and-pepper beard. 'Let's have a look.' Spike hands him the guitar, and Rick takes what feels like far too long to check it out. Visual inspection complete, he sits on a small wooden chair in the corner of the shop and starts to strum.

Spike sucks in his lips and pretends to admire the instruments on the walls of the shop. It seems wrong, Rick playing *his* guitar; he became twitchy even when Lou asked him to show her some chords.

'Yeah,' Rick murmurs. 'S'nice, Spike. A good, rounded tone. I could probably give you a hundred and fifty.'

'You're joking?' Spike spins round from the bass he's been studying. 'Is that all?'

Rick shrugs, carefully places the guitar back in its case and retrieves his still-smoking cigarette from the ashtray by the till. 'Tough times, mate. Recession, in case you hadn't noticed.'

'Yeah, I know.' Spike's stomach feels leaden.

'I'm telling you, reselling it isn't going to be easy. I don't want to be stuck with it, taking up space . . .'

Spike blows out air and digests the figure. He's being ripped off, and could probably get twice the amount if he sold it privately through a small ad. But Hannah's hen weekend is in two weeks' time, which means Lou has to decide whether or not to go pretty much right away. He *needs* Lou out of the picture, and giving her money is the only way he can think of to make it happen. 'Two hundred?' he suggests.

Rick puckers his bottom lip and grinds out the roll-up. 'One-sixty. That's my final. Sorry, mate. It's all I can do.' Great. A hundred and sixty quid for a quality guitar that cost more than that *thirty-four-bloody-years-ago*.

'Right. Okay.' Spike tries not to show any emotion as Rick counts out the tatty notes, and slips them into his jeans pocket as if the small, precious wad is no more significant than a shopping list. In reality, though, it's the passport to an entire, uninterrupted weekend with Astrid. Which means, he reflects, as he leaves the dusty shop, that it's worth it.

Is it morally wrong to sell something like that, he wonders? Of course not. Things are just *things* Spike tells himself; it's life's experiences that matter, and Spike considers himself a free man, unencumbered by material possessions. So he hasn't sold out – he's made a *considered investment*. And forty-eight hours in bed with Astrid is well worth £160.

Even so, his heart falters as he climbs the stairs to the flat. Suddenly, Spike fears that what he's doing is actually *very* wrong, and will result in some kind of terrible karmic retribution. He freezes on the landing, blood draining from his face as he desperately tries to remember if, in his haste to get his hands on some cash, he forgot to lock the door.

No, surely he didn't. He never does that. Yet the door

is a few inches open, and somebody is definitely pacing around inside his flat.

*

Spike doesn't feel brave or strong enough to charge in and grapple with whoever is in there. 'Right, so you really don't mind,' comes the voice. *Lou's* voice, on the phone. He nearly weeps with relief. Lou, who's pacing around with the phone, smiles as he walks into the living room. 'I feel like I'm letting you down,' she goes on, 'but at least we'll see you at the wedding . . .'

It's Hannah, Spike realises as Lou chatters on about wedding dresses ('I'm sure it's lovely, you're just nervous, that's all . . . no, of *course* you're not going to look like a nurse, daft thing, whatever put that idea in your head?'). Hannah, the blonde beauty with a fit, toned body, whom Spike has always suspected doesn't entirely approve of him. Still gripping the phone, Lou sneezes several times into a tissue. She resumes the chat, punctuating it with the loud, open laughter that seems to burst out of her mouth only when she's talking to one of her friends. She finishes the call. 'That was Hannah,' she says unnecessarily.

'Right.'

'I was just telling her I won't be able to go on the weekend.' Lou shrugs. 'She sounded a bit disappointed.'

'Er . . . what are you doing home?' he asks. 'I thought someone had broken into the flat.'

'Why?'

'Well, the door was open.'

'Was it? I mustn't have shut it properly. I came home early. This cold's really come on and Dave was quite sympathetic for once.' She pauses, studying his face as if detecting something – the tiniest tic, or his hair looking messier than usual – which might alert her to the nature of his morning activities. 'Where have you been anyway?' she asks.

'Just out and about.' *Don't panic. She asked in a normal voice, not accusingly.* 'I popped into Sound Shack actually,' he adds with a grin. 'Spoke to Rick about the acoustic.'

'What about the acoustic?' Lou pauses. 'Oh, Spike, you're not seriously thinking of selling it.'

'Sold it, honey,' he says grandly.

'What? You're joking! It's your oldest guitar. Your parents bought it for you! What would they think?'

He shrugs. 'They probably don't even remember it.'

'Of course they do! God, you can't get rid of it . . .' She sneezes again, her eyes moist and sore-looking.

'Well, it's all done and dusted.' With a resigned smile, he extracts the wad of notes from his pocket and hands it to her.

'I don't need this!' she exclaims. 'I feel terrible, like I'm responsible for you doing that . . .'

'Hey,' Spike cuts in, hugging her. 'You're not responsible. *I* did it, because you've been working your socks off and I don't want you to keep going on about it, okay? It's done. Finito. And the money's yours.'

Lou pulls back to study his face, then kisses him firmly on the lips. 'You're such a darling. Honestly, Spike, I can't believe you did this for me.' She smiles up at him, showing the gap between her teeth. Lou's so cute when she looks at him like that, Spike thinks, and he buries his face in her springy curls, even though they smell slightly of deep-fat fryer. It's not that he wants to split up with Lou. Theirs is an old-slipper sort of relationship: worn slippers with flattened backs which, although they hardly set your pulse racing, are somehow deeply comforting.

Unlike that guitar, he tells himself firmly, hoping to quell another pang of regret. That's just . . . *old*. Then Spike imagines some cocky little sod swaggering into Sound Shack and buying it – the type who wants a guitar to prop up in his living room as a 'thing' – and realises his face has set in an unbecoming scowl.

'You okay?' Lou is studying him intently.

'Er, yeah. Just thinking about my CV actually.'

She raises her brows in amusement. 'Well, I'm looking forward to seeing it. And, Spike . . .' She pauses. 'I'll be different when I come back from the weekend, okay? I probably just need a bit of time with Sadie and Han. It'll be good for me. Help me get back on track. I mean, they're still doing what they set out to do, aren't they? Hannah's doing really well at Catfish, and I know Sadie's at home with the babies but she wanted that too, she was desperate for kids with Barney, and she'll probably go back to teaching at some point . . .'

Spike nods. 'Yeah. It'll be good for the three of you to get together.'

'That's what's wrong, Spike,' she declares. 'I've let this crappy job take over my life and I need to get my priorities right and be focused.'

'I know what you mean.'

'And I miss them,' she adds. 'I know I've got plenty of friends here, but us three – it's as if we're somehow . . . connected.' Spike nods, picturing the girls' dowdy yet cosy flat in Garnet Street, all of them bunched around the kitchen table and everyone laughing and knocking back Spanish plonk as he regaled them with tales from the music business.

Right now, Spike feels as vibrant and alive as he did in the old days, as if his world has just opened up with a myriad of possibilities. He has Lou who adores him and is awash with gratitude, and Astrid waiting for him in her chemise. Spike senses his lips curling into a smile as he reflects that life really couldn't be much better right now.

SEVENTEEN

To: loucostello@yahoo.com;
    sadievella38@hotmail.com
From: hannahcmcshane@virgin.net

Dearest girls,

Can't believe the three of us are going to be together in one week's time. I'm so excited I can't tell you and am counting the sleeps like a little kid. The hotel's booked – I thought it sounded smart and boutiquey before someone on TripAdvisor said they'd found earwigs in the shower and an old sandwich poking out from under the bed. Oh well! It's all I could get on the cheap and it does have a swimming pool. Anyway, who cares what it's like? We'll hardly be there anyway.

Can't WAIT to see you. It's been a funny old week – loads on at work with a new wedding stationery range, which I should be finding easy with my own nuptials thundering towards me . . . but somehow I'm not. I've had to work really late a few nights, and Ryan's been looking all hurt as if I'm trying to avoid him. Which I'm not. Sometimes, though, I wonder if it's easier for him and the kids when I'm not around.

I know I've never really mentioned any of this. I guess it's because I've been trying to convince myself that it'll turn out fine somehow. But now I'm scared that it won't. Living here feels like I have to be on best behaviour all the time. The kids are so rude and surly – Ryan does his best but it's a real pig-in-the-middle situation for him, and they ARE his flesh and blood. Anyway, they make it pretty clear they don't want their beloved daddy to get married again. I made the big mistake of going into Josh's room the other evening (I knocked first) and said, 'Hi, how you doing,' that sort of thing. He had some music on and I said, 'Oh, I really like this band . . .' He gave me this disgusted look, like he might vomit right there on the carpet. I backed out of the room and went downstairs and poured myself a huge glass of wine, which I tipped down without even swallowing. It's a new skill I've learned. Remind me to show you in Glasgow!

There's something else too. I was putting a wash on this morning and I always check the kids' pockets because they're usually crammed with sweet wrappers and headphones and sometimes even an iPod or two. And I found a crushed cigarette packet in the back pocket of Josh's jeans. It had one in it – Marlboro Light. Everyone was out, and I was SO tempted to nip out to the back garden and smoke it (even though I've not had a fag for thirteen years and even then, as you both know, I was such a crap, part-time smoker). But I managed not to, and now I can't decide whether to tell Ryan. If I do, I'm a disgusting snitch and there'll be no hope of getting along better with Josh. And if I don't, I'm not fulfilling my role as WIFE TO BE by withholding vital information.

Anyway! Sorry to rant on, just needed to spill it all out and we hardly ever get the chance to talk properly on the phone these days. I probably just need to get away for a couple of days. I need some time with my favourite girls. Our train tickets are booked – I chose the East Coast line so we can all travel together. Sadie, I'll meet you at King's Cross, and Lou, you can collect your ticket at York station. We'll be banging on the window in case you're having a last-minute snoggy farewell with Spike and forget to jump on.

Oh, and listen – I don't want the typical matching T-shirts type hen party. No bunny ears or L-plates either, not even ironically. Hope you don't think I'm being a spoilsport and not getting into the spirit. All I want is for the three of us to be together again like old times.

Hannah checks her watch. It's 11.30 am – still half an hour before Petra's due, by which time Ryan and the kids should be back from the swimming pool. After six months here, Hannah still finds herself growing more agitated by the minute as a Petra visit approaches. She checks her hair, her face – even the state of her fingernails – and has already wiped the worktops and mopped the kitchen floor. It's silly really. Why should she care what Petra thinks of her?

The sharp ping of the doorbell makes her flinch, and Hannah quickly shuts her email and hurries to answer it.

'Hi, Petra,' she says at the door. 'Ryan and the kids are still at the pool but they shouldn't be too long. Come in . . .' It still feels weird, inviting Petra into the house in which she brought up her babies and played her cello and lived with her family for a decade.

Petra, clad in a camel jacket and elegant black trousers – what the magazines would describe as 'key pieces' – follows Hannah to the kitchen. 'I hoped they'd be ready,' she remarks, glossy dark hair bouncing around her pointy chin. 'We've got a lot to pack in today.'

She talks about them as if they're a project, Hannah thinks as she fills the kettle. 'Er, I think they were expecting you at twelve,' Hannah explains.

Petra frowns. 'It was definitely eleven-thirty. I wanted to make the most of the day.'

'What have you got planned?' Hannah asks, selecting the china Orla Keily mug from the cupboard for Petra and not the one emblazoned DANGER: RADIOACTIVE MATERIAL! CONTAINS PLUTONIUM SUSPENSION, which she's been carting from flat to flat since college.

'Well, I thought we could do Miró at the Tate,' Petra explains, 'then there's an open-air mime show at the South Bank I thought we'd check out. Have you heard about it?'

'Er, I think so,' Hannah fibs. 'It sounds great.'

Petra has parked her bony rear on a kitchen chair and smiles her thanks as Hannah hands her her tea. Petra's nails are manicured; perfect pink ovals like delicate shells. Hannah imagines them glinting under the spotlight as Petra performs Bach's Cello Concerto number something-or-other at the Festival Hall. Although she's never seen Petra play live, she's watched some of her performances on YouTube, having stumbled upon them accidentally after typing 'Petra Lennox Cellist' into the search box. She's also spotted a few lusty comments directed at Petra on there.

'They should be here pretty soon,' Hannah says unnecessarily, perching on the chair opposite her.

'Yep, hope so.' Petra smiles tightly. Hannah hasn't spoken to her since earring-gate, two weeks ago now, and the subject of potentially festering lobes hovers uneasily between them. Hannah wonders how Petra would react to news of Josh's Marlboro packet.

'Oh, *here* they are,' she cries, leaping up at the sound of Ryan and the kids tumbling in.

'Got these for you, sweetheart . . . oh, Petra, didn't expect . . .' Ryan stops in the kitchen doorway, smiling inanely and clutching a bunch of sweet peas, which Hannah quickly takes from him as if relieving him of a crying baby.

'Hi, Mum,' Josh says, stepping forward to give his mother a stiff hug.

'Hello, darling. Hi, Daisy, love.' She kisses her daughter's cheek and stands back to appraise her. 'Goodness,' Petra laughs. 'What have you done to your hair?'

Daisy frowns. 'Er . . . nothing, Mum.'

'That's what I mean. It's all tangly, sweetheart.'

'Well, I've just been swimming and Dad said we had to hurry—'

Petra rolls her eyes indulgently. 'Well, anyway, get your things together – and please brush your hair, Daisy – and let's be off.' *Yep, got to look immaculate for a scintillating afternoon of mime.* As the kids head upstairs, Petra's gaze settles briefly on the sweet peas, which Hannah has arranged hastily in a vase.

Now that Ryan's here, she can legitimately escape from the kitchen in which the temperature seems to have plummeted by about ten degrees. 'I hope Daisy's bringing plenty of books this weekend,' Petra tells Ryan. In the utility room, Hannah drags a washload from the tumble dryer into a laundry basket. She's kept the Marlboro Light packet, hiding it behind a broken Bakelite radio which sits on the shelf. Not to show Ryan, or as evidence to present in court, but because she doesn't know what else to do with it.

'I'll remind her,' Ryan says. 'We borrowed a couple from the library last week. I suppose it's just finding the right ones to spark her imagination.'

'I just think,' Petra adds, 'that she should be on more challenging books, Ryan. Especially after what they said at parents' night.'

'Yes, but we can't *force* her to read, can we? We can't strap her to a chair with an open book on her lap and—'

'Yes, *okay*, Ryan, I get the picture.' Hannah stops and listens. She knows Daisy's a reluctant reader. Ryan tries to encourage her, spending a small fortune on Amazon, and

Hannah has asked Daisy if she'd like to be read *to*, which she seemed to regard as immensely patronising, as if Hannah had suggested making little Play-doh animals together. Carrying the overloaded linen basket, Hannah strides through the kitchen, keeping her expression neutral.

As she escapes to her bedroom, Josh and Daisy pass her wordlessly as they make their way downstairs.

'So,' Petra says in the hallway, 'have you got over your earring thing, Daisy?'

'Yes, Mum.'

'Were you upset about it?' Petra asks in a gentler tone.

'Yeah. No. It's all right,' she mutters.

'The thing is, Ryan,' Petra adds, 'I don't think Daisy would have even got the idea in her head if Hannah hadn't suggested it . . .' Gritting her teeth, Hannah lowers the basket onto her and Ryan's bed.

'Hannah didn't suggest it,' he says lightly.

'She did, Daddy!' his daughter cries. 'Hannah said I could have it done for the wedding when we went shopping.'

'I'm sure that's not right,' Ryan starts. 'The way Hannah explained it, *you* asked her, Daisy, and kept going on . . .' Hannah's entire body is now rigid with rage. Her heart is thumping and her breaths are coming in rapid gasps.

'Well, it's not really appropriate, is it?' Petra says, and Hannah realises how much she hates that word: *appropriate*. 'You can have it done one day,' Petra goes on, 'when you're a teenager. Just not yet, okay?' Now Hannah is trapped, not knowing what to do next. She *should* go downstairs to say goodbye to the kids before they're whisked off by their mother. Yet she knows she won't be able to do this and appear calm and pleasant – like someone who might one day merit the title of stepmother.

'Yes, Mum,' Daisy says. There's more chattering then, and they're all sounding more jovial now as the children leave. Hannah hears Ryan calling goodbye from the front door.

Hannah glowers down at the pile of laundry, which she was about to – *helpfully* – sort out. Right now, she could cheerfully chuck it out of the window. Petra's voice drifts up, amused, yet still faintly accusing: 'Daisy, you *still* haven't brushed your hair.'

Hannah stands in the middle of the bedroom and waits. She knows that Ryan will be mortified – and here he comes now, leaping upstairs. He walks into the room, places a hand on each of her shoulders and looks her right in the eye. 'I suppose you heard all that, did you?'

'Yes. You know, what I really wanted to do was haul Daisy into Claire's Accessories and *force* her to have it done, but I thought you might be just a tiny bit upset.'

He sniggers mirthlessly. 'I thought that was your game, you evil woman. It's a wonder you didn't do it yourself with a rusty needle.'

'Well, I was tempted. I had one ready in my bag.'

Ryan smiles wearily and rubs his hands over his forehead. 'Jesus, Han. I'm so sorry. It's bloody ridiculous . . .'

'It's not your fault,' she says firmly.

'Petra can be such a cow sometimes . . .'

Hannah shrugs. She *won't* slag off Petra, or Daisy for that matter, and clenches her back teeth together to stop bad words falling out. 'Are you . . .' Ryan hesitates. 'Are you sure you *want* this, Han?'

'Want what? You mean do I want *you*?'

Ryan nods, and anxiety flickers in his soft brown eyes. 'Of course I want you,' she exclaims, pulling him close. 'Of course I do. It's just . . .' She stops. 'It's pretty awful sometimes, and I know Josh isn't exactly my greatest fan, but he's a teenager and I'm sure it's all normal. But with Daisy, I think she really resents—'

'She's just a kid,' he says simply.

'I know. And it can't be easy for a little girl when her mum leaves.'

Ryan nods wordlessly.

'Listen,' Hannah adds, taking both of Ryan's hands in hers and squeezing them, 'I know it's not easy for you either, that you're caught in the middle. We'll work it out. I want you more than anyone I've ever wanted in my whole life.'

As soon as she's said it, she knows she means every word, and she's kissing him now, every cell in her body feeling alive. They undress and fall into bed, forgetting about tentative plans to see a film, or go out for lunch. As Ryan pulls her towards him, and she breathes in the sweet warmth of his skin, Hannah realises she has everything she could possibly want right here.

EIGHTEEN

When Lou was a student living in Garnet Street, she occasionally fantasised about her Future Life. It wasn't that she didn't love living with Hannah and Sadie; they were a gang, with Johnny upstairs an honorary member. Yet Lou had always been aware that this was a temporary setup. That one day, when her Future Life began, she'd open her fridge and find more than a lump of antique cheese and a carton of suspect milk. There'd be fresh fish, from a proper fishmonger's, an array of exotic vegetables like pak choi, and other mysterious edible plants she didn't know the names of yet. The kind of things Johnny sometimes threw into his curries and stews. She'd live in a light, airy flat, with a roof terrace or even a small garden where she'd create beautiful jewellery by day and throw grown-up drinks parties with Spike by night.

Out of the three girls in Garnet Street, Lou had been the only one to make a token effort to cook, and it was that that had lured Spike to her. Spike, the sexy, mysterious older man who played guitar like a dream and had shown up at a Christmas party at the girls' flat, passed out on the two corduroy beanbags in the living room and tucked into the lavish breakfast Lou had knocked together the next

115

morning. Although Spike had a room in a shared house across town, he soon became a near-permanent fixture in Garnet Street. When Hannah and Sadie had moved on, Lou and Spike decided to rent a one-bedroomed place together.

Lou had felt confident then, during those early years, that her Future Life would be a joint project. Spike was spontaneous and fun, always up for mischief, and would write songs for her on his old acoustic guitar. Music, he assured Lou, was his path in life. Sixteen years on, that path has led him to a kind of no-man's-land consisting of holding out for gigs, something that actually happens only once or twice a year, which leaves an awful lot of time for lazing in front of the gas fire in their flat.

Lou's Future Life hasn't quite turned out the way she planned either. If there is pak choi in the fridge, it's been snatched from the pov shelf – her nickname for the 'poverty shelf' in their local supermarket where perishables teetering on their sell-by date are sold off for 10p after 9 pm. Which is why Lou Costello, aged thirty-five with a First in silver-smithing and jewellery, is lurking in the supermarket on a Thursday night, watching intently (although not too obvi-ously, she hopes) as a staff member wends her way around the aisles with a sticker gun.

The sticker gun, which is used to mark reduced items, has assumed a ridiculous importance in Lou's life. What's even sadder, she thinks now, grabbing a discounted net bag of tangerines, is that she's almost started to *enjoy* it. Lou experiences a distinct frisson as she snatches a knocked-down packet of only slightly wizened mangetout and a perfectly acceptable wholemeal loaf.

'How're you doing tonight, love?' Lou stops poking at 10p punnets of mushrooms (they're only a *little* bit slimy) to see Lenny, a middle-aged smallholder with a deeply grooved forehead, brandishing his fully-laden basket beside her.

'Not bad, Lenny,' Lou replies with a smile. As he nods his approval at her basket, Lou remembers with a start that Lenny only ventures out at this late hour to grab reduced provisions to feed his pigs. Whereas Lou is shopping for herself and Spike, actual *human beings*. An image of her Future Life roof terrace floats teasingly into her mind.

After paying at the checkout – Lou always senses a pitying glance from the pretty blonde girl on the till – she packs her reusable cotton shopping bags and steps out into the dusk. Something else is bothering her as she marches home. What was she thinking, buying tons of fresh stuff when she's catching the 2.30 pm train to Glasgow tomorrow, and won't be home till Sunday night? All this food is for Spike. She must feel guilty, Lou realises, or, more likely, she's fallen into a habit of babying her boyfriend, without even realising it.

Still, her spirits rise at the thought of boarding that train tomorrow. Apart from seeing Hannah and Sadie, it'll be good for her and Spike to have a weekend apart. He's been irritating the hell out of her lately, with his perpetual sniffing and checking of nasal hair. She's sick of rounding up the mugs he routinely leaves dotted around the flat – not only in obvious places, like on the rug or his bedside table, but in more surprising locations such as perched on top of the toilet cistern. Maybe she'll come back from Glasgow in a slightly more tolerant frame of mind. She might even start to fancy him again.

Lou has turned off the main road and is heading down a residential street of neat redbrick terraces when she sees a girl striding towards her. Her fine-boned beauty catches Lou's eye; high, sharp cheekbones, full lips, fair hair swishing this way and that. She's engrossed in a call on her mobile and looks familiar, Lou realises now, although she can't figure out where their paths might have crossed. Not at the pov shelf, that's for sure.

'Yeah, that'd be cool, I can do that no problem,' the girl is saying. Lou knows that voice: posh, with husky under-tones. The kind of voice you could imagine selling you hair colour or eyelash extensions. She thrusts her phone into her jeans pocket, and as they're almost face-to-face now, Lou flashes her a bright smile.

'Hi,' says the girl vaguely.

Lou stops. It's bugging her that she can't place her. 'Sorry,' she says as the girl passes her, 'but I know you from somewhere, don't I?'

'Umm . . .' She turns and looks at Lou quizzically. 'Er, yeah . . . I think we might've met.'

'*I* know. You were at that gig at the Horse and Hounds, weren't you? You're a friend of Charlie's. Spike, my boyfriend, did that acoustic set – d'you remember? Just before Christmas. We chatted at the bar?'

'Oh, yeah! You're Lou, aren't you?' She smiles broadly and turns a bit pink. 'Of course I remember you.'

'Your name's slipped my mind,' Lou adds apologetically.

'Astrid.'

'Oh, that's right.'

'Spike was good, wasn't he? Great voice, really held the audience in the palm of his hand. Has he been writing any more songs?'

'Um, not lately, no.' Lou doesn't want to start discussing Spike's preference for lying in front of their gas fire. She sees Astrid glancing down at her bulging shopping bags.

'Are you a musician, Lou?' she asks. 'I'm sorry, it's rude of me, but I can't remember . . .'

'Oh no,' Lou laughs, the bright orange sticker on a packet of egg noodles catching her eye in the dusk. 'I'm a jeweller. Well, I used to be – I haven't done much lately. I've been working at Let's Bounce . . .' Astrid looks blank. 'It's a soft play centre,' Lou adds. Still blankness. 'You know – for kids to throw themselves round while their parents sit at the tables, depressed, reading newspapers, before vomiting on the carpet.'

'Oh!' Astrid's nostrils flare a little.

'I mean it's the kids who throw up,' Lou explains with a laugh.

'Well, I'm glad to hear that. I don't mean glad that the kids are *sick*, but . . .' Astrid chuckles uncomfortably.

'Anyway,' Lou says quickly, a packet of withered mangetout tumbling onto the pavement as she grabs her bags, 'I'd better get back. I'm going away for the weekend and these are Spike's emergency rations.' She snatches the mangetout and jams them on top of a plastic bag of sweaty carrots.

'You mean you stock the fridge for Spike when you go away?' Astrid laughs. 'God, Lou, he's a lucky man.'

'Oh, I know it sounds pathetic.' Lou feels her ears burning hot, glowing like those stickers. 'But I don't want to come back on Sunday to find his poor, withered skeleton on the sofa. Anyway,' she adds, realising that skeletons don't actually wither, 'I kind of owe him. Without Spike, you see, I wouldn't be going at all.'

Astrid's eyes widen, clear and blue as a cloudless sky. 'Why not?'

'Well, it's a bit of a shock actually, but he sold his guitar to pay for my trip, which I feel terrible about. I mean, it's not his *only* guitar – he had five at the last count and how many guitars does one person actually need? But it was the first one he ever owned . . .'

'That was . . . generous of him,' Astrid says weakly, looking distinctly uncomfortable now. And no wonder, Lou thinks as they say goodbye and set off in opposite directions. What must Astrid think of her, needing Spike to sell a treasured possession just so she can go away for the weekend? She doesn't know, of course, that Lou pays for virtually everything: bills, rent and the lion's share of the food. With a shudder, Lou quickens her pace, vowing to be more like . . . like *Astrid*.

Now there's a girl who looks as if she's got her life sorted out. She's bright, confident, astoundingly beautiful – and positive too. While all Lou can see in Spike these days is a slightly crumpled middle-aged man with nasal hair and a collection of ancient ointment tubes, Astrid sees a beacon of talent who can *hold an audience in the palm of his hand*. Maybe, Lou thinks, lugging her bags upstairs to their flat, she should try to be more encouraging.

In the kitchen, Spike is spreading Marmite onto a thick crust. She plants a speedy kiss on his cheek as he folds it over to form a sturdy sandwich.

'Hi, babe,' he says with a full mouth. 'Good day?'

'Not bad. Had a quick drink with Steph and a couple of others, then got you some provisions.'

'Did you? That was good of you . . .' Together, they start to unpack the shopping. Lou briefly inspects each item before placing it in the fridge, hoping she won't return to find him collapsed on the floor, poisoned by egg noodles.

'I met a fan of yours on the way home,' she says teasingly.

'Yeah?' His face brightens. 'Who was that?'

'Astrid. Nice girl, friendly, very pretty. You probably don't remember, but she was at that gig at the Horse and Hounds. She was singing your praises today . . .'

'Was she?' His face contorts into an almost comical frown.

'Look at you, all bashful!' Lou chuckles, prodding him in the ribs. 'People do remember you, you know. You should be playing all the time. If a chick like Astrid thinks you've got something . . .' She waggles an eyebrow suggestively.

'Yeah, well . . .' He blows out air and takes an enormous chomp of his Marmite sandwich.

'In fact, I think she has the hots for you, Spike,' Lou adds.

'Oh, for God's sake!' he blusters, cheeks bulging with bread.

'C'mon,' she says, grinning, 'you're not wearing too badly for an old fella.' She beams at him, overcome by a sudden rush of affection. Then, wrapping her slender arms around his shoulders and reaching up to kiss his Marmitey lips, she feels, for the first time, that she might even miss him a tiny bit.

NINETEEN

Sadie is installed on the sofa with a plastic pump clamped to her left breast. It's a manual pump, kindly lent to her by Polly-the-banana-freezer who she ran into at another gathering of mothers and babies. It has a small handle, a rubbery attachment device shaped like a miniature satellite dish, and its purpose is to suck every drop of milk from her body.

She has been pumping for six weeks now – well, no, it hasn't been *quite* that long, but that's how it feels. It's been two episodes of *The Sopranos* anyway, and an awful reality show about a sixteen-year-old whose parents are throwing her a lavish party. There are diamond earrings as a present, plus a car the girl can't even drive yet, the keys for which her mother has clamped between her teeth as she bursts out of an enormous crepe-paper cake. It's making Sadie feel quite nauseous. She's glad the babies are being settled by Barney in the bedroom; she wouldn't want them getting overblown ideas about their own future birthday parties. She peers down at the clear plastic bottle and sees that she has now successfully pumped about three millimetres of milk. It looks as if she's just wrung out a breast pad. Sadie has never felt more bovine in her entire life.

To allow her maximum pumping time, Barney has been a star tonight, taking charge of bathtime and tidying up the house. She can hear him murmuring to them now, sleepily. She checks the bottle again. If the milk level's gone up, she can't detect it. Perhaps it's evaporating in the bottle, or her breasts are now completely empty and will shrivel up like forgotten party balloons if she keeps this up for much longer. Whatever's going on, it's clear that her boys will be feasting mostly on formula while she's away. A lump forms in Sadie's throat; she can't help thinking that Proper Mothers manage at least a year – heck, she once spotted a woman at a coffee morning allowing her three-year-old a quick slurp up her T-shirt. She also suspects that, despite Polly's encouragement in the swimming pool, she really shouldn't be going away at all.

'How are you getting on?' Barney appears in the living room, clad in PJ bottoms and a faded yellow T-shirt. His eyes look scratchy and tired.

Sadie grimaces and indicates the bottle. 'It's not the most effective milking method, I have to say.'

He comes over, perches on the sofa arm beside her and strokes her dishevelled hair. 'Never mind. We'll be fine with bottles and there's probably enough there for one tiny feed each if they're really missing you.'

'D'you think they will?'

Barney shakes his head. 'I'm sure we'll manage. It's only two days . . .'

'Are they asleep now?' she asks.

Barney grins. 'Yep, thankfully. Double shot of whisky did the trick.'

She smiles and resumes pumping, aware of Barney's barely-disguised mirth at Polly's contraption. Perhaps it's not so strange that they've had sex just the once in almost a year. It's not that she doesn't find him attractive; those cheeky green eyes, the tousled sandy hair, the shapely jaw and extremely lovely, muscular legs all add up to a pretty agreeable package. Yet these days, bedtime is for sleeping – the deepest sleeps she's ever had in her life. 'Barney,' she murmurs, 'are you *sure* you're going to be okay?'

'Yeah!' He exhales loudly, bringing the hair-stroking to an abrupt halt. 'God, Sadie, what kind of dad d'you think I am if I can't manage to look after my own children for one weekend?'

*

Eight hours later, at 6.35 am, Sadie is checking her bedside cabinet for her train tickets to Scotland. She also rummages through the vast pillow-bag, her handbag and various nooks and crannies around the house before realising that of course she doesn't have them, because Hannah did all the booking. The plan is to meet Hannah at King's Cross and travel up together, meeting Lou when she hops onto the same train in York. Yet she's still niggled by the possibility of forgetting something.

Barney and the babies are still asleep, for which Sadie is overwhelmingly grateful as she needs all her faculties to triple-check everything all over again. She surveys her suitcase, which is lying open on the living room floor. She's folded everything neatly, in the hope that it looks like the suitcase of a sorted woman like Polly who travels regularly. Sadie had planned to take only her smartest clothes, then lowered her criteria and packed anything that wasn't hopelessly ancient or stained with babyfood goo. Which has left precisely three outfits: a gauzy top and a pair of thankfully flattering jeans – though she still can't squeeze into her favourites – plus a printed shift dress and a sexy black LK Bennett number, which she bought in a fit of rebellion on eBay one night after a 3 am feed.

Still in rumpled pyjamas, Barney wanders into the living room. 'All ready then?'

'Yes, I think so,' Sadie replies, eyes fixed on her suitcase. 'I had this sudden panic about not knowing where my passport is, then remembered I'm only going to Scotland.' She laughs, and at the sound of Milo and Dylan waking, hurries through to the bedroom with Barney in pursuit.

'They'll be fine,' Barney keeps insisting, pulling off the top he slept in, taking another almost identical one off the radiator and putting it on. He then pulls off his PJ bottoms – Sadie is startled by this sudden display of semi-nakedness, and isn't entirely sure it's suitable for young eyes – before retrieving his boxers and jeans from the floor and dressing quickly.

'I'll drive you to the station,' he adds later, sloshing coffee into mugs.

'No, you don't need to do that. It's hardly worth it, getting the boys loaded into the car . . .'

'We'll walk then,' he insists. 'Looks like a nice morning. We want to see Mummy off, don't we, boys?' Milo scowls from his high chair and Dylan flings his blue rubber spoon onto the kitchen floor. Oh, they know all right: that their deserter mother is heading off for two days of frivolous, milk-free fun. Despite his display of jollity, Sadie detects a vein throbbing urgently around Barney's temples.

As soon as they're outside, Sadie pulling her wheeled suitcase and Barney pushing the buggy, she realises why she'd wanted to walk to Hissingham station alone. It was so she'd be able to compose herself, to make the mental switch from mother to woman-about-town, which feels as feasible as transforming herself into Liz Hurley. With Barney and the babies beside her, she's still Mother, spying a blob of something on one of Milo's shoes, and wondering if Barney will sterilise the feeding bottles and stick to the babies' nap time schedule. She wants to remind him, but fears that he might snap her head off and doesn't want to leave on a sour note.

'Fifteen minutes to go,' Barney remarks as they arrive on the station platform.

Sadie nods. She wants the train to come now, this instant, so she'll no longer have her beloved babies staring gravely at her, knowing she's going to dress up and dance and consume large amounts of alcohol.

As the train pulls into Hissingham station, she kisses Barney full on the mouth and each of her babies' foreheads in turn, and quickly steps on. The door closes, and through the smeared glass she sees a streak of undiluted panic shoot across Barney's tired, handsome face. There's a red button by the door, for emergencies. But that's in case of accidents or someone keeling over with a heart attack – not for a petrified mother who's worried that her husband will forget to use nappy rash cream. She blinks at her beloved Barney, longing to launch herself through the door and bury herself in his sweater. It's only Scotland, she reasons; what about Polly, straddling continents? At least she'll be in the same time zone. And Barney's right – they'll be *fine*.

The train edges forward and Sadie is waving now, sensing her bottom lip wobbling as Milo's face crumples and he tears off a shoe and throws it onto the platform. She's still waving, a wide smile cemented onto her face, and Barney's waving back, mouthing the words, 'Have fun.' Or it might possibly be, 'Oh fuck.'

TWENTY

Sadie trots across the concourse, dark hair piled up, lips cherry red, clearly not registering the admiring glances she's attracting. *God, look at her,* thinks Hannah, watching her friend for a moment, taking in the glossy heels, the well-cut jeans, the little blue top and jacket and the cluster of besuited men who are checking her out as she scans King's Cross station. 'Sadie!' Hannah yells with a wave. Seeing her, Sadie's face breaks into a colossal grin and she hurries towards Hannah, clacking across the concourse and letting go of her case to envelop her friend in a hug. 'You're here,' Hannah exclaims. 'You're actually here and you look fantastic!'

'So do you,' Sadie says, her dark eyes shining. 'I can't believe we're going to have all this time together. It's ridiculous how little I see you. You'd think I lived on Pluto or something.'

'It feels like it sometimes,' Hannah laughs as they head for the kiosk to stock up on coffees and baguettes for the train.

'And when we do see each other, it's so rushed,' Hannah declares.

'Or we're busy mopping up puke . . .' Sadie adds,

referring to her sole visit to Hannah's new home with the twins, soon after she'd moved in with Ryan.

'The babies were tiny,' Hannah reminds her, 'and no one cared anyway. Ryan's been through that stage, remember. He's not freaked out by a little vomit.'

'Daisy and Josh looked pretty horrified, though . . .'

'Well, they would.' Hannah bites her tongue as they check the board for the Glasgow train's platform number.

'What d'you mean?'

'Just . . . you know . . . kids. They get horribly queasy about stuff like that.'

'Oh yeah.'

Hannah is relieved to let the subject go. She didn't send the last email in which she'd blurted out the truth about Ryan's kids. That wasn't why she'd written it, she realises now; it was just to vent, to 'confess' to the two people who knew her best, without actually alarming or panicking them. Before she met Ryan and his offspring, Hannah had never kept anything from Sadie and Lou. And here she is now, harbouring a walloping secret: that the thought of marrying Ryan, no matter how much she loves him, makes her stomach lurch as if she's strapped onto a rickety roller coaster, which looks as if it might possibly veer off the rails. Spilling out the terrible truth would, Hannah feels, put something of a dampener on her hen weekend.

'Ryan was really good about it,' Sadie recalls. 'You know, Han, I knew he sounded right for you, especially after Marc with the T-shirt drawer thing – but that kind of cemented it for me, his swift action with the J-cloth.'

Hannah laughs. 'He has his advantages. Anyway,' she adds, taking a sip of her coffee, 'did you check out our hotel? What did you think?'

'Looks fine to me . . .'

'I hope it's okay. There were a few dodgy comments on TripAdvisor.'

'I don't care what it's like,' Sadie declares. 'I'm getting away from the village and that's good enough for me.'

'But I thought you *liked* it . . .' Hannah frowns.

'Oh, I do, it's great, and it's a much better place to bring up the boys . . .'

'But . . .' Hannah suppresses a snort. 'You kind of went like this' – she winces dramatically – 'when you said "village".'

'I did not! I just said . . . village.'

'You did it again,' Hannah teases. 'Every time you say "village" you get this funny expression . . .'

'Oh, shut up,' Sadie blushes.

'*Village*,' Hannah rasps into her ear, showing their tickets at the barrier and experiencing a small thrill at seeing the word 'Glasgow' on the illuminated board. People have the wrong idea about the city, she reckons; even her parents, who've been there on countless visits, always seemed to regard the city as if it were a slightly dangerous boyfriend, luring their baby away from the nest.

As for Little Hissingham – Hannah can, in fact, understand Sadie's involuntary wincing. It's pretty, with the pub and the cluster of cottages huddled around the primped village green. Yet there's a flatness about it, as if a big, long sigh is hanging in the air. Although Hannah can see the *point* of the countryside – and she had a fun evening, the one time she stayed over at Sadie's – she still can't quite imagine her friend fitting into that world.

By the time they've boarded the train and found their seats – Hannah plonks herself next to a man in a salmon-pink polo shirt – Sadie's already filled Hannah in on the numerous coffee mornings and infinite traybakes on offer, being quizzed on her preferred method of conception *and* contraception and told in no uncertain terms to freeze bananas.

129

'Jesus,' Hannah breathes, dumping their baguettes on the table. 'I've always imagined you and Barney sitting by a river somewhere, with a lovely picnic in a proper wicker hamper . . .'

Sadie shakes her head vehemently. 'We never do that. Actually, I don't even know if there *are* any rivers nearby. The thing I didn't realise about the countryside is, you're not actually allowed to walk through most of it.'

'Why not?' Hannah thinks of her own childhood, spent scrambling freely on Fife beaches.

'Because . . .' She shrugs. 'There are animals, there's stuff growing eveywhere, or you worry that some furious farmer's going to charge at you with a gun.' The man in the salmon top emits a chuckle, and the girls cast him a quick look.

'So . . . what d'you do then?' Hannah asks Sadie.

'Stick pins in my eyes, mainline gin . . .'

Salmon Man looks up at the girls as they burst into laughter.

'God,' Hannah says, 'I don't blame you. So was Barney okay about you coming away, or is he going to decamp to his parents?'

'He was fine,' Sadie says firmly. 'Virtually shoved me out of the door. I mean, it *is* only two days and he's perfectly capable of looking after the babies . . . I *think*.' She pulls a mock-terrified face.

'I hope you don't mind me saying . . .' Salmon Man says, and Hannah and Sadie look at him expectantly. 'It might sound presumptuous,' he adds, addressing Sadie as their train pulls out of the station, 'but you don't *look* like a new mother to me.'

Hannah and Sadie fall silent for a moment. His voice is plummy, his face pinkish and chubby, his fair hair atrociously cut, possibly with shears. 'So what's a new mother supposed to look like?' Sadie asks.

He grins. 'Oh, you know. Covered in milk sick, absolutely knackered, whole set of luggage under the eyes . . .'

'Well,' Sadie says, 'I'm usually like that, but I chipped all the sick off myself in honour of Hannah's hen weekend.'

'You're on a hen weekend?'

'Don't say it,' Hannah chuckles. 'We don't look like the types to—'

'No, no, you *absolutely* look like you're about to terrorise the inhabitants of . . . where's this hen party happening?'

'Glasgow,' Hannah tells him.

He frowns. 'But aren't hen parties supposed to involve great gangs of women dressed identically in satin tour jackets, that kind of thing?'

'What makes you think we don't have satin tour jackets?' Sadie teases.

'And there's going to be a *small* gang of us,' Hannah adds. 'We're picking up our other friend, Lou, in York . . .'

'Right,' he says eagerly. 'So you're Hannah, and you're . . .'

'Sadie . . .'

'I'm Felix,' he says with a broad grin. 'And I think we should celebrate, don't you?'

Hannah looks at him blankly as he delves into a coolbox at his feet, her eyes widening as he produces a bottle of champagne. 'What's that for?' she exclaims.

Felix shrugs. 'Well, I'm going to drink it, of course. And I'd be very much obliged if you girls would help me.'

'Are you sure?' Hannah asks, frowning.

'Of course! I wouldn't be so greedy as to polish it off all by myself . . .'

'Well, if you insist,' Sadie adds, at which Felix waves down the lady with the snacks trolley as if she were a passing cab.

'Three glasses please,' he says grandly.

'We only do plastic cups.' She eyes him with suspicion.

131

'That'll do. Just a receptacle of some kind, thank you.'

With a barely perceptible pursing of the lips, the woman hands Felix the cups, which he accepts with gushing thanks and a wide smile. As she moves on with the trolley, and he pours out the champagne, Hannah catches Sadie's eye and smiles. She knows Sadie remembers this: drinking champagne from plastic cups on that last night together at Garnet Street. It whooshed to her head then, as it does now, making her feel giddy. As for Felix, this stranger in a particularly unappealing pink top – there's something about him, she thinks. When they'd first boarded the train, all she'd wanted was Sadie all to herself. But now, with the champagne flowing and the knots of tension disappearing from her shoulders and neck, Hannah isn't remotely taken aback when he looks at her and Sadie in turn and says, 'So, girls, tell me all about yourselves.'

*

By the time the train pulls into York station, an entire bottle of champagne has been drunk, a second has appeared and Hannah and Sadie have learnt that Felix, who owns cocktail bars in London and Manchester, is making the trip north to check up on his latest venture in Glasgow. He wants to know all about Hannah's paintings, and scrolls through every single image of her work on her phone, saying he's a dumbass about art but these are lovely. He listens to Sadie's tales of child-rearing with rapt interest, brushing aside her fears that she's being a baby bore. As Hannah describes the ice-spitting fridge, and Ryan's ex-wife, the three of them decide that Petra probably takes her cello to bed, kissing its little tuning pegs and caressing its woody curves.

As the train slows down before coming to a halt, Felix appears to be as excited as they are. 'There's Lou!' Hannah cries, leaping up from her seat.

Spotting them, and quickly kissing Spike's cheek, Lou charges towards the door, lugging a navy-blue bag emblazoned with gigantic poppies. She scrambles on to the train, makes for their table and hugs them both tightly. 'All set?' Lou asks, turning to wave Spike goodbye. Spike manages a closed-mouthed smile.

'Yes,' Hannah laughs, indicating her cup. 'And we've started already, thanks to Felix here . . .'

'Pleased to meet you.' Lou grins, offering him her hand.

'Look at Spike,' Hannah marvels. 'I haven't seen him for what – three years? And he hasn't aged a bit . . .' On the platform, Spike thrusts his hands into his pockets.

'That's the life of leisure for you,' Lou chuckles. 'It's like being preserved in aspic.'

'He's still cute, though,' Sadie teases her.

'Sadie's saying you're still cute!' Lou mouths through the window, causing Spike to frown uncomprehendingly.

Thank God they're here, Hannah thinks as Felix requests another cup from the trolley lady as she passes. The train lurches forward, and the three women turn to give Spike a final wave, but he's no longer looking in their direction. He's turned away, as if in a sulk, and is rooting about for something in the pockets of his slightly too-young-looking leather jacket.

TWENTY-ONE

As Lou's train pulls away, Spike takes his mobile from his pocket and grips it tightly as if it were a life-support device. He pauses before making the call. Who was that man sitting next to Hannah – some posh oik, by the look of him – who'd leapt up and lifted Lou's case up onto the luggage rack? There was champagne too, by the looks of it. Spike saw Lou smile her thanks, then start talking to him, all animated, while he stood there like a spare school dinner.

Lou looked pretty today, Spike reflects, with her striking auburn hair bouncing around her impish little face. She'd put on slim-fitting jeans and a soft green sweater he'd never seen before. But it wasn't her clothes, he realises now as he makes his way towards the station exit. It was her body language that seemed different. Despite Spike's plans for the rest of the day, he feels a sharp stab of annoyance. Why was she so pleased to be getting away from him? And why couldn't she be more like this at home – pink-cheeked and buoyant and looking glad to be alive, instead of scowling in that marshmallow dressing gown and forcing him to do his CV? If a jury of his peers were presented with the cold, hard facts about his affair with Astrid, would anyone really blame him?

'Sod it,' he mutters, leaving the station and dialling Astrid's number. It's only a fifteen-minute walk from York station to her house. Rather cruelly, the quickest route takes him past Sound Shack where, as if to maximise his pain, Rick has placed Spike's guitar on a stand in the middle of the window. Spike pauses, taking in the blonde wood curves, and the fretboard worn by his very own fingers. A price tag dangles from one of the tuning pegs: £425. £425? Is he taking the piss? Quickly, Spike turns and marches onwards, fury bubbling like lava in his veins. He's always considered Rick a friend, and has known him virtually all the seven years he's lived here. He's obviously not a real friend, though, ripping him off like that. Spike has experienced that a lot over the years – people who want to be his mate, just because of who he is. At least what he has with Astrid is real, he thinks, trying her home phone for the third time, then her mobile (where the hell is she? Isn't she busily preparing for his arrival, having a bath, delipidating or whatever it's called when women shave their legs, and smoothing lotion all over her body?). Her airbrushed bum pops into his mind and he feels a shiver of desire. *She* doesn't care about 'My Beauty', or any horse telly songs for that matter – she's far too young to remember Follyfoot. Nearing her street now, he tries her mobile again. Still nothing. *She's teasing me*, he decides, his heart filling with hope as he turns the corner and her house comes into view. Spike raps sharply on her front door. Nothing. He tries again, then steps back onto the pavement and scans the windows. No one there.

Deciding to adjourn to the olde worlde pub in the next street, he nurses a couple of watery pints before nipping outside and calling her again. Miraculously, she picks up.

'Hey, you,' she says, her voice tinged with amusement. 'You've called me, like, five times! Is everything okay?'

'Er, yeah!' He pauses and frowns. 'I just . . . well, I've

just seen Lou off and thought, if you're not doing anything . . . you do *remember*, don't you, that I'm a free man this weekend? Like, all weekend, because Lou's gone to Glasgow?'

'Yeah, 'course I do. I just got in actually.'

'Where have you been?' he bleats, starting to walk towards her house at a determined pace.

'The library.'

'The *library*?' Fantastic. He's sold his guitar so the two of them could have heaps of uninterrupted time together, and she's been at the library?

'Yeah, the library, Spike. You know – that building with lots of books in it. Why shouldn't I go to the library?'

'Oh, no reason.'

'You sound out of breath. Are you okay?'

'Yeah, I'm just walking.'

'Sounds more like a brisk canter, Spike. God, maybe you should stop smoking . . .'

'Yeah, anyway,' he cuts in, 'did you get some good books?' Then, realising how peevish that sounds, he adds, 'Because I don't think you'll be doing much reading this weekend.'

'Oh. Haha. No, well . . . I suppose reading can wait. So what time d'you think you'll be over?'

'Er . . .' He pauses, blinking at her freshly painted front door. 'Well, I'm sort of here now.'

'What, here? At my house?'

'Er, yeah,' he mutters.

She sighs then, a proper, exasperated sigh. 'Shall we finish this phone conversation and talk face to face?'

'That'd be good,' Spike says with a feeble laugh. Astrid is still clutching her mobile as she opens the door.

'Hi,' she says lightly.

'Hi, babe.' He steps in, kissing her cheek.

'So I'm assuming Lou got off okay,' she says.

136

'Yeah.' He looks at her, and the anticipation that's been building up all week ebbs away like water into sand. Something about Astrid's mouth set in a tight line tells Spike that the weekend isn't going to pan out as he'd planned, and for a fleeting moment he pictures Lou, with that round-faced little tosser on the train, laughing and guzzling champagne.

TWENTY-TWO

By the time Sadie's train reaches Newcastle, Barney is exhausted as he places his writhing children into their buggy in the living room. It's 3.30 pm – milk time if he were to stick to the rigid routine which seems to dominate their lives these days, although right now his sons seem keener on exercising their tiny lungs than feeding. How can babies make so much noise? It seems completely out of proportion to their size – high-pitched, urgent, desperate. He's tried to feed them, but they lurched away from the bottles as if he was offering them Jeyes Fluid. So what *do* they want? Why can't they communicate more clearly, and say, 'Sorry, Dad, but I'm not really in the mood for a bottle right now. What I'd really like is a walk in the park – to be out of this dingy little house?'

Anyway, what would happen if Barney ignored the routine and went off piste, treating them to, say, a bag of chips at 4 pm? Would he be arrested? Would Little Hissingham be consumed by floods, resulting in mass deaths? 'It says here that it's really important to establish a routine,' Sadie explained several months ago, waving one of those thick, glossy baby manuals at him, written by a smug woman emitting of-a-certain-age glamour, who'd

138

clearly never wiped poo off a baby's lower back in her entire life. So many of Sadie's sentences start with 'it says here'. *It says here that home-made baby food is better nutritionally. It says here that we used to have fun . . .*

Sex too, if Barney remembers rightly. They used to have that pretty regularly. That one time, a few weeks ago now, was the first in living memory and, frankly, only served to remind him of what he had been missing. Before that, he'd almost forgotten that it was something adults did. Then that night happened – so tender and lovely it had brought tears to his eyes – making Barney foolishly think that intimacy might be back on the agenda. He now realises it was a flukey one-off, and probably only came about because Sadie was delighted to be getting the hell out of Little Hissingham for two days. Since then, whenever he's tried to touch her in bed, she's gone rigid with tension as if he might be about to pelt her with ice cubes.

Perhaps it's moving here, to this bleak little dot on the map, which has pushed them apart. To Barney's prickling shame, it was his idea in the first place. As he manoeuvres the buggy outside, he remembers wanting to protect his pregnant wife and children from the noise and pollution and people shouting outside their Stoke Newington flat. And Little Hissingham was affordable – just – and within commuting distance of London and surrounded by fields. Fields he's since discovered aren't much use as there's no way of knowing which ones might contain a bull.

'Aw, lovely boys you've got there.' A middle-aged lady pauses to admire his sons as Barney reaches the park gates.

'Thanks,' Barney says as she falls into step with him.

'Aren't you a good dad, bringing them out? Your wife's a very lucky lady.'

'Er, I don't think so,' he blusters, 'I just do it, you know . . .'

As she turns off the path, Barney watches her growing smaller, feeling guilty now for thinking bad thoughts about routines and baby books. Sadie isn't lucky, he wants to yell after the woman; *he* is, for having the good fortune to have met such a clever, remarkable, sexy woman. They're going through a blip, that's all; isn't that how those child-rearing experts put it? *It's common for new parents to feel estranged from each other. A little distant and cold, and lacking the intimacy of their pre-parenthood life . . .*

It's drizzling now, settling on Barney's face like wet breath, but at least the boys seem less fraught. Glancing up at the sky, which has turned a moody, gunmetal grey, Barney decides to make a pit stop at the park café. That'll fill half an hour. Then, in another fifty-seven hours and thirty-two minutes, Sadie will be home and everything will be normal again.

'Hi, what can I get for you?' asks the perky young girl at the counter. She has a slight accent – Polish, perhaps – and a short, impish haircut. Her fringe is secured to one side with a butterfly clasp.

'Er . . .' Barney scans the menu on the chalkboard on the wall behind her.

There's no beer on offer, unfortunately, but the thought of coffee, and possibly something sweet and baked, is preferable to the nappy fug of home. 'An Americano please,' Barney says, 'and one of those little currant things.'

'Sure.' She flashes him a white-toothed smile. 'Cute babies,' she says handing him his coffee and pastry.

'Thanks,' he smiles proudly.

'They obviously enjoy being out with their dad.' He glances down to see both boys gazing up at the girl in wonder, transfixed her by her smiling, open face. Perhaps that's what they've been missing today: Sadie's feminine presence. Can he blame them for regarding a bearded male with dastardly bottles of formula as a poor substitute? He's frozen Sadie's precious breast milk in case of an emergency, a sort of 'keeping the best till last' approach.

'Yeah,' he says, grinning. 'I hope so anyway. They weren't happy a minute ago, though.'

'Look like you, don't they?' Barney meets the girl's unwavering gaze, wondering with mild alarm if she's flirting with him. No, surely not. He's thirty-six, a clapped-out dad in knackered jeans and a faded Kings of Leon T-shirt, and he hasn't even combed his hair today. 'Think so?' he asks.

'Oh yeah. Same eyes, same face shape around here . . .' She touches her cheek.

Barney looks back down at his children. Actually, he can't see any resemblance whatsoever; with their dark hair and creamy complexions, they're miniature Sadies. He's about to tell the girl this, then hesitates. With a small jolt, he realises he's avoiding mentioning his wife's name, or even the fact that his children have a mother. 'Well, bad luck for them,' he chortles awkwardly, fishing out coins and placing them on the counter.

The girl laughs. 'I wouldn't say that. Anyway, nice to meet you, um . . .'

'Barney.'

'I'm Magda.' Another big smile. God, she's commented on his eyes and now she's introducing herself. He feels his eyebrows shoot up cartoonishly.

'Well, thanks, Magda.' He picks up his tray.

'I'll take that for you. You've got your hands full with the buggy. Where would you like to sit?'

'Oh, anywhere,' he murmurs, scanning the numerous empty tables. As he pushes the buggy towards the window, he wishes there were other customers in the café. Then he'd feel less exposed and self-conscious.

'Here you go.' Placing his tray on the table, Magda turns and heads back to the counter. Of course, it wasn't really him she was flirting with, Barney realises now; it was universal-dad-of-cute-babies, like that Athena poster guy clutching the child to his bare chest. The very idea of comparing himself to a male model, shot in black and white, almost makes Barney laugh out loud. Lately, he's wondered if the real crux of the matter is that his wife no longer fancies him.

Vaguely aware of Magda throwing him the odd glance, he recalls how he first glimpsed Sadie five years ago at a party in an impossibly smart Covent Garden flat. Barney knew Daniel, the host, from drama school, and Sadie was a friend of Daniel's girlfriend. As a jobbing actor, Barney had led a haphazard existence, trying not to notice that his resting periods were becoming longer, punctuated during one bleak year by an appearance as an armed robber on *Crimewatch*. It had become clear that he had to come up with a viable alternative. Two significant things happened at Daniel's party: he'd got chatting to the director of a charity who asked him to stop by for a 'chat' – nothing as formal as an interview – the following week. And he'd met Sadie Vella, a stunning brunette with melty brown eyes and curves to make any grown man collapse in a heap. A week later, Barney had a job and, more significantly, was pretty certain he'd met the love of his life. A year later, they married at Wood Green registry office in a flurry of confetti and kooky speeches from their gang of excitable and by now mutual friends.

The twins had felt like a gift, the icing on the cake. They *are* a gift, Barney thinks now, seeing Magda tip her head to one side and smile indulgently at his sleeping children (has he contravened The Schedule by allowing them to doze off?). But maybe it's too much for Sadie, looking after them full time, especially out here in the middle of nowhere. It's obvious now that they should have stayed in north London, near their friends, in a city with a billion things to do. It wouldn't matter that the tiny local playground has been vandalised or that there were takeaway cartons strewn on the ground. A bit of graffiti and litter never hurt anybody.

'So,' Magda says, coming over to wipe the table next to his, 'what are you up to for the rest of the day?'

'Er . . .' Barney's mouth is crammed with currants and he quickly gulps them down. 'Just going with the flow I guess.' *Don't read anything into this. Magda's only making conversation because you're the only customer in here on a drizzly Friday.*

She nods, rearranging the daffodils in the small blue vase on the adjacent table. Although he tries not to look, he can't help but notice her darting gracefully between the other tables in a cute denim mini skirt over leggings, and a spotty top that hugs her slight, boyish frame. He flinches as his mobile rings, as if Sadie might have somehow spied him glancing at Magda from her Glasgow-bound train.

'Hey, mate! How's it going? Sadie off on that hen weekend?'

It's Pete, Barney's best mate from secondary school, a chick-magnet who, at thirty-six, has so far managed to breeze through life without acquiring any responsibilities beyond a small mortgage on his airy Clerkenwell flat. 'Yeah, left this morning,' Barney replies, realising he's carefully omitted the word 'she'. 'Pretty excited, yeah,' he goes on. 'So, everything OK?'

'Yep,' Pete says. 'Hope you're enjoying your day off, though I guess it's not exactly a holiday being in charge of those two monkeys . . .'

'Oh, it's been fine,' Barney says jovially.

'Good man. Anyway, listen, I'm finishing up early today so I thought I'd drive out to see you, have a couple of pints in your village pub, the what-ever-it-is . . .'

'The Black Swan.'

'Yeah. Nice place. So what d'you think?'

'I, er . . .'

'I know you've got the kids,' Pete adds, 'but it's warm and sunny and they'd be okay outside in the beer garden, wouldn't they?' Barney looks out again, willing the drizzle to stop and the moody grey sky to turn blue. 'I mean, no one would call social services for that, would they?' Pete chuckles.

'Nah,' Barney laughs, 'I reckon we'd be fine. Weather's a bit dismal here but it might perk up. And it'll be great to see you. You can crash on the sofa if you like.'

'Great. Just feel like getting out of London, to be honest.'

Barney finishes the call and, balancing his cup on his plate with one hand, and steering the buggy with the other, he makes his way back to the counter.

'Bye, Magda,' he says with a big smile, buoyed by the prospect of Pete's visit, even more so now as the rain has stopped, and weak sunlight is filtering through the clouds.

'Bye, Barney. See you again soon, I hope.'

'Er, yeah. Me too.' As he barges towards the exit, clumsily knocking against a large plant, he tries to arrange his flushed features into a coping-dad face. Even though absolutely *nothing* has happened, he decides not to mention any of this to Pete.

TWENTY-THREE

Ladies and gentlemen, we apologise for this delay to our 12.30 service from King's Cross to Glasgow Central, caused by signalling problems in the Newcastle area. We hope to be moving again shortly and will keep you informed of further developments. Again, we are sorry for any inconvenience this delay may have caused . . .

Lou doesn't feel that any apology is necessary. She's relishing the banter with Hannah, Sadie and Felix, and she's grateful to be away from Let's Bounce and Spike, beached on the sofa, clutching the remote control to his chest. 'So you and your boyfriend have been together since college?' Felix asks. His hearty guffaws and startlingly direct questions are refreshing, Lou decides as he tops up her cup.

'Yep, sixteen years now,' she replies. 'I think that qualifies for some kind of long-service award, don't you?'

'He came along when she was a little stripling of nineteen and spoiled her fun,' Hannah chuckles.

Although Hannah is joking, Lou has always suspected she doesn't entirely approve of Spike. 'He must have something, though,' Felix insists. 'Something that's kept you together all this time.'

Lou rolls her eyes and grins. 'Yeah, I suppose he must. Um, let me think . . .'

Sadie and Hannah burst out laughing. 'He *looked* like a nice guy, dutifully standing there and seeing you off,' Felix offers.

'Oh, he is,' Lou agrees. 'He's very, er . . .' What should she say? When it comes to his glittering qualities, her mind is a complete blank. 'He's very . . . loyal,' she adds, realising she's made him sound like an elderly dog. 'And he's house-trained, *most* of the time.'

'D'you have any children?' Felix wants to know.

She shakes her head. 'Nope, none of those.'

'Want any?'

Lou almost laughs at his bluntness. 'That's so personal!' Hannah protests. 'God, Felix. You're like some probing, on-the-couch interviewer. Are you sure you run bars and aren't really a psychotherapist or something?'

Felix chuckles. 'No, I'm just interested in people, that's all. It helps with business, understanding what makes people tick. And, you know, my job is all about bringing people together so . . .' He smiles affably. Lou studies his expressive face, the mobile brows, the hazy grey eyes, the way he shoves back his messy fair hair distractedly. He's tipsy, she decides, but not drunk. His top has a small splash of champagne on the front.

'Well,' Lou says carefully, 'I would like kids actually, but Spike's not keen.'

Hannah frowns at her. 'Really, Lou? I didn't think you did. You always said you weren't sure, that you weren't convinced that you and Spike—'

'I've kind of changed my mind,' she says quietly.

'Have you?' Sadie asks. 'Why d'you think . . .'

'I had a false alarm a couple of months ago,' Lou cuts in, wondering what's possessing her to divulge such personal information on a busy train with a stranger sitting here.

146

Before now, she hadn't even mentioned any of this to Hannah or Sadie. The champagne's helping, of course, yet there's something else too; something about Felix's presence that's drawing out how she really feels.

'What happened, Lou?' Hannah asks gently.

'Well, I didn't know what to think, not really. I was scared at first, but then, as the days went on, I thought . . . why not? I'm thirty-five and there's no reason on earth why I shouldn't have a baby.' Without warning, Lou's eyes fill with tears, and she quickly blinks them away.

Hannah places her hand over Lou's. 'So you were happy about it?'

'Yeah, after the initial shock. It was strange, feeling secretly thrilled and excited when I'd never been broody before. Although I'm with kids all day, and half of them are usually screaming, I realised I really, really wanted to have the baby.'

A hush falls over the table. 'Did you tell Spike how you felt?' Sadie asks.

Lou nods. 'He wouldn't really discuss it. Kept shrugging it off, avoided talking about it because, you know, it wasn't planned. Actually, he was a grumpy bastard the whole time.'

'Why?' Sadie asks. 'Didn't he want the baby?'

'Obviously not.' Lou grimaces. 'But anyway, I was just really late and it turned out to be nothing, like Spike hoped it would be. And now,' she continues briskly, 'I look at you, Sadie, with two babies, managing to do it all as if it's come so naturally and, to be honest' – she pauses for another sip of champagne – 'I honestly don't know if I'm mum material, and even if I *am*, we probably couldn't afford it.'

'You really think it comes naturally?' Sadie exclaims. 'God, Lou, I wish it did. I'm terrified half the time, being in sole charge of Milo and Dylan even though I should know what I'm doing by now.'

'But should you?' Felix asks. 'Who says you should?'

'Oh, everyone! The coffee morning women with their baby slings and frozen bananas . . .'

'You probably just need to get away for a bit,' Hannah suggests. 'You've had virtually no time off since they were born.'

'What about Barney?' Lou asks. 'How's he with the babies?'

'As scared as I am,' Sadie says. 'I don't know. We don't really talk anymore – at least not properly. He says I'm always quoting from baby books . . .'

'Barney's lovely,' Hannah tells Felix. 'He's this sweet, kind, capable man . . .'

'And what's yours like?' Felix asks. 'Your man, I mean?' From his magic coolbox, he produces a box of truffles with an embossed gold lid and proceeds to hand them around.

'Wow. Thanks.' Hannah pops one into her mouth. 'What's Ryan like? Well, he's a dad, he's got two kids, we're getting married in two weeks . . .'

'You did that wincing thing!' Sadie exclaims. 'You know how you said I winced every time I said village? You did it just then when you said *married*.'

'No I didn't,' Hannah protests.

'You did! And I'm sorry, Lou,' Sadie turns to her, 'but you did it too, when you said *Spike*.'

The three girls are laughing now, tucking into Felix's truffles and pronouncing them delicious. Lou glances first at Hannah, then Sadie, wondering how she's managed to lose touch with the intricacies of their lives. They'd known everything about each other back in the Garnet Street days when every minuscule event had been discussed late into the night. Hannah has fallen silent now, and is licking a chocolatey smear from her finger, as if building up to share a secret of her own. Something's preying on her mind, Lou can tell; something bigger and scarier than pre-wedding stress. 'Are you okay about the wedding?' she asks hesitantly.

Hannah nods. 'Yes, of course I am.'

Lou shoots Felix a quick look, wishing now that it were just the three of them at this table, even though he's turned to the window and is gazing out at flat fields. 'I'm sure it'll be fine,' she says firmly.

Hannah turns to look at her, inhales deeply and sips from her cup. 'It's not the wedding, Lou. And it's not me and Ryan I'm worried about. It's Josh and Daisy.'

'What about them?' Lou asks, frowning.

Hannah shrugs. 'They bloody hate me.'

'They can't!' Lou gasps. 'Why on earth would they hate you?'

'Well, they make it pretty clear that they do.'

'But you've been so nice to them,' Sadie cuts in. 'What kind of stuff do they do?'

Hannah smiles ruefully. 'Oh, it's not horrible pranks or anything. I haven't had frogs put in my bed – yet. It's a lot more subtle than that . . .' She proceeds to fill them in on the shopping trip and the interrogation about not believing in God. 'There's another thing,' she adds. 'I found a Marlboro packet in the pocket of Josh's jeans.'

'Have you told Ryan?' Lou asks.

'No, not yet . . .'

'You should!' Sadie declares. 'You should frame the packet and hang it up for him when he gets home.'

'It's tempting,' Hannah murmurs.

'Well, I'm sorry, Hannah,' Felix scoffs, turning towards her, 'but you don't strike me as wicked stepmother material . . .' She forces a smile, and Sadie and Lou are agog as she describes the stony silences, the hostile glares and Daisy showing her every damn page in the wedding album. She tells Felix about her studio, and how lucky she is to have it despite Daisy reminding her over and over that it used to be Petra's music room. 'I don't even paint anymore,' she confesses. 'It's just a pretend studio full of my stuff, with the ghost cello watching over me . . .'

'Ghost cello?' Felix repeats, raising his brows.

'It feels like it's still there sometimes,' Hannah declares, her cheeks flushing.

Felix frowns. 'Only if you *let* it be there,' he suggests gently.

'Well, it's kind of hard not to . . .'

'But you *do* still want to get married?' Lou cuts in. 'I mean, you're not having second thoughts, are you?'

'Am I?' Hannah drains her cup. 'I really don't know.'

'You're having doubts?' Sadie asks, frowning. 'Seriously?'

Hannah pauses. 'I . . . I just can't figure out how I'm ever going to fit into that family.' Lou studies her friend, and although she wants to say it'll be okay, she doesn't know how to make it sound convincing. She sees a flicker of fear cross her face, and for a moment she sees the eighteen-year-old Hannah again, fresh from her village in Fife in her checked shirt and dungarees, stepping into the grown-up world, trying to look as if she knew what she was doing. As their eyes meet, Hannah holds Lou's gaze for a moment. Then Hannah grins broadly and says, 'God these truffles are moreish, Felix, I'll have to have my wedding dress expanded at this rate.' And she pops another one into her mouth.

TWENTY-FOUR

Spike has been in bed with Astrid for less than an hour and already it appears that she wants him to leave. 'I've just got things on later,' she says, sitting up and peering at the old-fashioned alarm clock on her bedside table, as if she's suddenly become incredibly short-sighted.

He gazes forlornly at the most beautiful back he's ever laid eyes on, resisting the urge to reach out and touch it. All that time wasted before he'd been able to get hold of her; then she'd insisted on knocking together a late lunch (it was hungry work, browsing books in the library, Spike thought dryly) before making umpteen calls, checking her emails and putting on a *wash*, for God's sake. He was honoured that she hadn't decided to clean the kitchen floor.

'What kind of things?' he asks in what he hopes is a tone of mild interest.

Astrid swings out of bed, pulls on plain white knickers and jeans and does up the clasp on her bra. 'Just . . . a meeting. A work thing,' she replies with her back to him.

Another 'work thing', right at the end of the afternoon? Astrid's job has started to seriously impinge on their time together.

'D'you really have to go?' he asks lightly.

151

'Yeah. Sorry, babe.' Well, that's just great. Spike has started to obsess over the measly £160 Rick paid him for the guitar; and now, with Astrid clearly on the verge of kicking him out, he feels even more ripped off. The sex was okay, although not quite up to their usual enthusiastic standard. Astrid is almost fully dressed, as if she'd just wanted to get it over and done with, like having her teeth scaled and polished.

Spike feels used. Now he knows how women feel when they complain about men being cold and uncommunicative after sex.

'Damn,' Astrid mutters, checking the clock again. 'I've really got to go, Spike.'

'Well . . . couldn't you cancel it, just this once?'

'What are you, hairy boy? My keeper?' Astrid laughs, turning to face him as she sweeps back her honey-coloured hair with her fingers, then bends to pick up one of his socks from the floor and drops it onto his bare chest. She has yet to put on her top. The sight of her standing there, all slender in that rather sensible white bra sets something stirring in him again. Yet he's being kicked out, discarded without a second thought, like a takeaway carton.

'No, I don't mean that, I just mean . . .' He shrugs, affecting nonchalance. 'I just thought you might have a bit more time to . . . y'know. Hang out.'

'Well, I don't,' Astrid says briskly. She plucks her lilac top from the back of a chair, and disappointment pools in Spike's stomach as she slips it on.

'Maybe I could just hang around here, watch a bit of telly until you come back?' he asks hopefully.

She shakes her head firmly. 'Sorry, babe. C'mon.'

With a petulant sigh, Spike climbs out of bed and strides brazenly across her bedroom, gathering up his clothes from her oatmeal rug. At least she called him babe just then, not hairy boy. Where had that come from? The 'boy' part was fine, the 'hairy' part less so; Spike has always assumed she *likes* his manly chest. She's always stroking and kissing and pressing her cheek against it, as if it were a much-loved pet. He frowns down at it now and quickly pulls on the fresh white T-shirt which he'd laundered specially on a hot wash while Lou was packing for Glasgow.

'Ready?' Astrid asks impatiently.

'Yeah. Just got to find my shoes.' He glances around her bedroom.

'Did you leave them in the bathroom?' Christ, she's like an over-zealous chambermaid, pressurising him to leave the room so she can get on with servicing it.

'Er, yeah, I might have.' He stomps out and finds them kicked off by the loo, feeling foolish now as he returns to her boudoir, naked from the waist down and clutching them. Wordlessly, he pulls on his boxers and jeans, retrieves one sock from the bed and looks around for the other one. No sign of it, and Spike isn't prepared to humiliate himself by trying to find it with Astrid watching, virtually drumming her nails on the bedside table. Who needs socks anyway? he thinks rashly, pulling on the one he's managed to find, then lacing up his shoes. 'Right, I'll be off then,' he announces, striding out of her bedroom and marching downstairs.

'Oh, Spike . . .' Astrid hurries after him. 'I'm sorry about this. It's just not the best time, okay?'

He shrugs. 'It's *fine*. It's just different for me, you see. You're single, you can do what you like. My life's more . . . *complicated,* so I guess I build up these opportunities in my mind, and they mean a lot to me . . .' That's good. He can see Astrid's expression softening, like ice cream.

'Look, babe,' she starts. He catches his breath, waiting for her to say *sorry for being so cold with you, darling, sorry for the library, the meeting and calling you hairy boy, let's go back to bed and start all over again . . .*

'I feel a bit weird, Spike,' she adds, biting her lip.

'What about?' For a terrible moment, he thinks she's going to tell him she's pregnant.

'I . . .' Astrid clears her throat. 'I wasn't going to mention it but . . . I ran into Lou yesterday.'

'Did you?' He'd been hoping she wouldn't bring this up, and feels the blood drain from his face.

'She was heading home and I'd just been to the gym . . . I didn't want to stop and chat but I saw her checking me out and it turned out she remembered me from your gig, the one before Christmas . . .'

Spike nods slowly. His lips have completely dried out, and his tongue feels as if it might be permanently gummed to the roof of his mouth.

'So we stopped and chatted,' Astrid continues, 'and she was so friendly and nice, it made me think, is this right? Sleeping with you when you've got this lovely, sweet girlfriend at home, who obviously adores you . . .'

'I . . . I don't understand why you're saying this,' Spike blusters. 'Yeah, Lou's great, she's loyal and faithful, but you and me – well, it's really nothing to do with her . . .'

'Loyal and faithful!' Astrid cries, pink patches springing up on her cheeks. 'You make her sound like a puppy. You'll be praising her for peeing on newspaper next.'

'Well, I didn't mean . . .'

'*And* you've been with her for about a hundred years. Of course it's to do with her. And I just felt, I don't know . . . such a hypocrite, kind of small and pathetic, being all friendly with her in the street.'

'Listen,' Spike insists, his sockless foot starting to feel clammy already, 'with me and Lou it's just . . . just *stale*, that's all.' He shrugs helplessly, trying to evoke sympathy. 'We're like flatmates, okay? There's no spark.'

'You mean,' Astrid says carefully, 'you don't sleep with her anymore?'

154

'Well, uh . . .' Spike can sense himself flushing. 'We do share a bed, yeah . . .'

'No sex though?' Astrid's finely-arched brows shoot up.

'Well *yeah*, once in a blue moon, but it's quite an empty experience, to be honest.'

'Oh, poor baby. How awful for you.' Astrid smiles tersely. Five minutes ago, she'd been desperate to kick him out so she could rush off to her precious meeting. Now, when it comes to grilling him on the state of his relationship, it seems she has all the time in the world.

Astrid is focusing hard on his face. Spike is finding the intensity of her blue-eyed gaze a little unnerving. 'Would you consider leaving Lou?' she asks in an eerily calm voice.

'Huh? You want me to leave Lou?' He's completely confused now. He's crazy about Astrid – loves her even – and he's certainly never met anyone he's desired more. And he'd assumed she was happy with their arrangement – that she preferred it that way, in fact.

'It's not about what I want,' she says sharply. 'It's about you, Spike. What *you* want. D'you want to leave Lou?'

He exhales loudly, wanting to leave now and hurry home to the sanctuary of his woman-free flat. Christ – he's spent all week fantasising about the various scenarios he and a naked Astrid could possibly find themselves in. He hadn't imagined being made to feel like ten tons of crap in her hallway. 'I . . . I don't know really,' he mumbles.

'Don't you?' Her nostrils flare a little. 'It's a simple enough question.'

'I know. I suppose I haven't given it much thought . . .'

Astrid musters a smile, and Spike is relieved to see her face soften again. 'I'm not saying this to make you feel awkward,' she says in a gentler tone. 'I just think Lou deserves some consideration, especially as she's thoughtful enough to stock your fridge so you don't go hungry while she's away.' Spike looks at her bleakly, feeling like a scolded schoolboy. 'Want to think about what I've said?' Astrid asks.

Spike nods again and turns for the door. 'Yeah. I'll call you, okay?'

Astrid steps forward and kisses him. Then, as if determined to thoroughly confuse him, she adds, 'You do that. See you around, hairy boy.'

TWENTY-FIVE

'God, Felix,' Hannah says, 'we're all talking about our lives, guzzling your champagne and eating your truffles and we've hardly asked about you. You must think we're so rude and self-obsessed.' In truth, she wants to veer the conversation away from Daisy and Josh.

Felix chuckles and sips from his cup. 'Oh, you don't want to know about my sad little life.'

'Come on,' Lou exclaims. 'It's hardly sad – you've got bars dotted all over the country – and you can't tease all this information out of us and tell us nothing.'

'I didn't tease it out,' he says in a mock-hurt voice. 'You just told me.'

'I suppose we did,' Sadie laughs. 'But what about you? Are you married, Felix?'

He pauses, and for the first time, seems to lose his composure a little. 'I was almost married,' he says carefully.

'Almost?' Hannah repeats gently, noticing with alarm that his grey eyes have misted over and his pale lashes are fluttering as if to bat away sudden tears. Hell, now she wishes they'd stuck to the topic of *her* marriage.

'What happened, Felix?' Lou asks kindly.

'My intended . . .' He presses his lips together, as if

mustering strength. 'Well, let's just say she had it off with my best friend Rashley – my best man, in fact – and chose the night before our wedding to make the big confession.'

Hannah, Sadie and Lou fall silent. Felix rolls a stray truffle across the table with a finger. 'That's terrible,' Hannah breathes.

'God, how awful for you,' Lou exclaims. Felix sniffs loudly and the girls glance at each other, wondering what to do next.

'At least you knew,' Hannah offers, 'before you went through with it.'

Felix nods and offers them a wobbly smile. His eyes aren't just moist now; they are filling with tears, threatening to spill over any moment. 'Bet you wanted to kill him,' Sadie offers.

'Well, yes, but I'm just a big old coward really, so I just . . .' He shrugs. 'I just retreated from the scene.'

'And the wedding was cancelled?' Hannah asks.

'Absolutely, leaving a whopping three-tier cake with mine and Amanda's name on it in rather tacky gold icing.' He forces a laugh, and Hannah touches his arm.

'Oh, Felix. And here I am, moaning about Ryan's kids . . . it makes my worries seem pretty pathetic.'

'Mine too,' Sadie adds. 'I mean, however tough it is at the moment, at least I *trust* Barney . . .'

'Me too,' Lou adds. 'Spike wouldn't have the energy to get up to anything anyway.' Everyone sniggers, lightening the mood.

'Right,' Felix declares, wiping his eyes with the back of his large, fleshy hand as he stands up unsteadily. 'Now if you'll excuse me, girls, this business has made me quite upset, and I think we're out of supplies so I'm going to get myself a little something from the bar.'

'Of course,' Hannah says, leaping up and quickly moving aside to let him pass.

'Can I get you something?' he asks.

Hannah shakes her head firmly. 'No thanks . . .'

'No, we're fine,' Lou adds as he totters along the aisle and disappears to the next carriage. Hannah, Sadie and Lou stare at each other. 'Jesus,' murmurs Sadie.

'Poor man,' Hannah adds, and Lou nods in agreement. 'Imagine his girlfriend doing that.'

'And imagine having a friend called Rashley,' Sadie jokes, 'and using phrases like "had it off".'

'At least he didn't marry her,' Hannah adds, feeling strangely loyal to this drunk, jilted man, and unwilling to discuss him with other passengers in earshot – passengers who've been throwing each other amused and exasperated glances as Felix's voice boomed through the carriage.

'He seems heartbroken,' Lou adds. 'I wonder how long ago it happened?'

'Must be pretty recent,' Sadie observes, 'to make him well up like that.'

Hannah nods, and the girls contemplate the awfulness of such deceit, until Felix reappears, looking a little more together now, clutching a coffee.

They finish the truffles, the conversation switching to lighter matters such as where they might go tonight. Twenty-five minutes later, as their train approaches Glasgow Central station, it would appear that Hannah, Sadie and Lou have made a new friend.

TWENTY-SIX

Back at his flat, Spike decides he's misjudged Astrid Stone. He had her down as a free spirit, a beautiful creature concerned only with having fun and fantastic sex, the kind of girl who relishes kissing a guy she's just met, virtually pulling him into a damp alley. So it seems bizarre, and totally out of character, that she's demanding he split up with Lou.

He paces around the small kitchen, filling the kettle, sloshing water into a mug containing the last teabag, then realising he didn't actually boil it. He doesn't want tea anyway. He wants – no, *needs* a drink, more than he's needed one in a long time. Astrid has as good as dumped him – insulted him, anyway, with all that hairy boy business – and Lou will be two hundred miles away in Glasgow by now, so wrapped up in her beloved friends' company that she won't have given him a second's thought. It's pretty special to be rejected by two women in one day.

Spike takes a gulp of cold tea, spits it out in disgust onto a collection of dirty mugs heaped up in the sink, and peers into the fridge. No wine or lager in there – just wholesome veggies, which Lou is always so eager to foist upon him. She'll be suggesting colonic irrigation next. There are chicken breasts too, flabby and beige and completely unap-petising. Spike bangs the fridge door shut so hard its Wallace and Grommit magnet pings off, and he inhales deeply, overcome by a desire to rebel.

Maybe Charlie will come out tonight. It's not even six o'clock, and the whole of Friday night beckons. He pulls his phone from his pocket, sees a missed call from Lou and plays her voicemail message. *Hi love, on the train, bit delayed but never mind, having such a laugh with this guy, tons of champagne and truffles* . . . There's a gale of laughter in the background. *Bye, honey!* she trills. Having a laugh with what guy? What, the stranger who helped with her suitcase? And what's she on about truffles for? Maybe he misheard. He knows he should call her back, but right now, still agitated over Astrid, he isn't sure he'd be capable of sounding normal. No, alcohol is what's needed. He calls Charlie, and while the phone rings, he rifles through the cupboards for a beacon of hope in the form of a forgotten bottle of beer or wine or even some liqueur chocolates left over from Christmas.

'Hey, mate,' Charlie says, 'how's it going?'

'Good, good,' Spike replies.

'Much on this weekend?' Charlie is obviously somewhere lively and bustling, having a great time.

'Er, not really,' he says. 'Lou's away, y'know, off to Glasgow with her friends so I thought I'd see what turns up.'

'Ah, right . . . well, hopefully something will. Listen, mate, I'll catch up in the week, okay? I'm doing a sound check for this band, this studenty thing . . .'

'Are they any good?' Spike asks, pulling out a bottle and examining the label: Cabernet Sauvignon. Yesss! *Cabernet Sauvignon Red Wine Vinegar.* Ah.

'Not bad,' Charlie says, then to someone else in the background, 'Yeah, just mic up the bass, would you? I'll

161

be with you in a tick . . . Er, you can come tonight if you like,' Charlie adds, clearly distracted now as someone is shouting for him in the background. 'Mitchell Hall. The band'll be on just after nine. I can put your name on the door . . .'

'Yeah, maybe. There's a few things happening but I might drop by . . .'

'Need a plus-one?'

'Er, no. It'd just be me.'

'Right. Great. Well, maybe see you later, mate.' There's a shriek of feedback in the background, and Charlie is gone.

Spike hangs up and stares at the bottle of vinegar on the worktop. Well, he's not going to drink that, even if it does have wine in it. Reaching up to the wall cupboard, he searches among Lou's cereals – gravelly mixtures that look as if they've been swept up from the bottom of a budgie's cage – until, right at the back, he spots a large, dusty green bottle. Spike takes it out. Père Magloire Fine Calvados, reads the elegant type on the label. Isn't calvados brandy? And this Père Magloire – there's a picture of him, some old bloke in a kind of robe and a nightcap, like Wee Willie Winkie's. A priest, maybe. So it's practically *religious*.

Spike pulls off the stopper, inhales the potent aroma and pours out a generous measure into a Let's Bounce mug, its logo arranged in a jaunty curve. Taking a large gulp, and perching on a kitchen chair while the warmth spreads to his throat, Spike decides that perhaps this Friday night isn't going to turn out too badly after all.

TWENTY-SEVEN

Ryan and Petra treat each other with the utmost courtesy. There's something about his ex-wife that makes people do things for her: open doors, walk on the roadside of pavements to protect her from being splashed or mowed down by oncoming trucks. Ryan did this instinctively when they were together. Her diminutive stature made him feel more solid and masculine, which he quite enjoyed, although he'd also found her brittle nature unnerving. Lurking at the back of Ryan's mind had been the perpetual low-level worry that one day, without warning, Petra might literally snap.

He's making her coffee now – strong, black, no sugar, in the bone china cup that she likes – while Josh and Daisy gather together the last of their things for a weekend at her place. 'So I thought we might pop into the Portrait Gallery,' she tells Ryan as he places the cup in front of her.

'Right, what's on?' he asks.

'A pop-art exhibition, pretty child-friendly. I think they'd like that, don't you?'

'Er, yeah. Sounds good.' Petra is perched on the edge of a kitchen chair as if wary of sullying her small, hard bottom and is taking small sips from her cup.

'And I thought we might do a bit of shopping,' Petra

adds, fixing him with her almond-shaped grey eyes. Her black bob is immaculate, as if expertly smoothed into place during the millisecond she'd spent waiting at Ryan's front door before he'd scampered to open it.

'Looking for anything in particular?' he asks.

'Well,' Petra shrugs, 'I really should get the kids something nice to wear for your wedding, seeing as you don't seem to have got around to it.' She emits a tinkly laugh, and Ryan can't decide if she's being snide or not.

'We've tried,' he murmurs, 'but there's been a distinct lack of enthusiasm, to be honest.' Petra raises her brows, the tiniest gesture that says, *That's because they don't want you to marry that silly artist girl*. Ryan takes a big gulp of coffee, willing the kids to hurry up. It isn't that being alone with Petra makes him feel uncomfortable exactly; he's known her since university, when they were just eighteen years old. It's more a sense of sadness that this single, fragile-looking woman of thirty-seven, whom he'd once loved to the point of distraction, feels it necessary to adopt such a cool, businesslike manner with him. It unsettles him to see Petra sitting three feet away from the gigantic stainless steel fridge that used to be *their* fridge – chosen by her – and whose contents she would carefully monitor to ensure nothing slimy ever lurked at the back.

Petra sniffs and frowns. 'I think I can smell gas, can you?'

Ryan lurches forward, realising he's been leaning against the oven's gas controls, inadvertently turning one on. 'Oh, God,' he says, quickly switching it off and swooping towards the table to pick up Petra's empty cup. Realising he's treating her as if she were an invalid, or royalty, he gives himself a mental shake.

'So how long's Hannah away for?' Petra asks as he washes then dries the cup, for far longer than is necessary.

'She's back on Sunday night.'

'So it's her hen party, is it?' Petra hadn't had one before she and Ryan had got married; she'd had an *intimate dinner with friends.*

'I suppose so,' Ryan replies, 'but really, it's just a chance to get together with her best friends. They hardly see each other these days.' Hell, what's taking the kids so long? Ryan wants to yell upstairs to tell them to get a move on, but doesn't want to make it sound as if he's desperate to chivvy Petra out of the house.

'Not long till the big day now,' Petra adds, glossy lips forming a teasing smile.

'Nope. Just a couple of weeks now . . .'

'All organised?'

'Well, yes. We've kept it pretty simple, just the registry office and a bit of a buffet and party afterwards . . . nothing flashy.'

'A buffet?' she repeats. Ryan is aware of how Petra feels about buffets: food sitting out for too long, prodded by too many fingers.

'It's less formal than a sit-down thing,' he explains, starting to sweat now.

Petra smiles. 'I know you, Ryan Lennox. Bet you're stressing and panicking like mad. I can see it all over your face.'

'Well,' he says, wondering what she can see exactly, 'I just want it to go smoothly, you know . . .'

'. . . And I bet Hannah's being all casual and free-spirited about it, taking everything in her stride.'

'Um, she's managing it pretty well,' he says, a trace of irritation in his voice. Hell, what *are* the kids doing upstairs? After all this time – three years since she left him – Petra still possesses an uncanny ability to read every thought that's skittering about in his brain. Yes, he's stressing, and not only because of his flappy suit trousers or the fact that, now he thinks about it, perhaps a buffet seems a bit

165

cheapskate after all. And what if Petra's right – not that she's *said* anything exactly – and the food is all curled-up and sad-looking? Even more alarming, he has a horrible feeling that, ever since they started making wedding plans, Hannah has acquired the air of someone who would dearly love to run away.

'Anyway,' Petra says, 'I bet she's excited.'

'Who?' he asks.

'Hannah, of course!' Ryan blinks at his ex-wife. What kind of comment is that? He can't say she *isn't* excited; yet if he agrees, he'll be implying that she's over the moon to be marrying him, fantastic prime catch that he is. And Ryan doesn't feel like a catch. He feels weighed down with the baggage of his first failed marriage, plus his children who make no secret of the fact that they resent Hannah being part of his life. How will it be when they're married? Will everything magically sort itself out? 'You'll have to ask her – she's probably cursing the day she said yes,' he says with forced joviality, awash with relief as the children appear with their packed weekend bags.

'Ready at last.' Petra smiles at her children, then turns back to Ryan. 'So, empty house this weekend, huh?'

'That's right.' He leans back, taking care not to switch on the gas again.

'What'll you do?'

'Oh, I don't know. Got a bit of work to catch up on. We're pitching for this new bar snack range and I've got to dazzle Marcus with some brilliant ideas first thing Monday.'

'Oh,' Petra chuckles. 'Well, we'd better let you get started then. Don't want to get in the way.' With that, she clops to the front door, swooping out to her little red car into which the children hop obediently, before turning to wave goodbye.

Petra waves too, which is unusual. Her smile is brighter,

her brittleness momentarily softened by . . . what exactly? Pity for Ryan that he's marrying the sort of woman who has a hen weekend? Petra is starting her car now – a shiny red Corsa whose interior smells new, even though it's four years old. 'It's not that kind of hen party,' he wants to call out, but she's already pulling away.

TWENTY-EIGHT

When Sadie studies her reflection in the mirror on the scuffed lime-green wardrobe in room 232, she sees not a mum of two, with tension and tiredness clouding her eyes, but the woman she used to be.

Sadie Vella, who graduated from Glasgow School of Art with a First in textile design and for whom the whole world was waiting. Not a dishevelled mother who gets ticked off by strangers for losing her babies' shoes. Hannah is curled up on her own bed in their bleak but perfectly serviceable triple room, applying mascara with the help of a mirrored compact, and Lou is in the bathroom, wrapped in a towel and teasing out her wet curly hair with a comb. What Lou sees in the mirror isn't a picker-upper of squished chicken nuggets, or a fisher-outer of rank nappies from the ballpool. She sees her younger self, cheeks radiant, eyes shining and alive. 'I don't think we should go to the old places,' comes Hannah's voice from the bedroom. 'Let's just go out with open minds and see where we end up.'

'See where the night takes us,' Lou chuckles, wandering back into the bedroom to join them.

'We could try Felix's bar,' Sadie suggests.

'Funny, wasn't he,' says Hannah, 'with the coolbox picnic and everything?'

'Truffles!' Lou laughs, smoothing moisturiser onto her face. 'Who travels with a supply of truffles?' Her mobile rings, and she retrieves it from her single bed. 'Hey, Spike. I tried to call you earlier. Everything okay?'

'Yeah, pretty good,' he says. 'So how was your journey?'

'Such a laugh,' Lou enthuses. 'We met this man who runs cocktail bars. He had a whole stash of champagne with him, and *truffles*, can you believe it? We were just saying, who on earth travels with—'

'You sound drunk,' Spike cuts in.

'Oh, I'm not. Just a bit . . . well, *happy*, I guess.' Still gripping her phone, Lou tips the contents of her make-up bag onto her bed.

'So what was this guy like?' Spike asks.

'Funny. Strange. Not strange in a creepy way or anything, but there was something about him, you know? The way he drew things out of us, how we really felt about our lives and where we're all going . . .' She laughs. 'I don't know. It sounds a bit mad. We were probably all just over-excited.'

'Yeah, sounds like it,' he says curtly. 'So . . . you sat there with this weird stranger, drinking his champagne, telling him your innermost secrets?'

Lou stops rummaging through her make-up and frowns. 'It was just a laugh. God, he was only being friendly . . .'

'I just don't like the idea of it, that's all.'

Hannah and Sadie are looking quizzically at Lou. She rolls her eyes and inhales deeply. 'I am a grown-up, honey. I think I can just about look after myself.'

'Yes, but he could have spiked—'

'What, the champagne? Don't be crazy. Anyway, we saw him taking out the cork right in front of us.'

'The truffles then,' he continues sulkily. 'He could've put something in those . . .'

169

'You think he might've *drugged* the truffles?' Lou's shoulders are bobbing up and down now, and Hannah and Sadie have clasped their hands over their mouths to stop themselves from laughing.

'Not necessarily. I just think . . .'

'. . . Like, injected something into their little chocolately middles?' Lou adds.

'I'm just concerned, that's all. It sounds completely bizarre . . .' *Of course it does*, Lou thinks: *me enjoying myself, talking to a man, the four of us whiling away the journey by having a bit of fun.* She decides not to mention Felix's tearful outburst, which Spike would decide made him sound doubly weird.

'There's no need to worry,' Lou says sweetly. 'We've arrived here in one piece . . .'

'Good. Glad to hear it. Anyway, have a great night,' Spike adds, sounding a little friendlier now. 'I'd better go. I'm starving – just popping out to the chippie.'

'Oh, aren't you having a stir-fry? I bought you all those—'

'No, I'm not!'

'Okay, okay! God, I only asked . . .' Lou shakes her head despairingly. 'What's so offensive about a stir-fry all of a sudden?'

'Just don't fancy it,' he growls.

'Fine. Enjoy your chips then,' she says coolly.

'Thanks. I will.' Finishing the call, Lou tosses the phone onto her bed.

Hannah gives her a knowing look. 'That didn't go too well, then.'

'Bloody hell,' Lou exclaims, exhaling loudly. 'I can't tell you how glad I am to be here with you two instead of at home with him.'

'That bad?' Sadie raises a brow.

'Oh, not really.' Lou catches herself. 'He's probably just

had a boring day, sitting at home on his own with no one to talk to and nothing to do.'

*

By 6.30 pm, Sadie has changed into a wrap dress, with her freshly washed and blow-dried hair tumbling lushly around her shoulders. She had almost forgotten her hair could look good, and barely recognises herself. *I wish Barney could see me*, she thinks, grateful that their quick phone chat was perfectly pleasant – reassuring, actually – and not a snippy exchange like Lou and Spike's. *I wish I could show him that I'm still the same old Sadie underneath . . .*

Her face changes then, her brow crinkling with worry. Thinking about Barney has made her recall his terrified expression as her train pulled out of Hissingham station, which has led her swiftly to thoughts of her beloved babies, and whether Barney's planning to stick to the correct bedtime routine tonight. *Structure*, one of those hectoring baby books said, *will help you to manage your twins so they fit into your life, and not the other way round*. It seemed almost cruel, Sadie thought at first, and went against her instincts to just hold and feed and love her children as she saw fit. But then, what did she know? And Barney had just flapped about on the sidelines, trying to help in his dithery way, with a perpetual air of panic as if a bomb might be about to go off in his face.

Now, despite her polished appearance, Sadie's breasts feel as if they might be in danger of exploding at any moment. They'd been okay as she'd showered and dressed in the gloomy bathroom, but thinking about home has triggered her milk production with gusto. It's uncanny, the way her body reacts, as if she no longer has any control over what it might do.

171

Stepping back into the bathroom, in which the white tiles are decorated with silhouettes of ladies with parasols, she pulls down the top half of her wrap dress so it hangs in soft folds around her waist, and frees her breasts from her gargantuan black bra. God, they're huge. They look like joke boobs that someone's stuck on her for a laugh. While Sadie has always been curvy, since having the babies her body has retained an extra layer of soft, spongy motherliness, which renders certain cuts of clothing unwearable. High necklines, for instance, make her look as if she has a bolster stuffed up her top. But never mind that. Right now, she must relieve the pressure by expressing milk into the chipped sink.

It feels like there's an awful lot of it, probably due to all that expressing last night, which has propelled her body into production overdrive. Leaning over the washbasin, she manages to squeeze a little from each breast, figuring that this probably wasn't the image the designer had in mind when he was creating the dress. She dabs at her chest with some loo roll, squeezes herself back into her hammock-like bra and pops in breast pads, just in case. Feeling slightly more comfortable now, Sadie yanks up her dress, slicks on a fresh coat of lipstick and steps back into the bedroom with renewed optimism.

'Wow, look at *you*,' Lou exclaims, leaping up from the bed and snatching her vintage beaded handbag from the floor.

Sadie grins. 'Well, you know. I like to make an effort. It's not often one of us is getting married, is it? Come on, let's go.' She glances at her friends, aware of an unspoken agreement that whatever they said on the train had just popped out, and that of course Hannah will put on her oyster dress and silver tiara and marry Ryan Lennox as planned. Grabbing her bag from the bed, Sadie also makes a silent vow to stop fretting about what might be happening back home, and to make the most of every minute of her two days off the leash. But first, she might just call Barney to check if he's remembered to put nappy rash cream on Dylan's bottom.

TWENTY-NINE

When Sadie left, the babies screaming as her train pulled out of Hissingham station, Barney had envisaged a bleak weekend of feeling helpless and hopeless. He'd even come up with the emergency strategy of visiting his parents if things were really spiralling out of control. His mum would cook a roast, fuss over the babies and tell him how well he was doing, barely managing to refrain from ruffling his hair and tickling his chin – and for the duration of his visit, Barney would almost believe that she was right. What has actually happened, though (apart from the pleasing exchange with Magda in the café) is that Pete, his old mate, has shown up. Eager-eyed and claiming to be delighted to have escaped London, he dumps a pack of beers on the kitchen worktop.

'Shall we go out for a little stroll then?' Pete asks, laughing at how middle-aged that sounds.

'Why not?' Barney says, grinning, and brushing aside a niggling feeling that Sadie wouldn't entirely approve of this sudden amendment to the schedule. 'Stroll' is Pete's code word for drink and, luckily, the weather has perked up enough to make sitting in the Black Swan's beer garden seem like a perfectly reasonable thing to do. To salve his conscience, Barney dresses the boys in warm fleeces, padded jackets and gloves, even though they're clearly uncalled for, slinging the gigantic baby-survival bag over his shoulder.

Now, at the pub, while Pete's inside at the bar, Barney tries to remember the last time he was in licensed premises. The guys at work often go out, especially on a Friday, but he's stopped doing that unless it's a birthday or some other special occasion. Barney doesn't *resent* it exactly, yet the lack of a social life has left a distinct void, which he has no idea how to fill.

'Here you go.' Pete places two bottles of Grolsch on the wooden table.

'Grolsch,' Barney says approvingly. 'I haven't had that for years. I can't believe you remember I used to drink it.'

Pete grins, scanning the beer garden in which all manner of receptacles – wheelbarrows, tyres, a wicker basket strapped to the front of an ancient bike – are overflowing with spring flowers.

'You were the only one who did,' he jibes. 'Pretentious twat.'

Barney laughs, feeling good about being with an old friend who knows him not as a work colleague or that new bloke who's moved into that pretty little cottage with his wife and twins. 'Yeah, well, you smoked unfiltered French fags,' he sniggers, 'and usually had some Sartre or Camus novel sticking out of your back pocket if I remember rightly. Which you never read.'

'Yeah, I did!' Pete exclaims, looking hurt.

'Okay, so which ones did you read? Name 'em.'

Pete frowns and chews his lip. 'There was that French one.'

'They're both French,' Barney sniggers, and they continue their good-natured banter. Pete seems to be improving with age, Barney thinks wryly – unlike him, who appears to be

175

deteriorating rapidly with new furrows and eye bags appearing by the day. Whereas Barney is always a bit scruffy, Pete has that self-assured groomed look, and the grey that's beginning to fleck his dark hair is only serving to heighten his appeal. Barney has already noticed a pretty girl with blonde pigtails casting Pete a quick glance as she clears the glasses from an adjacent table. As he jiggles the buggy with one hand, and lifts his glass to his mouth with the other, he's enjoying observing the effects of Pete's charm. It's like dipping his toe back into the place where the rest of the human race has been all along.

Dylan and Milo are snoozing now, reminding him that they should actually be in their cots and not a pub garden, surrounding by people drinking. As Pete regales him with tales from work – he imports wine, which doesn't sound like real work in Barney's opinion – he starts to wonder if 7.20 pm still qualifies as daytime, or if his babies are now officially on their first-ever night out.

'Fancy another one?' Pete asks, already getting up from the bench.

Barney glances furtively at his children. They seem fine – still asleep and blissfully unaware that they've been brought to the pub. And it's so tempting to stay here a little longer, surrounded by adults, feeling like a normal human being again.

'Yep, I'll get these,' he says quickly, heading for the pub's entrance. *Thank God they're not super-advanced talkers*, he thinks with a smile at the bar. *At least they won't grass me up*. Yet, as he strides back outside and hands Pete his beer, seeing that his boys are now awake and alert, he senses that he may be overstepping the mark. 'Hell,' he mutters, taking his seat at the table. 'I shouldn't have let them have that nap. It'll be really tricky to get them down tonight.'

Pete guffaws. 'Jeez, mate. You talk as if you're running

an army camp. No one does that now. It's all meant to be much more fluid, isn't it? Let them sleep when they're tired and er . . . do stuff with them when they're not.'

Barney snorts. 'I'm sure you're really up to speed with the latest parenting trends, Pete. Like, what kind of stuff?'

Pete laughs again and sips his pint. 'Oh, I dunno. Baking?'

'They're not quite ready to be let loose in the kitchen, Pete . . .'

'No, I don't mean on their own. I mean with supervision.' He casts the babies a fond glance as they gaze up at a hanging basket with rapt interest. 'Good-looking kids, aren't they?' he adds. 'Lucky they take after Sadie and not you. How's she doing anyway? I'd never have had her down as a country girl.'

'She's fine,' Barney says firmly. 'Well . . . I guess we're both still settling in but it takes time, doesn't it . . .'

'How long've you been here now?'

'Six months, and we've still got to learn the country ways . . .' He affects a ridiculous West Country accent.

'But you,' Pete observes, 'at least you're on that train to London five days a week, escaping it all . . .' *That's it*, Barney thinks. *Work's not just work anymore. It's my great escape.* 'What about Sadie,' Pete goes on, 'tied to the house with the babies all day? I mean, I'm sure she's doing a great job but—'

'Well, she *is* allowed out,' he says tetchily.

'You know what I mean.'

Barney feels his face reddening and focuses on the alluring amber of his beer. 'To be honest,' he says carefully, 'I don't know how she feels about living here, or staying at home with the kids, because we don't really talk anymore. It's kind of . . . different, you know? Sort of . . . *practical.*'

Pete frowns, clearly not getting it. 'What's practical? Moving to the country?'

'No, I mean me and Sadie. There's so much to get done,

and remind each other to do, that it doesn't really leave any time for anything else.'

'You mean . . .' Pete pauses. 'You just tell each other what to do all the time? Like, bark orders?'

'Er, well, Sadie tells *me*,' Barney chuckles, trying to lighten the atmosphere. It's too late, though. He's done it: been honest about him and Sadie, for the first time since his sons' birth.

'That doesn't sound good, Barney,' Pete says quietly.

'Ah, so now you're a relationship expert as well,' Barney jokes.

Pete smirks. 'I don't mean that. I just mean . . . maybe you both need a little break from the nappies and all that.'

Barney shrugs. 'Not much chance of that. My parents love the kids, but if we've left the boys alone with them for even five minutes it's been, "Barney? Sadie? One of them just coughed! Is that okay?" And Sadie's parents are in Liverpool,' he adds, 'so . . .' He glances towards the pub door where two young women are heading outside, chatting and carrying drinks.

It's *her*. Magda from the café, in a cute navy dress with a pale pink cardi over the top. Her painfully skinny auburn-haired friend points to an empty table. 'Oh, look,' Magda exclaims, 'it's the sweet twins! Hello, Barney.' She hurries over to the buggy and bobs down to greet his children.

'Er, hi, Magda,' Barney says, amazed yet thrilled that she's remembered his name. 'This is, um . . . Pete.'

Barney has never believed that a smile is actually capable of lighting up a face, but Magda's does. 'Hi, Pete, this is my friend Amy.'

Amy smiles too, then says in a soft Yorkshire accent, 'These are the cutest babies I've ever seen.'

'They're Barney's,' Magda tells her.

'Oh! You're so lucky.'

'Thanks,' he says humbly.

Magda turns, as if about to make her way back to the table they'd earmarked, just as an elderly couple sits down at the vacant seats. Well-heeled couples and families are occupying most of the other tables, and Barney is relieved to see a couple of children here – okay, school-aged children, teenagers actually – but children all the same. 'Okay if we join you?' Magda asks.

'Sure,' Barney says, taking a fortifying gulp of his beer. At least Pete will no longer be able to dissect his marriage, he reflects, as the girls perch on the seats and fuss over Milo and Dylan.

'So how d'you two know each other?' Pete asks, looking from Barney to Magda.

'We don't really,' Magda explains with another sweet smile. 'We were just chatting earlier in the café where I work.'

'Where are you from, Madga?' Pete asks, putting on his *terribly-interested-in-you* voice.

'I'm from Poland, Amy's from Leeds . . .' She smiles. 'And you?'

'Oh, I'm a north London boy, same as Barney,' Pete says, triggering a flurry of nostalgia in Barney's stomach. They're chatting about the girls' photography course now – that's how they met and became friends. Barney slips into the background, lifting Milo, then Dylan, out of the buggy and onto his lap, whilst marvelling at how speedily Pete zooms back and forth from the bar to buy the girls more drinks, and how easily he's slipped into conversation with them. They're so young – early twenties at most – a couple of students with part-time jobs. Yet the way Pete is chatting away, anyone would think they had acres of common ground.

'So how about you two?' Magda wants to know. 'How d'you know each other?'

'We're old schoolmates,' Pete explains. 'That's – God – a *scarily* long time ago . . .'

'Noooo,' Madga says. 'Not that long ago.'

Pete smirks. 'It was, trust me, and he was the brainy one, getting all the grades while I got kinda distracted.' He shrugs flamboyantly in a 'what can you do?' way. 'I messed up. I'm just the dumb friend.'

'I'm sure you're not, Pete,' Amy says, touching his knee. What Pete's doing now, Barney realises, is playing the lovable klutz. He's witnessed this tactic before. For a brief period in his mid-twenties, Barney went out with a girl who pretended she couldn't operate a screwdriver, just because she thought it was cute.

'But you've done so well,' Amy adds, removing her hand, 'with your wine business and everything.' Barney glances down at his T-shirt. There's a yellow blob near the neck where Dylan spat his lunch at him.

'Well, y'know . . .' Another of Pete's self-deprecating shrugs. 'Anyway, shall we have one for the road, Barney? What d'you think?'

'Better not,' Barney says quickly, having declined the last round. 'I really should get these little men home.' Carefully, and overwhelmingly grateful that they don't howl in protest, he places his children back into their buggy.

'Oh, that's a shame,' Magda says lightly.

'Well, *you* could stay out a bit longer, Pete,' Barney adds, hoping he doesn't sound like his dad.

'Are you staying at Barney's tonight?' Amy asks.

'Yeah. Listen, I'll just come back with you,' Pete says, a trace of reluctance in his voice.

Barney is up on his feet, gripping the buggy handles expectantly. It's almost half eight, the family with teenagers have gone, and yellowy lanterns have been switched on among the flowers in the horse troughs. The beer garden has taken on a decidedly evening feel. 'Well, we'll leave you girls to it,' he says with a broad smile.

'Thanks for the drinks,' Magda beams at Pete. 'And nice to see you again, Barney.'

'Nice to see you too.' Barney is eager to leave now, to get his babies bathed and tucked up in their cots and for all to be right with the world.

'Pete,' Amy calls after them, 'we're doing a photo shoot tomorrow, just pictures around the village for Magda's assignment. D'you both fancy coming along?'

'I'd love to,' Pete enthuses. 'I'm really interested in photography.'

'Are you?' Barney looks at him incredulously.

'Yeah. It's something I've been getting into recently . . .'

Barney makes a peculiar noise at the back of his throat. 'Since when?'

'Since . . .' Pete shrugs. 'Just *lately*, that's all.'

'Right. Since you got your new iPhone.'

With a roll of his eyes, Pete turns his attention back to the girls. 'Well, *I'd* like to come. It'll be interesting . . .'

'Might pick up some new techniques,' Barney murmurs with a snigger.

Magda smiles brightly. 'What about you, Barney? Are you free tomorrow?'

'Well, not really,' he blusters. 'I've got the kids . . .' He indicates them sitting contentedly in their buggy, as if Magda might have forgotten who his kids are.

'Oh, the babies will be fine,' Magda insists. 'It's all outdoors, they'll enjoy it and it won't take too long . . .'

'Love to,' Pete cuts in eagerly. 'C'mon, Barney, we're not doing anything else tomorrow, are we?' Barney shakes his head mutely, imagining Sadie's stern gaze shooting all the way down from Glasgow.

'Great,' Amy says warmly. 'Around eleven, by the lake in the park?'

'Sure.' Pete grins. 'See you then.' Barney forces a smile, and as they turn to leave he glances anxiously around the

181

beer garden to see if any of these watchful village types have been paying attention to their exchange. *Not that I'm doing anything wrong*, he reminds himself firmly, steering the buggy out through the gate and towards the sanctuary of home, where he plans to salvage whatever tattered fragments he can from the kids' bedtime routine.

THIRTY

Sadie, Hannah and Lou have been installed in the low-lit bar opposite their hotel for less than half an hour, and already Sadie has confessed that she and Barney have had sex only once since she was six months pregnant. She glances down at her shoes. They're not flat, battered Hissingham Park pumps with half the sparkles fallen off, or even marginally smarter coffee-morning shoes. They're Sexy Sadie shoes – patent beauties with precarious four-inch heels. 'I'm sure it's normal,' Hannah says. 'You're knackered, you don't have the time. It's like your priorities have changed. Things'll get easier when the babies are a bit older . . .'

'. . . Like at university,' she says with a wry grin. 'Oh, you're probably right. It's just that other mums seem to manage it.' She does this a lot these days; says 'mums' instead of 'women'.

Sadie smiles, catching the eye of a tall, dark-haired man with glasses who's standing in a small group by the bar. 'Well,' Hannah adds, 'it sounds completely normal to me, not feeling like throwing yourself around the bedroom . . .'

'You're saying normal a lot,' Sadie says with a grin. 'D'you think we are normal, the three of us? For our age, I mean? When we were in Garnet Street, I always thought we'd have everything sorted out by now. Thirty-five seemed so old!'

'I thought I'd have a roof terrace,' Lou murmurs, 'and my jewellery would be stocked at Liberty, and Spike and me would have made lots of beautiful babies. What about you, Han? Did you think you'd be married by now?'

'Maybe not the married part,' Hannah says thoughtfully, 'but when I used to think about the kind of man I'd like to end up with, not the Marcs of this world but the one who was really *meant* for me . . .' She pauses, looking up from her glass. 'He was like Ryan. He really was. When I met him, there was none of the usual game playing or that time-wasting stuff and . . . well, it was as if he'd been there for me all along.'

Lou frowns and pushes back hair from her eyes. 'What about Daisy and Josh, though? How are you going to deal with that?'

Hannah shrugs. 'I suppose it's pretty common for kids to hate their prospective stepmother. Maybe that's just going to be part of getting married.'

Sadie pauses. Outside, the street is thronging with smart couples and large, sprawly groups of students. The bar is packed, and the man in glasses keeps glancing over. Sadie's wine has topped up the effects of Felix's champagne, and she wonders, wildly, what's making the three of them so keen to convince each other that everything's all right. Why has Lou sacrificed her jewellery-making to work at Let's Bounce and keep a man who barely has the energy to scratch his own arse? And why should Hannah put up with Josh and Daisy's hostility? Perhaps this weekend, as well as being their great escape, is their chance to figure out what they need to do when they get home. 'I think we should make a rule,' Sadie blurts out.

'What kind of rule?' Hannah asks.

'An honesty rule. A sort of truth or dare . . .'

'I'm *not* running down Buchanan Street naked,' Lou declares.

'No, not that kind of dare,' Sadie laughs. 'I mean, we're only here for two days, right? And the three of us haven't been together like this since . . . when?'

'Your wedding,' Lou murmurs.

'Yeah. And that was four years ago. So I think, as we're here, we should start telling each other exactly how we feel and stop all this pretending.'

'You start then,' Hannah says with a grin. 'You tell us what you're thinking about now, apart from that man in glasses who keeps looking at you . . .'

'What man in—'

'She hasn't noticed!' Hannah sniggers to Lou.

'Okay,' Sadie laughs, 'I sort of registered him, but here's the really sad thing. I'm not thinking about whoever might happen to be looking because I'm wondering whether Barney's used up my breast milk, which he's meant to keep for emergencies, and if he's tried to put them down to bed too early to get some peace and quiet and they won't settle . . .' She tails off. '*And* I think my breast pad's leaking.'

'Can't see anything,' Lou reassures her.

'So you reckon it's a national state of emergency in Little Hissingham tonight?' Hannah asks.

'Yes. No, not really. Now I'm thinking he's taken the boys out this afternoon, and got chatting to some gorgeous young single mother who thought, "Oooh, look at him, managing all by himself with those babies . . ."'

'You're insane,' Lou laughs, shaking her head.

'I know. I'm just a power freak, Lou. I rule Barney with a rod of iron, poor sod, and I'm paranoid . . .'

'Me too,' Lou cuts in. 'You know what? One time, a couple of weeks ago now, Spike was ill with some kind of terrible gastric flu – well, a cold really – and I thought I could smell something off him.'

'What kind of smell?' Hannah asks.

Lou shrugs. 'Kind of . . . sweet. Vanilla-ish. Like . . . body lotion or something.'

'You don't think he's up to anything, do you?' Hannah cuts in.

'No. No! God, he wouldn't have the energy. And he's, like . . . forty-eight . . .' Hannah gives her a look. 'I know,' Lou adds quickly, 'that forty-eight-year-old men have affairs, of course they do. It's not like there's an age restriction . . .'

'You don't think Spike is, though,' Sadie adds.

Lou shakes her head. 'No, I don't. It's just me being silly . . . anyway, guess what he's doing this weekend . . .'

'Playing a gig?' Sadie suggests.

'No. Staying home to write his CV!'

Hannah and Sadie burst into peals of laughter. 'Well. God,' Hannah exclaims, 'maybe this weekend's going to do him good. You know – shake him up a bit . . .'

'And maybe Barney'll realise that looking after the babies basically involves walking around the park about eight million times,' Sadie adds, 'and when I get home, he'll have put that gloomy little cottage on the market and found us a lovely flat.'

'Closer to London, you mean?' Hannah asks.

'Yes, like actually *in* it.' Sadie kicks off the shoe that's pinching her. 'You know what, though? I feel better already. Just being here, I mean. Escaping for a bit.'

Lou nods firmly. 'Me too. And maybe I'll resign from that crappy job when I get back.'

'And start making jewellery again?' Sadie asks. 'Could you make enough money doing that?'

'Well,' she says, grinning, 'I doubt it, I mean we'd probably starve, but at least I'd die happy . . .'

'What about you, Han?' Sadie asks, turning to face her. 'What about you and Ryan's kids?'

'Erm . . .' Hannah places her glass on the table. 'That's kind of tricky.'

'Can't Ryan do something about it?' Lou asks.

'He could, I suppose, but they went through hell when Petra left and I don't think he's prepared to do or say anything to rock the boat.'

Sadie reaches across the table to squeeze Hannah's hand. 'So . . . where does that leave you? I mean, you're marrying him, Han . . .'

'Oh, it's not that I don't want to be with Ryan,' Hannah declares. 'I just don't want to be with him the way we are, in that house. I could move out, get a little flat . . . we could even still get married, but live separately like Helena Bonham Carter and her man, the film guy . . .'

'Tim Burton,' offers Sadie.

'Yeah, like them . . .'

'Or Woody Allen and Mia Farrow,' Lou suggests.

'But they split up,' Sadie reminds her.

'That's because he started sleeping with her adopted daughter,' Hannah points out.

'Well, you could get your own place,' Sadie offers. 'I know it's not exactly conventional, and your parents might think it's a bit weird, but if it means having some distance from those horrible kids . . .'

'You know what?' Hannah says. 'They're not actually horrible. They're just horribly . . . *normal.*'

'Like us,' Sadie says with a grin.

'We're *so* normal,' Lou agrees.

'Let's get some cocktails,' Sadie insists, 'and toast our complete and utter normalness.'

'If we're going to have cocktails,' Hannah says, 'd'you fancy trying Felix's bar?'

'Yeah, maybe we'll get them on the house?' Lou suggests.

187

'Great idea,' Sadie says, forgetting her breast pad and even her babies for a moment as she throws her arms around her friends and hugs them as tightly as she possibly can.

THIRTY-ONE

Spike and Père Magloire are getting along great. He's never imagined being friends with some craggy old bloke in a robe and a nightcap, but now he feels like they've established a strong rapport. There had been a couple of inches out of the bottle when he discovered it, lurking behind Lou's cereals, and now there's only a quarter of the bottle left. That's the thing with quality booze, he reflects. You can enjoy yourself with no unpleasant consequences – which is the kind of set-up he thought he had with Astrid. But never mind her. Père Magloire is doing a sterling job of making him feel much better about all that. A distant memory causes Spike to smile – of him, similarly desperate for drink in Lou's Garnet Street flat, and unearthing a bottle even dustier than this one and straining it through her tights. He definitely has a talent for squirrelling out long-forgotten booze. Maybe he should put *that* on his CV.

By now – 8.37 pm – Spike is hungry and remembers, slightly too late in the proceedings, that it's not a good idea to drink on an empty stomach. After another fortifying sip of brandy, he places his mug on the living room carpet and makes for the bathroom to spruce himself up. The white T-shirt and jeans are fine; all he needs is a quick splash of water on his face, plus a cursory check of his nasal hairs and he's good to go.

At the chip shop at the end of the street, Spike buys a deep-fried sausage and a carton of pale, limp chips, plus a bottle of Croatian red wine from the off-licence next door. He carries his supper home and eats at the kitchen table, eyeing Lou's collection of beachy finds, which she's arranged on the shelf above the worktop. Delicate shells, twisted nuggets of driftwood and barnacle-encrusted pebbles are often starting points for her jewellery designs. He feels a tug of regret that she hardly ever makes anything these days, a feeling compounded by the realisation that the sausage, an unsettling combination of grease and an unyielding plasticky skin, has been a very poor choice.

Spike wipes the grease from his lips onto the back of his hand, fixing his gaze upon a cluster of spiky coral. Lou had been such a grafter at college, such a talented girl, winning prizes almost every year. She'd kept up the momentum for their first couple of years in York as an artist-in-residence . . . so what had happened? Maybe she'll stick to her word and get back into jewellery when she comes home, Spike reflects. Then she'll be happier. And he'll do his CV, he decides, feeling foolish now for going on about spiked truffles and realising, with a sudden inebriated pang, that he misses Lou, and that maybe it's for the best that Astrid has been so offish.

Sunday night, and Lou's return, now feels like a terribly long way away. He'll go to that gig, then – the one Charlie's doing the sound for. Have a night out, but not a *massive* night out, then get up early tomorrow and try to remember all his qualifications and jobs and any other qualities he can think of to put on his CV.

Yes, that's it, Spike decides, abandoning his half-eaten supper and the barely drinkable wine. He'll be sensible this weekend, using Lou's absence as an opportunity to clear his head. Right now, though, there's a little brandy left in the Père Magloire bottle, and a whole night of fun to be had.

THIRTY-TWO

Ryan has been thinking about new and inventive ways to market quirky bar snacks but keeps coming back to the fact that, really, all anyone wants is crisps or nuts. Ultimately, it comes down to crispy or crunchy – nice and simple and covered in salt. No one really wants little baked biscuit things. The laptop is hurting his eyes and brain, so he abandons it on the sofa, throws some random ingredients into the wok and pours himself a glass of wine.

Since Petra left with the children, Ryan has also pottered about in Daisy and Josh's bedrooms – he has reached the age where he potters, he realises – gathering up books, clothes and sweet wrappers from the floor and dragging their duvets up onto their beds. He found a wizened peach, its skin all baggy and wrinkly, a plate of toast crusts and a toffee, which seemed to have melted into the carpet – virtually all the food groups in his son's room. In Daisy's bedroom, the rug crunched with tortilla chips, clearly her salted snack of choice. God, his kids are phenomenally messy. Ryan used to be too, but he's had to force himself to invent routines and systems, all the stuff Petra used to take care of with alarming efficiency, to keep his family clothed and fed and in a reasonably hygienic state. And they're doing okay, they really are – which gives Ryan a faint glow of pride. He doesn't want to upset his family's fragile happiness by grumbling about messy bedrooms.

Now, having finished his uninspired supper, Ryan has drifted up to Hannah's studio. He's not sure why, and it feels vaguely like trespassing; he wants her to feel that it's *her* space, away from his children, who he knows can be surly (he's tried to tackle them on that score, only to be met with innocent shrugs and protests of, 'But I didn't *do* anything!'). It's a beautiful room during the day, a loft conversion paid for with one of Petra's performances in Berlin, with light flooding in and an uninterrupted view over the park. In the evening it becomes a cosy den, away from the domestic clutter of the rest of the house.

The landline rings, and Ryan snatches it from Hannah's desk as if caught doing something naughty. 'Ryan? It's me.'

'Oh, hi, Petra. Is everything okay?'

'Yes. Yes, everything's *fine* . . .' Only Petra can use the word to mean, actually, everything's totally *un*-fine. '. . . We're just going through Daisy's reading books,' she adds.

'She's done quite a bit of extra work during the week,' Ryan says quickly. 'Honestly, Petra, I think she's doing okay.'

'Well, she says so, but after that parents' evening . . .' *That* parents' evening. The one at which Daisy's teacher happened to comment – quite casually, Ryan thought – that when his daughter didn't know a word, she was inclined to just make it up. Well, Ryan made things up all the time. At work, he made up the fact that he gave a monkey's about two more fragrances being added to the Corsican-Maquis-in-your-toilet range. 'She was telling me about a proper short story she's written all by herself,' Petra continues. 'Something they were doing at school on the theme of . . . what was it again, Daisy?'

193

'An unforgettable experience,' Daisy pipes up in the background, sounding so much younger than she does face-to-face.

'Oh! Right. She didn't mention it to me. That's good, though, isn't it? That she's writing stories? I'll have a read of it when she comes back.'

'Would you mind emailing it over?' Petra asks. 'She seems really proud of it and I'd love to see it.'

Ryan's attention is momentarily caught by a young couple walking hand in hand across the park. He wishes Hannah were here now, and they could go out, see a film or have dinner, do things that normal couples do. 'I doubt if it's here,' he tells Petra, 'if Daisy was working on it at school.'

'Daisy says it is. Says there's a copy on Hannah's computer because they were told to finish it at home.'

'Really? Okay, give me a minute . . .' He fires up Hannah's PC. 'Could you ask Daisy what it's called?'

'Hang on a minute . . .' Ryan hears Daisy explaining something convoluted to her mother. 'She can't remember,' Petra says.

'Well, could you put Daisy on? Maybe we'll be able to figure it out.'

'Sure. Here you go. Daisy, Daddy wants to talk to you.' There's a shuffling noise as Petra hands Daisy the phone.

'Hi, sweetheart,' Ryan says. 'So, you want me to find this story of yours?'

'Uh-huh. Mum wants to read it.'

'Right, er . . . so you've no idea what you called it?'

'Mmmm . . . no.'

Ryan exhales, clicking open Hannah's document file. 'Can't see anything here, darling. It looks like work stuff, mostly, and pictures . . .'

'Er . . . I think . . . um . . .' She tails off. Ryan can imagine Petra standing over her, lips pressed together.

'Can you remember where it might be?' As Daisy umms

and arrs some more, Ryan glances outside. That couple has stopped in the park and are standing face to face, clutching each other's hands, their lips almost touching. 'I can't remember,' Daisy says, 'but I think I emailed it to Jess or Kira 'cause they wanted to read it . . .'

Ryan bites his lower lip and opens Hannah's sent emails file. He feels shifty, sifting through them. 'They'd better not copy it,' Daisy adds.

'No, I'm sure they won't. Look, sweetheart, I've looked through all Hannah's sent emails and I still can't see anything here. It'd have an attachment, wouldn't it?'

'Er . . . yeah, I think so.'

'Are you sure you need it right now? I can ask Hannah when I speak to her . . .'

'I *really* need it,' she exclaims, and now Ryan sees Petra, studying their daughter, suspecting that the story doesn't exist and that Daisy's just made it up to convince her that she's doing super-brilliantly at school. It would appear, Ryan thinks, that their daughter doesn't particularly like books which, in Petra's universe, is tantamount to admitting, 'Actually, Brahms isn't my thing.' People have been incarcerated for less, Ryan thinks darkly.

He carefully rechecks Hannah's sent emails file. 'Daisy, it's not here. I'm sorry. I'll have another look through all the documents and call you tomorrow, okay?'

'But I need it tonight, Dad!' Daisy's voice wobbles. 'Mum was testing my reading,' she adds in a murmur – Petra must have wandered off now – 'and I couldn't read *psychologist* . . .'

'Psychologist?' Ryan splutters. 'What on earth were you reading?'

'Just, I dunno, some book of Mum's. A grown-up one. Mum says the school ones are too easy . . .'

'Oh, Daisy, don't get upset. I promise I'll email it to Mum as soon as I've found it. Tonight, if I can.'

Daisy sniffs into the phone. 'Okay, Dad.'

Ryan finishes the call, mutters *psychologist, for crying out loud* under his breath and resumes his search. Yet the only sent emails are to Hannah's parents, to her friends at work, to Lou and Sadie and a couple of mates from back home in Fife.

He opens her draft file, wondering if Daisy had pinged the email into here by mistake. There's just one email, to Lou. Ryan pauses, blinking at the screen. Why has Hannah kept a draft?

It would be wrong to read it, and he isn't the prying type. He's only lowered himself to that kind of despicable, sneaky behaviour once in his life – when Petra announced she was leaving – and even then, he'd just had a quick pry through her texts, expecting to find outpourings of love to a conductor or violinist and discovered precisely nothing. But this email, stranded in Hannah's drafts file as if she'd intended to send it, then had a change of heart – why would she do that? Because it's *significant*.

Ryan clicks it open and glances over his shoulder towards her studio door, almost expecting her to bounce through it, explaining that plans have changed and she hasn't gone to Glasgow after all. He sees that Sadie was copied into the mail too, and stares, convincing himself that he's not reading it, not really. He's just skimming it. *So excited I can't tell you . . . counting the sleeps like a little kid. The hotel's booked . . . sandwich poking out from under the bed . . .*

Prickling with shame, but unable to close the email, Ryan averts his eyes to focus on the couple who are still standing out there, embracing. His eyes are dragged back to the screen. *It's been a funny old week – loads on at work with a new wedding card range, which I should be finding easy with my own nuptials thundering towards me . . . but somehow I'm not . . .* Ryan's back teeth have jammed together. *Ryan's been looking all hurt as if I'm trying to avoid him* . . . Well, things did feel slightly odd, he reflects, the few days before she went away. He put it down to prewedding stress and Hannah having so much on at work. *Sometimes, though, I wonder if it's easier for him and the kids when I'm not around* . . .

Is it easier? Yeah, probably, he thinks bitterly. I mean, here I am, having a fantastic time raking through your private mail . . . *I've been trying to convince myself that it'll turn out fine* . . . *I'm scared now that it won't. The kids are so rude and surly – Ryan does his best but* . . . *There's something else too* . . . *found a crushed cigarette packet in the back pocket of Josh's jeans* . . . *It had one in it. One Marlboro Light* . . .

Ryan gawps at the computer. Cigarettes? He rereads it in case his mind has flipped, and he's concocted the word in his head. But no. Hannah has not only discovered illicit smoking materials in his fourteen-year-old son's pocket, but also chosen not to say anything about it.

He inhales deeply and sits back on her swivel chair, a wave of sadness washing over him – for his son, who's been such a mardy arse lately and is secretly smoking, *deceiving* him, wrecking his health. And for Hannah, too: the sunniest girl he's ever met in his life, who changed his world when she strode into Nell's one damp evening and he knew, despite his intense shyness in those sort of situations, that he simply had to speak to her.

And he has to speak to her now, this instant. 'Han?' he barks as she answers the call.

'Hi, darling! How's things?'

'Er . . . good, good . . .' Ryan realises he hasn't a clue what he wants to say, or how he should say it.

'. . . so good to be back here,' Hannah is enthusing, sounding excited and shimmeringly alive. 'And the train journey, what a laugh, met this guy called Felix . . . tons

197

of champagne and *truffles*, can you believe it? That anyone would bring truffles on a train?'

'Ha . . . no,' he says flatly.

'. . . and we're so out of touch with Glasgow,' she goes on, 'that we decided to come to his bar, that's where we are now – hang on, it's a terrible signal in here, I'm going to take this outside . . .'

'Sounds like you're having fun,' Ryan says grimly. Unwittingly, he has slipped into disapproving parent mode. God, what's wrong with him? This is the woman he loves, sounding happier than he can remember, enjoying a night out with her best friends. *You don't want to marry me,* he thinks as her voice bubbles on. *You want to escape.*

'So what are you up to tonight?'

'Oh, er . . . nothing much. Petra picked up the kids, I've just been pottering about, this and that . . .' *Wondering what the hell to do about my son's nicotine addiction . . .*

A small pause. 'Well, um . . . have a nice evening. I'd better go back. It's still hard to hear, you keep breaking up . . .'

So would you, Ryan thinks, if you were me right now. 'Okay,' he mutters. 'Have a great night, give my love to everyone.'

'Yeah, will do. Love you, darling . . .'

'Love you too,' Ryan croaks. By the time he's finished the call, he's forgotten all about Daisy, eagerly waiting for him to email her her story so she can show it to her mother and feel proud. Because right now, Ryan feels crushed. Right now, with his children gone and his beautiful future wife in a cocktail bar owned by some guy she met on the train, Ryan Lennox feels utterly alone.

What should he do now? A long night stretches before him. With a sigh, and suddenly feeling heavy and old, he heads back downstairs to try and chip that toffee off Josh's carpet.

THIRTY-THREE

'Hey, hairy boy, you okay?' Spike pauses, finding it hard to form the right shapes with his mouth. He grips his mobile, wondering how best to put it that he doesn't appreciate this new 'amusing' nickname Astrid's come up with.

'Er . . . I've been trying to call you,' he says. 'I was thinking, now your meeting's over, at least I'm *assuming* it is, maybe I could come over . . .'

'Oh . . . I'm not sure,' she replies.

'Really? Well, we could go out then. There's still plenty of time. Charlie says there's this band on, don't know how good they'll be, but he's put my name on the door and I'm sure I can get you in—'

'No, sorry, I'm really tired tonight. I think I'll just stay in.'

'But it's Friday night!' he exclaims. The realisation that Astrid is considering throwing away this prime opportunity sparks a flash of instant sobriety.

'I know, hon, but I've been working a lot this week, you know? I just feel like lounging about, to be honest. I'm sorry. I know it sounds boring.'

She doesn't sound sorry at all, Spike decides, momentarily

distracted by a vision of Astrid lounging about in her neat, tasteful living room wearing not a bulky marshmallow dressing gown but that . . . French thing. What's it called again? A *chemise*. 'Well . . .' he drawls, closing the polystyrene carton on the kitchen table which contains his sausage remains, 'I think I'll go anyway, just to check them out. Okay if I pop by to see you later on? About half-ten?'

Say yes. Please, please, say yes.

'Um, no, Spike. Not tonight. I've told you, I'm really shattered.'

Because sitting in a meeting or doing a voiceover – ie talking into a microphone – must be completely fucking exhausting . . . 'So you don't want to see me at all tonight?' Spike asks coolly.

'I'm just not in the mood, okay?'

Brilliant. Spike senses his entire body slumping with disappointment. His greasy supper shifts in his stomach; maybe he should have had a stir-fry after all. 'Is it . . . something to do with me?' he murmurs.

'No, no, no . . . it's just stuff. I've got a lot on at the moment, Spike, and after we talked about Lou, I hoped, well . . . you might give it some thought.'

Spike opens his mouth, trying to make sense of what she's saying. 'So you're giving me an ultimatum to leave Lou? Is that it?'

'God, Spike . . .' Astrid laughs bitterly. 'Of course not. Look, maybe it's not really about Lou. It's just . . . our setup, you know? I mean, it's not really a relationship, is it?'

'Isn't it? What would you call it then?'

'I dunno. Just . . . a *thing*.'

Grabbing the bottle, Spike fills his grease-smeared wine glass with Croatian red and takes a big sip. 'I thought you liked it that way. I thought you were enjoying our . . . *thing*.'

'Well . . .' Astrid pauses, 'I was for a bit. But I just think it's best if we don't see each other anymore.'

'I don't understand!' Spike rages into the phone. 'It's like you've gone off me, all of a sudden, with this hairy boy business . . .'

'What?' Astrid exclaims. 'You're offended by me calling you hairy boy? It's just a joke . . .'

'Yes, I know that, but it's not very flattering, is it?'

'But you *are* hairy,' she says in a gentler tone. 'You're one of the hairiest guys I've ever met, and it's . . . it's nice, I like it . . .'

'Well, obviously you don't,' he splutters.

'I do! I did. Hairy is, um . . . *great*, Spike. It's just, I've been thinking about us, mulling it over and –'

Spike doesn't know what Astrid's been thinking because he hangs up on her and snatches the cigarette that's been trickling smoke from the conch ashtray. *Hairy boy.* How his life has plummeted since that brief flurry of attention, following that one hit record so long ago. Letters galore, flooding into his record company; scrawlings of love – some pretty lewd – and even the odd pair of knickers or bra stuffed into a jiffy bag. Then . . . nothing.

Gripping his wine glass, he makes his way unsteadily through to the bathroom and observes his tense reflection in the mirrored cabinet. His lips are stained black from the wine. He grabs Lou's spotty white flannel, wets it under the tap and rubs it vigorously over his mouth. Sod Astrid, he thinks angrily. She's been playing him along, knowing full well how much he's looked forward to this weekend – even selling his guitar, for God's sake. Well, two can play games. Balancing his glass on the toilet cistern, he whips off his T-shirt and peers down at his chest.

What is it about it that Astrid finds so offensive? Sure, it's hairy, but the hair is concentrated around the right area – ie, the chest zone, and not creeping upwards towards his

201

shoulders or round to his back. Nothing he can do about that. Yet . . . there *is*, isn't there? Women aren't hairy because they go to great lengths to get rid of it. Well, Spike will too. He'll show Astrid Stone what he's capable of, and then she'll be bloody sorry.

A wave of nausea hits him as he flings open the cabinet door. So Astrid wants smooth? He'll give her smooth. How hard can it be to wax your own chest? Teenage girls do it. Well, not their chests, admittedly, but their legs and under-arms and other areas he can't allow himself to think about. And chest skin isn't delicate. Spike's is probably as tough as rhino hide. He'll whip it all off, then he'll go round to see Astrid and surprise her – forget that band, they'll prob-ably be crap anyway. And Astrid will either be astounded and ravage him there and then, or find it hysterically funny or possibly even *touching* that he's done this for her. Either way, it's win-win.

Packets and cartons tumble out onto the peeling lino floor as Spike rifles through the cupboard. There it is: *Silken Glide ready-to-use cold wax strips for sensational smooth-ness*. Perching on the loo, Spike studies the blurb on the back of the lilac box. *Precautions*: *not suitable for use on face or head*. What kind of idiot would try to wax their own head?

He squints at the instructions. *Briskly rub the strip between your hands to warm and soften it . . .* Spike briskly rubs. *Now peel the two plastic layers apart and place one, wax side down, firmly onto your skin*. Spike presses it onto his chest, just above his left nipple. *Rub firmly and repeat-edly, following the direction of the hair growth*. What direction is that? Spike's chest hair doesn't seem to have a direction; it sprouts in unruly whorls, not unattractively he notices now, gazing bleakly down at the strip. He decides to rub in all directions, so at least some of his strokes will be right.

Now pull the wax strip back on itself as quickly as you can, in the opposite direction of your hair growth. There it is again. If he doesn't know its direction, how can he be sure which way to pull it off? Yet the longer he dithers, the more firmly the strip will glue itself to his skin – perhaps requiring a humiliating trip to the doctor's to have it removed. Gritting his teeth, Spike plucks a corner of the strip between his thumb and forefinger, pausing for a moment while sweat prickles his brow. He takes a deep breath and pulls hard, letting out a cry of anguish as pain sears through his body and the hairs are ripped out. 'Jesus,' he gasps, eyes watering, chest stinging like fury. He glances down at the newly-waxed area. It's bright pink, eerily shiny and almost hair-free. There's no way Spike can face waxing another section. He isn't a small man, and his chest hair extends upwards from his pubic region to just beneath his neck. It would take hours to wax it all, and involve acute pain. Spike has a newfound admiration for women who have Brazilians.

No, he'll have to abandon the project, he decides, glancing down to see that the waxed section has now sprouted angry red pimples. Great. So that's supposed to be more attractive than natural man-hair, is it? Spike tosses the box of remaining wax strips into the bath in disgust.

He'll just have to live with it, he decides. Maybe, when he's sober and steadier of hand, he'll be able to muster the courage to rip off the rest, or perhaps he'll just let the bald bit grow back and hope it merges in with the rest of the forest so Lou doesn't notice anything untoward.

And what about Astrid? What will she make of it? Replaying their phonecall, Spike doesn't believe she no longer wants to see him – not really. She was probably just in a mood, that's all. Hormonal, or playing a game to test his keenness. Next time she glimpses him naked, she'll probably laugh her head off and it'll help to break the ice.

Spike needs another drink, but even more than that, he needs people around him. He's spent too long by himself, eating vile, greasy food, getting drunk on brandy and Croatian plonk and waxing himself, and Lou's only been gone for about five hours. If he carries on in this manner, by the time she comes home on Sunday, he'll be hospitalised.

He pulls on his T-shirt and jacket and walks purposefully out of the flat, focusing his thoughts on the gig Charlie mentioned. Spike's chest is stinging, and he's left the used wax strip draped, like evidence at a crime scene, over the side of the bath. But, looking on the bright side, he tells himself as he quickens his pace, the night can only get better.

THIRTY-FOUR

Father and son have stopped to listen to a busker playing guitar outside the Metro station. It's a bustling Friday evening in Glasgow, and most people are more interested in being out, and getting to where they want to be, than in a skinny teenager with choppy red hair strumming a Bob Dylan song. But Johnny and Cal have stopped and are playing the 'how much to throw in the guitar case?' game.

'He's really good, Dad,' Cal says. 'I reckon at least ten quid.'

'I can't give a tenner to a busker!' Johnny exclaims with a grin, basking in the comfortable ordinariness of being out in the evening with his son. They've been to the cinema, the vast multiplex with all the escalators that Cal still enjoys riding up and down on, even at twelve years old. If this were a normal Friday night, they'd be heading back to Johnny's flat where Cal spends most weekends. They'd get up early, pick up some shopping and maybe, if Johnny was feeling generous, Cal would be treated to a strawberry tart from the posh new patisserie where everything comes in a fresh white box. Not this one, though. It's Cal's mother's birthday tomorrow – her 36th – and Rona wants to spend it with her son.

'Yeah,' Cal says, 'but we said that instead of giving small amounts to different buskers, we'd save up for the best ones.'

'Why did we say that again?' Johnny asks.

'Because otherwise we're giving the same to the good *and* the crap ones and that's not really fair, is it? He's worth a lot more than that old lady with the squeaky accordion you gave a quid to.'

Johnny laughs. 'Yes, but maybe she needed the money more than he does. Maybe she was a poor old granny with fifteen grandkids and he's got a rich mum and dad and is just doing this for fun. Maybe he gets more pocket money than you get in a whole *year*.'

Cal turns to him and frowns. 'So? He's still good, Dad.'

'So, I'm just saying.' With a grin, Johnny fishes out a two-pound coin from his wallet and hands it to his son. 'Here, give him this.'

'Dad! You're so tight.'

'Yeah, right, I just paid for our cinema tickets and bought you a massive carton of popcorn . . .' With a snort, Cal steps forward and drops the coin into the busker's fur-lined case. 'C'mon, we'd better go,' Johnny adds as the busker nods his thanks.

'Can't we stay out a bit longer? Just walk about a bit?' Like his father, and despite the fact that Cal has lived in Glasgow all his life, he still relishes the buzz of the city as it revs up for a weekend night.

'No, I'd better get you back,' Johnny says.

Cal makes a low grumbling noise, which Johnny feels like doing too. What he really wants to do is pick up a pizza and head back to his place – a small but perfectly decent two-bedroomed flat a couple of streets away from the art college. He wants to hang out with his son over a pizza with mushrooms, chatting about the movie and the fact that Cal's been picked for his school football team.

Not major, life-changing stuff. Just the minutiae of his son's life. They'd stay up late, but that wouldn't matter because there's no school tomorrow. Tonight, though, Cal must be returned to Rona and Tristan's vast Merchant City flat with its white rugs and white sofas and white bloody everything else as far as Johnny can work out. There's even a little white C-shaped rug that fits snugly around the loo.

He plucks his phone from his pocket and calls Rona. 'Hi, it's me, sorry we're running late . . .'

'That's okay. I was just about to phone you, though. I was getting a bit worried . . .'

'Yeah, the film was longer than I expected so . . .' Johnny tails off. He and Cal are passing a basement bar, a new cocktail place called Felix, its black and purple sign embellished with swirls. It looks posh, expensive and a tad pretentious. From up at street level, Johnny can see a woman sitting at the window, perched on a high stool, glass in hand, curly auburn hair springing around her face.

'Are you coming over now?' Rona asks.

'Yes. Yes, I am . . .' Johnny falters. He can't see all of the girl's face, just her cheek, her graceful neck and the dainty curve of her chin. But he feels as if his heart has stopped.

'Johnny?' Rona's voice snaps him back to reality. 'Is everything all right? You sound distracted . . .'

'Yes, yes, it's fine . . . sorry. Just thought I saw someone I knew.'

'Who?'

'Oh, just someone from years back . . .' He finishes the call and looks down at the girl in the window. She is wearing what looks like a vintage dress, black or navy with large bright flowers splashed all over it.

'C'mon, Dad.' Cal nudges him as the woman turns and, just as he thought, it's Lou Costello from Garnet Street. Lou, who Johnny hasn't seen since the day he moved out from the flat above hers, and in with pregnant Rona, trying to convince himself that it *would* all work out, and that his girlfriend was right – it was time to cut ties with his ramshackle student life and grow up and be a dad.

'Who is it?' Cal asks as Johnny slips his phone back into his pocket.

'Huh?'

'You told Mum you saw someone you know.'

'Oh,' Johnny laughs. 'Yes, I think I have. See that person in that bar down there, sitting right by the window?'

Cal squints and nods. 'Yeah.'

'Well, I think I used to know her years and years ago, before you were born . . .'

'Which one?' Cal asks. 'There's three of 'em.'

'What? Oh yes, so there are . . .' Next to Lou is a blonde girl – Hannah, he realises now – and sitting opposite them, raising a glass to her lips, is Sadie. All three, just like the old days. Johnny feels ridiculous staring down at the bar, but is rooted to the spot.

'Did you go out with them?' asks Cal with a sly grin. Lately, he's developed a keen interest in his dad's lacklustre love life.

'No,' Johnny laughs. 'I didn't go out with them, Cal. They were just friends. It is possible for a man to have female friends, you know.'

'Why are you red then?'

'I'm not! I'm just hot.'

'But it's *not* hot,' Cal insists. 'It's cold, Dad. You look really funny.'

'That's just me,' Johnny chuckles. 'I'm funny-looking, you should know that by now. C'mon, let's go, Mum's expecting you.' He starts walking with Cal jammed at his side.

'You must've gone out with one of them.'

'Well, I didn't, all right?'

208

'Not even before you met Mum?'

'Nope, not even then.'

'Why not?'

Johnny chuckles, wondering how to put it. 'They didn't fancy me, Cal.'

'Well, I think it's weird.'

'That they weren't all madly in love with your old dad?'

'*Noooo*,' Cal exclaims. 'It's weird that you didn't go in and say hello.'

'Um . . .' Johnny starts awkwardly. 'It's just . . . they looked like they were having a nice night and I didn't want to butt in and spoil it. Anyway,' he adds, making a conscious effort to slow his pace so Cal doesn't have to trot alongside him, 'I haven't seen them for years and it might've been awkward.'

'But it's rude not to talk to someone you know. *You* told me that.'

'Yeah, but they didn't see me, Cal. It's different.'

'Spying's rude too.'

'I wasn't spying!'

'Well, that's what it looked like. So anyway, which one did you fancy?'

'That is *so* private,' he chuckles, having regained his composure now that they're a safe distance from the bar. 'I couldn't even begin to share that information with you.'

'Which one did you like best then?' Cal wants to know.

'Oh, I liked all of them,' Johnny says truthfully. Hannah had been his mate; Sadie too, although he'd found her exotic beauty slightly unnverving. And Lou: well, she was the loveliest girl he'd ever met, but even if she had been interested in him before he'd met Rona, Spike was always there, glowering in the background. Johnny didn't believe in blurting out his feelings for someone who had a boyfriend, even if said boyfriend was incapable of keeping it in his pants for more than five minutes. So, in some ways, it had been the right thing to do: relocate with Rona to the furthest reaches of the suburbs, where he would immerse himself in impending fatherhood without the distraction of being utterly crazy about Lou Costello, and seeing her being betrayed by the man she loved.

Johnny had thrown everything into being a father to Cal. He'd been a part-time catering student while working in an Italian restaurant, and when his shifts had proved incompatible with parenthood, he'd started landscape gardening instead. Yet it still hadn't worked out. His remote and beautiful Rona had slipped away from him and into the burly arms of Tristan Hunter, a highly-respected heart doctor, the son of friends of her parents and someone far better equipped to offer a young boy what he needed. *He* hadn't minded getting involved with someone who had a partner already.

It's ironic, Johnny thinks, putting an arm around Cal's shoulders as Rona and Tristan's smart red sandstone block comes into view, that Scotland's top cardiologist appears to have no heart of his own.

*

Rona looks different tonight – slightly startled, as if her virtually line-free face would feel waxy to the touch. While he can understand that Rona might not wish to age prematurely, all these 'top-ups' she has seem totally unnecessary. Tristan, on the other hand, always looks plastic with no intervention whatsoever: six foot four inches of hulking manhood with a solid square jaw and weird, closely-cropped Action-Man hair.

He doesn't seem to be around right now, thank God. Tristan's presence never fails to make Johnny feel ill at ease, and his preferred topics of conversation – rugby, golf, the halogen lights they're having fitted in the kitchen – make him feel as if the lifeblood is seeping out of his body. Once, when Johnny tried to steer the conversation to football – which he and Cal follow avidly – Tristan eyeballed him as if he'd confessed that cage fighting was more his thing. Football, as far as Tristan is concerned, is a game for uneducated oiks.

'What have you got planned for tomorrow?' Johnny asks Rona, trying not to peer at her face to figure out where those fillers have been pumped in.

'Well, we'll start with the usual birthday breakfast,' she says with a smile.

'Waffles?' Cal asks eagerly.

'Yes, of course, darling. Bacon, maple syrup – the works. Then we'll go for a wander around town and have lunch, Tristan's taking us somewhere nice.'

'Sounds good.' Johnny digs into his jacket pocket, pulls out a card and a small parcel and hands them to her.

'Oh, thanks, Johnny! You needn't have . . .'

'It's just tiny.'

'You're very sweet.'

He shrugs, eager to leave now as he hears the bath draining – that vast oval bath, big enough to contain a hunk of buffed-up manliness. 'Well, I'd better be off. Okay if I come over about five-ish tomorrow?'

Rona smiles, and he notices now that her teeth look brighter than usual: startling Tipp-Ex-white, like a fluorescent strip. 'That should be fine.'

He hugs his son, and as he turns to leave, Cal gives him another sly grin. 'So are you gonna go see those ladies now, Dad?'

'What ladies?' Johnny asks with a frown.

'The ones in that place. The place downstairs.'

'Oh, I don't think so,' he laughs.

'What ladies, Johnny?' Rona teases. 'Planning a big night tonight, are you?'

211

'God, no,' he blusters, sensing his cheeks redden as Action Man appears in the hallway. He is liberally doused in citrusy aftershave and wearing some kind of stretchy lounge pants and a mottled grey top. He barks a man-greeting at Johnny, who tries to man-greet him back, wondering if there will ever be a point in his life when he'll acquire loungewear.

'What ladies in that downstairs place?' Rona asks again with a tinkly laugh. 'What are you up to, Johnny?'

'Nothing! It's . . . no one. Just some people I thought I knew . . .' He rakes back his hair distractedly. 'Anyway, I'm just going to head straight home.'

*

Lou Costello, he marvels, breathing in the crisp evening air after saying his goodbyes. Lou, Hannah and Sadie are here, which doesn't make any sense at all. Maybe he imagined it. Should he go back and see if they're still there? Of course not. He hasn't seen them for over a decade, and he can imagine what they'd think of him, disappearing like that. 'How d'you think it is for me?' Rona had snapped one long, bleak night with Cal writhing in her arms, 'when your best friends are girls? It's okay for you – your life hasn't changed one bit. But I'm completely alone. None of my friends have babies . . .' Johnny had thought it better not to remind Rona that none of *his* friends had babies either.

So he'd made a decision – to do as she demanded and cut ties with the girls, because the thought of it not working out with Rona when they had a child was terrifying. He'd stopped returning their calls, and when Lou had sent him a playful letter, he'd put it on top of the microwave until he could decide what to do with it. The next time he looked, it had gone.

Too agitated to go straight home, Johnny orders a pint in the dark, cavernous pub he used to frequent as a teenager. He chats briefly with several people he recognises, even securing a lucrative landscaping job for next month. Work is good, life is good, he reflects, stepping out into the street. He has a son he adores, and these days, even he and Rona have begun to enjoy a fragile sort of friendship.

As Johnny is feeling at one with the world, he decides to play a little game with himself. If he turns the corner and the first person he sees makes eye contact with him, he'll go back to the bar and see if the girls are still there. Johnny turns the corner. A couple are walking towards him. He wills at least one of them to glance at him, but they're locked in conversation and disappear into a side street.

That's that then, Johnny decides – a sign that he shouldn't go marching into that cocktail place and make an arse of himself. He doesn't drink cocktails anyway – at least he's never tried one he liked – and he wouldn't have imagined Lou and the others drinking them either. It was lager or cheap wine in the old days.

He's tempted to have one more go at the game. If he turns the next corner and there's a pigeon there, either flying or pottering about on the ground – he's not fussy – he'll walk right in and say . . . well, he doesn't know *what* he'll say. He'll just have to wing it.

No pigeons. Not a single one, when they're usually flapping all over the place, pecking at rubbish and scattered chips, even at night. Hell, he'll just go in, like Cal said he should. He'll just pop in and say hi, have a brief catch-up, and it'll be no big deal at all. Johnny marches faster now, heart pumping, no longer caring about pigeons. Will the girls even remember him? Surely they will. He doesn't think he's changed that much, and they certainly haven't from what he's seen. He pictures Lou perched on that chrome stool, laughing, hair springing around her adorable face, and his stomach flutters in anticipation.

213

So how *should* he make his entrance, he wonders? Pretend he's just happened to go in, as if he frequents cocktail bars all the time, and look around for some imaginary friend then just happen to spot them? How will he react if Lou explains that she and Spike split up years ago? He'll have to remember to arrange his features to look suitably devastated.

He arrives at the bar and stares down. It's them all right: Sadie, voluptuous in a drapey wrap dress, and Hannah, a bronzed beauty in a strappy top. And Lou Costello. Johnny stares, frozen in time, feeling as if his heart has stopped.

It *is* Lou, he's certain of that – but she's with a man, a big blond guy whose arm is casually slung around her shoulders. They're laughing, Lou and her boyfriend, looking totally carefree and happy on a Friday night. Johnny blinks, allowing himself to take in the scene. Then he turns on his heels, pulling up the collar of his jacket as a cold wind whips past him, and hurries home to his flat.

THIRTY-FIVE

Hannah isn't really a cocktail person but Felix isn't making ordinary cocktails. There are fresh raspberries and redcurrants and cloves in there, bursting onto her tongue. Felix likes to keep his hand in – and his immaculate staff on their toes – and Hannah suspects he also enjoys showing off, pouring liquids from a ridiculous height, his hands flying as he speedily chops fruit on a granite slab. When Hannah asks how he's managed to achieve all this, he explains, 'Well, my ex, Amanda, once said I'd never amount to anything. And I thought *okay* . . . I'm going to prove you wrong. So,' he grins, having joined them at their table now, 'you could say that being dumped was good for me.'

'Maybe it was,' she says with a grin.

'Anyway . . .' he says, pointing to the glass she's holding, 'what d'you think of that?'

'Delicious,' Hannah enthuses. 'Like liquid raspberries but with a kick . . .'

'Mine's like honey,' Lou adds. 'It's the nicest thing I've ever drunk in my life.'

'Mine tastes of fresh blackberries,' Sadie says. 'God, Felix, I don't want to drink anything else now.'

'But you must,' he insists. 'You see, what you've had so far was on the menu. You haven't had a bespoke one yet.'

'Bespoke cocktails?' Hannah repeats. 'How do they work?'

Felix grins. He is dressed in a sharp grey suit tonight, although his wayward blond hair appears to have been untouched since they said goodbye at Glasgow Central station. 'The idea is, you tell me which flavours you love and we put them together to make a unique cocktail that's especially blended for you.'

'But how do I know what goes together?' Lou asks.

'That's the whole point,' Felix explains. 'It's our job to *make* the ingredients go together, but the chances are they do anyway because they're tastes that you love, which tend to be from the same flavour spectrum . . .'

Sadie explodes with laughter. 'Are you for real, Felix? Or are you just winding us up?'

'Would I do that?' he laughs in mock-horror. 'No, it's part of what we do in all our bars. It's our unique selling point.'

'Do they cost a fortune?' Lou asks.

'Not to you – they're on the house . . .'

'But Felix,' Hannah exclaims, 'we've already had one on the house – '

'This is my wedding present to you, Hannah,' he says with a grin, 'and if you like it, I'll give you the recipe and you can serve it to your guests. You could even sneak some into your miserable stepkids' lemonades to perk them up a bit. So get thinking. I need three flavours each . . .'

'But how do we know you'll have the ingredients?' Sadie wants to know.

Felix raises a brow. 'We have everything here. We only need tiny amounts, that's part of the magic.' Hannah sees him glance towards the window, frown and look back again.

'What's up, Felix?' she asks.

'Oh, there was just some man out there a few moments ago, hanging about and staring in – at you three lovelies, I think . . .'

The girls turn to peer out, but all they see are people marching purposefully past the window. 'Was he cute?' Sadie asks.

Felix shrugs. 'Guess so. Tall, handsome, bit scruffy . . .'

'Maybe he was wondering whether to come in or not,' Lou suggests.

'We probably scared him off,' Hannah cuts in. 'We're bad for business, Felix. Anyway, I've thought of my three ingredients, okay? I love lemony things and dark chocolate and this might sound a bit mad, but I like spice, hot things, chilli . . .'

'That sounds good,' Felix says as Sadie winces. 'No, it really does. Now Lou, what about you?'

'Um . . .' She pauses, running her tongue over her teeth, thinking of the things she used to treat herself to before she stalked the supermarket sticker girl. 'Pomegranate, almonds and, um . . . strawberries.'

'Great.' He nods his approval.

'Aren't you going to write this down?' Hannah asks.

Felix rolls his eyes and chuckles. 'I can remember nine ingredients, you know. Sadie . . . your order please?'

'Er . . .' She tries to think, but the only flavours that pop into her mind are milk – not the kind you slosh into your tea but formula milk with its weird, faintly sweet smell, and breastmilk, siphoned off by that pump for hours and hours . . . 'Peach,' she says quickly, 'and caramel and, God, that sounds sickly, doesn't it . . .'

'Just say whatever comes into your head,' Felix urges her.

'Okay. Blackcurrants, but not like Ribena blackcurrant . . .'

'It's okay,' Felix chortles, hopping off his stool, 'that's one thing we don't do here.' And he's gone, leaving the girls to marvel at his bespoke cocktail concept, and to speculate whether his concoctions will be as delicious as promised. They've forgotten about that man Felix saw standing outside, and Sadie hasn't noticed that the dark-haired man in glasses, who'd glanced at her in the previous bar, has now walked into Felix's.

And when the drinks arrive, the girls are in awe. Sadie's is indigo, Lou's concoction is a delicate pink and Hannah's is citrusy lemon. As the warmth of the drink spreads down her throat, she pictures herself on her wedding day, having done the registry office part and moved on to the bar-cum-restaurant with friends and family. And in that moment, she can see that everything *will* be all right. 'This is amazing, Felix,' she murmurs. 'I'd really like to serve this at my wedding.'

'Be my guest,' he says.

'Would you . . . come and make it for us?' she asks hesitantly.

Felix smiles broadly. 'I'd love to, Hannah. It would be my absolute pleasure.'

'Really?' she exclaims.

'Yes, of course!'

Hannah laughs, taking another sip. 'I need to text Ryan and tell him right now.'

'It's hard to get a signal in here, I'm afraid,' Felix tells her.

'Okay. Won't be a minute.' She jumps off her stool and steps outside, sensing the worries of the past few weeks floating away as she pulls out her phone. Yet now, it seems far too convoluted to explain about Felix, bespoke cocktails and having just discovered their perfect wedding cocktail. As a smile spreads across her face, she simply texts LOVE U DARLING XXXX before skipping back inside.

218

THIRTY-SIX

The bleep of an incoming text jolts Ryan awake from a brief doze on the sofa. Hannah again. He reads her text, and is about to respond with LOVE YOU TOO when the landline trills to life.

'Dad? It's me. Where's my story?'

'Oh, Daisy!' Ryan looks at the digital clock on the DVD player. 9.47 pm.

'Did you email it yet? 'Cause Mum says it hasn't come and she wants me to go to bed now and I *really* want to read it to her tonight . . .'

Ryan takes a deep breath. 'Sorry, darling, but I've looked in every file and I can't find it. I should've rung to tell you, sorry . . .'

'But Dad!' she exclaims.

'I'm really sorry, Daisy, but I've done what I can, okay?'

'Did you really look everywhere? Are you sure?' Daisy's voice wavers.

'Yes,' Ryan says firmly, 'I did, darling, but tell you what – I'll have another really careful search and then, if I find it, I'll send it over first thing in the morning . . .'

'But you've already looked and it's my only copy!'

'Oh, Daisy, don't get upset. Mum's right, you should head off to bed now . . .'

'It took me hours and hours and HOURS!' she wails.

Ryan's brain aches as he tries to think of how to placate his daughter. 'Daisy, I'm sure it's . . . *somewhere*.' No, that's no good. She's crying now, and all he wants to do is spirit himself over to Petra's neat little flat in Crouch End and hold his daughter tightly in his arms.

'I bet Hannah deleted it,' Daisy weeps. There's a distinct absence of soothing words in the background from Petra, he notices. She's probably nodding in agreement: *Yes, that silly girl probably did delete it. Is it any wonder you're not getting good marks at school, poppet?*

'Hannah wouldn't do that,' Ryan insists.

'Yeah, she would!'

'Why on earth d'you think that? Listen, sweetheart, getting all worked up isn't going to help. It's just a story . . .'

'Just a story?' she chokes.

'No! Not *just* a story. We'll find it, and next time you write one you can tell me when it's done and I'll back it up on a memory stick.'

There's some muted crying, then Petra's voice filters down the phone, suggesting that Daisy really should go to bed now, seeing as she's *so* upset over this mess-up. Call over, Ryan sinks back into the vast beige sofa, chosen by Petra so the entire family could spend quality time watching movies together. But Petra always wanted to watch box sets of *Life on Earth*, or that movie about the penguins trooping across the Arctic or Antarctic or wherever it was, which the children only watched to please her. It occurs to Ryan that so much of his life, and the children's lives, have been shaped around trying to make Petra happy. She has that effect – an aura of brilliance, albeit as chilly as the terrain in that penguin film.

And yes, he should tell her about Josh's cigarettes, he decides. The thought of uttering those words to her makes him feel heavy inside, as if *he'd* bought them, offered one to their son and forced him to smoke it. Yet they have to discuss it, face to face. Hannah feels so far away right now, and Ryan must to talk to someone, so he picks up the phone and dials Petra's number. 'Hi again,' he says.

'Ryan? Are you okay?'

'Yeah . . . I'm just sorry, hearing Daisy so upset like that . . .'

'She'll be fine,' Petra says evenly. 'You know what she's like, blowing things out of all proportion, like the time Hannah suggested she get her ears—'

'But Hannah didn't—' Ryan stops himself. 'Um, look, Petra, I hope this isn't an imposition or anything, but I wondered if . . . would it be okay to come over?'

'What, tomorrow?' she asks lightly.

'Well . . . I was thinking more . . . tonight.'

A small pause. Ryan pictures her face: eyes steady, lips pursed. 'Um . . . okay . . . are you sure everything's all right? You sound a bit . . . stressed.'

His forehead creases as he grips the phone. Apart from dropping off or picking up the kids, he's never been over to Petra's. Before this grim Friday night, it's never occurred to Ryan that being there, in her orderly flat with the cello propped up on its stand, could make him feel better. But now he's pretty certain it would. 'I'm fine, Petra,' he says softly, 'but I'd just like to talk to you about something.'

'Sure. Are you going to drive?'

'No, I've had a couple of drinks, better call a cab . . .'

'Okay,' she says, more gently than usual.

'Great.' Ryan senses some of the tension in his jaw and shoulders ebbing away. 'I'll be over as soon as I can.'

THIRTY-SEVEN

The band are good, everyone keeps saying so. While Spike is happy to lurk about at the back of the hall, he's less keen on the constant questioning about his own musical achievements of late. 'Done any gigs lately?' asks Brian, a bass player with whom he's played in the distant past.

Spike shakes his head. 'Bit quiet lately, but there are a few things coming up . . .'

Brian nods and sips his beer. 'So what else is happening?'

Spike turns to face the stage, watching the energetic singer clutching the mic, sweat spraying in an arc from his shaggy hair. Perhaps Spike should furnish Brian with details of being dumped by his girlfriend-on-the-side and his recent adventures with Lou's wax strips. The effects of the brandy and wine have worn off a little, and despondency is starting to seep through his veins. 'Been pretty busy,' he hears himself saying. 'You know – applying for jobs, getting my shit together . . .'

'What kind of jobs?' Brian wants to know.

Spike glances at him. Something high up in the council's education department, with a wife and three kids, Brian has the air of someone who's been a fully-fledged grown-up from the age of twelve. A pale green T-shirt is stretched across his substantial belly, and his jeans look as if they might have been designed by George at Asda. 'Just something to tide me over until things start moving again,' Spike explains.

Brian nods sagely. 'I'm sure you'll pick something up.'

'Yeah.' The band finishes a song to enthusiastic applause, then crashes straight into another, for which Spike is hugely grateful. He checks his watch, wondering what Lou is doing now and sensing an acute pang of loneliness. The band are playing an encore now, and Spike realises with a start how young most of the people around him are, apart from Brian, who seems to be rooted to his side. 'So I was wondering,' his companion says as the applause finally dies down, 'if Lou would make something for Dawn's birthday? It's her fortieth so I'm looking for something special and unique, you know?'

'Um, yeah, I'm sure she would,' Spike mutters.

'I thought maybe she could incorporate Dawn's birthstone. It's amethyst. I wondered about something in silver, Lou works with silver, doesn't she . . .'

'Yeah, yeah,' Spike says distractedly. 'She's away in Glasgow this weekend, but I'll mention it when she gets back.'

'She's in Glasgow?' Brian asks with interest.

'Yep, with a couple of friends on a hen weekend . . .'

Brian chuckles, and his eyebrows squirm like fat caterpillars. 'Whoo. Wonder what *they're* getting up to . . .'

'I shudder to think . . .' Spike forces a smirk, feeling conspicuous now as people drift towards the exit in rabbly groups.

'So me and Tony and a few others are gonna try that new casino,' Brian is telling him, scouting around the hall for his friends. 'Fancy coming along?'

'Er, I think I'll give it a miss,' Spike says, unwilling to admit that, with Lou away, he needs to keep a tight rein on funds.

'Okay. Well, enjoy the rest of your night . . .' Mercifully, Brian has spotted his mates and strides towards them. Allowing them a couple of minutes to leave, Spike totters unsteadily towards the foyer.

'Hey, Spike, I've been looking for you!' Charlie is in front of him now, pink and sweaty and clutching a plastic cup of lager. 'So what did you think?'

'Great,' Spike enthuses, conscious of his tongue feeling unusually large and dough-like. 'You did a good job with the sound, mate. Nice balance.'

Charlie grins. 'Thanks. Listen, me and the band are going for a few drinks, thought we'd go to Bar Circa, that Spanish place . . . you can join us if you like.'

It's tempting, especially as Charlie is notoriously generous with getting the drinks in. But so, too, is nipping over to Astrid's to try and talk some sense into her. The surge of lustful longing is almost too much to bear, and he's sure she didn't mean to dump him. Maybe she'd started her period or something. 'Thanks,' he tells Charlie, 'but I've got something on, this, er . . . party thing I've been invited to . . . maybe I'll drop by later.'

'Sure,' Charlie says with a nod.

As he leaves the venue, setting his internal compass on a straight course to Astrid's, Spike pulls out his phone. Hell, a missed call from Lou, and now it's ringing again. He strides on before calling her back, trying to steady himself so he'll sound normal and sober. 'Hey, I've been trying to call you,' Lou exclaims, sounding all happy and sparkly. There's a colossal amount of chatter and laughter in the background.

'Have you? Where are you now?'

'Just stepped out of this bar for a minute . . .'

'Right, well, sorry . . . I was at a gig, this band Charlie was doing the sound for . . .'

'Oh, was it fun?'

'Yeah, pretty good . . .'

'So what are you up to now?' Lou asks.

I'm standing in front of Astrid's house, he thinks, *feeling completely depressed.* 'Er, just heading home . . .'

'Not going on anywhere else? I bet you are! Are you with Charlie now?'

'Nah, I'm a bit tired to be honest . . .' *Tired, emotional and feeling like a complete jerk . . .*

'Oh,' Lou says. 'Well, we've had a great time so far, thanks for asking . . .'

'I was just going to ask! You haven't let me get a word in . . .'

'Sure you were,' she laughs. 'Well, since you're so interested, we had a few drinks at a place across the road from the hotel, and then we met up with Felix, the truffle man . . .' There's an outburst of rowdy laughter, but Spike no longer cares that everyone appears to be having a better time than he is, because a few feet away, in Astrid's pale-cream living room, a man is casually browsing the CDs on her shelf.

'. . . Bespoke cocktails!' Lou continues. 'Like, you can choose anything, any ingredient at all and Felix will blend them to make . . .' He switches off, watching as the man turns – a tall, handsome, musclebound bastard – and speaks to someone out of sight. The man selects a CD from the shelf. *Who the fuck are you?* Spike wants to yell.

'Spike? Are you listening?'

'Er, yeah, sorry . . . um, where are you again?'

'At Felix's cocktail bar – well, just in the doorway actually, can't get a signal inside . . . Oh, Felix is here now, he's come out . . .'

'Has he really?' Spike growls.

'Don't be so grumpy. You'd really like him, Spike. He's a scream . . .' Spike inhales sharply, gaze fixed on that blond freak-boy who looks about twenty. 'You'd have loads in common,' Lou continues, 'and guess what? He knows you!'

'Uh?'

'I mean, he remembers your song, don't you, Felix? D'you want to talk to him?'

'No!' Spike barks. Speaking to a stranger is the last thing he wants to do right now.

'Spike, my man!'

Spike winces at the loud, brash voice in his ear. 'Er, hello,' he says ambling away from Astrid's house.

'So, fancy this, huh? Amazing!'

'Yeah, amazing.'

'Been hearing all about you,' Felix says. 'I've often wondered, you know, what happens when someone has such a big hit, and then . . .'

'Uh-huh,' Spike mutters.

'It must be strange for you . . .'

'Yeah, kinda,' Spike growls, turning into the street where Sound Shack is and deliberately looking away as he passes it.

'Great song, though,' Felix blathers on. 'La-laaaaa . . .' Oh no. He's started to sing loudly over the background hubbub of the street. Worse still, someone else has joined in.

'Okay!' Spike snaps, but no one seems to hear – it sounds as if the whole damn town is joining in now. He finishes the call without saying goodbye, his jaw rigid with fury.

*

The door swings back with force as Spike storms, damp and dishevelled, into Bar Circa. It smells of cheap lager and wet jackets and at first, he can't spot Charlie or any of the band members. The bar is packed with people yelling to be heard, and virtually all the girls are skimpily dressed in minuscule skirts and strappy little tops. Under normal circumstances, he might have paused to take in the view, but right now he's far too agitated to appreciate shapely legs or death-valley cleavages. Now he's started to warm up, Spike has become conscious of a faint odour coming from his moist leather jacket – fuggy and foodie, not unlike the whiff from Lou's hair when she returns from Let's Bounce. Spike pulls his jacket off and slings it casually over his shoulder. Now worrying that that looks awkwardly posed – a male model stance from his mother's Grattan catalogue – Spike stuffs it under his arm like a small, damp pet and squeezes his way to the brass-railed bar.

'Hey, glad you made it.' Charlie has landed beside him and slaps him on the back with unnecessary force.

'Yeah, just thought I'd drop by,' Spike mutters.

'Good party?'

'Huh?'

'That party. Take it you didn't stay long?'

'Er, no, wasn't really in the mood,' he explains with a shrug.

'Right. Anyway, come over and meet everyone . . .' As he follows Charlie towards the cluster of band members, Spike decides he isn't in the mood for this either. He feels hot, tired and vaguely nauseous from the cheap perfume fug, mixing in with whiffs of brandy that are wafting up into his throat.

'Jamie on drums, Justin on bass, Simon on guitar, Rod on vocals, not forgetting Harry the roadie . . .' Charlie is making a big show of introducing each person as if they're on stage. Spike nods, trying to appear fully engaged, yet only half-listening. At least Charlie hasn't mentioned 'My Beauty', so he might possibly be spared further humiliation tonight. Not that any of these guys are old enough to remember his sole hit. They're probably still studying for their A-Levels, Spike thinks dryly as a bottle of Stella appears miraculously before him. 'So where are you playing next?' he asks the singer.

'Glasgow,' Rod explains. 'We should probably crash soon, get a few hours' kip at the hotel. We're meant to be on the road by ten tomorrow.'

Spike checks his watch. It's only midnight; what a bunch of lightweights, he thinks darkly. 'When he says hotel,' adds Harry-the-roadie, 'he's using the term loosely.'

'Right,' Spike chortles. 'So where are you staying?'

'Some hovel about ten minutes away,' Rod explains. 'Stinks of fried breakfast, wet dog, wet dog *turd* actually . . .'

Everyone laughs, and Spike has to stop himself from telling them that he used to tour too. 'That's funny,' he offers. 'My girlfriend's in Glasgow right now.'

'Yeah?' Harry says. 'What's she doing up there?'

'She's on a hen weekend with her friends.'

'Right, so it's going to be a quiet, low-key kind of thing,' Rod chuckles.

Spike grimaces. 'Well, it's not meant to be a big, wild weekend . . .'

Charlie and the band are all smirking knowingly, and Spike feels irritation bubbling up once again. 'But that's not what it sounded like when I spoke to her earlier,' he adds, unable to stop himself. 'There was some guy there, some posh creep who'd tried to pick her up on the train, plied her with drink, and he was tagging along for the night, sounded like they were all out of their skulls, to be honest . . .' A rich burp pops up, reeking of sausage. Charlie is frowning at him as if he has something strange and horrifying growing out of his nose.

'Well, it's a hen party,' Harry offers with a shrug. 'What else are they going to do? Sit around having tea and cakes?'

'Yeah, but it's not meant to be a wild weekend, remember,' Rod adds with a guffaw.

'You don't think . . .' Charlie frowns, meeting Spike's gaze. 'Lou wouldn't get up to anything, would she? Not your Lou. She's such a great girl.'

'Of course she wouldn't,' Spike exclaims. 'I just . . .' He shrugs, wishing he had some chewing gum to take away the bad taste in his mouth.

'So what are you worried about?' Charlie wants to know.

'Nothing.' Spike shakes his head firmly and swigs from his bottle.

'He's just jealous,' Rod guffaws. 'Jealous of his girlfriend letting her hair down while he's stuck with us sorry lot.'

Spike forces out a dry laugh and tries to relax.

'Well, mate,' Harry-the-roadie says with a smirk, 'you could come up to Glasgow with us, check out what she's up to. We've got room in the van.'

'I might just be tempted,' Spike chuckles.

'Yeah, Lou would love that,' adds Charlie. 'You showing up out of the blue, ruining her fun.'

As they banter on, Spike tunes out. He no longer wants to be standing here, pretending he's having a great Friday night out. What he really wants to do is to beam himself into that Glasgow bar and punch Felix in the face.

He says his goodbyes then, deciding that he needs to go home, sober up and wrestle his tangled thoughts into order. 'Well, it's been great meeting you all,' he says stiffly, placing his empty bottle on a cluttered table, 'but I think I'm going to crash.'

After a small flurry of backslaps and you-take-care-mates, Spike starts to head for the exit. 'Like we said, Spike,' Harry calls after him, 'we've got room in the ambulance if you change your mind . . .'

'Ambulance?' Spike echoes. Although he feels vaguely unwell, he can't imagine that a hospital visit is necessary.

'Our tour bus,' Rod explains with a grin. 'Hardly luxury but it gets us about.'

'We're leaving around ten,' Harry adds.

'I'll bear that in mind,' Spike calls back.

'Hey, Spike!' Charlie yells. 'If you do go, I suggest you wear two socks instead of just the one, yeah? It can get pretty chilly up in Glasgow.'

THIRTY-EIGHT

Sadie has drunk two more bespoke cocktails and feels just fine – better than fine, in fact. The last time she socialised was at a Little Hissingham coffee morning. She's now perched on a stool with her best friends, surrounded by beautiful people – *everyone* looks beautiful to Sadie tonight. She wants to call Barney, to tell him she loves him and the babies so much, and to say sorry for going on about schedules like some tedious headmistress at a strict boarding school.

And now, perhaps fuelled by Felix's caramel cocktail, she's no longer an addled mother but dancing with her friends, feeling slightly off kilter at first because she hasn't danced in a very long time. It's like sex, she thinks: you stop doing those lovely things you used to take for granted, then you try it once and it's okay, it's *better* than okay, and you realise what you've been missing. Sadie's thoughts are racing, any trace of self-consciousness gone. She's dancing, unaware of the breast pad which has worked its way up to the neckline of her dress and is about to make a bid for freedom.

When the tall, dark-haired man in glasses asks her to dance, she smiles and turns towards him, recognising him from the last bar. It's so *friendly* here. It's where she belongs. When the breast pad pops out of her dress, she just laughs, kicks it aside and keeps dancing . . .

Sadie Vella is so happy she could cry. Anything she does right now is just fine, because she loves Hannah and Lou and Barney and the boys, and right at this moment, life is pretty damn perfect.

THIRTY-NINE

Ryan's taxi pulls up outside Petra's ground floor flat. The living room curtains are drawn at the bay window, with soft light behind, and even from the street her place has an aura of stillness and calm. Ryan pays the driver, clears his throat and absent-mindedly smoothes down his hair as if about to embark on a blind date. Then he knocks quietly on Petra's front door and waits.

'Hi,' she says with a smile, stepping back to welcome him in.

'Hi.' He smiles awkwardly. 'I hope you don't mind . . .'

'Of course I don't. Come in, I'll get you a drink. What would you like? Beer? Glass of wine?'

Ryan shakes his head as he follows her to the kitchen. 'I'd just like a coffee if that's okay.'

Petra smiles, her raised eyebrows registering surprise as she scoops coffee into the cafetière. 'Are you okay, Ryan? Is something going on?'

'Um . . . sort of.' He perches on the edge of her kitchen table, watching as she takes a mug from the cupboard. Petra looks different tonight; her hair is softer, more natural, her pale, earnest face free of make-up. Instead of her customary crisp white shirt – Ryan always wonders how she manages not to cut her neck on those collars – she's wearing a black long-sleeved top and stretchy black trouser things which Ryan assumes are for yoga. It's the sleepy, night-time Petra whom he hasn't seen for a very long time.

She turns and hands him the mug of coffee. 'Shall we go through?'

'Yes, okay.' He follows her into the living room and they sit a little awkwardly on her low oatmeal-coloured sofa.

'So?' She fixes her clear grey eyes on him.

'Well, I er . . .' he starts.

'Dad?' comes Daisy's voice from the bedroom she shares with Josh. 'Daddy, is that you?'

'Yes, Daddy's here,' Petra calls out softly, 'but it's after midnight, darling. Go back to sleep . . .'

There's a thump of feet and the squeak of a door, followed by the sound of Daisy padding towards them.

'Dad!' she exclaims, appearing in the living room doorway. 'Why are you here at night?'

'Er, I've just come to see Mum.' He smiles broadly, kissing the top of his daughter's head as she wraps her arms around him.

'Have you brought my story?'

'No, no . . . . but I'll find it. I promise. Or you can help me look for it when you're home on Sunday.'

She pulls back, her smile wilting. 'Why did you come then?'

'Daisy.' Petra stands up and places a hand on her daughter's shoulder. 'Sometimes me and Daddy just need to talk.'

'What about?' She frowns and bites her lip.

'Just . . .' Her mother shrugs. 'Just things, sweetheart. Things we don't really get the chance to talk about at any other time.'

'Were you talking about *me*?'

'We weren't talking about anything yet,' Ryan says with a chuckle. 'I've literally been here about five minutes.'

Daisy throws him, then her mother, a quizzical look. 'Can I have a hot chocolate?'

'No,' Petra says with a laugh. 'Bed, Daisy. Come on now, we've got a lot to fit in tomorrow.' Reluctantly, Daisy turns and heads for her room.

Petra looks expectantly at Ryan. He sips his coffee, which is lukewarm now, and swallows hard. He doesn't want to tell her; the Marlboro packet no longer seems like the massive deal it had a few hours ago. Hadn't he sneaked a few ciggies behind the sports block when he was Josh's age? 'Petra,' he murmurs, 'Josh has been smoking.'

She is perfectly still, clear-eyed, lips poised. 'Has he? Are you sure?'

Ryan nods. 'Yeah.'

'How d'you know? Have you smelt it or something?'

'No, I just stumbled on an email of Hannah's where she was telling a friend . . .'

Petra frowns. 'She was telling a friend, but hadn't told you?'

Ryan exhales. This was what he's been thinking too, turning it over and over in his mind. It's what bothers him most about the whole thing. 'Maybe she felt she shouldn't interfere,' he suggests, 'or she didn't want to get Josh into trouble.'

'But she caught him smoking! And didn't even say . . .'

'She didn't catch him exactly,' Ryan says quickly. 'She found a packet with one in it in his jeans pocket.'

'But would her loyalties be with Josh rather than you? I wouldn't have thought so . . .'

Ryan tenses at the word 'loyalties'. What about his loyalty to Hannah who'll be his wife in just two weeks' time? He shouldn't be here at Petra's at twelve-thirty at night. Yet who else can he talk to about Josh? 'I don't know what's going on with Hannah,' he says carefully. 'It's as if there's this whole other thing going on that I know nothing about.'

'What kind of thing, Ryan?' Petra's eyes are filled with concern.

He shakes his head. 'I'm not sure. I just . . .'

'I thought you must be worried about something,' she adds gently, placing a delicate hand on his knee, 'if you've been looking through her emails.'

'I didn't mean to pry,' Ryan insists. 'I was only looking for Daisy's . . .' He stops himself.

'Ryan . . .' Petra's hand is still there, small and warm on his knee. 'No one just stumbles on other people's mails. We read them because we're looking for something, and we only do that when we think something's wrong.'

Ryan blinks at her. Calm, wise, beautiful Petra with her sharp cheekbones and almond-shaped grey eyes. 'You're right,' he murmurs. 'You're absolutely right.'

'So . . .' Her voice is soft, her house so calm and still he can feel his heart thudding. 'Is there something . . . ?'

He looks at her, his ex-wife who decided she no longer loved him three years ago, and realises, with a crushing certainty, that it's happening to him again. 'Petra,' he says, 'we've planned this wedding and it's all going ahead, but I know, when we say those vows, it's going to be all wrong . . .'

'Why?' she asks gently.

'Because Hannah doesn't want to marry me,' he says.

FORTY

Johnny Lynch is sitting on his small sage-green sofa with his laptop open beside him. Lou has been easy to find and, not for the first time in his life, Johnny gives a brief, silent thanks to Saint Google. He studies her home page:

Lou Costello Jewellery Designs
- Home
- Gallery
- Contact artist

Contact artist. Of course he can't. After all this time, having abruptly cut ties, he can't just lurch back into her life. Anyway, if that really had been her, Sadie and Hannah in that pretentious-looking basement bar – which is highly unlikely, Johnny decides – then Lou will hardly be picking up her emails right now.

Instead, he browses Lou's gallery pictures as he sips a beer. Her jewellery is quite breathtaking, and Johnny isn't even a jewellery person. Each piece is incredibly delicate, like a precious thing found on a beach. Bracelets resemble shards of shell and coral, and a pearl-encrusted brooch looks as if it might have been plucked from the seabed. For one mad moment, Johnny considers posing as a buyer and emailing to ask for more details. As Lou hasn't put any prices on the site, it would be perfectly feasible. But what would be the point? It would just be weird, and Johnny has lived alone for long enough – nine years now – to be aware that weirdness can creep up on you without you noticing. If he hadn't had Cal to think about, Johnny is pretty confident that he'd have descended into Weirdness Central by now.

He sits back, sipping his beer, thinking about Cal nagging him to go in and speak to those girls. How spineless is he, not even having the courage to do that? What kind of message is he sending his son? Cal wouldn't have held back. He's the kind of boy who'll march into any situation – first evening at scouts, a birthday party where he barely knows a soul – and within minutes everyone knows what Cal Lynch is all about.

Johnny clicks on 'Contact'.

Lou Costello, Flat 2, 67 Winston Street, York YO16 7AZ.
Phone: 01906 334774
Email: enquiries@loucostellojewellery.com

It's all there, laid out on his screen. A landline, not a mobile. Well, that's better than nothing. He could phone right now even though, at 12.37 am, it's far too late to be calling anyone. If she doesn't answer, there might at least be a mobile number on the answerphone message. And if she *does* pick up, he'll know it wasn't her in that bar.

Picking up the handset, Johnny starts to tap out her number. At the penultimate digit, he pauses, his finger hovering over the button. A few millimetres, one tiny movement of his index finger – that's how close he is from speaking to Lou Costello again. He jabs at the 4, catching his breath as it rings and the answerphone kicks in. *Hi, can't get to the phone right now, please leave a message after the beep. Thanks. Bye!*

Brisk, perky, just like the Lou he remembers. At the sound of her voice, Johnny is left momentarily speechless. He opens his mouth. There are a few seconds of crackling, then the beep. 'Er, hi Lou, it's me! Erm . . . Johnny. D'you remember? From upstairs at your old Glasgow flat? God, I know it's been years. Look, I know it's horribly late and you'll probably think this is completely bizarre . . .' He's sweating now, and nearly loses his grip on the handset. 'Um, I was out tonight and I noticed these people in this little cocktail place in Bath Street, can't remember what it's called, and I thought I saw you! Sitting at a table by the window with two girls who looked just like Hannah and Sadie, and you were there too, at least someone who looked exactly like you, with your boyfriend . . .' He stops abruptly. This is coming out all wrong. Fuck, he sounds completely berserk, like some mad stalker, prone to peering in through windows at bunches of girls having a perfectly nice Friday night out. 'Er . . . but of course, if you are in Glasgow, you won't be picking up this message,' he adds with a strained chuckle. 'So anyway, bye!'

He slams the handset down and sinks back into the sofa. 'Bloody idiot,' he mutters out loud. Leaning forward then, and pressing his knuckles so far into his temples that it actually hurts, Johnny decides that the only thing for it is to take himself to bed. He turns off his laptop and tips the rest of his beer down his throat. Then he marches through to his small, orderly bedroom to pull off his clothes, crawl under the duvet and try to convince himself that his deranged call to Lou Costello had never happened.

FORTY-ONE

Barney has cocked up big time. His sons are merrily kicking and swiping at the dangling objects on their gigantic activity arch as if it's the middle of the day and not an ungodly 1.15 am. He's tried everything to coax them cotwards: singing, rocking, bathing them and feeding them copious amounts of milk. He's even changed them into fresh sleep-suits in case his initial choice had been uncomfortable or regarded as a style faux pas.

'Are they normally as lively as this?' asks Pete, regarding the scene with undisguised relief that, for him, this is a one-off and not a regular occurrence.

'No,' Barney says, trying to keep the agitation out of his voice. 'Not when Sadie's here. They're usually in bed by about nine.' He stops himself from adding, *That's because Sadie has strict schedules to be adhered to, and this is what happens when you flaunt the rules.* There's no 'winging it' with babies, he realises now. When Sadie was pregnant, he'd imagined the two of them continuing to travel, as they had pre-children: trekking through Peru or India, each transporting a baby on their backs. Now, it feels like an almighty feat to strap them into the car and drive them to his parents' place in Hertfordshire.

What had he been thinking, allowing his children that long, luxurious evening nap in the beer garden – so close to bath and bedtime – while he and Pete chatted up two young girls?

'Wonder what their photo shoot will be about tomorrow?' Pete muses, installed in the comfiest armchair in the room and sipping from his bottle of beer.

Barney glances at him. With Milo on his lap and the *My Little Farm* picture book open in front of him, he tries to convince himself that it's *fine* to meet up with the girls tomorrow.

'God knows,' he murmurs, pointing to one of the pictures. 'Horse,' he adds, 'look, Milo, horse. *Neeeeiiigh* . . . just don't embarrass me, all right? I live here, remember, and Magda works in the café in the park.'

'What would I do to embarrass you?' Pete exclaims, observing Dylan as he crawls across the rug towards his father.

'Cow. Moo . . . . Oh, I dunno. Flirt madly, try to get off with a twenty-year-old.'

'Twenty's all right!' Pete protests. 'Twenty's hardly, y'know, jail-bait.'

Rolling his eyes, Barney turns the page, reaching down to lift Dylan up onto his other knee while keeping Milo firmly clasped on his lap. 'Look,' he says brightly with both sons now staring intently at the book. 'That's the farmer's wife. *Lady* . . .'

Dylan stiffens. 'Mama . . .'

'Yes, Mama . . .'

'Mama,' he cries, more forcefully now, causing his brother to flinch.

'Well, no, it's not really Mama,' Barney explains. 'It's just a lady – the farmer's wife – and she doesn't look *anything* like Mama, does she, with that funny bun hairdo . . .'

'Mama!' Dylan cries, swiping at the page.

'I think she quite liked me,' Pete muses.

'Who?'

'Amy . . .' He grins smugly.

'But I thought you were seeing . . .'

'MAMA!' Dylan cries as Barney quickly turns the page.

'No,' he murmurs. 'Mama gone . . .'

'*Waaaagh!*' Dylan yells.

'I didn't mean Mama gone, not real Mummy, she's only in Glasgow, I mean the book one, we've turned the page now . . .' He looks down. While Milo is whimpering, Dylan's mouth has opened in a great circle of misery as he thrashes around on Barney's lap.

'It was only a casual thing with Christina,' Pete explains, seemingly immune to Dylan's anguished cries. 'And Amy's cute, don't you think . . . God, are babies always like this?'

'Yeah, no, they're just unsettled . . . look, could you go to the fridge, top shelf, there are two bottles in there . . .'

Pete holds up his bottle of Becks. 'It's okay, I've only just started this . . .'

'Not beer! *Milk*. There are two bottles, defrosted, that I've kept in reserve. There's only a little bit in each but it'll probably be enough to send them off . . .'

'Er, right.' Pete stands up and places his beer at his feet, but doesn't seem to be going anywhere.

Barney looks at him. 'The fridge, Pete. In the kitchen.'

'Oh, yeah.' Pulling his lips tight, Pete gives the wailing babies a worried glance as he hurries out of the room.

Barney breathes deeply as he hears the fridge door open. 'Right,' Pete mutters, as if confronted by a virtually insurmountable task. 'You mean this bottle on the shelf in the door, right?'

'Yep. Bring two, though. They haven't got their heads around the concept of sharing yet.' Despite the now stereo crying, Barney is trying to sound light and jovial for his old mate who's schlepped all the way out to deepest Cambridgeshire to see him.

Pete reappears in the living room and thrusts the two bottles at Pete. At the sight of them, Milo and Dylan wail and kick furiously. 'No, I should have said they don't like it fridge-cold . . .'

'Er . . . what should I do then?' Glancing down at the distraught babies, Pete takes several steps back. 'Heat it up in the microwave?'

'No!' Barney exclaims, louder than he intended.

Pete frowns. 'Why not?'

'Because it could burn their mouths . . .'

'God, Barney,' Pete guffaws. 'I might not have kids, but I *am* capable of microwaving a couple of bottles without heating them to, like, two hundred degrees . . .'

'Yeah, I know,' Barney snaps, 'but the books say microwaves heat liquids unevenly and there can be dangerous hot spots.'

'Right,' Pete says slowly.

'It's just . . .' Barney shrugs, deciding not to even attempt to talk his friend through the workings of the bottle warmer, 'it's safer to run them under the hot tap, if that's okay.'

Pete smiles condescendingly. 'Sure. I think I can manage that.'

Barney waits, jigging his children rhythmically on his knee. It takes Pete what feels like forever to warm the two stubby bottles and thrust them at Barney.

'You couldn't feed Milo for me, could you?' Barney asks.

Pete stands before him, gripping the bottles like a couple of grenades. 'Well, um . . . I've never actually held a baby before. And babies don't like me. They think I'm a terrifying, horrible man. Look . . .' He focuses hard on Milo and Dylan who are no longer crying but gazing expectantly at Pete.

Barney laughs. 'Looks like you've bonded already. Here you go . . .'

'Well . . . . All right then. If you're sure . . .' Pete hands him one of the bottles, then cautiously lifts Milo from his lap.

'Of course I'm sure.'

'I just don't know how to . . . *do* this.'

'Just sit down with him and pop the teat in. Nothing to it . . .'

'Okay . . .' Pete treads gingerly towards the armchair, carrying Milo as if he were made from the finest glass, and lowers himself into it. 'Just pop it in?' he repeats.

'Uh-huh.'

'What are you sniggering at?'

'Just this. You and me, feeding a baby each. Who'd have thought . . .'

'Yeah.' Pete chuckles as Milo starts to suck vigorously on the teat. 'Actually, this isn't so bad. I don't see what people make so much fuss about. All those books, the parenting classes – God, it's hardly rocket science is it?'

'Well, there's a bit more to it than this,' Barney says with a grin.

'Is there?' Pete pauses. 'Yeah, well, I suppose there's the nappies and being woken up at night occasionally, and maybe not being able to go out as much as you used to . . .'

No, Barney wants to tell his friend. *Of course there's all that, but that's fine, that's all perfectly manageable compared to what it does to you as a person, and the woman you love, the sexy party girl with feline eyes who suddenly, without warning, decides that you're a crappy excuse for a father. Not that she says so exactly, at least not with words. But with a look* . . . Barney is chewing this over when Pete cries, 'Oh, fuck!' and Milo emits a startled peep as the top plops off the bottle and milk sloshes all over Pete's left trouser leg.

'Oh my God,' Barney exclaims.

'What happened?' Pete cries.

'You mustn't have put the top on properly!'

'I didn't *touch* the top. I just took it out of the fridge like you said . . .'

'You can't have, you must have fiddled about with it . . .'

'Why the hell would I fiddle—'

'Well, it's never fallen off like that before . . .'

'Can't you just make up some more?' Pete asks.

'No! It's not actually physically possible . . .' Pete peers at him uncomprehendingly. 'That was one of the reserve bottles,' Barney snaps over Milo's cries, 'the stuff I'd kept back in case of emergencies.'

'What stuff?'

'Breast milk.'

'What, this is breast milk?' Pete glares down at his wet trouser leg. 'Like . . . *out of Sadie?*'

'Of course it's out of Sadie! Who else would it be out of?'

'Well, I . . .' He studies the milk stain with revulsion. 'It just feels a bit weird, that's all . . .'

'It *is* natural, you know . . .'

'I know, I'm sorry,' Pete mutters, standing up and cradling Milo to his chest before handing him back to his father.

'It's okay,' Barney mutters as Pete picks up a discarded bib from the coffee table and tries to dab himself dry. 'Just don't mention this to Sadie, all right?'

Pete frowns, and Barney notices that a large, damp patch has appeared on the armchair. 'Why not?'

He breathes slowly, wondering now if his oldest friend will ever come out to visit him again. 'Because,' he says quietly, 'it took her about four hours to express that milk.'

FORTY-TWO

There are three answerphone messages when Spike returns home. One is from his mother who, for some unfathomable reason, thinks he's keen to hear about Annie Bartholomew, an old neighbour of theirs – correction, not Annie Bartholomew, a joyless crone who'd once knifed a football Spike had kicked into her garden. No, the hot news concerns Annie's daughter who'd been happily married and then gone off – just like that – with her daughter's best friend's father. *Nice of Annie to visit . . . we do like visitors, you know. Breaks up the long days. But Annie's daughter, you remember the blonde one, big legs, she's gone off the rails . . . don't know what she sees in him, always thought he was a layabout . . .*

Spike tunes out, removing his footwear and rubbing the sore bit where his bare left heel has been rubbing violently against the back of his shoe. 'And on top of all that,' his mother adds, 'Annie's had bother with that catheter.' Spike shudders, making a mental note to never turn into the kind of person who relishes talking about other people's malfunctioning internal organs, even if he lives to be a hundred and five, which is unlikely, considering his lifestyle. 'We haven't heard from you for a long time, Donald,' his

246

mum goes on. 'Why don't you and Lou come up sometime? We'd love to see you – *both* of you – and could you please thank her for that brooch she sent for my birthday? It's very pretty, bit modern for me but I'll try wearing it on my camel coat . . .'

Spike flicks on the gas fire and sits cross-legged on the living room carpet, noticing a smattering of crumbs embedded in it. Why does his mother still insist on calling him Donald? Spike's real name is Donald Wren. Not just a bird, but the smallest, least significant native bird in Britain – although Spike often consoles himself with the fact that it could have been worse, it could have been Puffin or Tit. Even so, Spike grew up always knowing he'd be a musician, and that Donald Wren was no name for a star. He's been Spike since he was thirteen years old. As his mother's voice warbles on, he gets up and flops onto the sofa. The cushions are squashed flat from his earlier lounging, but he can't be bothered to plump them up. That's the kind of thing Lou does – plump cushions, wipe the kitchen worktops, place packets of mangetout in the fridge. If she *is* up to something with that Felix and it splits them up – and by now, Spike's pretty sure she isn't – he wonders if living a single man's life, with no cushion plumping going on, would not be that bad after all. 'Anyway, bye, Donald,' his mother trills. There's a pause, as if she expects the machine to say 'bye' in response. 'Er . . . I'll just go then,' she mumbles, unable to disguise the hurt in her voice.

'Hey, Lou!' chirps Steph, Lou's work friend, as the second message clicks in. 'I know you're away, hope you're having an amazing time, just wanted to let you know I'm having a girls' night round at my place next Thursday, about eight-ish . . . make sure you keep it free, okay? There's quite a few coming over . . .' Spike frowns at the phone, wondering why thirty-something women insist on referring to themselves as 'girls', and why they enjoy clustering together in girly groups whenever they get the chance. It's not that Spike doesn't *like* Lou's friends. In fact, he always enjoyed being around Sadie and Hannah in Garnet Street, especially when they were drifting around all damp-haired and towel-clad after a bath. Yet he always suspected that, no matter how friendly they were with him, he was somehow hovering around the edge of the group, and never wholeheartedly welcomed in. Perhaps they were in awe of him. That was probably it, he concedes as Steph finishes her message with an irksome 'bye, sweetie!'

The third message starts to play. *Er, hi Lou, it's me! Erm . . . Johnny . . .* At the sound of his voice, Spike springs up as if jabbed with a cattle prod. *D'you remember? From upstairs at your old Glasgow flat? God, I know it's been years. Look, er, I know it's horribly late and you'll probably think this is completely bizarre . . .'* Jesus Christ. Spike thought that hanger-on had disappeared from Lou's life years ago. *This might sound mad but I was out tonight and I noticed these people in this little cocktail place in Bath Street, can't remember what it's called, and I looked down to the basement and I thought I saw you! Sitting at a table by the window with two girls who looked just like Hannah and Sadie, and you were there too, at least someone who looked exactly like you, with your boyfriend . . .'* Her boyfriend? What the hell is she up to? *Er . . . but of course, if you are in Glasgow you won't be picking up this message . . . so anyway, bye!*

Spike blinks at the phone, all traces of alcohol instantly evaporating from his bloodstream. He needs to hear that message again to make sure he hasn't gone stark raving crazy. It's a clunky old answerphone, and in order to play it again, he'll first have to listen to his mother rambling on about catheters, and Steph's girly invitation.

All through the messages, he sits, tension building in his

shoulders and brain until it's Johnny Lynch again, who just *happened* to spot Lou and the others sitting in a bar by the window – was he stalking them or what? And who the hell was this 'boyfriend' – Felix, the ponce with the truffles? Lou must have been kissing him or wrapped up in his arms at the very least. Spike's fury morphs into acute anguish as he stands up, swipes ineffectually at the cream plastic phone on the coffee table and marches through to the kitchen – *their* kitchen, where Lou has cooked him billions of meals, with a slight overreliance on the wok, maybe, while he chatted about the details of his day. The first tear startles him, oozing without warning as he lowers himself onto a chair. He's crying over Lou and this *boyfriend* in Glasgow, and he's crying over sleeping with Astrid, which he should never have done, and the guitar his dad bought him, having saved up the money for months because Spike – sorry, *Donald* – had begged for one.

He virtually gave away the guitar to Rick at Sound Shack – let a precious thing go, just like that. And now he's lost Lou too. It was karma, he thinks bleakly. If he hadn't sold the guitar, simply so he could spend all weekend having it away with Astrid Stone, then his life wouldn't be one great bloody car crash right now.

Blundering back into the living room, Spike looms over the phone, hands bunched into tight fists. Then he picks up the receiver and dials Charlie.

'Hey,' Charlie says, 'you all right, Spike? Get home okay?'

'Er, yeah. Yeah. Um . . . just wondered, d'you have that guy's number, what's-his-name . . .'

'Huh?'

'The roadie. The one in the Spanish bar. Henry, was it?'

'It's Harry . . . why?'

Spike purses his lips and exhales, making a noise like

air hissing out of a punctured tyre. 'Um . . . you know, I was thinking I might go to Glasgow with them in the morning, just for a laugh.' He chuckles unconvincingly, fixing his gaze firmly on the brandy bottle on the coffee table, as if it might somehow anchor his thoughts.

'You mean you're going to check up on Lou?' Charlie exclaims. 'Just because she put some pissed bloke on the phone to you?'

'No!' Spike retorts. 'Of course not . . .'

'So why d'you want to go, then?'

'I just . . .' He takes a deep breath. 'Just thought I could come along for the ride,' he adds feebly, 'so if you could give me that number . . .' That's better. He needs to make it sound like a jaunt, rather than a desperate attempt to salvage his relationship.

Charlie makes a snorting noise. 'No need, Spike. He's right here. We came back to their hotel bar for a little nightcap. I'll put him on . . .'

'Hey, Spike,' Harry says, sounding even younger on the phone than he did in Bar Circa.

'Er, hi. I was just wondering, are you, er . . . still heading up to Glasgow tomorrow?'

'Yeah, 'course we are . . .'

'You know what?' Spike is pacing his living room now, hoping it'll make him feel calmer. 'I think I'll come, if you're still all right about that. Just for the ride . . .'

'Right, and your girlfriend just happens to be there on that hen weekend,' Harry reminds him with a snigger.

'Yes. Yeah, she is! So it'll be, er . . . good. To see her, I mean . . .' There's an awkward pause, and Spike feels himself breaking into a sweat.

Okay,' Harry says warily. 'Well, we've got room like I said. Can you come over before ten? Know where we're staying?'

'Yeah, I know it . . .'

'See you bright and early then.' There's a burst of laughter in the background, but Spike doesn't care. He's going to Glasgow tomorrow – in an ambulance – to reclaim the woman he loves.

FORTY-THREE

Sadie wakes up just before seven, taking in the unfamiliar layout of the room. Pale light filters in through a sash window, and there's already the hum of city traffic in the street below. Sadie remembers her bespoke cocktail, although she can no longer recall what was in it – something vaguely toffee-ish – and she remembers dancing like she hasn't danced in years. But after that, it's all just a blur of somehow making their way back to the hotel and something about the lift being broken . . . then . . . nothing.

Despite her hangover, Sadie is shimmeringly awake. The babies have usually been up for at least an hour by now, and even with a fuzzy head, she is no longer capable of sleeping in. She glances to the left: no Barney, of course. Instead, in the single bed next to hers, Lou is sleeping, her hair fanned out on the pillow, one bare foot poking out from under a crumpled white sheet. Sadie can't see Hannah but she's probably still asleep, bunched up under the fleecy blanket.

Sadie tries to will herself back to sleep, thinking she should make the most of this opportunity. Isn't a lie-in the thing she's craved most during the past few months?

Not today, though. It's no use. Every time she closes

her eyes, they ping straight open again. This is it then, she reflects, studying a ragged crack in the ceiling. She's spent a whole night away from her children – in *another country* – and it would appear that everything is okay. The sky hasn't fallen in, the police haven't called her; there haven't even been any panicky phone calls from Barney. Just a brief chat late yesterday afternoon, when he'd been waiting for Pete to arrive. Sadie's glad that Barney has had adult company. She knows how empty and hollow adult-free days can be and wants his first experience of being in sole charge of the children to be as pleasant as possible.

With a small pang, Sadie wonders what they're doing now. They'll be up, of course – although perhaps not Pete. Barney will probably be feeding the boys, or warming bottles – she hopes he won't put the boys in their bouncy seats and prop up their bottles on rolled-up blankets, as she once caught him doing. That's not recommended in the baby books.

Sadie sits up in bed, now a little anxious at the thought of her precious babies feeding from bottles not being held by actual human hands. No, she's just being silly. Something else is niggling her, something about last night in Felix's bar. A wave of anxiety washes over her. Surely she didn't do anything truly awful. No, Hannah and Lou would have stopped her.

The sloshing of water in the bathroom gives Sadie a start. She realises now that the furthest bed doesn't contain a sleeping Hannah after all. Slipping out from under her sheets, she catches her reflection in the mirrored wardrobe door. Her eye shadow is still on, all smudged and smeary, and a trace of wonky red liner outlines her lips. Sadie hasn't slept with make-up on since her student days. Her mobile rings, and she grabs it from the bedside table. 'Barney! Hi, how's things?' She's thankful he can't see the state she's in.

'Fine, all good . . . so how's it going with you? Have a fun time last night?'

I have absolutely no bloody idea . . . 'Yeah, it was great, just a few bars, you know . . . bit of dancing and stuff . . .' She clamps her mouth shut, conscious of a vein throbbing in her forehead.

'You sound a bit rough,' he says teasingly.

'No, I'm fine, just woken up. How about you? Did Pete stay over?'

'Yeah, we just had a few beers, y'know . . .'

Sadie bites her lip. In the bathroom, Hannah is humming softly. 'It sounds really quiet now. Are the boys okay?'

'Yep, just had breakfast . . .'

'Did they settle last night?'

'They were fine, stop worrying . . .'

Sadie frowns. She hadn't said she was worried, yet her voice must be laced with anxiety. A fragment of memory sneaks into her mind. Of her, dancing – not with Sadie or Hannah, but someone else . . . 'I'm not worried,' she says firmly. 'I know you're totally capable, and if I'm sounding weird it's probably just being away from the babies and feeling—'

'You don't sound weird,' Barney corrects her. 'Just a bit tired, that's all. I shouldn't have rung you so early, but . . .' He pauses. 'I miss you, Sadie.'

'I miss you too,' she murmurs. 'So what are you up to today? Is Pete staying for a while?'

'Yeah, I think so – just see what happens I guess . . .' They finish the call, with Sadie silently cursing herself for sounding so shifty. 'Han?' she murmurs at the bathroom door.

'Uh-huh?'

'You're up early. Are you okay?'

'Yes, I'm good . . . I'll be out in a minute if you want a bath. Don't worry – you don't have to use my water, although I haven't even cut my nails . . .'

Sadie takes a deep breath, trying to shake off her unease as Hannah emerges in a bath towel and gives her a quizzical look. 'So . . . how are *you* feeling?' she asks with a grin.

'I'm all right . . . I think. Bit fuzzy. Boobs sore from not feeding.'

Hannah frowns. 'Anything you can do about that?'

'Express milk,' Sadie says, wincing. 'I'll do it in the shower in a minute.'

'Right . . .' Hannah hesitates.

'Um . . . how much did I have to drink last night?'

'Not loads. Apart from that champagne on the train, maybe two or three cocktails . . .'

'Is that all?' Sadie exclaims. 'Because all I can remember is being in Felix's bar, chatting and then dancing, and then it all goes . . .' She shakes her head fretfully. 'It's all blurred. I think one of my drinks might've been spiked . . .'

Hannah smiles kindly. 'Sadie, they weren't spiked. Think about it – how long is it since you've had a drink?'

Sadie frowns. 'Well, I haven't drunk at all since having the kids, with breastfeeding . . .'

'Really? Not one drink?'

'No . . .'

'And during your pregnancy . . .'

'None then either.' Surely that makes her a good person – one who, before yesterday, hadn't had a sniff of alcohol for over a year. 'Blimey,' she murmurs, 'I didn't realise it had been that long.'

Hannah smiles. 'No wonder it rushed straight to your head. So don't worry. It didn't mean anything . . .'

'*What* didn't mean anything?' Sadie shrieks, waking Lou who springs up in alarm.

'Just, you know . . .' Hannah takes her arm as they perch side by side on Sadie's unmade bed. The patent shoes lie accusingly on their sides on the floor, and the contents of Sadie's bag have spilt out beside them.

'Tell me I didn't sleep with anyone,' she breathes.

'Of course not! You were just having a great time, that's all . . .'

Sadie shudders. She knows what that means. Lou is also at her side now, warm and comforting in rumpled polka-dot pyjamas. 'You were dancing,' she offers. 'That's all, really . . .'

'And one guy in particular was pretty taken with you,' Hannah adds.

'Who?' Sadie croaks.

'Dark hair, glasses, don't know his name,' Lou says, 'but you were just having a laugh, not much more to it than that . . .'

'Not *much* more?'

'. . . Well there was that *little* kiss,' Hannah adds.

'A kiss?' Sadie turns pale. She kissed someone? That wasn't part of the plan. What the hell was she thinking?

'Just a peck really,' Lou says quickly as Sadie sweeps her hands across her face. 'A little peck, like a bird. It was nothing . . .'

'*Less* than nothing,' Hannah insists.

Sadie places her hands on her knees and looks at each of her friends in turn. 'Honestly? You're not just trying to make me feel better?'

'Honestly,' Lou says firmly. 'It was just harmless fun.'

Sadie exhales loudly, telling herself that a peck is really nothing – God, she routinely pecks the hostesses at all those coffee mornings she goes to. Yet how would she feel if Barney was indulging in a little 'harmless fun' back home in Little Hissingham right now? There's no such thing, she realises – and besides, she's a *mother*. A breastfeeding, veg-mashing, picture-book-reading mother in her big bra and pants.

'Stop worrying,' Hannah says gently. 'If you'd done anything else we'd have told you. It was just that kiss – I mean peck – apart from the other little thing . . .'

'What?' Sadie asks, heart pounding. 'What the hell did I do?'

Hannah's mouth quivers, and a bubble of laughter bursts out before she can stop it. 'You gave him your number,' she giggles, 'written in lip liner on a breast pad.'

FORTY-FOUR

The Glasgow morning is bright and blue-skied with the sharpness of spring in the air. Hannah's brain feels a little cloudy, and there's an ache in her calves from dancing, but she feels glad to be alive. As she turns into Sauchiehall Street, on a vague quest to fetch decent coffees, she experiences a rush of gratitude towards Sadie and Lou for sharing this weekend with her. Whatever decision she makes, she feels now, will be the right one.

It's 9.35 am and the street is already beginning to fill up with Saturday shoppers and *Big Issue* sellers starting their day. Despite being gone for so long, Hannah still feels at home here. Seeing a bridal shop, Hannah stops and looks into the window. The bride's dress on the headless mannequin looks stiff and unyielding in cream satin. But the dress next to it, designed for a bridesmaid perhaps, in a stunning poppy red, is lovely. Do bridesmaids ever wear red? Is it for a guest, perhaps? Hannah stares at the beautiful knee-length, sleeveless, nipped-in-at-the-waist dress and she wants it.

She can't have it, of course, because she's already bought a dress, and isn't there some superstition about the colour? *Get married in red, wish yourself dead,* an aunt of

Hannah's had once muttered at a family wedding when the bride had worn daring fuchsia. Not that Hannah believes such rubbish. Anyway, the shop doesn't open until 10.30 and it's probably hugely expensive. Walking on, Hannah calls home. When Ryan doesn't pick up, she tries his mobile.

'Hi,' he says gruffly.

'Sorry, have I woken you up?'

'No, no, it's just . . . How are you anyway? You're up early . . .'

'Just thought I'd call to prove I didn't get completely wasted last night,' she says with a grin. 'I'm not even lazing in bed. The other two are – I've been sent out on a mission for coffees . . .'

'Right,' he says vaguely.

'Are you okay?' she asks, registering music in the background: classical music, something sombre and dark, not Ryan's usual kind of thing at all.

'Yes, I'm fine,' he says dully.

'Well, you don't sound it,' she persists. 'I did wake you up, didn't I?'

'No, it's *fine*.' The music is louder now – mournful and stirring, quite beautiful, and at odds with a street full of shoppers on a Saturday morning.

'What's that in the background?' she asks.

'Just music,' Ryan says.

'Sounds like a cello. It's lovely actually. Have you gone all classical since I've been away?'

'No, it's just . . .'

She pauses, holding the phone to her ear. 'Ryan . . . what *is* that music?'

'Um, Elgar's Cello Concerto Number One.'

Hannah has stopped in front of a department store in which everything is 70% off. 'I didn't know you had that,' she says quietly.

'I . . . I don't,' he mutters. 'It's, um . . . Petra playing.'

'Petra's playing her cello at our house?'

'No . . . I'm at Petra's.'

Hannah blinks at her reflection in the shop window. It's okay, she tells herself. Something's happened – Ryan's had to drive over to Crouch End to sort out something to do with the kids. 'Why? What's happened?'

'Er, nothing . . .'

'Why are you there then?'

'I just needed to talk to Petra about something last night . . .'

'You stayed the *night*?' The music has changed, becoming lighter and brighter, swooping up and down with such lightness and beauty that Hannah could cry. Tears prickle her eyes, and she blinks them away.

'Yes, on the *sofa* . . .' he says defensively, the music fading as, presumably, he takes his phone somewhere more private.

'Ryan, what's going on?'

'I . . . I read your email—'

Hannah's entire body goes cold. 'Which email?'

'I didn't mean to,' he says quickly. 'I was looking for Daisy's story, the one you let her write on your computer . . .' He pauses, and without having to ask, Hannah knows which email he means. 'The one you sent to Sadie and Lou,' Ryan continues. 'All the stuff about the kids, them hating you, you finding a packet of cigarettes in Josh's pocket . . .'

'I . . . I didn't know whether to . . .' Hannah feels as if her heart is in her throat.

'And about you dreading getting married to me.'

'I'm not dreading it,' she exclaims. 'That's *not* what I meant, Ryan, honestly . . .' She looks around at the bustling street, and can still see the burst of red in the wedding shop window.

'Yes you are,' he snaps. 'You told Sadie and Hannah but you haven't said a word of any of this to me.'

'Ryan, you know it's not easy living with—'

'So I came over last night because of the cigarettes, he's our *son*.'

'I know he's your son!' Hannah barks.

'And I needed to talk it over with Petra.'

'Yes, I'm sure you did,' she says firmly, 'and that's fine, but you need to know that I didn't tell Sadie and Lou about all that, I didn't send the mail, in fact I never intended to. I meant to delete it . . .'

'Well, it still doesn't make me feel great,' he mutters.

'I don't feel great either, knowing you slept at Petra's!'

'On the *sofa* . . .'

'Really?'

'Yes, really!' he shouts. Hannah stands dead still. The cello music has stopped, or at least he's far enough away from Petra that she can't hear it. Beside her, an elderly lady pulls out a handful of biscuits from her coat pocket and scatters them on the street. A flurry of pigeons descend to feast on them.

'We should talk about this when I get back tomorrow,' Hannah says, breathing steadily to level out her voice.

'Yep.'

'And . . . whatever you think, whatever I wrote in that email you have to know that I love—' she starts, but her words are cut short, not by the cello virtuoso, but by Daisy who yells, sounding as if she's millimetres from the phone, 'Daddy, Mummy says breakfast is ready! She's made pancakes.'

'Erm . . . right,' Ryan says, clearing his throat.

'I'll let you get on with your breakfast,' Hannah says coolly, glaring down at a pigeon that's pecking close to her feet.

'Um, okay. I'll call you later.'

261

'Enjoy them,' she says tersely. 'Enjoy those *pancakes* . . .'

'All right,' he snaps, and before finishing the call Hannah hears Petra's perky voice in the background, possibly enquiring whether Ryan would like her to cut the pancakes into teeny pieces and feed him morsel by morsel herself.

*

Hannah has forgotten about her mission to bring back three lattes and has passed numerous coffee shops by the time she swerves, mindlessly, off Sauchiehall Street. *Pancakes.* She didn't even know Ryan liked them. Marching determinedly up the steep, straight hill, she pictures Petra topping up the kids' glasses with cranberry or blueberry or some other health-giving purplish juice, and Ryan's white porcelain cup with fresh coffee.

It hasn't taken much, she thinks darkly, for the family to come back together. *Just one day.* It should have been an omen – that plain little nurse dress, which Hannah probably chose precisely because it was so inoffensive and therefore unlikely to trigger adverse reactions from Daisy or Josh. *That's* what she's done, she realises now: tried to make herself as unobtrusive as possible. Unobtrusive and so damned *nice* – letting Daisy use her computer, and even offering to type up the story.

And that shopping trip – what had happened there? Hannah was virtually accused of starving the child, forcing her to tramp the West End streets fuelled only by a lump of dry bread, and dragging her off to have her – what was Petra's phrase again? – lobes punctured! Well, she's sick of being nice. Maybe that's why Hannah doesn't paint any more – there's no room for ideas with all the niceness clogging up her brain. As she catches her breath and stops to take in her surroundings, she realises she's standing in front of 61 Garnet Street.

Hannah stares up at the tall tenement block and a flood of memories come rushing back. So many parties, Hannah reflects, all thoughts of Petra and pancakes and Elgar's whatever-it-was ebbing away as she feels herself tumbling back into the past. A woman's face appears at the first floor window and Hannah quickly turns away. She looks over the city, feeling a calmness descend as she takes in the jumble of buildings fading into the hazy hills beyond. Hannah hears a door opening and someone coming out, and when she turns again she sees it's her old front door, still painted a gloomy maroon, with all the bells for the flats on the right. An older woman, in her fifties perhaps, is stepping out into the street, her flame-red hair piled up artfully with large, perilously heavy-looking earrings dangling at her cheeks. 'Are you lost or something?' she asks pleasantly.

'Oh, no . . .' Hannah shakes her head quickly and smiles. 'This might sound silly but I used to live there. I suppose I've just come for a look.'

'When was that?' the woman asks.

'Well, I left thirteen years ago now . . . there were three of us, all students.'

'Ahh.' The woman grins, her green eyes twinkling playfully. 'We must have bought it from your landlord. Orange wallpaper?' She grins and raises a heavily-pencilled brow.

Hannah laughs. 'That's right.'

'Sparkly lino on the bathroom floor?'

'Yes, that was ours . . .' The woman pauses, not seeming in any hurry to leave, and Hannah glances quickly at the second-floor flat. 'We were friends with the guy upstairs,' she adds. 'Johnny Lynch – did you know him?'

'Johnny?' the woman repeats. 'Yes, he moved out just before the baby was born. Not ideal, is it, all those stairs with a pram . . .'

Hannah shakes her head.

'. . . Shame it didn't work out . . .'

'Didn't it? We kind of lost touch . . .'

'Us too, for a while,' the woman explains. 'We'd become pretty friendly in a short time. He was a chef back then . . .'

'He was still on his catering course when I knew him.'

'Well, my husband manages a restaurant,' the woman continues, her earrings swinging like pendulums as she talks, 'and Johnny worked for him for a while. But the shifts weren't fitting in with his new baby, and I don't think . . .' She presses her lips together and frowns. 'Things weren't good between him and Rona. It wasn't really anyone's fault. You know how it is with a new baby . . .'

'Oh yes,' Hannah fibs.

'They thought that having a bigger place out of town would help.' Hannah nods, willing the woman to go on. 'Then, sadly, they split up . . . and now he's back.'

'What, in Garnet Street?' Hannah exclaims.

'No, but just round the corner . . .' The woman points up the hill, indicating the adjacent street. 'Can't remember the number, but Johnny's flat is at the furthest end, top floor.'

'Really?'

The woman nods. 'Good friends, were you?'

'Oh yes.' Hannah laughs. 'Sometimes I think that without Johnny, we'd have starved or at least had malnutrition.'

She chuckles warmly. 'Well, as I said, he's given that up. He's been gardening these past few years, has an allotment somewhere. He and Cal are up there most weekends.'

'Cal?' Hannah repeats.

'His son. Must be about twelve now – I lose track. You should pop round and see him. Bet he'd love to see you.'

With that, the woman turns to go. Hannah stands in

the now deserted street, then heads up the small hill and round to the left, to the very last door in the terrace. Outside Johnny's flat, she casts a quick look up at the cloudless blue sky. Her finger hovers over the buzzer which reads FLAT 2B J LYNCH, and her heart quickens as she presses it.

FORTY-FIVE

The morning is going well. While Pete has dozed off on the sofa bed, shrouded in a spare duvet and seemingly unperturbed by the activity going on around him, Barney has put on a wash, wiped down the kitchen and swept the floor, all the while keeping an eye on his babies who've been mercifully content on their play mat with its various stuffed cotton animals.

He is multi-tasking. That's something men aren't supposed to be able to do. Well, Barney can, *and* he's been up since 5.47 am, having fed and dressed his sons and changed their nappies twice (remembering to use their nappy rash cream and scented sacks which, to his mind, smell far worse than anything that spurts out of a baby's bottom). He's starting to flag a little now – on a normal day, a weekday that is, he'd have merely sat on the train to King's Cross, caught the tube to Holborn and installed himself at his gloriously uncluttered desk. At this point – it's just gone 10 am – he'd be peeling the plastic lid from his morning Americano and taking that first delicious sip. Barney hasn't had time for coffee yet – he's barely had time to pee – and nor has he had the chance to reflect on his and Pete's forthcoming meeting with Magda and Amy in one terrifying hour's time.

Barney cringes as this unwelcome thought darts through his brain. It just feels *wrong* somehow. Pete hasn't helped either. He could have dropped Sadie's name countless times, but for some reason seems to have chosen not to. With a small shudder, Barney picks up Dylan and settles into the armchair. He holds him close to his chest, breathing in his sweet, delicious scent in the hope that his baby's innocence will somehow cancel out the uneasiness brewing inside him. He glances over at Pete, who has opened his eyes on the sofa bed, and is stretching his entire body so his long, hairy feet poke out from the bottom of the duvet. 'Morning,' he says with a grin.

'Morning. Plenty of beauty sleep?'

'Yeah,' he chuckles, 'just about.' In fact, Pete looks irritatingly perky considering he's spent a night on the least comfy sofa bed Barney has ever owned in his life.

'Look, Pete . . .' Barney starts, holding up Dylan who's gazing at their house guest with interest. 'I don't think I'll come and meet the girls if it's okay with you. I'm kind of busy with these two. You go, hang out for as long as you want, pick up some photography tips, and I'll make you something to eat later if you're not . . .' he wiggles an eyebrow '. . . caught up in other things.'

Pete props himself up on an elbow and frowns. 'But they want to see the babies.'

'What?' Barney looks at him incredulously.

'I mean . . .' At least Pete has the decency to blush. 'You saw what a fuss they made of them at the pub. They're obviously the kind of girls who love kids.'

'They don't care about my babies, Pete!'

'No, they really do.'

Barney shakes his head disbelievingly. 'You're saying you want to use my children as girl-pulling accessories, is that it?'

'No, I don't mean that.'

'I could hire them out,' Barney teases, 'for a reasonable fee.'

'Oh, fuck off . . .'

Barney turns away, placing Dylan back on the play mat and picks up Milo's bib from yesterday off the living room floor. Hell – it says Monday on the front, and yesterday was Friday. Parenting police will be called and he'll have serious questions to answer. 'Listen,' he adds, sounding less prickly now, 'I don't really care whether they like babies or not. The point is, I'm married. You might've forgotten that . . .'

'Of course I haven't! God, I love Sadie, she's the best girl in the world. But this . . . this is nothing. We're only meeting up in the *daytime*. It's just a bit of harmless—'

'So nothing ever happens in the day, does it?' Barney asks with a straight face.

'Well, I suppose it *can*, in the right circumstances, but it's not like that, is it? You're reading far too much into it.'

'Oh yeah,' Barney snorts. 'It's just a photography lesson. I forgot.'

Tutting loudly, Pete tosses the duvet aside and sits up in his white T-shirt and grey boxers. 'I did notice that you never mentioned Sadie's name, or being married, at any point yesterday, you poor single dad, you . . .'

Barney blows out air loudly, causing Milo to stare up at him and Dylan to giggle in delight. 'I don't know what you're on about.' He shrugs and turns away. 'It just didn't come up.'

'Of course it didn't,' Pete snorts.

'Well, it just didn't,' Barney says, heading through to the kitchen for milk. 'And anyway, I do wear a wedding ring . . .'

'I don't think Magda noticed,' Pete calls out after him, 'or maybe she likes married men . . .'

'Oh, shut up,' he says as Pete follows him, throws open the fridge, extracts a bottle of apple juice and slugs from it. 'I just feel a bit uncomfortable about it. I mean, the two of them are so *young* . . .'

'God, you're making them sound about fifteen,' Pete exclaims.

'Okay,' Barney says hotly, placing a bottle in the bottle warmer. 'I'll keep you company but *please* don't come on strong. I've got to live here, remember, and Madga works in the café in the park . . .'

'I'll behave,' Pete says.

'You'd better.'

'Don't look so scared. I'm sure they don't bite . . .'

Barney shakes his head despairingly. 'I've nothing to be scared of, Pete. I mean . . . we're just going to meet up for a bit of a chat, right?'

'Yep,' Pete says, his eyes glinting with anticipation. 'Nothing more dastardly than that.'

FORTY-SIX

Well, of course Johnny's not in. It's Saturday morning, and he's a dad – he'll be out taking his son to football or something. By the time she's returned to Sauchiehall Street, Hannah has reassured herself that Ryan probably *did* sleep on Petra's sofa. To further raise her spirits, she reminds herself that there wouldn't be any room for a six-foot male in Petra's bed anyway – not with that cello tucked up beside her. Even so, the thought of going home – back to Ryan's – fills her with dread. Why the hell hadn't she deleted that email? Perhaps, she reflects, a small part of her had wanted him to find it.

The stunning red dress catches Hannah's eye again as she strides past the bridal shop, and she quickly turns away. She's been so engrossed in her own thoughts that she's forgotten all about nipping into Costa to buy coffees, and she's also failed to notice the tall, long-legged figure heading towards her on the opposite side of the pedestrianised street. He's carrying two carrier bags laden with shopping, and although his dark brown hair needs a comb, he's still handsome, still the kind of man women notice. But Hannah doesn't see him glance over in her direction and do a quick double take.

What Johnny Lynch sees at twenty past ten on a blue-skied morning is a beautiful woman in faded jeans, her fair hair pulled back in a ponytail, her face fresh and pretty without a scrap of make-up. He watches her striding determinedly, this old friend whom he'd dropped, like the others, simply because he'd been told to. No, not *just* because Rona had demanded it, but because he knew it was right, and that he had to stop seeing them – Lou especially. Because he'd kissed Lou that morning after the last party – and if Spike hadn't been sleeping a few feet away he'd have kissed her a whole lot more. And was that any way to behave when his girlfriend was scared and pregnant?

Johnny opens his mouth, ready to call out Hannah's name, but something stops him. If he runs over to her now, he'll have to feign surprise that it's not just Hannah who's here in Glasgow, but all three of them, and he doubts if he could carry that off. Hannah has passed him now, growing smaller down the street. He watches her, wondering why he's rooted here with his carrier bags, letting her go. He feels a pang so sharp it's almost a physical pain.

He starts walking then, quickening his pace, not noticing the shoppers or buskers or *Big Issue* sellers because his gaze is fixed upon the blonde woman with the ponytail ahead. And he *can't* let her go. He can't just let the chance pass him by the way he did last night. He no longer cares what he'll say or what she'll think. He sees her stop and glance towards the posh patisserie on her right. He knows the shop well, because Cal always nags him to go in. Sometimes Johnny lets him choose something, though not every time, because the place is so pricey that he can knock together an entire roast dinner for the price of one of those strawberry tarts.

Hannah pushes open the gleaming brass door with the French flag bunting flapping above it and goes in. Johnny approaches the shop and sees her waiting in the small queue.

Just go in, be normal and buy something. Buy a tart for Cal, it'll be a surprise for him when he comes back from his mum's this afternoon. Johnny clears his throat as he opens the door, wishing he'd shaved this morning and fitted in that haircut last week, wishing he'd at least *combed* his hair this morning and that he wasn't carrying two bulging carrier bags and wearing a baggy old sweater that he really should have parted company with some years ago.

He steps into the shop, breathing in the sweet pastry smells. With all his dithering, two people have joined the line after Hannah. 'Three lattes to go please,' she says. The two elderly women between them are chatting away, saying the weather's fine now but there's still a bite in the air, and Hannah's coffees are handed to her in a cardboard holder.

She takes them, and Johnny starts to feel trapped between the old ladies and a large middle-aged man who's come in behind him, breathing loudly and nasally on the back of his neck.

In the periphery of his vision, Johnny sees Hannah glancing towards him, perhaps with a flicker of recognition – but no, she hasn't realised who he is. Why would she notice a scruffy guy in a ratty old sweater with an unraveling elbow? Women are different: they take good care of themselves, they look bright and fresh even first thing in the morning. Not that Johnny can really remember what a woman looks like first thing in the morning.

Clutching her coffees, Hannah is pointing at something, although Johnny can't make out what it is. Resting her tray of coffees on the glass-topped counter, she fishes her purse from her bag and hands over some money. The shop lady places a large, flat white box beside her coffees. Johnny scrutinises his shoes, heart racing now, hoping she'll stride right past him. He feels hot and hemmed in and is overcome with self-consciousness. Three lattes mean all three of them are definitely here, and how can he possibly face Lou? And now . . .

Hannah is standing before him with a huge smile on her face, blue eyes bright, cheeks flushed pink, and both hands full with the coffees and that big flat white box. 'I thought it was you,' she says.

Johnny is aware of the enormous smile spreading across his face as he puts down his shopping. 'I thought it was you too, Han. God, I can't believe it.'

The elderly ladies look irritated, and Hannah says, 'We'd better go out. I think we're clogging up the shop.'

'Here, let me take that box,' Johnny says quickly. The heavy-breathing man opens the door for them, and they step out, both of them laughing at the absurdity of running into each other like that. Outside the shop, they stand and look at each other.

'Johnny Lynch,' Hannah says, 'after all this time. And, God, you've forgotten to buy your . . . what were you getting in there anyway?'

'Oh, I er . . .' He pauses, momentarily trying and failing to name one thing he might want to buy in a patisserie, and remembering Cal's incessant nagging as he stood outside the cocktail bar last night. *Why don't you just go in and say hello?* 'I wasn't buying anything,' he says with a laugh. 'To be honest, I just came in to say hi.'

FORTY-SEVEN

Ryan sits in the kitchen watching Petra tipping chickpeas, chopped garlic, olive oil and something brown and gloopy from a jar into the blender. She turns it on, the room filling with its frantic whir, then she spoons the contents into some kind of gnarled, recycled cardboard tub. Petra is making hummus for a picnic. 'Won't that go soggy?' Ryan asks.

'No,' she says with a small frown. 'These are great – we can throw them away when we're done instead of carrying nasty plastic tubs around.'

'Oh,' Ryan says, wondering if he's included in the 'we'. No reason why he should be, just because he spent last night on Petra's sofa. They still haven't properly addressed the issue of Josh smoking, having veered into the even more worrying territory of the state of his relationship with Hannah. He's aware that spending the whole of Saturday together would feel weird for both of them, yet the thought of heading back to a stark, empty house is hardly tempting either.

'I'm glad you're coming,' she remarks, topping up his mug from the coffee pot. 'The kids'll enjoy you being there.'

'Are you sure that's okay?' he asks.

'Of course, unless you've other things to do . . .'

'No, no,' he says quickly. 'I don't have any other plans for today.'

'Well, thanks,' she teases him. 'I'm glad we're filling up your otherwise desolate, empty Saturday.'

'I didn't mean that. I just mean . . . It'll be nice, that's all.' What's happened to Petra's Saturday plans, he wonders? The pop art exhibition and all the other educational trips?

'You can help if you like.' She flashes him a broad, almost flirtatious smile. Ryan blinks at her.

'Sure. What d'you want me to do?'

'Fancy making some sandwiches? There's bread in the bread bin and ham in the fridge.'

With a nod, he assembles the ingredients and sets to work, noting that Petra's ham isn't the normal supermarket type that he buys, but posh stuff, hand-sliced from some deli and wrapped in waxy paper with a green gingham design. Her butter isn't Kerrygold but French, *extra-fin*, with a peasant riding a donkey on the wrapper. 'I thought you wanted to take the kids to the Portrait Gallery today,' he says casually as Petra starts to pack the provisions into a hamper on the table.

'Oh, it's such a nice day, it seems a shame to be rushing about all over the place.'

'I suppose so.' Ryan is a little apprehensive now about how this picnic will turn out: his first family outing with Petra in more than three years. Perfect Petra, with her wicker picnic basket and swanky butter who's now, he notes with a jolt of alarm, pulling out a bottle of champagne from the fridge. 'What's that for?' he asks lightly.

'My birthday.' She grins and tosses back her hair which gleams inky-black in the morning sun.

'But . . . isn't your birthday next week?'

'Yes,' she says quickly, 'but seeing as we're all together, I thought I'd celebrate early. I mean, this doesn't happen very often, does it?'

'What, your birthday?' He feels stupid now for trying to make a joke.

'No – *us*.' Her eyes meet his, causing a strange fluttering in his stomach. 'So what d'you think?'

'What, take the champagne? Yeah. Why not?'

With a smile, she sweeps through to the living room, leaving Ryan to cut more ham sandwiches, quartering each round into the neat triangles he knows Petra will approve of. She's only suggested a picnic to celebrate her almost-birthday, he tells himself. As far as Ryan can see, dutifully wrapping the sandwiches in the greaseproof paper she's put out for him, there's absolutely nothing wrong with that.

FORTY-EIGHT

If Johnny had ever imagined meeting Lou Costello again, he hadn't envisaged having two carrier bags bulging with assorted groceries plus a bright blue bottle of Toilet Duck at his feet. But here he is now, with not just Lou, but Hannah and Sadie too – the Garnet Street Girls. They're tucking into an extravagant brunch in an airy pub with jazz playing quietly in the background as they fill him in on the past thirteen years of their lives.

And if Lou had ever imagined running into Johnny again – which she has, countless times, when Spike's behaviour has soared up the irritation scale – she'd never have imagined he would have grown into such a ruggedly beautiful man.

She is sitting beside him, and every now and again his arm brushes against hers. It's not his *actual* arm – just his baggy-elbowed sweater sleeve. Yet each time it makes contact, she feels a small jolt which takes her away somewhere else, away from this trendy pub populated by a young, mildly hung over clientele to a place where she's conscious of every nerve in her body. Hannah, Sadie and Johnny are showing each other pictures on their phones. 'That's Dylan,' Sadie explains, 'and that's Milo, looking scrubbed and presentable for once . . .'

'They're *so* like you,' Johnny exclaims. 'God, Sadie, the double whammy – you must be so proud.'

'I suppose I am,' Sadie laughs, bringing up another picture. 'Anyway, this is Barney, my husband. It still sounds funny saying that sometimes, even though we've been married for four years . . .'

'Well, he's a lucky guy,' Johnny says with a grin. 'And you're a country girl now, huh?'

'Yeah, or trying to be . . .' She laughs again. 'But really, I don't know about Barney being lucky. Right now, I think I'm the lucky one.' She looks around the scratched oak table and smiles. 'Here I am, away for the weekend with my favourite people in the world – apart from my family, I mean. That's a different kind of favourite . . .'

'I know what you mean,' Johnny murmurs, shifting in his seat, making Lou flinch as his sleeve tickles her arm.

Sadie's eyes have moistened. 'It's funny – I was expecting Barney to be calling every ten minutes, asking what he should do about this, and where do we keep that . . .'

'You expected him not to cope,' Hannah cuts in.

Sadie nods. 'But he's only phoned once and everything's fine . . .'

'You're virtually redundant!' Johnny teases her.

'Yeah. I guess I am. It still feels strange, you know, being away from my kids . . .' She grins, spearing a mushroom with her fork. 'But it feels great too.'

'Like the old you?' Lou suggests.

'Yes, just about.' More coffees arrive, and the conversation veers towards Johnny's allotment and his green-fingered lifestyle these days. Lou wants to ask him so much, but everyone is talking over each other, butting in in that way that old friends do. She places her cutlery on her plate, barely having made headway into her meal.

'So how about you, Lou?' Johnny has turned to her.

'Oh, you know . . . crappy job, dingy little flat, but I'm

278

working on it – I'm coming up with some kind of plan
. . .' She stops, realising she hasn't the faintest idea of what
that plan might be, and hoping he doesn't ask for further
details. She senses her cheeks reddening and takes a big
swig of coffee.

'So . . . you're still with Spike?' Johnny asks.

Lou feels all eyes on her. 'Yeah, still ticking along.'

'And, er . . . how is he?' Johnny asks brightly.

'Oh, he's great! Just the same.' She pauses. 'Well, you
know what he's like.'

'Just the same, yeah?' Johnny repeats.

Lou nods, realising he's moved slightly closer to her now,
and that his woolly sleeve is in constant contact with her
bare arm. 'Yep, pretty much,' she says, turning to smile at
him, hoping to convince her old friend that as soon as she
gets back to York, she's going to put her plan into action.
Yet, when his soft grey eyes meet hers, Lou knows he
doesn't believe her at all.

FORTY-NINE

There's nothing wrong with being in Hissingham Woods with two girls, Barney tells himself – nothing at all. It's just *harmless fun*. So here they are, clutching silver reflectors and, well, not doing much else to help, admittedly, but Magda and Amy are obviously quite happy for them to be here. Barney isn't so sure that Sadie would be happy, but if she does find out – which she won't – Barney will explain the situation for what it is: just a pleasant outing, all Pete's idea. No, there's nothing wrong with watching Magda take pictures of Amy, who arrived in a bluish-green cobwebby top which, after she disappeared behind a tree and whipped off her jeans, now appears to be an extremely tiny, fragile-looking dress. All this is *fine*, Barney reassures himself, because his babies are here. Babies are wholesome. Nothing untoward can ever happen when they are around.

'That's great,' Magda enthuses, taking shot after shot as Amy moves ever-so-subtly, raising a shoulder, tilting her chin, and sort of collapsing back against a sturdy oak as if suddenly needing it for support. 'Let's go further into the woods,' Magda suggests. 'There's a place where this little bit of sunshine comes in between the trees, it's really beautiful.' And now, with the reflector trapped under his arm while he pushes the buggy with difficulty along the muddy path, Barney is starting to think maybe it's *not* okay, and that they're stepping into dangerous territory.

Amy is now lying in that wisp of a dress, on a scattering of leaves and twigs as if she's fallen into a dead faint. 'That looks *really* good,' Pete observes sagely. 'There's a lovely feel to it, the way the dress and, er . . . the browny textures of the ground are merging,' he continues, as if he sees himself as creative director of *Vogue* and not a wine importer who buys cheap plonk from God knows where and knocks it out at vastly inflated prices.

Having been relieved of reflector-holding duties – 'Maybe Pete should do that, being taller,' Amy points out helpfully – Barney crouches down in the dappled shade from where his children are regarding the proceedings with interest. Maybe it's educational for them, he thinks, with a growing sense of unease, watching a young woman writhe on the ground like that.

'Now that's beautiful, I love the languid, sensual feel of that,' Pete enthuses as Amy stands up, picks out a few twigs that have become lodged in the holes of her dress and flops her head to one side, as if something's wrong with her neck.

'Yes,' says Magda. 'It's like . . . she's part of the forest, you know?'

'Yeah,' Pete said thoughtfully. 'She really is.'

'Like a little fairy.'

'Uh-huh.'

'Or a nymph,' Magda adds, moving in a little closer.

'Exactly,' Pete agrees. 'That's exactly what I was thinking.' Pete is somehow – although only just, Barney suspects – preventing his tongue from lolling out and dragging across the forest floor. What *are* they doing here?

Barney's knees click painfully as he straightens himself up. He's old enough to have dodgy knees, yet is behaving like a teenager, going into the woods with girls. He needs

281

to get away *now*, be responsible and remove himself and his children from this wood nymph photo shoot situation. Magda takes a few more pictures, and just as Barney is about to say something, she announces, 'Well, I think we're done for now . . . I've got everything I need.'

'That's it?' Pete asks, unable to conceal his disappointment.

'Yes, the pictures look great. We should get something to eat, don't you think?'

'That's a great idea,' Pete replies, and Amy murmurs in agreement.

'I'm not really hungry,' Barney lies. With all the multi-tasking this morning, all he's managed to cram into his mouth are the remains of Milo and Dylan's baby porridge, which tasted like food for the ill. No wonder they often spit it out.

'Well, I am,' Pete remarks. 'I'm starving. Breakfast was hardly forthcoming this morning, was it, Barney . . .' Barney presses his lips together and chooses not to answer.

'We could go to the pub,' Magda suggests as they amble back along the winding path to the place where Amy left her jeans. She disappears behind a tree and comes back fully clothed, now a little less nymph-like.

'I'd better not,' Barney says quickly. 'In fact, I should get the boys home for lunch, it's almost one . . .'

'That's in the schedule, is it?' Pete teases.

'No, I'm just saying . . .'

'I thought you packed those jars of sloppy stuff in there?' Pete adds, indicating the baby-essentials bag, which now has a few leaves stuck to it.

'Er, I don't think I did actually . . .'

'I'm sure you did,' Pete says, grinning infuriatingly, clearly delighting in winding him up. 'Chicken and sweetcorn casserole, wasn't it, and some of those little biscuit things.'

'No, I don't *think* so . . .' Everyone looks at him

expectantly. But he can't go back to the Black Swan, not for a second visit in twenty-four hours. 'Sorry, I really need to get home,' he says firmly.

As they reach the edge of the woods, he senses Magda glancing at him. 'Well, maybe we all could meet up some other time,' Amy says lightly. Barney feels better out here in the sunshine – less trapped with the clear blue sky above him.

'That'd be great,' Pete enthuses, flipping his phone from his pocket in one swift movement. 'What's your number, Amy?'

Barney hovers as she tells him, gripping the buggy handles, and Magda bobs down to bid the children a fussy goodbye.

'I'll see you around, Barney?' she adds, straightening up as they prepare to part company.

'Yes, I'm sure you will.' He forces a small grin.

'I work Mondays and Fridays in the café. I'll show you the pictures next time I see you, okay?'

'Yeah, great . . .'

She gives him a warm smile. 'Your babies are lovely but it must be such hard work. I don't know how you do it.'

'Well, y'know.' He shrugs, feeling his cheeks burning, and is relieved when they finally part company with the girls.

'Poor single dad,' Pete murmurs as they stride back towards Barney's house.

'Shut up.'

'Poor Daddy, managing to look after two babies all on his own with no woman to help him.'

'Fuck off, David Bailey,' Barney splutters, bursting out laughing despite himself.

They reach Barney's front door and awkwardly ease in the buggy. 'Honestly,' Pete adds, mimicking Magda's soft, wispy voice, 'I don't know how you do it.'

FIFTY

The drive to Glasgow in the band's converted ambulance has been horrendous. Spike's lower back aches and he has a crick in his neck. He's often thought how much he'd enjoy being back here, checking out his old haunts. Yet now, with his aches and pains, plus a lingering wine/beer/ Père Magloire hangover and the horror of Harry's erratic driving, all he wants is to be in bed. Glimpsing his reflection in the 'superloos' at Glasgow Central station, he decides he doesn't look super at all. His face is clammy and beige, like one of those chicken fillets Lou left for him in the fridge back home.

Spike splashes cold water on his face, wipes it dry with his sleeve, then fishes out his wallet from his pocket and counts his money carefully beside a washbasin. £32.47. It's not a lot, admittedly, to see him through the rest of today, and Saturday night, plus whatever tomorrow might throw up. But he'll manage. If Lou *isn't* up to anything – and Spike now feels utterly confident that she isn't, which makes him wonder why he endured that stomach-swirling journey – then he can probably sneak into the girls' hotel room tonight and kip on their floor. Surely they wouldn't mind. He can also borrow a bit from each of them for the train fare back to York – spread the cost. In fact, the prospect of being among Lou and her friends as they lie on their beds, painting their nails and indulging in all that lovely girlie grooming makes him feel momentarily better.

Spike glances around the superloo, scanning the row of cubicle doors. Satisfied that he's in there alone, he pulls up his plain black T-shirt and inspects the waxed area just above his left nipple. The spots have died down, thank God. The rectangle is still creepily bald, though – just the one strip, as if someone had started to mow a lawn and given up when the rain came on. Picking up his rucksack from the floor, and trying to summon up a sense of positivity, Spike struts up the stairs and out onto the bustling station concourse.

Outside, he pauses to light a much-needed cigarette and takes in the lively street scene before him. Glasgow feels buzzy and youthful, and Spike senses his crippling tiredness subside as he makes his way towards Puccini's, an old-fashioned Italian café. They'd all hung out here – the Garnet Street Girls, that twat Johnny and a gaggle of art students who'd cottoned onto the fact that you were allowed to dawdle over one cup of coffee for an entire afternoon. Spike pushes open the heavy wooden door, inhales the aroma of coffee and pizza and steps in.

Puccini's looks just as he remembered. There are still plastic red-and-white checked tablecloths, pleasingly mismatched wooden chairs and oil and vinegar dispensers on each table. Three of the dozen or so tables are occupied by people at various stages of lunch. 'Okay if I just have a cappuccino?' he asks as a waiter approaches him.

The man nods and motions for Spike to sit at the nearest table. Disconcertingly, although Spike has placed his order, the waiter continues to stand over him with his small grey pad, his hair slicked close to his almost spherical head. 'Um, actually, I think I will have something to eat,' Spike mutters. He takes a quick look at the menu. 'A small margherita pizza please, and a cappuccino.'

The waiter nods and returns to the kitchen. Christ, what was that about? Perhaps he's a bit smelly from being trapped in an ambulance with those prepubescent musicians. While he waits, Spike weighs up his options as to what to do next.

He could head straight round to the girls' hotel – he has the address – or call Lou and find out what they're doing right now. Yet if he alerts her to the fact that he's come all this way, and she *has* been up to something with that fuckwit Felix, she'll have a chance to cover her tracks. A sense of unease creeps over him as he fears he's made a terrible mistake. After all, Lou has never done anything to make him distrust her. Oh, there was that one time in her kitchen in Garnet Street, when he'd glanced in and seen her in a horribly intimate clinch with Johnny – but surely that hadn't meant anything.

Spike's pizza arrives, the dimples in its cheesy topping forming rock pools of yellow oil. He hacks into the burnt crust, then abandons his cutlery, tears off a hunk and gnaws at it. Whilst mildly more palatable than that sausage last night, it's a pretty poor excuse for a margherita. His coffee, too, is unsatisfying, becoming oddly grainy as he reaches its murky depths. Spike starts to crave one of Lou's stir-fries with prawns, noodles and leafy bits which she flings so artfully together. Having gamely choked down what he can, Spike abandons the remaining half of his pizza and requests the bill.

At least the place is still cheap – £7.60 for the pizza and coffee. As the waiter turns to squirt the next table with something chemical and presumably germ-zapping, Spike slips a hand into his jacket pocket.

No wallet. He tries his other pocket, then the inside ones and the pockets of his jeans. 'Shit,' he whispers, bending down to open his rucksack on the floor and rifle through its contents as surreptitiously as possible. One pair of Levis, one T-shirt, one pair of fake Calvin Klein boxers. Toothbrush, toothpaste, razor and roll-on deodorant tightly wrapped in a plastic bag. And that's it. Spike is sweating now as the waiter prowls the vacant tables.

To affect a relaxed demeanour, he continues to sip from the coffee cup, even though there's nothing in it apart from some tarry residue. He keeps on pretending to sip until the waiter disappears into the kitchen.

This is it. His only chance. Spike stands up slowly as if he might be about to stretch. He looks at the exit, just a few strides away. Then, taking care not to make any sudden movements while slipping his rucksack onto his shoulder, he glances anxiously towards the kitchen door. It's still closed, and the waiter's in there, probably plating up another slab of oily dough. Spike springs for the exit, flying out into the street past a newspaper vendor and a large group of old people who veer back as he charges past. 'Oi!' is all he hears as he darts down a side street, which stinks of garbage, and up a small ramp and down again into the bowels of a multistorey car park.

Spike leans back against a concrete wall, his breath coming in painful gasps. His wallet. His soft black leather wallet, a present from Lou, with £32.47 in it. Gone, just like that. He must have dropped it, or maybe someone nicked it. He wants another cigarette – his body is crying out for nicotine – but he fears that the waiter is prowling about in the labyrinthine car park and might smell it and track him down.

Spike bides his time until it seems safe to leave, then makes his way out, checking the street first in case that waiter's out there. He walks briskly with his head down, telling himself that of course his wallet is sitting waiting for him in the superloos at the station. All he has to do is retrieve it and everything will be fine.

FIFTY-ONE

Sadie really needs to phone Barney. Apparently she kissed the face off some stranger last night – she knows that this is what Hannah and Lou really mean by a little peck, a bit of *innocent fun* – and she needs to hear her husband's voice to reassure her that her life isn't over. Just talking to him for two minutes will stop her from freaking out that he knows what she's done, that images of her attached to the face of some man in glasses haven't been transmitted on Sky News.

Right now, though, it's impossible. Together with Lou, Hannah and Johnny, she is on a walking tour down memory lane, and every time she hangs back to try and make the call, someone cajoles her to stop dawdling and keep up, to check out that bar they used to drink in and see how posh it is now and *oh look, Sadie, there's that hairdresser's where they put the thick yellow tramlines through your hair, remember, when you'd just wanted coppery highlights? And you wore a hat for a week until you could afford some home colour to dye it yourself?*

Lou is equally keen to peel away from the group, not to call Spike to check up on his fresh vegetable consumption but to talk to Johnny alone. What was it like, she wants to ask him, splitting up with Rona when they had a child? As they walk in the sunshine, Lou keep stealing glances at him as he banters with Hannah, reassuring her that those kids *will* come round and accept her, and how could they not be delighted to have such a cool stepmum? The more Lou thinks about it, the more she's convinced that she really does need a plan. Hannah is getting married – despite her doubts, Lou doesn't believe for an instant that she'll call off the wedding – and Sadie has a family of her own. But what does Lou have? A duff job and Spike on the sofa. If Johnny managed to part from the mother of his child, why can't Lou disentangle herself when all she and Spike have to tie them together is a sixteen-year history and some crappy furniture? He cares for her though, she reflects as everyone heads into a charity shop. He really must do. Otherwise he wouldn't have sold his guitar to pay for this trip.

Lou glances around the shop. She usually loves charity shops and this one is a cut above the rest, an explosion of colour with everything presented with care. Old vinyl records are displayed on a wall, and vintage clothing is artfully hung beside retro kitchenware and jewellery. Yet Lou is distracted. Johnny turns from a rail of jackets, catches her eye and smiles. Lou smiles back, conscious of her ears reddening as if he can read her private thoughts. How the years have changed him, Lou thinks as he moves on to the old Levi's and checked shirts. He's filled out just a little, softening his lanky frame and the sharper angles of his younger face, and it suits him.

They leave the shop, and Johnny touches Lou's arm and points across the street. 'Look,' he says. 'That's the barber's where one of the staff rushed out and asked you to marry him, remember?' She laughs, having long forgotten the incident. Things like that don't happen to her anymore.

They stop off for coffee, the rapid-fire catch-up between

the girls and Johnny having slowed down to a more mellow pace. 'So Johnny,' Hannah says, putting an arm around his shoulders, 'what happened with you and Rona?'

Johnny pauses. 'Well, I used to think it was having Cal pretty young,' he begins, swirling the wooden stirrer around his cup. 'You know what it's like, Sadie, with babies . . .'

'Oh yeah. It changes everything. Not just the practical stuff, but the the way you are together . . .'

Johnny nods. 'So there was all of that. We were young and thrown in at the deep end. But now' – he glances at Lou – 'I don't think it was anything to do with Cal at all. Having a son is amazing, so I don't regret me and Rona, not a bit. I just think maybe the two of us weren't right, and never would have stayed together even if she hadn't got pregnant.'

'Johnny,' Hannah says hesitantly, 'why did you stop being in touch with us? We all tried to call, and I think Lou wrote to you too.'

Lou looks away as Johnny sips from his cup. 'Yes, I know. It sounds pathetic now, but back then we were still trying to figure everything out, making it up as we went along really. And it's what she wanted . . .'

'Rona didn't want you to be friends with us?' Lou exclaims. 'Why not?'

Johnny exhales. 'She felt . . . threatened, I guess. She knew how close we all were . . .' He turns to Lou and smiles. 'I'm sorry. And yes, I did get your letter, Lou.'

'Did you?' She shuffles in her seat and wills Hannah to fire another pertinent question. But there's just an awkward pause, and Lou senses Hannah and Sadie looking curiously at her, then at Johnny. Hannah removes her arm from around his shoulders and clasps her cup.

'I should've replied,' Johnny adds, 'or at least explained.'

'Oh, that was years ago now,' Lou says quickly. 'I'd forgotten all about it.'

'Well, never mind,' Hannah says briskly. 'We're all here together now and that's all that matters. We won't lose touch again.'

Everyone agrees, and when Sadie goes up to the counter to pick a selection of cakes for everyone, Hannah insists on helping her. Lou can sense Johnny looking at her and it feels as if her heart has been put on hold.

'We're not going to lose each other again, are we?' he asks gently.

'No, Johnny,' Lou murmurs, silently thanking Hannah and Sadie for taking a terribly long time to choose those cakes. 'I really don't think we are.'

FIFTY-TWO

Spike had forgotten it costs 30p to get into the superloos. *30p for a pee*. Promising he won't use any of the facilities and only wants to get his wallet back, Spike gushes his thanks as the sympathetic attendant opens the glass barrier for him.

Of course his wallet isn't sitting patiently beside the basin where he washed his face. It's nowhere to be seen, which leaves him no option but to call Lou and admit that he's followed her to Glasgow. 'Why?' she'll ask, at best taken aback but more likely, he realises now, pretty pissed off. And what can he possibly say? That he blagged a lift because Johnny Lynch – whom neither of them has seen for over a decade – happened to leave a weird message on their answerphone, about seeing Lou out on the town with her supposed boyfriend? Spike's head is pounding but he doesn't even have the money for a Paracetamol. He's overreacted like a complete idiot, and on top of all that he'll have to explain that not only has he rocked up to gatecrash her girlie weekend, but also has zero pence to his name.

Spike has never felt smaller, or more foolish, in his life.

He leaves the loos and steps out into the smoky fug outside the station, trying to calm his racing thoughts. He's stranded in Glasgow, a city in which he no longer knows anyone – at least no one he's been in touch with for years now. He's all alone.

Get a grip, he tells himself angrily. *You know this city like the back of your hand.* First priority, he decides, is to get some money. The only way he might possibly do this – ruling out snatching a handbag or begging in the street – is to utilise one of his many talents.

The afternoon is turning warmer now, and Spike can't remember seeing a bluer sky. As he lights a cigarette, an idea starts to form – one which offers him a glimmer of hope. Spike is starting to feel more human now, his hangover finally clearing as he heads away from the station. Taking care to avoid Puccini's, he quickens his pace, determined to get himself out of this mess.

*

Spike rarely feels more at home than when he is in a music shop. There's something about looking at row upon row of guitars and knowing that he can play any one of them that makes everything seem right in his world. He *loves* playing guitars in shops. Someone always listens, even though they pretend not to; it's one way of gaining an audience these days.

While Sound Shack is a mess, strewn with dog hair and chewy bones, this cavernous, three-storey building is neat, professional and entirely dedicated to the discerning musician. The ground floor has all the woodwind instruments, and drums are up on the second; Spike is reassured to see that the basic layout hasn't changed. Taking the stairs two at a time, he gallops up to the first floor where the guitars are displayed. Here, although he pretends to browse the instruments, he's really checking out the staff. There are only two currently on the shop floor: a teenager in a shrunken grey T-shirt, and an older man with a gingery beard, taking a guitar from the wall and handing it to a middle-aged man in a baseball cap.

No, they won't do. To them, Spike's just any one random bloke who's just happened to walk in off the street. The younger guy would have been in primary school or possibly nursery when Spike lived in Glasgow, and he can tell the bearded one has an attitude. Spike's spirits sink, weighed down by the pizza in his belly and an unavoidable sense that he is well and truly stuffed. He'll have to call Lou, he decides, studying a wire rack bearing packets of strings.

'Spike?'

He spins round and hesitates for a second as a heavy-set man with a shaven head beams at him. 'Terry!' he exclaims. 'You're still here . . .'

'Still hanging on for my sins,' Terry says with a grin. 'Should've got a proper job by now . . .'

'Yeah.' Spike chortles, stuffing his hands into his jacket pockets. 'Good to see you, though. How's it going?'

Terry shrugs. 'It's *going*. Tough times but we're okay, y'know? So what are you doing here? Thought you moved away years ago.'

'I did, I have . . . just up for a visit.'

'Right. Still got family up here?'

'Not in Glasgow, no. The old folks have moved out – they're in sheltered housing now, down on the coast . . .'

'Aww, hope they're doing all right,' Terry says.

Spike nods and sucks his teeth, regretting having mentioned his ageing parents and eager to move on to the matter in hand. 'Anyway, just up to see a few old friends,' he says quickly. 'The thing is . . .'

'Still with lovely Lou?' Terry asks with a smile.

'Oh yeah.' Spike nods, allowing Terry a few moments to reflect on the wonderfulness of his girlfriend.

'Doing her jewellery, is she?'

'Uh-huh. Still pottering along . . . .'

Terry scratches his head and steps back, giving the impression that, niceties over, he should really get on with doing something more productive. 'So, er . . . are you looking for anything?'

Spike exhales and glances around the shop. 'Not exactly. I've . . . had a bit of a disaster, Terry, to be honest.'

'Yeah? What happened?' A deep crevice appears between Terry's bushy grey eyebrows.

'Just got here, like, just got off the train . . . and had my wallet stolen.'

'Jeez.' Terry frowns. 'You mean all your cards gone, everything?'

'Yeah.' Spike casts his gaze at the faded carpet tiles.

'Called the police? And your bank?'

'Yep, it's all in hand.' Spike brushes back his hair distractedly. 'The thing is, Terry, I know it's a big ask . . .'

'Sure,' Terry says, frowning. 'I can lend you . . .' He takes his wallet from his back pocket and opens it. 'Only got a fiver in here, can't really leave the shop to go to the bank, but would that be enough to get you to your friend's place?'

Spike's cheeks flame instantly. 'Er . . . thanks, but I can't take your money. It's my own stupid fault. I should've taken better care of it. You see, what I was wondering is . . .' He turns towards the rack of guitars on the wall and winces. 'I couldn't, um . . . borrow one for a bit, could I? Just for an hour or so?'

The crevice between Terry's brows has deepened to a geographical fault. 'What for, mate?'

'Well . . . I was thinking of busking.'

'Seriously?' Terry says with a barking laugh. 'You don't need to do that. Take the fiver. Look, I can probably get you another, would a tenner do? Hey, Norm!' The boy in the shrunken T-shirt turns round.

'No, no, I can't take anyone's money,' Spike cuts in, panic rising in his throat. 'I . . . I'd feel really bad. And look . . . Lou's up here with me and we planned to go for dinner tonight, it's a sort of special occasion . . .'

'Her birthday?' Terry suggests.

'Yeah. Exactly. So I need . . .' He throws open his arms in a *women, what can you do?* kind of way. 'I need quite a bit and I can't ask you for that. So I thought . . . I'd need an hour, two at the most . . .' Terry scratches his chin and glances at the guitars on the wall. 'Just anything you can spare,' Spike adds. 'I'll take really good care of it, I promise.'

Terry's mouth has set in a firm line. 'Well . . . Mike'll go mad if he finds out. But he's on his lunchbreak so I might be able to help you out.'

'Thanks, mate,' Spike murmurs.

Terry twitches his head in the direction of the stock room. 'C'mon. Let's see what we've got. But I've got to tell you, Spike, any damage . . .'

'Absolutely. I'll guard it with my life.'

Ten minutes later, Spike emerges from the shop, gripping the handles of a guitar case, ready to play what is possibly the most important gig of his life.

FIFTY-THREE

Petra was right. Her gnarled recycled cartons don't go soggy when filled with gloopy substances. They are a miracle of modern construction and, as she lays out the picnic on a large crocheted rug, Ryan can't help feeling a little in awe. It's one of those perfect picnics you glimpse sometimes, wondering how on earth the family managed to put it all together. There are dips, crudités, a berry salad, a carrot cake and the posh ham sandwiches. There's Ryan's ex-wife looking elegant in a simple grey shift and sandals with a tiny heel, and the two beautiful children they made. There's chilled champagne, proper glasses, sunshine and all of Hampstead Heath spread out before them.

Josh and Daisy aren't even arguing. They're sitting together a few metres away, chomping on sandwiches while Daisy fires questions about secondary school, which Josh is even deigning to answer.

'This is nice, isn't it?' Petra says, selecting a celery stick and biting it delicately.

'It's lovely,' Ryan says. 'I should be working today but . . .' He shrugs and chuckles, reclining on the rug. 'I guess the bar snacks can wait.'

Petra smiles and falls silent again, and Ryan senses that she'd like to say something more.

'Lucky with this weather,' he adds quickly to fill the space.

'Yes.' More silence. Josh and Daisy are wandering towards the pond now to throw their crusts to the ducks. Fourteen years old and a *smoker*, for God's sake, and Josh still won't tolerate crusts.

'So, what d'you think about the smoking thing?' Ryan asks.

'We should talk to him of course.'

'Yes, we really need to.'

'I think we should both do it together,' Petra says, turning to him.

'You're right,' Ryan says. 'United front and all that. But not today, huh? This is just too nice.'

Petra nods. 'We need to choose our time. It's not easy, is it? We're so rarely together these days . . .'

That's what happens when a couple breaks up, Ryan thinks dryly. 'Well, we'll just have to plan it, grab some time when it's just us . . .' *And no Hannah*, he means. 'When Daisy's not earwigging,' he adds quickly.

'Yep,' Petra says firmly. 'I'm sure we can do that.'

Ryan studies her face. She is sitting up straight, long, slender legs stretched out, crossed at the ankles. There's a sadness in her eyes which he hasn't seen for a long time. She's usually so brisk at handover time; brittle and impenetrable. 'Is everything all right, Petra?' he asks gently.

'I'm fine,' she says with a smile that doesn't reach her eyes. 'It's just . . . I do regret it sometimes, you know.'

'What d'you regret?' he asks, startled.

She lowers her gaze. 'What I did three years ago. Leaving . . .'

'Do you? Leaving the kids, you mean?'

Her grey eyes are fixed on him now. 'Yes, but not *just* the kids. Us too.'

He looks past her, at their children who are messing about, trying unsuccessfully to skim stones across the water. *Because you haven't met anyone else?* he thinks. *Because you're all alone with your cello in that perfect little Crouch End flat?*

'Why, though?' he asks. 'You seemed so sure when you left.'

She shakes her head, pushing her hair back distractedly. 'I was a mess back then, Ryan. I can't tell you how hemmed in I felt, trying to keep everything going. It's not as if I have a regular job that can just be slotted in . . .'

'Like mine?' he asks curtly.

'I'm not belittling what you do, but you *know* what my life is like. You know the schedules, rehearsals, touring . . . it just became impossible. Half the time when I was away, I was eaten up with guilt . . .'

'But the kids were fine,' Ryan cuts in. 'They had me, didn't they? I might not be perfect, but we muddled along . . .' She throws him a resigned look. 'I did my best,' he adds. 'You didn't think they'd be better off without you, did you?'

'In some ways, yes.' Her eyes mist with tears and she places her hand on his arm. 'I know you were doing your best,' she adds softly, 'and I couldn't have had my career without you. But the way I saw it, it was all such a terrible compromise . . .'

'I don't know what you mean,' he mutters.

'I mean,' Petra says, more forcefully now, 'your life's always been more stable, and I knew that the kids would know where they were and you'd always be home, making dinner . . .'

'. . . while you flew off to China or Brazil or Berlin or wherever . . .'

'It's what I do, Ryan!' she exclaims, swiftly removing her hand. 'But now they're older and I know they could cope with me being away, because they're settled. And that's mostly because you've done such a great job with them.'

Jesus Christ. Ryan thought he'd been asked along on a simple family picnic, and now he's being given a performance review. 'Thanks,' he mutters.

'Look how happy they are,' she adds, indicating the two of them perched at the edge of the pond.

Ryan nods wordlessly. 'Petra, are you actually saying you want me and you to try again?'

She presses her lips together and nods, her eyes filling with tears again.

'But . . . I'm getting married in two weeks' time . . .' *To someone who feels trapped, possibly even as 'hemmed in' as you claim to have felt three years ago. I'm clearly good at making the women I love feel imprisoned . . .*

'Well,' Petra clears her throat. 'I had to tell you what I've been thinking.'

Ryan glances distractedly around the heath. He *could* do it. He could set Hannah free to pursue her art without grumpy stepchildren impinging on her life. 'The kids would be pleased,' Petra adds tentatively.

'Yes, they probably would be.'

He's looking away now but can sense Petra studying him. An elderly couple walks by, arm in arm, and they murmur something and smile. *I probably look like I have the perfect family*, Ryan reflects, *with the good-looking children and the beautiful wife and the wicker hamper.* But it doesn't feel perfect. He wants Hannah to be in Petra's place, and a pang of missing her sweeps over him. 'Maybe,' he murmurs, 'it would be better if the kids lived with you.'

'What?' Petra looks aghast.

'Well, you know they're not exactly a hundred per cent delighted that I'm marrying Hannah . . .'

'Yes, because they don't want to share you,' Petra declares. 'They love you to bits. It's hard for them, Ryan.'

'And I love them,' he shoots back, 'more than anything, but I can't let them dictate how I live the rest of my life.'

She blinks at him. 'You mean . . . you'd seriously make them move out?'

'God, Petra, you're making it sound as if I'd be putting them out on the street. They'd live with you – their mother. You've got a lovely flat, plenty of space . . .'

'It's only two bedrooms, and what about their schools?'

'Well, we'd have to figure something out . . .' He knows, as soon as he's said it, that it's not what he wants, and he's sure it's not what his kids want either. Daisy and Josh belong with him.

'But . . . what about my work?' Petra asks coolly. Ryan looks at her, marvelling at how quickly she's transformed from being Petra the guilt-ridden mother to Petra the concert cellist. Petra for whom, if push came to shove, Elgar would always come before any real, living person.

Her entire demeanour stiffens as she starts to pack the remains of the picnic back into the hamper. The cartons have started to wilt now, and the berry salad has barely been touched. 'Maybe we should ask them,' he adds, 'and see what they think.'

Petra nods curtly, lips pursed, eyes guarded. 'We should think about it. We shouldn't rush into anything.'

'No, of course not.'

'And we need to talk to Josh about the cigarettes.'

'Yes, of course we do.' Ryan stands up, strides to the water's edge and puts an arm around his son and his daughter. Josh is only two inches shorter than he is, his baby softness morphing into sharp cheekbones and a handsome face. Turning to him, Daisy grins and snuggles closer.

They could all live together – his family – and Petra could cook her delicious meals, when she was around. Instead of the top floor being a jumble of Hannah's paintings and art materials it could be serene again with a chrome music stand placed like a spindly sculpture in the middle of the floor, and the cello parked in the corner, watching over the room like a stern aunt.

Ryan knows he could have all that again, but right now his daughter is demanding that he shows her how to skim a stone properly. He selects a flat, smooth pebble that's cool in his hand, throws it hard and fast across the water and hopes for the best.

FIFTY-FOUR

Two hours after leaving Little Hissingham, Pete calls Barney with the gleeful announcement that Amy has texted him already.

'That's great,' Barney says without conviction, simultaneously trying to clean Milo's bottom with a wet wipe. While Barney grips the phone, Milo makes his escape, crawling away at speed and daubing the living room rug with poo.

'You'd better come clean with Magda,' Pete adds, 'before you run into her again, you single dad with the adorable babies, managing all on your own . . .'

'Oh, fuck off,' Barney says, realising that he, too, is now crawling, in hot pursuit of his son. Dylan, who's strapped in his bouncy chair with splatters of mustard-coloured baby food all over his front, wails to be let out.

'Aren't you going to tell her you're married?' Pete wants to know.

'Yeah. No. God, it's not really important, is it . . .' *Hell, how can so much poo come out of one little person?* He grabs Milo and plonks him, still dirty-bottomed, on his lap.

'Well, it's probably quite important to Sadie,' Pete reminds him.

'Yeah. Listen, I don't really have time to talk right now . . . I'll call you later.'

Barney hangs up, still clutching Milo and gazes bleakly at the brownish stains on his freshly-washed jeans. Now, to make matters worse, Pete's phone call has rekindled Barney's guilt. He looks around the room in mild panic. There's poo on the floor so he can't liberate Dylan from his seat yet. His jeans are dirty, yet he can't change them until Milo is firmly encased in a fresh nappy. And only then can he turn his attentions to the rug. So many tasks have piled up, just when he'd been congratulating himself for coping so well. The room smells like a sewer, and he's lost one of the boys' baby shoes too; it must have fallen off when they were in the woods. And the buggy's a disgrace, its wheels caked with mud which he'll have to scrub off before Sadie comes home and wonders where the hell he took them. She's only been gone for a day but he has never known such crushing exhaustion in his entire life.

Breathing deeply, he cleans Milo as best he can, puts a nappy on him and, with Dylan's cries dying down to a whimper, places his brother in the seat beside him. Then he sets to work on the rug. Pausing for breath, he glances up at the framed wedding photo on the mantelpiece. Sadie looks ravishing – all full red lips and tumbling wavy hair, like a young Sophia Loren. God, she was gorgeous. Still is, of course, when she's not barking at him, being the parenting Führer. The phone rings, and he dumps the wet cloth on the rug and rushes to answer it in the kitchen. 'Barney? It's me.'

'Oh, hi, darling. How's it going?' His fingers smell terrible, he realises now.

'Good. Great . . .' Sadie says.

'Have a wild time last night?' Barney wills her to say yes and tell him all about it, to distract her from quizzing him about how things are at home.

'Not really, just a few drinks, bit of a dance at the end of the night.'

'Oh, come on,' he teases her. 'It can't have been that tame.'

'Well, it was!' she says tetchily. 'We just had a nice night, that's all.'

'Right, *okay* . . . .'

'How are the boys?' she wants to know.

'They're fine, been really good.'

'They don't sound fine. They're crying!'

Barney glances at his sons, willing them to be quiet. 'Yeah, well, they're just a bit hungry, I'll feed them in a minute.'

'You'd better go then,' she says sharply.

'Okay! I will, I just answered the phone . . .' God, what was he supposed to do? Leave it ringing, making her panic even more?

'I tried your mobile a couple of times this morning,' she adds.

'Sorry, out of charge.'

'And the house phone. I tried that too.'

'Like I said, we went out for a walk.' Christ, had he said that?

'You sound a bit stressed,' Sadie observes.

'Just busy. You know what it's like.'

She chuckles mirthlessly. 'Yes, sort of. I *can* relate . . .'

'Yeah, I know. Stupid thing to say.'

'Anyway, you said you were just about to feed the boys . . .'

Barney breathes deeply, wondering how this conversation has gone so wrong. 'It's okay. They've quietened down a bit now.'

'That's good . . .' She clears her throat. 'Um, Barney, thanks for this. For letting me . . . no, not *letting*, you never make me feel like I need permission to do anything . . .'

'Of course you don't,' he says, relieved at the softening of her tone.

'But thanks anyway. It's been . . . good for me to get away.'

'I'm glad,' Barney says.

'It's . . . sort of like I'm *me* again,' she adds hesitantly, 'and it's made me realise I haven't exactly been a bundle of fun lately.'

'Sadie, it's fine,' Barney says, his guilt kicking in again now. 'You've just been under a lot of pressure . . .'

'I don't want to be like that any more,' she says firmly. 'I love you and I love the boys, and I miss you all, you know . . .'

'We miss you too.'

'I haven't messed it all up, have I?' she blurts out.

'Of course not! You haven't messed up anything. You're a fantastic mum, and more than that, you're the love of my life, you know that?'

'Well, I hope so.' She lets out a small laugh.

'You are. You completely are.'

'You're mine too,' she says.

After the call, with the boys in a happier mood and content to kick around on their play mat, Barney walks around the house in a semidaze. What was that about – Sadie worrying about messing things up and blurting out her feelings for him? *She knows*, Barney thinks, sweat beading on his brow. *Somehow, she knows I've been in the woods with a couple of twenty-year-olds*. After feeding the babies he takes them out again, marching around the village and avoiding the park, even though Magda isn't working in the café today. *You're a bloody lucky man*, he keeps reminding himself. *Don't mess it all up.*

Later, he decides, when the boys are settled in their cots, he'll wipe the food smears off the worktops and high chairs and investigate the whiff that's started to come from the fridge. Then he'll take the baby listener out to the back garden and delve into the shed where Sadie's bike is lying all buckled and broken. There's a mountain-biking centre nearby, with a repair shop, which he thinks is open on Sundays. Tomorrow, he'll load the babies into their car seats and Sadie's bike into the boot, and the three of them will drive to that bike place in the hope of putting everything back together again.

FIFTY-FIVE

'I'd really better be going,' Johnny says reluctantly. 'I'm supposed to be picking up Cal from his mum's at four.' He and the girls are still in the café, having ordered yet another round of coffees which, he suspects, no one really wants, but has given them an excuse to spin out their time together.

'Where does she live?' Sadie asks.

'Not far, just over in Merchant City.' Johnny feels a twinge of guilt; usually he's so keen to collect Cal from his mother's that he shapes his entire day around it.

'We could all come with you,' Hannah teases him. 'We could turn up en masse, terrify the poor boy . . .'

'I want him to meet you all,' Johnny says quickly, 'but yeah – it might be a bit much for him today.' A bit much for Rona, he means, and he can picture Action Man's scathing gaze if he did show up with three women. *Still rollicking around with your old student mates, Johnny? Anyway, better dash, I'm on call, got lives to save . . .*

'I'd like another quick look around town anyway,' Hannah says.

'Me too,' Sadie adds as a small silence descends, and Johnny focuses on the collection of cups and plates on the table.

'Well, if it's okay with you, and please say if it's not, I'd like to come with you,' Lou says suddenly.

Johnny turns to look at her. 'Yeah! Yeah, that'd be fine . . .'

'I don't mean going to Rona's place,' Lou adds quickly. 'I just mean I'd like a walk, mooch around for a bit. Might check out some of the other vintage shops, so I could head over that way with you if it's okay . . .'

'Of course it is. Shall we go then? I tend to get the evil eye from Tristan if I'm late.'

Johnny tries to affects a breezy demeanour as he and Lou part company with Sadie and Hannah outside the café. Yet it's proving to be a challenge. He feels like a teenager again, a teenager who cannot believe his good fortune to have found a glittering excuse to be with his favourite girl. Lou is chatting animatedly as they walk, the skirt of her patterned dress swishing around her slim calves, her neat little feet encased in flat red ballet pumps. Lou's auburn hair is just as she wore it in Garnet Street, as if the defiant curls have resisted any attempts to tame them. Her face is pink-cheeked and pretty, her eyes sparkling and alive as she stops to admire the jewellery in a posh boutique.

'This is gorgeous,' she enthuses. 'I'm sure I remember the name from college . . .' She peers at the label attached to a necklace made from fine interlocking silver hoops.

'Your stuff's lovely too,' Johnny ventures.

'Oh, I haven't made anything in ages. I keep intending to, but in the evenings I don't seem to have the energy and the weekends . . .' She shrugs. 'They sort of pass me by in a thrilling whirl of domesticity. Anyway,' she adds, 'I don't have any materials at the moment. We're kind of going through a bit of a cash crisis.'

'Isn't Spike working?'

Lou shakes her head and laughs dryly. 'I'm not blaming

him, though. I could get it together if I really wanted to and had the motivation.'

'You should. You really should make some space for it, Lou, because the pieces I saw on your website—'

'You've looked at my website?' she exclaims.

'Yes, I did.' He feels his cheeks colouring. 'I looked at it last night actually.'

Johnny focuses hard on the necklace in the window, conscious of Lou studying his face.

'Well . . . I'm flattered. So what did you think?'

'Really impressive. It's a nicely designed site.'

'Thanks. A web designer I know offered to do it in exchange for some jewellery. But I need to start doing the stuff everyone tells you to do – the marketing, the getting out there and selling myself.' Lou pauses and smiles. 'And I guess I've never been very good at that.'

'I wish I could help,' Johnny says.

Lou laughs, sending a tiny jolt of electricity through him as she tugs gently on his arm. 'You already have. I can't tell you how lovely it's been seeing you again. And isn't it weird, you looking at my website last night when I was probably only a mile away, sitting in Felix's bar with Sadie and Han . . .'

'It's bizarre,' he agrees. His ears feel as if they're sizzling now.

'And d'you know what?' she adds as they turn the corner and make their way past a stag party, one member of which has 'Clive – Doomed Groom' emblazoned across his black T-shirt – 'I've got this feeling that things are going to be different when I get back to York, I really do, probably because I *feel* different.'

'Do you?' he asks. 'Why d'you think that is?'

'Oh, I don't know,' Lou says blithely, and for a moment Johnny allows himself to think it's because of him. But of course, it's being away with her old college friends that's lifted her spirits. 'Maybe it's seeing you,' she adds.

'Oh, I tend to have that effect on women,' he jokes feebly.

'You know what I mean,' she murmurs.

Johnny glances at her as they walk, trying to read the expression on her face. Whether she really meant that or not, he's seized by an urge to take her hand in his; the hand he's wanted to hold since he first met her sixteen years ago.

Just do it, he tells himself. What will she do – pull her hand away and run off screaming? *If I see a pigeon*, he tells himself, *I'll hold Lou Costello's hand.* They take a right turn, heading towards Rona and Tristan's smart red sandstone block. Just ahead of them, a boy of around Cal's age in low-slung jeans tosses his half-eaten packet of chips in the vague direction of a bin. It collides with its side, bouncing backwards and scattering pale yellow chips on to the ground, and Johnny has never been happier to see pigeons descend in his entire life.

FIFTY-SIX

Spike is playing, and it feels good. His fingers are agile, his lack of self-consciousness perhaps aided by the last traces of his hangover. He is standing in front of a particularly crappy shop filled with 99p T-shirts, lurid cheap handbags dripping with gilt chains and other assorted tat. Yet Spike doesn't care; he's just grateful to have found a pitch. He learnt enough about busking etiquette in his youth to know that you're not supposed to set up too close to another musician. He is singing a love song. It was inspired by Astrid, and he wrote it literally in a fever; it had come to him when he'd been virtually dying of flu a couple of weeks back. However, now she's clearly ousted him in favour of some big blond freak, he likes to think his lyrics run deeper and are really about enduring love.

Lou. It's about Lou, Spike realises, his voice ringing clear and pure across the street, the voice he'd almost forgotten he had. He starts changing the lyrics to whatever comes into his head on this beautiful spring day. He wants Lou, and he's singing his heart out for her.

Why has it taken him so long to realise this? As Spike launches into the third verse he pictures the provisions she'd lovingly bought for him: the noodles and mangetout and chicken. He loves that girl, he reflects, his voice cracking a little as a pound coin lands in the open guitar case. Another follows it, and he smiles his thanks each time, grateful that it's going down well, this love song he's now virtually making up as he goes along.

A small crowd has formed in front of him. A boy has stopped, clutching a guitar case of his own. *I can't be past it*, Spike decides, *if a teenager wants to listen to me*. Then, past the boy, Spike sees someone else: a girl walking towards him with curly red hair in a black dress with flowers all over it and little pumps on her feet. Pretty girl, he thinks, watching her gradually come into focus. She smiles at her boyfriend who's holding her hand, the way Spike and Lou held hands what feels like eight hundred years ago. Then Spike ceases to notice the small audience that's gathered around him, or even a little girl who runs forward and showers coins into the guitar case.

'What's up?' a man yells as Spike suddenly stops playing.

'Play!' the little girl demands. But Spike can't play because he's staring into the middle distance where the girl he loves, the girl he's travelled all the way from York in a clapped-out ambulance to see, is strolling along in the sunshine holding the hand of Johnny Lynch.

FIFTY-SEVEN

It doesn't fit, Spike being here on this sunny afternoon in Glasgow. It can't be, Lou thinks; it's just a man with longish dark hair in a battered leather jacket – hardly an unusual look for a busker. She keeps telling herself this – it *can't* be Spike, he's at home in York, doing his CV – even as he charges towards them with his guitar still strapped on.

'What the hell are you—' she shrieks, springing apart from Johnny as Spike swipes wildly at his jaw. 'Spike, for God's sake!' Lou screams as he misses his mark.

'Just get away, Lou,' he shouts back, this time landing a punch on Johnny's cheek before two men grab him, pulling him back, yelling, 'Jesus, calm down! Leave him alone . . .'

'What are you doing with Lou?' Spike roars, trying to launch himself towards Johnny again, but held back firmly by the two bigger, stronger men.

'You'll get arrested, mate!' one of them barks.

'Sort yourself out,' the other one tells him. 'If you've got a problem, deal with it. You can't just attack someone in the middle of the street—'

Lou stares at Spike. He's actually followed her here. She glances at Johnny who looks dazed as he holds a hand to his cheek. Blood is leaking from a cut. 'Are you all right?' she asks, reaching out to touch his face.

'Yeah, I'm okay,' he mutters, flinching.

'What are you *doing* here?' she snaps, whirling back to face Spike. 'What the hell are you playing at?'

He opens his mouth as the two men loosen their grip on his jacket. 'You're with him,' he splutters, indicating Johnny who's pressing a hankie against the side of his face. 'You came up here to be with him, didn't you?' Shaking his head as one of the men lets him go, shortly followed by the other, he fixes Lou with an anguished gaze.

'Of course I didn't! Are you crazy? Hannah ran into him in a shop – she was buying coffees and there he was and we've just been hanging out. I don't know what you *think* we've been doing . . .' She glances back to where Johnny was standing, but he's gone.

'You were holding his hand,' Spike growls.

'Yes, because we're friends, for Christ's sake. God. Can't I spend time with old friends?'

'Oh yeah. All the touchy-feely-huggy stuff. I'd forgotten about that.'

Lou's eyes narrow as she throws him a look of disgust. 'How did you get here anyway?'

'I, um . . . got a lift,' he mutters, lifting the guitar strap over his neck.

'Really? And what was your plan – to ruin my weekend? Well, you've done that now . . .'

Spike shakes his head. 'That's not why I came. He – Johnny – left a message on our answerphone last night. Said something about seeing you in a bar with your boyfriend . . .'

'But he can't have,' Lou exclaims. 'He would have spoken to us, wouldn't he? And anyway, Johnny hasn't got our home number . . .' She frowns, remembering now that he was looking at her website last night.

'So who's this boyfriend?' Spike asks sulkily.

'I don't know what the hell you're talking about. It was probably Felix . . .'

'Oh, *Felix*,' he sneers. 'Truffle man. That's all right then.'

Lou blinks at him in bewilderment, then turns slowly and starts to walk away. 'Lou! Please wait!' he yells after her. When she keeps on walking, Spike breaks into a trot, still gripping the guitar and calling her name, too distraught to notice a bunch of kids descending to gather up the money from the case on the ground.

FIFTY-EIGHT

'How did you find out?' Josh asks dully. Ryan, Petra and their son are sitting around Petra's kitchen table, Daisy having been asked to remain in the living room watching the penguin DVD.

'Hannah found—' Ryan starts.

'Oh, right, *she* told you,' Josh mumbles, picking dirt off his thumb with a fingernail.

Ryan observes his firstborn across the table. Being a dad wasn't supposed to be like this; it was meant to be about keeping them fed, warm and in a reasonably hygienic state, and taking them on fun outings. 'Actually,' Ryan says, keeping his voice level, 'Hannah didn't tell me. Yes, she found a Marlboro packet in your jeans pocket, but she didn't say anything to me.'

Josh looks up at his father. 'So how d'you know?'

'I just do, okay?' Ryan mutters, wondering how it's all switched around so he's ended up the one being interrogated.

'You might as well tell him, Ryan,' Petra says gently.

He looks at his ex-wife who, just a couple of hours ago, was gently suggesting that the two of them might try again. The very idea is ludicrous; it's Ryan who feels hemmed in when he's with her, the way she once claimed to feel with him. 'Hannah wrote about it in an email,' he says, clearing his throat.

'What, she wrote about *me*?' Josh barks. 'Who to?'

'Just her friends. In fact she didn't even intend to send it.'

'Why did she write it then?'

Ryan takes a deep breath. Explaining why will mean telling Josh just how difficult Hannah finds living with them all, when he's spent the last six months pretending that everything will sort itself out. 'She wrote it because she was fed up,' he says flatly. 'She finds you and Daisy hostile' – Ryan sees Josh's eyes darken but carries on regardless – 'and I think she needed to splurge it all out, to share it with people who'd understand . . . do you know what I mean?'

Josh shrugs. 'Not really.'

'Well . . . she's really close to Sadie and Lou and I suppose she felt better offloading to them.'

'What else did she write about me?' Josh asks warily.

Ryan pauses. 'Just that you're not especially friendly, that she doesn't feel welcome in our house . . .'

Josh looks as if he's about to defend himself with his usual *but I didn't do anything!* then decides he'd better not. Ryan glances at Petra, willing her to say something, to at least give the impression that they're in this together.

'So why did you read it then,' Josh asks, 'if it was meant to be secret?'

'I didn't mean to,' Ryan says hotly. 'I was looking for your sister's story to send to Mum . . .'

'Yeah, but how come you thought an email was a story?'

'I didn't!' Ryan barks. 'It was . . . a mistake. I stumbled upon and it and I read it and maybe I shouldn't—'

'I think you're just trying to get us off the subject of you smoking,' Petra says firmly.

'They were Eddie's,' Josh mutters. 'Not mine.'

319

Ryan blinks at him. 'But you had them in your pocket.'

'Yuh. I . . . I tried one . . .'

'So you *have* been smoking,' Ryan observes, trying to sound like an outraged dad, but knowing his heart is no longer in it.

'No, Dad. Not really.' His son's eyes are large and dark, and for a brief moment Ryan sees his little boy again, his funny son who loved Peter Pan and built pirate ships out of enormous cardboard boxes.

'What d'you mean?' Petra asks.

'Um . . . I had a little try and started coughing and couldn't manage any more. Eddie laughed and wouldn't even give me five quid.'

Ryan stares incredulously. 'What was the five quid for?'

'A bet,' Josh mumbles, his cheeks flaming pink. 'I did it for a bet.'

'Well,' Petra says firmly, 'I hope you're not going to do it again.'

Josh shakes his head. Then he turns to his father, a flicker of a smile playing on his lips: 'So, Hannah found 'em and didn't tell you?'

'Well, it looks that way,' Ryan says.

Josh smiles then – actually cracks a grin, dispelling the cloud of tension that's been hanging over Petra's kitchen table. 'Is that it then?'

'Is that what?' Ryan asks.

'Is that the end of the big talk?'

'Don't be cheeky, Josh,' Petra snaps. 'I don't find it funny.'

'Oh, come on.' Ryan catches her eye, and her expression softens a little. 'We all try things, don't we?' he adds.

'Not really, Ryan, no.'

'Well,' he says with a shrug, 'I think most of us do. So yes, Josh . . . that's the end of the big talk.'

FIFTY-NINE

Johnny's face has stopped bleeding by the time he arrives at Rona's apartment. As he sits at her granite-topped island unit, all that remains of Spike's outburst is a small crust of semidried blood and an ache that's radiated towards his ear. Cal is perched on the stool beside him, regarding him with large, serious eyes as he slurps Nesquik through a straw. 'Does it still hurt, Dad?' he asks.

Johnny shakes his head and musters a smile. 'A bit. It's getting better already though. I'll survive.'

Cal frowns, clearly turning over the simplified version of events that Johnny gave him. 'So,' he says carefully, 'you met your friend, and her boyfriend saw you and he thought you were stealing her off him?'

'Yes.' Johnny nods. 'Sounds mad, doesn't it? Not the kind of thing that usually happens to your dad.'

Cal removes his bendy straw from the glass and sucks out the remaining microdribble of Nesquik. 'Was it one of those ladies in that place last night?'

'Er . . . yes, it was.'

'Where were you going?' Cal wants to know.

'Well, actually, we were on our way to pick you up. She wasn't planning to come – she was going to shop for clothes or something – but she would like to meet you sometime.'

'Would she?' Cal asks. 'What's her name?'

'Lou.'

Cal sniggers. 'What, like the *loo*?'

Johnny laughs too, causing a spasm of pain to shoot from his nose to his ear. 'Yeah, I guess so. I never thought of that.'

Cal sucks the end of his empty straw. 'Can I still meet her?'

'Um, probably not now. I'd imagine she's gone back to the hotel to sort things out with her boyfriend, and anyway, she's going back home to York tomorrow.'

'How far's that?'

'Well . . .' Johnny shrugs. 'It's quite a long way, about four hours' drive . . .'

'But . . .' Cal turns to him, deadly serious. 'I could meet her another time. We could visit.'

With a smile, Johnny puts an arm around his son's shoulders. 'After what happened today, I don't think that'd be such a good idea.'

They fall silent then as Tristan's voice booms through from the bedroom: 'I don't know what he's thinking, getting into a bloody fight on the way to pick up his son. It's ridiculous, Rona, God knows what the real story is . . .'

'It *is* the real story,' she spits back. 'What are you implying – that he started a fight in the street? He's not like that . . .'

'He's a father,' Tristan snaps. 'What kind of father turns up to pick up his son covered in blood?'

They carry on, perhaps forgetting that Johnny and Cal are perched at the kitchen island, and Johnny tries to engage his son in bland conversation, asking what he thinks they might need to do at the allotment tomorrow. 'Er, dunno, Dad,' Cal murmurs, his face clouded now.

'Whatever you think,' Rona snaps, 'at least he bloody cares about his son. All you care about is your damn self.'

'Hey,' Johnny says quickly, 'maybe we should get going, huh? Is your bag ready?'

'Yeah, nearly. I'll just go and get it.' Cal hops off his stool and hurries to his bedroom, clearly keen to escape too.

'Sorry about that.' Rona stands in the kitchen doorway in a pretty pale blue sleeveless dress – a birthday dress – her hair piled up artfully.

'It's all right,' Johnny says. 'Not your fault.' She steps towards him, tilting her face this way and that as she examines the cut on his cheek. 'There's still a bit of blood,' she says, tearing off a sheet of kitchen roll, wetting it under the chrome tap, and gently dabbing his face.

'Thanks.' Johnny feels small, being attended to by his ex-wife, and Tristan's hostile vibes filter through from their bedroom.

'Poor you.' She stands back and smiles ruefully. 'So, who was this friend you were out with?'

'Er . . . Lou Costello.' Sensing his cheeks flush, he quickly adds, 'She's here with Hannah and Sadie for Hannah's hen weekend. And for some reason Spike took it upon himself to come up too.'

'Why?' she asks incredulously.

Johnny shrugs. 'Seems to have got it into his head that she was up to something.'

'*He's* one to talk,' Rona declares.

'Yeah. Well, hopefully they'll sort things out.'

Rona nods. 'He was always a bit of a loser, wasn't he? Remember that time he strained wine through Lou's tights at that party?'

Johnny chuckles. 'I thought that was pretty resourceful actually. Anyway, I haven't even asked – how's your birthday so far?'

'Oh, this morning was lovely,' Rona says blithely, proceeding to wipe the immaculate worktop with a cloth. 'We had the birthday usuals – waffles, strawberries, little bit of champagne . . .'

'That sounds nice . . .'

'All bought and prepared by me,' she adds softly.

'Oh.' Better keep it neutral, Johnny decides, with Tristan lurking moodily just a few metres away. 'And he really surpassed himself with the present this year,' she adds with a roll of her clear blue eyes. 'Gave me £200 to buy myself something.'

'Wow,' Johnny says flatly.

'Nice to see romance isn't dead.' Rona laughs bitterly.

Johnny looks away and is more than relieved when Cal appears with his backpack on, baseball boots laced up and ready to go.

'So, we'll be off then,' he says, briefly kissing Rona's cheek.

'Yep, okay. Come here, Cal. Give me a hug.' He puts his arms around her waist and squeezes tightly.

'Bye, Mum,' he says with a grin.

'Enjoy the rest of your birthday,' Johnny adds.

'Thanks.' Rona smiles, and as he and Cal turn to go, she calls after him, 'You should get in touch with her.' Johnny throws her a quizzical look. 'Lou, I mean. Where's she living these days?'

'York,' he says lightly.

'Well, you should call her.'

'Maybe.' Johnny shrugs in Rona's hallway.

'I know you want to,' she adds, 'and I really think you should.' He smiles then, and is seized by an urge to hug her, although with Tristan likely to appear at any moment he decides that this might be unwise. Instead, he strides out into the fresh, cloudless day with his son, figuring that one angry altercation is quite enough for one day.

SIXTY

Lou is alone in the hotel room, perched on the edge of her single bed. She's called Hannah and Sadie to tell them about Spike showing up, and the scene with Johnny, and although they want to come back, she's suggested they stay out for a little longer. She needs a Big Talk with Spike, and as she knows from experience, this is unlikely to be a calm, measured discussion. 'I'll call you,' she told Hannah, 'as soon as I know what the hell's going on.'

Right now, though, after dumping his bag in her room and suddenly remembering the guitar case still sitting out in the street, Spike's rushed back to retrieve it. He tried to kiss Lou as he was leaving, but she'd recoiled in disgust. He's taking much longer than she expected. She wants him back here, right now, so they get this talk over and done with.

Lou stands up, tips her cold tea into the washbasin and glances around at her friends' things scattered around the room – Hannah's summery dress and Sadie's sexy high shoes – suddenly wishing that Spike would disappear into the atmosphere like a bad smell, and that she and her friends could try to salvage the rest of the weekend. The thought of not being able to say goodbye to Johnny triggers an ache in Lou's gut, but there's nothing she can do about that now. Although she now has his number, he's unlikely to want to see her again after Spike's spectacular display.

The trilling phone makes her flinch. Spike's ringtone, coming from somewhere in his rucksack. The phone has stopped ringing by the time she finds it in one of the small outside pockets. Missed call from Ast. Who's Ast? Lou does a quick mental flick-through of Spike's friends, but can't think of who it could be.

She places his phone on the cheap laminate desk then, feeling uneasy, unlocks it and scrolls through his contacts. There it is – *Ast* – after Andy and before Ben. Back on his home screen, she sees that the mysterious Ast has left a voicemail message. If she plays it, he'll know she's been prowling around in the inner sanctum of his mobile. But after today's episode, Lou doesn't really give a damn what he thinks,

Hey, Spike, the girl's husky voice starts, *hope you're okay . . . It's me, Astrid, Saturday teatime-ish . . . look, hon, I'm really sorry. I should probably have been straighter with you but there's a couple of things . . . well, you already know I felt a bit weird after running into Lou that day . . .*

Lou feels as if her heart has stopped.

. . . I mean, Spike, you're a lucky guy! She's such a sweet girl and I don't think you should throw it all away . . . A short pause. Lou's breath is coming quick and shallow as, still clutching Spike's phone to her ear, she lowers herself back onto her bed. *. . . There's another thing too. Something I should have told you about. It's nothing serious but I've kind of met someone through work. Still early days but I'd feel bad, you know? And it's not like me and you were ever going to go anywhere . . .*

Tears are falling now as Astrid says *bye, lots of love* – not because of the cheating, which Lou should have known about, she should have spotted the signs. No, Lou's tears are for all the time spent, the years wasted. She's crying for the life she's stumbled into, for every minute she's spent at Let's Bounce in a synthetic brown tabard and for every squashed nugget she's scraped off the floor.

SIXTY-ONE

'Hope you got what you needed,' Terry says with a grin as Spike hands him the guitar.

'Yep, did pretty well,' Spike says, 'considering I haven't done it in a long time.'

'Bit rusty, were you?' Terry chuckles, opening the case and lifting out the guitar.

'Well, you know what it's like . . .'

'. . . Like riding a bike,' Terry remarks, pausing to frown at a chip in the wood on the side of the guitar. Spike blinks at the mark, praying that it's just a trick of the light. 'What's this?' Terry asks.

'Er, I dunno,' Spike murmurs, sounding amazed. Hell, it must've happened when he'd lunged at that arsehole, Johnny-bloody-Lynch. Spike is horribly aware of his nasal breathing as Terry frowns at the chip.

'Mike'll go mental when he sees this.'

'I'm sure it was there all the time,' Spike says quickly, still conscious of a faint smarting in his right knuckles from where they collided with Johnny's cheekbone.

'I don't think it was, mate. God, Spike, I thought I could trust . . .'

And so it starts: the wrangling, with Terry saying Spike

will have to pay something as the guitar can no longer be sold as new.

'It's just a tiny scratch,' Spike protests, wondering now if this is his favourite shop after all. 'I mean, it's hardly visible to the naked eye.'

'My eyes are naked,' Terry huffs, 'and I can see it a mile off.'

'But I told you, I don't have any money. My wallet was nicked . . .' Spike is starting to sweat now, and a faint thudding has started up in his temples.

Terry frowns at him. 'What about your busking money?'

'I don't have it,' Spike mutters.

'What, you didn't make any?'

'It was nicked,' he growls.

Terry blows out a loud gust of air and throws Spike a pitying look. 'Not your day, is it? First your wallet, then all your takings . . . hang on a minute. I'll see what Norm thinks, maybe we can fix it . . .' Terry places the guitar in the open case on the floor and mooches off to the back room to find his colleague.

Spike stares down at it. He could wait, and perhaps they'll be able to smooth out the dent with some kind of magic filling stuff, but he isn't prepared to stay and find out. For the second time that day, Spike runs, taking the carpeted stairs two at a time and bursting out onto the street before fleeing towards Lou's hotel.

It's only a few doors away. He dives in, startling the girl at reception and barks, 'What room are they in?'

'Sorry?' the girl says, frowning.

'Er, I think Hannah booked it. Hannah McShane – there's three of them. One's my girlfriend. What's their room number?'

The girl blinks at her screen. 'It's 232 but I'm not supposed to – '

'Thanks,' he says, turning to run up the stairs to the

second floor. He arrives at the girls' door and gives it a firm rap. 'Lou?' he says in an urgent whisper. 'It's me! Quick, let me in . . .'

There's a muffled exchange inside the room, and an agonising few seconds tick by as he waits. As the door opens slowly, he's already spilling it out: about the chipped guitar and Terry being different these days, totally over-reacting, wanting *money* off him . . . Spike tails off and peers around the room, first at Lou who's perched on the edge of her bed like a little doll – a doll with red, puffy eyes. 'Lou?' he croaks. 'What . . . what's up?'

Lou remains silent, her mouth set in a firm straight line, and beside her, Sadie regards him with a caustic gaze. 'I think you know what's up,' Lou spits out.

'What? No . . . I really don't . . .' Something tightens in Spike's stomach as he sees Lou inhaling deeply, drawing herself up, becoming stronger and a little less doll-like, in fact, no longer doll-like at all. She wipes a hand across her wet cheek and juts out her chin. 'You missed a call while you were out,' she tells him. 'You left your mobile here in your rucksack.'

'Er, did I?' He quickly skims the room for it, trying to ignore Hannah, who's staring at him icily.

'It's over there,' Lou adds, pointing to the dressing table. 'Astrid called.'

'Uh?' He tries to form an expression of incredulity, as if Astrid is someone he knows vaguely – has maybe run into once or twice – but that he'd be no more perplexed if Barack Obama had called him.

'You know,' Lou continues, her voice eerily steady now. '*Astrid*. She left you a voicemail message.'

'Did she?' he says faintly, finding it all too much being trapped in this dingy room with three pairs of eyes beaming hatred at him.

'Yes, you'll see it's been played,' Lou goes on, 'but you

can listen to it again if you want. It's not good news, though. It's definitely over between you two. She doesn't feel good about you having a girlfriend, and anyway, she's met someone else.'

'Jesus,' he blurts out. 'It's not . . . it's not what you think, okay? It was nothing! Look, can we talk, Lou – just me and you? Can we go somewhere . . .'

'*You* can,' Lou cuts in, her eyes glistening with tears once more, but tears of fury, not hurt. 'You can get out of here right now and go home.'

'But . . . but I can't!' he cries. 'Please. Hannah, Sadie, could you just give us a few minutes? We really need to talk about this. I can explain . . .'

'*Why* can't you go home, Spike?' Hannah asks coolly.

'Because I lost my wallet and all the money I made busking was gone by the time I went back to get the guitar case . . .'

'Guess you'll be walking to York then,' Lou says firmly. 'Now get out, Spike. Just get the hell out.'

SIXTY-TWO

The hotel pool is called 'The Lap of Luxury' which must, Hannah thinks, be someone's idea of a joke. It's deep in the bowels of the basement, is barely larger than the average tablecloth and has a distinct air of being underused. While there's no discernable algae on the water's surface, there's a faint whiff of damp costumes and smelly feet.

Lou and Sadie are already in the jacuzzi by the time Hannah joins them, heads resting on its tiled edge. 'You okay, Lou?' she asks gently, stepping into the feebly bubbling water.

Lou smiles stoically. 'Yes, I think so. I'm just sorry this has screwed up your weekend.'

'It hasn't,' Hannah declares. 'We've found Johnny again, haven't we?'

'Anyway,' Sadie cuts in, placing a hand on Lou's arm, 'it's not as if you could help it – Spike turning up like that.'

'Maybe,' Hannah adds tentatively, 'it's for the best, Lou. That you found out, I mean. Have you any idea how long it's been going on?'

Lou shakes her head. 'A while, I think. It sounded that way from her voicemail message . . .'

Hannah studies her friend, cautious of saying anything

negative about Spike. She's seen enough friends split with long-term boyfriends and have everyone pitch in with how despicable they always thought he was, only for them to promptly get back together again and make babies. 'So,' she says, 'is this it, d'you think?'

'God, yes.' Lou looks at Hannah, her expression defiant. 'You know my only regret?' Her eyes moisten now, and she rubs her wet fingers across them.

'What is it?' Hannah takes hold of her hand.

'There was this one time, years ago now, when I thought Spike might be having a thing with someone else. I can't even remember her name, but she had a blonde plait coiled on top of her head like some kind of weird loaf thing. She came to that party we had – the last one in Garnet Street . . .'

'I remember her,' Hannah says.

'There was something that night,' Lou continues. 'That girl spent most of the party smoking in the kitchen, but now and again I'd see her give Spike this look, and he'd give her a look back, and I just had this . . . hunch. And I told myself it was probably nothing, or I'd drunk too much and was feeling emotional because you were leaving, Han.' She pauses, stretching her toes out of the water. 'Now,' Lou adds, 'I know that hunches are usually right.'

'Why didn't you ask him about that girl?' Hannah asks gently.

'Because,' Lou shrugs, 'I was in love, I was twenty-two and stark raving mad. And my parents thought he was awful, remember – some dirty old man who'd got me in his clutches and God knows what he was going to do with me.' She laughs bitterly. 'So I *couldn't* believe he was cheating. I kept thinking, if I could push any niggling doubts out of my mind, everything would be okay.'

'Well,' Sadie murmurs, 'I reckon you've had a lucky escape.'

'You know what I think?' Hannah adds.

'What?' Lou asks.

'We need to get out for a bit. Blow the cobwebs away.'

'What've you got in mind?' Sadie asks.

'Well . . .' Hannah grins. 'I hadn't really planned to do this on our weekend away. But then, I hadn't imagined any of this – us meeting Felix, finding Johnny again, Spike turning up . . .'

'It should just be three of us for a while,' Sadie declares.

'I was thinking that too,' Hannah says, 'especially as Felix wants us to pop into the bar later tonight.'

'Dare I go back?' Sadie shudders.

'Of course,' Hannah laughs. 'But let's get dry and make the most of the rest of the day.'

'Where are we going?' Lou wants to know.

'Just a little jaunt. We should get moving though, because we've got to to be at Felix's at ten . . .'

'What's with the schedule?' Lou asks, frowning.

Hannah turns to her and smiles. 'You'll see.'

*

The red-lipsticked girl at reception had told Hannah about the nearest car hire place, tucked away in an industrial unit by the Clyde. They are finally doing it – heading north to Loch Lomond, like they'd always planned to as students – music blaring as they leave the city behind. Hannah is driving, feigning confidence as she has never been behind the wheel of a Beetle before. There was no choice, though. In fact there'd only been one available – not red like Johnny's dented old model but unashamedly pink. Hannah rarely drives in London but now, as the glassy-smooth loch comes into view, she realises she's lost her customary nervousness behind the wheel. Lou inhales a lungful of cool air as they follow the twisting road alongside the loch. For the moment, Spike and her dingy flat feel a long way away. 'I'm going to redecorate when I get back,' she announces suddenly, turning to Sadie.

'Are you? You mean, so it feels like a fresh start?'

'Yeah.' Lou laughs, her gaze caught by a speedboat zipping across the water. 'Some people get their hair chopped short when they split up with a boyfriend. And here I am, thinking of light blue for the living room . . .'

'You're going to do it yourself?' Hannah asks.

Lou nods. 'Remember how many times we discussed getting rid of that orange wallpaper in Garnet Street?'

'And all the times we said we'd persuade Johnny to drive us up here? We never got around to that either,' Sadie chuckles. 'Why didn't we just do it?'

'Too busy,' Lou suggests with a smirk.

'Too busy doing what?' Sadie asks.

Lou looks at her friends, knowing they'll have to turn back soon to return the car, and that this, like every tiny chapter of their lives, will soon be over. That's the thing about being young, she reflects: you really do think everything will carry on, just the way it is, like the winding road they're following now. But life changes and everyone grows up. None of them would dream of straining wine through tights any more. Well, maybe Spike would, if he was really desperate. 'How could we possibly have thought we were busy?' Hannah muses, slowing to take a perilous turn. 'What were we doing anyway?'

Lou laughs, pulling out the band that's been securing her hair. 'Just living, I guess,' she says.

SIXTY-THREE

For a brief period in his early twenties, Spike had been assigned a car and driver by his record company. This driver, an elderly man called George, was at Spike's beck and call, ferrying him from venue to venue for interviews and TV performances. Although that was twenty-odd years ago now, Spike still recalls the Merc's soft Caramac-hued leather and the back of George's reassuringly grey, neatly-clipped hair as he drove. If he really concentrates, he can almost spirit himself back to those happier times, which is precisely what he's trying to do now from the passenger seat of a van filled with rolls of carpet that's being driven at a terrifying speed by a man called Ralph.

'You like Judas Priest?' Ralph barks, jolting Spike from a semi-slumber. He suspects it's rude to sleep, or even feign sleep, when hitchhiking. Ralph probably only stopped and offered him a lift in exchange for some banter and a few laughs, but Spike feels that his store of humorous material is rather depleted right now.

'Judas Priest!' Ralph exclaims, giving Spike an agitated look. 'D'you like 'em?'

'Er, yeah,' he fibs.

'You into music?' Ralph wants to know, swivelling his

fleshy face towards Spike for longer than is probably recommended in the Highway Code.

'I'm a musician actually,' Spike says.

'Yeah? Play in a band or what?'

'Um, I've got a few things on the go . . .'

The brief silence that follows is filled with the frantic strains of Judas Priest. Spike's thoughts wander to Lou, and what she might be doing right now. 'You know,' Ralph muses, 'I'm sure I know you from somewhere.'

Spike gazes at a sleek grey Porsche speeding ahead. 'Yeah?'

'What bands have you been in?' he wants to know.

Just tell him, then he'll stop jerking his head round and keep his mind on the road. 'There've been a few things over the years,' Spike says airily, 'but the thing you probably remember is a song called 'My Beauty' that I recorded when—'

'Not that horse song?' Ralph exclaims, oblivious to the frantic beeping behind him as he veers into the outside lane.

'That's the one.' Spike's expression has set like cement.

'God, yeah, I remember that,' Ralph guffaws, and launches into an out-of-tune rendition of the song.

Spike glances down and checks his watch. They have just passed Carlisle and, by his reckoning, it will only take another three hours to get to York.

SIXTY-FOUR

Their last supper is a simple Italian. Not at Puccini's – Johnny mentioned that no one goes there anymore – but a small basement candlelit place where the girls are given a corner table. 'What's going to happen, Lou?' Sadie asks.

Lou places her cutlery neatly on the side of her plate. 'Well, Spike will have to come and collect his stuff, I suppose. Not that he's got much – guitars, a few books, his clothes and some manky old tubes of ointment in the bathroom . . .'

'I mean apart from that.' Sadie sips her wine and regards Lou over the rim of her glass.

Lou fixes her with a steady gaze. 'I've decided I'm going to cut my hours at the hellhole and start work on some new jewellery.'

'That's fantastic,' Hannah exclaims. 'Are you going to tell Dave when you get back?'

'Yep,' Lou says firmly. 'And eventually, if I can get things going again I can quit completely.' She shrugs and smiles. 'No, I *will* quit. I'm also going to look for another artist-in-residency post, like I should have done years ago, even if it means moving . . .'

'Where to?' Hannah asks.

'I don't know.' Lou grins and tops up her glass of red. 'Anywhere really. You know, it's actually a lovely feeling to know that whatever I do, I won't have to discuss it or do any persuading. It's just *me*.'

'Will you manage, though,' Hannah asks tentatively, 'paying the rent and everything all by yourself?'

'I do that anyway,' she says with a rueful smile. 'And because Spike won't be lying around in the day with the gas fire on full blast . . . God,' she pauses to tear off a scrap of pizza crust, 'I'll be loaded.'

Lou can sense her friends studying her, perhaps suspecting that she's just putting on a brave face. 'So it's definitely over with Spike,' Hannah ventures, unable to erase the trace of hope from her voice.

'Oh yes,' Lou declares. 'I was working it all out when we were in the jacuzzi. He sold that guitar – the one his parents bought for him – so I'd go to Glasgow leaving him completely free for his weekend of fun . . .'

'And now she's dumped him,' Hannah observes.

Lou nods. 'So the pour soul's alone and it's all been for nothing. Sorry, though, Han,' she adds, 'I think it might be a tiny bit awkward if he comes to your wedding.'

'Oh, I'm sure we'll manage to have a good time without him,' Hannah smirks.

'He'd bought his suit and everything. Well, not *bought*, Charlie said he had one he could borrow . . .'

Sadie twirls the remains of her spaghetti around her fork. 'You are still going to go through with it, aren't you, Han? The wedding, I mean?'

Hannah nods and smiles. 'Yes, of course I am. I just had a wobble over him spending last night at Petra's – I mean real, serious jealousy that actually made me feel sick . . .' She pauses. 'It made me realise, despite everything, how much I love him.'

'What about Daisy and Josh?' Sadie asks.

'Oh, I'm sure, when I get home, the kids will still be . . .' She laughs, trying to find the right words, '. . . still his kids. I mean, they'll be around forever, won't they? Bringing bags of stinking laundry home when they're students, phoning up to say they can't get their washing machines to work when they're thirty-five . . . they love him to bits, you know. And now, after being away with you two, I feel . . . sort of hopeful that things will turn around.'

'You really think so?' Lou asks.

'Yes, I do,' Hannah says firmly. 'God, it might be a complete disaster and they'll resent me even more when I'm their dad's wife, and I'll sneak into their rooms and find little Hannah voodoo dolls with pins stuck in . . .' The waitress refills their glasses and deftly clears away the clutter of plates.

'Han,' Sadie says when they're alone again, 'I've decided I'm not bringing the babies to your wedding.'

'What?' Hannah exclaims. 'We don't mind, you know' – she's slipped into we-speak, she realises – 'even if they bawl the registry office down when we're saying our vows. Isn't that supposed to happen at weddings? And there'll be other kids there – Ryan's sister is bringing her three kids and his friend Adam has a newborn . . .'

'I just don't think we should,' Sadie explains. 'You know how many times me and Barney have been out on our own since we had the boys?' Hannah and Lou look blank. 'None,' she announces.

'Really?' Lou gasps.

'Yep, really. Shocking, isn't it?'

'But who will you leave them with?' Hannah asks.

'Barney's parents,' Sadie says.

'Will they be okay with looking after the kids?' Lou asks, frowning.

'They'll be fine, even if they don't do things the way I

would. Anyway, it'll be good for the boys to get to know their grandparents better, and me and Barney . . .' She grins and opens the dessert menu with its old-fashioned, wedding-invitation-style script. 'Well, that means we'll get to spend the night in a hotel, doesn't it?'

'Careful,' Hannah sniggers. 'You know what happens on these drink-fuelled nights, *especially* at weddings . . .'

'I don't know what you mean.' Sadie's dark eyes gleam in the light of the stuttering candle. 'I'll be tucked up in bed in my sensible pyjamas with a book by nine o'clock.'

'You haven't done much reading on this weekend,' Lou remarks.

'Well, I've been a bit busy.'

'We've noticed.' Hannah smiles teasingly. 'I take it he hasn't texted you yet?'

'No, thank God,' Sadie exclaims. 'But listen, what I was thinking is . . . coming to your wedding on our own might make me and Barney feel a bit more . . . *together*. We need to do something, I've realised that. Something weird's happened to me since we had the boys . . .'

'What kind of weird?' Lou asks.

Sadie shakes her head. 'I've become this . . . routiney person, obsessed with everything being absolutely right and by the book. As if it'll all fall apart unless we stick to the schedules I've set up. And just being away for one night has proved that it won't, that I *can* relax and just be myself and maybe, more than anything, that's what me and Barney need right now.'

'It sounds as if you're blaming yourself for everything,' Hannah says, touching her hand.

'I'm not. It's up to me *and* Barney to make it work, but . . .' Sadie's eyes mist as she takes a deep breath. 'I think,' she continues, 'if I had more in my life to think about, then I wouldn't blow little things out of proportion . . .'

'Are you thinking of going back to work?' Lou suggests.

'Maybe. I hadn't planned to, but maybe in a few months' time, I'll look into going back part-time. I might even start designing again too.'

'What, lingerie?' Hannah grins. 'You really should. You're wasting your talents, you know . . .'

'Well, I've been wondering,' Sadie says, 'whether there's a market out for there for maternity and nursing underwear that's not hideous, and bras that don't look like awful satin hammocks . . .'

'Would that mean moving back to London?' Hannah blurts out. 'I hope it does. God, I'd love it if you were near me. I need an ally . . .'

'Well, a bit closer maybe, if I was teaching . . .' Sadie tails off. 'I'll have to talk it over with Barney.'

'Go on,' Hannah urges her. 'Use all your persuasive womanly powers.'

'You should mention it on Han's wedding night,' Lou suggests, 'at that hotel. And don't wear your sensible nursing bra either. Dig out one of your hand-made corsets from the old days.'

'You know,' Sadie says, smiling mischievously as the waitress approaches to take their dessert orders, 'I might do just that.'

*

'I've got a proposition for you, Hannah.' Felix places three tall glasses of inky liquid on their table and perches on the vacant fourth chair.

'Felix, she's marrying Ryan,' Sadie teases, placing a conciliatory hand on his arm. 'I'm sorry, but it's all sorted . . .'

'You break my heart,' he declares with a shake of his head, 'but listen – I've had an idea about those wicked little stepkids of yours, Hannah . . .'

'What's that?'

'You need some space, right? Somewhere you can call your own, at least for a couple of hours or so . . .' He pushes back his badly-cut choppy blond hair.

'She needs a shed,' Lou smirks.

'Well, I was actually thinking of my flat. It's in Bow, so not far from you . . .'

'You'd be like Woody Allen and Mia Farrow,' Lou exclaims.

Hannah laughs, fishing a perfectly-formed blackberry from her drink and popping it into her mouth. 'Felix, I think you're great, but I'm not so sure about you and me as flatmates, you know?'

'Yes, but I'm up here for the next twelve days and later on I'm in Bath, scouting for premises for a new place. You could use it for a bit of respite.'

'I can't just *use* your flat,' she exclaims.

'Ah, but you'd be doing me a favour,' he explains. 'You see, I've hardly been there these past few months and it's been empty for far too long.'

'You'd like me to flat-sit for you?' she asks.

Felix nods. 'God, one of these days I'm going to come back and find a load of squatters lying pissed on my Heal's rug.'

'I'll roll up the rug first,' Hannah teases him, 'if I'm planning on having a few drinks.'

Felix touches her arm, his cheeks flushed, his beady little eyes framed by pale lashes. 'I can tell you're a well-brought up girl, Hannah. But there's another thing too. It's a soulless place – I've only had it for a year, never had the time to do anything with it. And I've seen your paintings, had a good old prowl around on the web and I know this isn't the usual sort of thing you do, but . . .' He hesitates, smiling in recognition at a group of smart thirty-somethings who've swept into the bar, all toffee tans and Armani.

343

'You want me to do your portrait?' She sips the black-berry cocktail, heady and fruity with a potent kick.

'God, no,' Felix guffaws. 'It's traumatic enough having my passport photo done. No, I mean . . . I wondered if you'd paint a mural for me in the living room. Nothing huge – just something to personalise the space, give it some life. I was thinking of something around the window in the living room – it's got a fabulous view and I'd like to make a feature of it. I'd pay you of course.'

'I wouldn't take any money from you, Felix,' Hannah exclaims. 'You've kept us in cocktails these past couple of nights and anyway, I haven't painted for months and I need a project. So yes, I'd love to do it.'

Felix beams at her. 'That's fantastic. What time's your train home tomorrow? I'll have a spare key cut and meet you at the station.'

'We leave at three.'

'Okay, I'll call you in the morning.' Felix stands up, picking up the empty tray.

'Felix,' Hannah calls after him, 'can I ask you something?' He nods and heads back towards their table.

'What is it, Han?'

'I . . .' She hesitates. 'Why have you been so generous these past few days? There was all that champagne on the train and cocktails both nights. We must've cost you a fortune . . .'

'Well,' he blusters, and even in the dim light she can tell he's blushing. 'I guess I'm just the sharing sort.'

'But there's more to it than that, isn't there?' Hannah pauses. 'I don't want to seem ungrateful, but—'

Felix nods. 'You're right. I guess I was just lucky to meet you girls at a particularly, um . . . I don't want to sound overdramatic but . . .'

'A particularly what, Felix?' Lou asks, frowning.

Looking around, he fixes his gaze on each of the girls

in turn. 'You remember I told you about my wedding that never happened?'

'Uh-huh,' Sadie murmurs.

'Well, it was supposed to be yesterday.'

'What?' Hannah exclaims. 'You mean . . . you'd only found about your girlfriend and that other man—'

'Rashley.' He nods. 'Yep – the big announcement was on Thursday night.'

'So, while we were all drinking your champagne on the train, you should've been getting married?' Sadie blurts out. 'God, Felix. I wish we'd known.'

Felix nods, pressing his lips firmly together. 'I had to get away. They don't need me here' – he gestures around the packed bar – 'in fact the place runs better when I'm not around, getting in the way, insisting on my ridiculous bespoke cocktails, which my staff reckon are the most ridiculous idea they've ever heard . . .'

'Why didn't you tell us it'd just happened?' Lou asks softly.

Felix sighs. 'I couldn't, not with you all heading off to celebrate Hannah's wedding. I didn't want to put a dampener on your celebrations.'

'You did anything but,' Hannah says warmly. 'It was lovely meeting you.'

'And running into you three has got me through these past couple of days,' he declares. 'D'you know, I was all set to down all that champagne by myself. God knows what state I'd have been in if you hadn't been there. I'd probably have ended up in the Royal Infirmary having my stomach pumped.'

'Glad we could help,' Sadie says, touching his arm.

'You definitely did me a favour.' He smiles now, absent-mindedly picking up Hannah's glass and taking a sip. 'Seriously, you took me out of myself and made me think, well, if I can meet three lovely girls who are happy to hang out with me and don't write me off as a complete fuck-up . . .'

'Of course we don't!' Hannah exclaims. 'I just wish we hadn't gone on about our own problems.'

'Maybe that's exactly what I needed,' he says. 'It helped to put things into perspective for me as if . . .' He shrugs. 'I don't know. This sounds crazy but it was as if I was *meant* to meet you.'

'Oh, Felix.' Hannah puts her arms around him and hugs him tightly. 'I can't believe you were meant to be getting married yesterday.'

'Me neither.' He pulls away and smiles at her. 'Perhaps I had a lucky escape. Anyway, I'd better go hassle my staff. They'll be wondering what's wrong with me. And, Hannah, I'll be back in London a week on Thursday . . . I know you'll be busy with the wedding so I don't expect anything finished by then . . .'

'Well, I'll see what I can do,' she smiles.

'I'll leave it completely up to you.'

Hannah nods, draining the remains of the blackberry concoction, just as her old friend Johnny walks in through the door, bang on time at 10 pm.

SIXTY-FIVE

Lou wakes up on a hazy Sunday morning in a bed that's not her bed. It's not her bed in the hotel room, either. It's an unfamiliar bed in an unfamiliar room.

She sits up slowly, studying the grey and cream striped double duvet and the pale blue blind filtering soft morning light. Lou's entire body is tense and her eyes feel scratchy and dry. She studies the cream-coloured wardrobe and the framed film posters on the wall. One depicts a pensive Steve McQueen in black and white above a blur of cars with the film's title, *Bullitt*, in red.

'Why are you on the sofa, Dad?' The child's voice gives her a jolt.

'Because a friend stayed over,' comes the reply as Lou leans back against the plump pillows, closing her eyes as snippets from the previous night start to replay in her mind.

She remembers the four of them, crammed around the small circular table at Felix's bar until Johnny checked his watch at ten to twelve and said he had to go. He didn't usually use a babysitter on his Cal nights but, well, he hadn't been able to resist coming along.

A small smile tweaks Lou's lips as she recalls Johnny hesitating, clearly not wanting to leave, and something

347

else – perhaps the effects of Felix's blackberry cocktail, or that voicemail message from Astrid – pulling her out of her chair and across the floor towards him where she'd murmured, 'Can I come with you? Just to talk, like we used to?' And now she replays Johnny saying yes, of course, as she glanced back to see Hannah and Sadie grinning like mad and quickly trying to straighten their faces.

They'd come back here to Johnny's flat where he'd let them in quietly and introduced her to Miriam, the babysitter with blazing red hair and colossal gold earrings dripping with beads.

Then . . . chatting. Nothing more than chatting late into the night until the sky lightened with streaks of mauve. Johnny said she could sleep in his bed, he wouldn't hear of putting her on the sofa, not when she was travelling tomorrow. 'It's hardly going to be arduous,' she'd joked. 'I'll just be sitting with Sadie and Han for three hours, drinking coffee.' He'd insisted, though, whispering apologies for the state of the place as he hastily smoothed out the duvet.

And now, as Cal says, 'Which friend stayed over?' Lou recalls a kiss, brief yet head-swimmingly lovely, a goodnight kiss like she'd never had in her life.

'Her name's Lou,' Johnny tells his son.

'Lou's boyfriend punched you!' the child exclaims. 'What happens if he finds out she stayed here?'

'I don't think he will,' Johnny murmurs. 'Anyway, listen, d'you want some of that chocolatey Weetabix?'

'Did you get strawberry tarts yesterday?'

'No, they didn't have any . . .'

'Ugghhh,' Cal groans.

'I know,' Johnny says levelly. 'You're *so* deprived. You should probably get on to social services . . .'

Lou hears the clink of crockery as she steps onto the

grey carpet. She is wearing a plain black T-shirt, man-sized, plus the sensible white cotton knickers that she often suspected Spike found faintly disappointing. What kind of underwear would Astrid wear for him? she muses. Complicated basques and corsets like the kind Sadie made for her degree show? Lou's phone beeps with an incoming text, and she retrieves it from the pocket of her jacket, which is draped over a chair. ARE YOU ALIVE? reads Sadie's text. Lou smiles and texts YES VERY just as there's a soft knock on the bedroom door.

'Hi,' she calls out. 'Come in.' The door opens, and Johnny peers around it.

'Sleep okay?'

'Yes, really well.'

He pauses, as if fearing that he might be trespassing in his own room. 'I'll make you some breakfast. Feel free to have a shower if you like . . . there's a dressing gown on the back of the door.'

'Thanks. And . . . thanks for last night, Johnny. Sorry for keeping you up so late.'

'Well,' he says with a smile that warms her heart, 'we had a lot to catch up on, didn't we?'

*

If hearing about Josh and Daisy had made Lou wary of getting to know other people's children, Cal dispels her fears in an instant. 'I told Dad to go into that place and talk to you,' he says cheerfully, shovelling Weetabix into his mouth, 'but he wouldn't. He always says to me to be polite and talk to people but *he* wouldn't—'

'Cal,' Johnny says hotly, 'it wasn't exactly like that.'

Lou laughs, seeing him flush as he fills her mug with coffee. 'Yeah it was.' Cal grins at Lou. 'Dad was *spying* on you.'

'Were you, Johnny?' She mock-frowns at him. 'I'm very flattered actually.'

'Yeah, okay, Cal,' Johnny mutters, plucking toast from the toaster. 'Anyway, you'd better hurry up and get dressed because we've got a few jobs to do at the allotment this morning. You're welcome to come too, if you like,' he adds, turning to Lou.

'I'd love to,' she says, 'but I'd better get back to the hotel and pack. We've got to check out by twelve, and I think Hannah wants a quick whirl round the shops before we catch our train.'

'Some other time then?' Johnny asks.

Lou glances at him as he busies himself with screwing the lids back onto the jars of jam and Nutella on the table. 'Yes, I'd love that.'

'Are you coming to stay again?' Cal asks eagerly.

'Well . . .' She shrugs and glances at Johnny. 'Maybe. We'll see.'

'Or we could visit you, couldn't we, Dad?'

'Er, yeah. Sometime maybe . . .' Clearly flustered, Johnny places the jars back in the cupboard.

'I hadn't finished with that,' Cal reprimands him. 'I was gonna have Nutella on toast.'

'But you've had cereal . . .'

'I'm still hungry.' Cal fixes his gaze on Lou as his father hands him the sticky jar. 'You live in York, don't you?' he adds.

'Yes, that's right,' Lou says, surprised. 'Have you ever been there?'

'Yeah, we went on a school trip. We went to this massive church.'

'It was probably York Minster. It is pretty massive . . .'

Cal wrinkles his nose as he twists the lid off the jar. 'That was a bit boring. But then we went to a theme park and there was this motorbike ride and it went from, like, dead still to—' He makes a whooshing noise and shoots his flattened hand across the table. 'And I was sick,' he adds gravely, 'like, seven times.'

'That's awful, Cal,' Lou exclaims. 'What happened?'

'It did something to my brain,' he says with a trace of pride.

'He got concussion,' Johnny says, pulling up a chair and sitting beside his son. 'Something to do with the velocity. He was fine, though. But if we do visit Lou sometime' – he catches her eye across the table – 'and go to that theme park again, we'll maybe give the motorbike ride a miss.'

'Awww.'

'But there are loads of other rides,' Lou reassures him. 'There are at least three roller coasters as far as I remember, and one of them has a double loop.'

'Will you go on them with me?' Cal wants to know.

'Yes, I love roller coasters.' Lou takes a sip of her coffee and munches a slice of toast.

'Dad hates 'em,' Cal says darkly.

'Well, aren't I just a pathetic specimen of a father,' Johnny says briskly, clearing the table as Lou gets to her feet.

'Hardly,' she says with a smile. 'But look – I'd better get back. It was nice to meet you, Cal' – he nods and licks the Nutella spoon – 'and Johnny, thanks for giving up your bed for me.'

'No problem,' he says as sees her to the door. 'Your train leaves at three, right?'

'Yes.'

'We'll come and see you off . . .'

'Oh, you don't have to—' She stops herself and looks at him, knowing she wants him to, very much.

*

351

Three suitcases rattle and bump along the pavement as Hannah, Sadie and Lou make their way towards the station. 'What d'you think?' Hannah asks, indicating a dress in the window of a chic wedding boutique.

'It's gorgeous,' Sadie exclaims.

'It's got your name on it,' Lou says, craning forward to read an imaginary label. 'Hannah McShane, it says right here. And look – the shop's open.'

'Well,' Hannah says, her blue eyes shining, 'I'm sort of thinking . . .'

'What – for the wedding?' Sadie exclaims. 'But I thought you already had a dress.'

Hannah pulls a wry smile. 'I have but . . .' She hesitates, turning away from the window to face her friends. '. . . I don't know what I was thinking when I chose it. It's plain cream – sorry, *oyster* . . .' She winces. 'And now I think I bought it because it's the sort of dress I thought a sensible bride should wear. But it's so . . . *nothingy*. As if I was desperate not to offend anyone or make the children think I was somehow trying to take their mother's place.' She shakes her head, conscious of how ridiculous she sounds. 'It's the kind of dress I reckoned Daisy and Josh couldn't possibly find fault with, and now I'm thinking . . .'

'. . . That's not really the way to choose your wedding dress,' Sadie offers.

'But then,' Hannah murmurs, pulling out her phone from her pocket, 'Daisy is really good with clothes . . .'

'But she's only ten, isn't she?' Lou laughs.

'Yes, but you should see the way she throws things together. Hang on a minute . . .' Hannah steps towards the window, framing the searing red dress on the screen of her phone.

'What are you doing?' Sadie asks.

'Getting a second opinion,' Hannah murmurs, sending

352

the image as a text along with the message: OKAY FOR A BRIDE?

'And *our* opinion doesn't count,' Sadie teases.

'Yeah, we know nothing,' Lou adds. 'We've only known you since you were eighteen years old . . .' Hannah's phone beeps and she peers at Daisy's reply: YEAH.

'Is that all she said?' Lou asks, frowning, 'Just *yeah*?'

'Well,' Hannah laughs, slipping her phone back into her pocket as she pushes open the door of the shop, 'from Daisy Lennox that probably counts as a big thumbs-up.'

*

Two hours later, at Glasgow Central station, Hannah, Sadie and Lou exchange slightly stiff hugs with Cal, who's clearly not the hugging type and keeps asking his dad if he can have a bagel from the kiosk. Then Johnny and Felix hug and kiss each of the girls in turn before they climb aboard their train.

Hannah has the key to Felix's flat in her bag and a new, tissue-wrapped dress in a smart paper carrier bag, which she places carefully on the overhead shelf. As the train edges forward, the three girls wave through the dirt-speckled window at a man in an aquamarine top, blond hair askew, and a dad in a sweater, clutching the hand of his boy.

SIXTY-SIX

Lou unlocks the door to the flat, steps into the hallway and inhales the aroma of home. There's a lingering hint of stale fried food, not unlike the smell at Let's Bounce. Leaving her case in the hallway, she goes through to the kitchen and studies the items on the table.

There's a half-empty wine bottle, a mug of black tea and a cardboard carton from the chippie. Lou sniffs the bottle, wincing at its acrid smell, and opens the lid of the carton. There are a few chips in there, pale and flabby, like slugs, and a dark brown, wizened lump which, on closer inspection, appears to be the end of a sausage. One of the fat chips has a cigarette stubbed out into it. It looks, Lou thinks, like a crime scene. She drops the mess into the bin.

Luckily, she had the foresight to eat on the train as she hadn't expected Spike to have left her much in the way of food. Yet when she opens the fridge she sees that the chicken, noodles and veggies are still there, waiting expectantly, all looking rather sweaty and sorry for themselves. She bins the chicken and noodles, decides the vegetables might just about be okay and wanders through to the living room. On the coffee table sits another bottle – empty this time. Calvados, with a picture of a man in a sort of nightcap on the front. Where had that come from? Lou doesn't like brandy and she can't remember buying it. She deposits it in the recycling box, a memory gradually pulling itself into focus – of her and Spike, catching the Dover to Calais ferry, and being so thrilled by the concept of duty-free that they'd come home laden with ciggies for him and wine for her and the brandy because they'd thought it so Continental and exotic. It had seemed a little less so in their scuffed flat, and so it had been shoved to the back of the cupboard. Hot tears fill Lou's eyes suddenly, and she heads to the bathroom for loo roll.

Here, she surveys the open wax strip packet in the bath, and the tubes and pots lying all over the floor as if they've thrown themselves out of the cupboard. Lou bristles with unease as she puts everything back, wondering now if someone has been here – some intruder who had the audacity to sit at the kitchen table eating his sausage and chips while drinking their booze, then trashing their bath-room. She inspects the room carefully, searching for further evidence of wrongdoing.

Draped over the side of the bath, alongside her flannel, is a solitary wax strip. Lou picks it up gingerly and exam-ines it, realising it's covered in dark curly hairs. What kind of sicko burglar would take a little break in the proceedings to wax himself? Yet there's no evidence of anyone having broken in – no tampering with the door, no windows forced open. With sickening clarity, she realises it must have been Astrid. Spike must have had her over after Lou left for Scotland. They probably got pissed together, then Astrid must have raked through Lou's private possessions and treated herself to a little Silken Glide session, making herself all smooth and lovely for Spike . . . well, she's clearly not a natural blonde, Lou thinks, shuddering as she drops the strip into the bin.

In the bedroom, Lou inspects the bed. While Spike's side

has clearly been slept in, hers looks undisturbed. He could have arranged it that way, of course, but anyway, she's past caring now and, as Sadie pointed out, she's had a lucky escape. Just a pity it didn't happen thirteen years earlier when Lou had watched him making cow-eyes at that woman with the hair like a loaf. While Lou is hardly in a celebratory mood, her fury is beginning to ebb away and she feels momentarily calm. She replays the scene as the train pulled into York station just an hour ago, when Hannah and Sadie had hugged her goodbye, asking over and over if she wanted one or both of them to come to the flat with her. It wouldn't be a problem, they said; they could stay over and make their way south tomorrow. Barney could take an extra day off and Hannah's boss would understand. 'I'll be fine,' she'd said firmly, and now, as she wanders into the bedroom and opens the wardrobe, Lou knows it's true.

She carries the chair from beneath the small window, places it in front of the wardrobe and clambers onto it so she can reach the top shelf. With difficulty, because so much junk is jammed in all around it, she pulls out the huge, heavy box containing her jewellery materials, gripping it tightly as she steps back onto the floor. Lou carries it through to the kitchen. From the box she takes out her sketchpad filled with jewellery designs, and the ultra-sharp hard-leaded pencils she likes to work with, and starts to draw.

SIXTY-SEVEN

'I shouldn't have read it,' Ryan says softly, pulling Hannah towards him in bed. 'I should have respected your privacy and I'm sorry.'

Hannah studies his face on the pillow and traces her fingers down his arm. 'Maybe I shouldn't have written it. It's one of those things you do in the heat of the moment without thinking . . .'

'Couldn't you have told me?'

'About the cigarettes?' Hannah asks.

'No, not that . . . God, that seems like nothing now. Just a few puffs . . .' He laughs softly. 'By his age, I was already making cocktails from whatever my parents had in their drinks cabinet. No, I mean the other stuff, about the way the kids are with you.'

'I didn't think I needed to. I thought you could see it happening every day.'

'Maybe I could,' Ryan says, dropping his voice to a whisper as Josh's bedroom door opens and he plods to the bathroom. 'But I pretended everything was okay. Maybe . . .' He pauses, as if unsure whether to go on. 'Maybe that's what I did with Petra too, telling myself we were fine . . .'

Hannah's fingers come to a halt on Ryan's skin. 'Daisy said you had a picnic on the Heath yesterday.'

'Yeah, that's right,' he murmurs.

'How was that?' Hannah asks lightly as the loo flushes and Josh makes his way back to his room.

'It was . . . weird. She actually suggested that maybe me and her could try again,' he says quickly.

'What? You're kidding!' Hannah's forgotten about the unspoken nocturnal whispering rule.

Ryan shakes his head. 'I don't think she meant it, not really. It's probably just the wedding, the thought of me getting married again . . .'

'God, Ryan,' Hannah mutters. 'That's unbelievable.'

He pulls her closer, kissing her lips. 'Honestly, I don't think she really wants to. It's just . . . her life isn't turning out the way she'd imagined. Petra's put her music before everything else – she admitted that – and I guess if she hadn't, she'd still be giving cello lessons to reluctant kids.'

'Daisy and Josh are lucky, though,' Hannah ventures. 'At least you've always made them the centre of everything.'

'Well, I don't know about that. Yesterday, I suggested to Petra that maybe they should live with her.'

'They can't do that!' Hannah exclaims.

'Why not?'

'Because *you* don't want that, do you?'

'Not really but—'

'What kind of life would they have? Oh, I know there'd be plenty of exhibitions and museums and *mime shows* . . .'

'But what you said in that email, you're right – this is your home too, and it's not fair . . .'

'You'd do that for me?' she asks incredulously.

'Well, yes – for us.'

'But this is their home, Ryan. It's where they've lived all their lives, their friends are nearby, their schools . . . what did Petra say?'

Ryan turns to look at her, finding her hand beneath the duvet. 'She didn't look overjoyed, I have to say.'

'All the more reason not to then,' Hannah declares. 'You haven't mentioned this to them, have you?'

'No, I thought we should talk about it first.'

'Please don't, Ryan. They'd think it was because of me, that I don't want them here – and I do. All this time, I've been thinking I'll try this, I'll do that, trying to *make* them like me . . .' She shrugs. 'Maybe I just can't. And maybe it'd be better if I didn't keep trying, if I was just *myself* . . .'

Ryan slides his arms around her back and pulls her towards him. 'Are you sure,' he says gently, 'that this is what you want? Me and my kids and our terrible ice-spitting fridge?'

She looks at Ryan and leans in to kiss him. 'I think,' she whispers into his ear, 'I could actually grow to love that fridge.'

*

It's gone midnight by the time Sadie and Barney have settled the babies to sleep, although Barney suspects that Sadie wanted to keep them awake, to cuddle and kiss them as if she'd been away on a six-month trip and not one meagre weekend. He's been desperate to show her her gift, the way he used to be during their first few Christmases together when each of them would go to extravagant lengths to source quirky, personalised presents. Last Christmas, to his shame, he'd suggested they skip presents, what with having moved house only a few months previously and, anyway, wasn't this house their present to each other? He tried to make up for it today, taking the boys and Sadie's bike to the mountain-biking centre where, with the help of a couple of enthusiastic teenage boys and a whole heap of components, he'd managed to restore it to its former glory.

'My God, it's perfect,' Sadie exclaims, gripping his hand as they stand in the back garden. 'It must've taken you all weekend! How did you manage it with the boys around?'

'Ah well,' he says, 'you're always saying men are no good at multitasking. But the truth is, I don't know what you do all day . . .' She tries to swipe him, laughing, and he catches her in a big hug. 'Let's go in,' he murmurs. 'It's freezing out here. I'll bring in your bike – I only put it out there so you wouldn't see it . . .'

As he wheels it into the hall, she's tempted to check on the babies again, the way she usually does every twenty minutes or so. But no – they'll be fine. She really doesn't need to keep creeping into their bedroom throughout the evening. Sadie hasn't asked Barney whether he used nappy rash cream either, or grilled him on what the boys had for every meal while she was away. She hasn't even commented on the grubby bib poking out from under the cooker, or on the faint poo smell that's lingering in the air. No, she's stopped all that. She's trying, anyway. Trying to loosen the reins.

Later, as she's about to sit beside him on the sofa, she notices a dark stain on the armchair. Although she manages not to ask what happened, Barney catches her studying it. 'Just a bit of spilt milk,' he says quickly.

Sadie smiles. 'Well, if that's the worst thing that happened while you were in charge . . .' She doesn't finish, because her husband is pulling her towards him and kissing her full on the lips.

SIXTY-EIGHT

After work on Monday Hannah cycles straight home, then drives over to Felix's place. She's pleasantly surprised that Josh and Daisy agreed to come with her. Perhaps it's because she didn't appear as if she desperately wanted them to, but just presented it as something they might like to do.

'This is so posh,' Josh marvels as she lets them into the third-floor flat. 'Is he rich?'

'I don't know,' she says, laughing. 'It's lovely, though, isn't it?'

'It's beautiful,' Daisy murmurs beside her. Together they wander from room to room. It feels still and calm and is pleasingly white – *pure* white, with no scuffs on the walls from kids casually brushing against them. There's no faint air of chaos, no crucial school trip forms lying scrunched up on worktops or laundry half-pulled out of the tumble dryer in an unwieldy clump. Felix's flat is clearly the home of a single person who employs a cleaner to dust the wafer-thin TV before hoovering the cream Heal's rug.

They step into a kitchen which feels as if no food has ever been prepared in it. There's a small chrome rack of spices, seemingly unused, and apart from the gleaming cone-shaped kettle, the wooden worktops are bare. 'There's no . . . stuff here,' Daisy remarks. 'I like it.'

'Yeah, I'd love to live somewhere like this,' Josh enthuses.

'Me too,' Hannah says, realising it's the kind of place she *used* to fantasise about – didn't she and Lou once spend an entire evening in Garnet Street describing their perfect future lives? Lou's had been all about gin and tonics on the roof terrace – she hadn't even liked gin and tonic then, but had been confident that it was something she'd be able to train herself to enjoy. Hannah's future life had been different. She'd have a flat a little like this one – tons of light, no clutter, every item chosen with care. But now, she decides there's something soulless about it. It's almost *too* perfect. 'This is the wall Felix wants me to paint,' she explains, bringing them back to the living room. 'What d'you think I should do?'

'I don't know,' Josh mutters as Daisy wanders away to continue her explorations. 'Aren't you scared of messing it up?'

'Well, if Felix doesn't like it, he can always paint over it . . .'

'I mean, aren't you nervous?' he says, frowning.

Hannah smiles. 'No, I'm really not. I know what you mean, though – it's a big responsibility. But I'm just going to go with what feels right . . . for instance, I know it's going to be abstract, and I think I know the kind of colours I'm going to use . . .' Josh mumbles something into the baggy neck of his murky green T-shirt.

'Sorry, Josh? I didn't hear—'

'I said thanks for not telling Dad about the cigarettes. I know he read the email . . . you'd already found them and decided not to tell on me, hadn't you?'

'Er . . . yes,' Hannah says hesitantly. 'I didn't really think it was my place, Josh—'

'Well, thanks,' he grunts.

'Er, that's okay . . .'

'Are you going to live here, Hannah?' Daisy demands, having reappeared in the living room doorway.

'No, of course not,' she exclaims. 'What makes you think that?'

'You just said it's your place. I heard you . . .'

Hannah steps towards her and, without considering whether it's okay or not, takes Daisy by the hand. 'That's not what I meant,' she says gently. 'Me and Josh were talking about something else. This is Felix's place, and I'm going to come here some nights after work, and maybe most of next weekend – you can come too, if you like. You're good with colour, you have a real eye for it and maybe you can help me.'

'Okay,' Daisy says warily.

'But I'm not moving here,' Hannah adds firmly. 'Me and your dad are getting married in twelve days' time, sweetheart. We're going to be together, in your house, if that's okay with—'

''Cause Dad gets lonely when you're not there,' Daisy cuts in, impervious to Josh's glare.

'Does he?' Hannah asks, frowning. 'I thought you all had a nice time when I was away, with the picnic and everything.'

'Mum and Dad were talking about us,' Daisy mutters.

'Shut up, Daisy,' Josh growls, throwing her a furious look.

'They were!' she counters, eyes flashing as she whirls round to face him. 'You heard them when we were sitting by the pond. Dad wants us to go and live with Mum and go to new schools where we won't know anybody and not even have our own bedrooms and I'd have to share with—'

'Daisy, he doesn't—' Hannah touches her arm, but she backs away.

'He does! I heard him, and Mum doesn't want us, so where are we going to live?'

'Please, Daisy!' Hannah exclaims, putting her arms around her and studying her tear-stained face. 'He *doesn't* want you to live with your mum. He wants everything to stay just the way it is, okay? He just mentioned it because he thought maybe you haven't been that . . . happy lately. Maybe it's been weird for you with me around.'

'It's not,' Daisy chokes out. 'It's good and I like it. I don't want everything to change again.'

'I . . . I promise it won't,' Hannah stammers as Daisy looks up at her, teary-eyed. 'Listen – why don't we start thinking about this mural tonight? I'll sketch out the window and the proportions of the room, and when we go home we could have a play around with some colour up in my studio. What d'you think?'

'All right,' Daisy murmurs, biting her bottom lip.

'I've got some ideas,' Josh says hesitantly.

'No you haven't,' Daisy scoffs. 'You're no good at drawing, you don't have any ideas about—'

'Hey, you two,' Hannah cuts in, realising she's slipped into using Ryan's conciliatory tone, the one reserved for squabbles at breakfast over who gets the last of the orange juice. 'The more ideas we have, the better. My plan is to sketch out some options and text them to Felix.'

'When's it got to be finished by?' Josh asks.

'There's no deadline,' Hannah says, 'but he arrives a couple of days before the wedding. My plan is to have it all finished by then.'

'That's not long, is it?' Josh wonders aloud.

Hannah smiles, taking her sketchpad and pencils out of her bag and perching on the arm of the putty-coloured sofa. 'Between the three of us,' she murmurs, already seeing wavering stripes, like ribbons around the window, 'I'm sure we can do it.'

'Of course we can,' Daisy says with a grin.

Josh looms over Hannah, his glance flicking from the open page in her pad to the elegant window she's sketching. 'What's Felix like anyway?' he asks.

'I think you'll like him,' she says. 'You'll meet him at the wedding. He's funny and there's something about him . . .'

'You're good at drawing,' Daisy observes.

'Thanks, but this is just a scribble really.'

'What d'you mean, there's something about him?' Josh asks.

'I don't know how to explain it,' Hannah says, sketching the individual panes, the hazy outlines of the trees and the neat brick terraces beyond. 'I suppose he's just good at bringing people together.'

SIXTY-NINE

Spike knows he should be grateful that Charlie and his girlfriend Toni have taken him in, but at forty-eight he feels he really shouldn't be lying on a sofa bed in someone else's living room, awake at 4.47 am, with the next day stretching bleakly before him. Pulling the duvet around his shoulders, he pads over to the computer at the desk in the corner and turns it on.

Spike isn't sure about the etiquette of using Charlie and Toni's PC but at this ungodly hour he doesn't really care. He opens a new Word document and starts to type.

Darling Lou,

I know you've told me not to phone or come round so I'm writing this instead. Well, typing actually – you know how terrible my handwriting is. What can I say, darling? I've let you down, not just recently but for years, by not supporting you and seeing you trying so hard and taking that crappy job . . . what can I do to make it up to you? I love you, Lou. You're my soulmate . . . Spike stops, picturing Lou rolling her eyes at that. He erases it and writes: *You're everything to me. The most beautiful, talented girl I've ever known. Please, Lou, let's sort this out. I'll change. We'll get a better flat and you won't have to pick out nappies from the ballpool or come home stinking of chips. Not that I ever thought you stank. And I need to sort myself out, I realise that, and be a proper boyfriend – maybe we should get married. What do you think? And have a baby? I've never felt ready for parenthood but now I know how selfish I've been. I realise you're not getting any younger . . .*

No, God, he can't put that. *If you want a baby I'm happy to start trying right now.* No! That makes it sound like he's expecting to walk back in and jump her bones. He pauses, his brain whirling, wishing there was a guitar here so he could at least put all of this into a song instead, he's better at that than writing letters . . . Taking a deep breath, and wondering if Charlie and Toni have any wine in the fridge, he signs off: *I love you, Lou-Lou, please never doubt that. Spike xx.*

He takes a moment to steady his breath, then switches on the printer which sounds horribly loud and rattly in the middle of the night as his letter scrolls through. Spike peers at it, trying to reassure himself that he doesn't need reading glasses – it's just the font, that's all. He should have used a bigger font.

He rereads it with difficulty, folds it in half and wonders how he'll ask Charlie for an envelope without arousing suspicion. Then he turns back to the computer, opens a new document and starts to type:

Donald Wren: Curriculum Vitae

SEVENTY

It's a fine, dry Tuesday morning and Sadie is out on her bike. She doesn't cycle the way Hannah does. She's not a daredevil city cyclist, zipping between traffic and haring around roundabouts without flinching. She prefers a more sedate approach, taking in her surroundings and rarely breaking into a sweat. Perhaps, she thinks, this is what living in the country is all about.

Passing the small row of shops – the Spar, post office and a curious place that sells everything from kites to reconditioned sewing machines – Sadie heads for the park. She hadn't planned to go any further, but she won't get this chance very often – Barney is working from home today and has persuaded her to go out for an hour or so. She leaves the park, following the steep, curving hill out of the village, then turns off along a narrow path still mulchy from last autumn's leaves.

Hissingham Woods, the sign reads, with a picture of an acorn. *Public right of way.* All these months they've lived here, although she's known roughly where the woods are, she's never got around to finding her way into them. Sadie breathes in the rich, damp scent of foliage, making a mental note to bring Barney and the babies here. Since Glasgow,

Sadie has no longer felt trapped in a fug of motherhood. While she'd expected to miss her boys, she'd been unprepared for the gnawing ache of longing which had engulfed her as the train had approached King's Cross, growing even more intense as she'd caught the local train to Little Hissingham. The difference now is that she knows it's possible to physically separate herself from them, that Barney is a perfectly capable father who can cope admirably when she's not around.

She cycles on, following the path deeper into the woods until it opens out into a glade – a perfect picnic spot, the kind of place she'd imagined they'd come to all the time when they moved to the country. She and Barney tend to take the children out in shifts – her on weekdays, him at weekends. Well, that should change, she decides. They should all hang out together as much as they can.

Sadie stops and lays her bike on its side, finding a place to sit. As she pokes a finger into the back of her trainer to rub a sore spot – a minor injury from dancing in heels – something catches her eye in the grass.

It's a tiny shoe in soft, biscuit-coloured leather. Dylan's shoe, bought by Sadie's parents – one of the many parcels they'd arrived with when they'd shown up in hospital after the birth. It's slightly flattened and damp, she notices, slipping it into her pocket. She brushes grass from her jeans and picks up her bike, feeling uneasy now. As she cycles home, no longer noticing the smells and sounds of the woods, a single thought turns over and over in her head: Barney said he'd taken the boys to the park. *He never said anything about the woods.*

Letting herself into the house, Sadie can hear Barney and the boys in the living room. Instead of popping her head round the door, she wheels her bike through to the back of the house and into the garden shed. She props it against the wall and takes a deep breath. 'You're going to turn into a shed man,' she'd teased Barney when they'd bought this place.

'What do men do in sheds anyway?' he'd asked.

'They tinker,' she'd said. 'You're going to be a tinkering shed man.' Sadie doesn't know how long she's been standing here, but she knows it's too long to appear normal. Aware of her thudding heart, she rehearses her opening line: 'Look what I found in the woods.' *You said you took the boys to the park. You never said anything about the woods . . .*

She heads indoors, gripping the baby shoe tightly. As she enters the living room, her boys gaze up delightedly from the rug. She turns to Barney and opens her mouth, then freezes. 'You got a text,' he says coldly, striding towards her with her phone in his hand. 'Here, you'd better read it.'

With a frown, Sadie takes it from him and peers, wordlessly, at the message on display: GREAT TO MEET YOU SADIE. HOPE TO REPEAT SOMETIME? ANDREW X

SEVENTY-ONE

'Have you done any bar work before?' asks Ben, the manager of Bar Circa, in the side room reserved for private parties.

Lou pauses, then decides to be honest. 'Not since I was a student. I worked in a club for a few months in Glasgow – that's where I studied – and for the past year or so I've been at Let's Bounce.'

'The soft play centre?' Ben's eyebrows shoot up in amusement.

'That's right,' Lou says, surprised that she hasn't had to explain what it is.

He laughs. 'I've got a two-year-old, took him there a couple of times . . .'

'Very brave,' Lou says with a smile.

'So what d'you do there?'

'Um, pretty much everything. Work in the café, supervise the play area, clear up, just throw myself into the general mayhem really . . .'

'I can imagine. To be honest, I don't know how you can stand it . . .'

She chuckles, warming to this engaging, amiable young man. 'I think I've stood it for long enough, actually. That's why I'm here.'

He nods understandingly. 'So how did you end up working there?'

'Needs must,' she says quickly. 'I'm actually a jeweller. I was doing pretty well before the recession, but a few independent shops closed and I just wasn't selling enough. I had to find something else . . .'

'And you're thinking of leaving Let's Bounce?'

'Oh yes,' she declares. 'You see, working here would be perfect. Your ad said you were looking for someone for evening shifts . . .'

'That's right.'

'And what I really need to do is free up my days so I can focus on . . .' She hesitates, unsure of how to phrase it without putting down bar work.

'Focus on what you really want to do?' Ben suggests.

'That's right.'

He smiles. 'That makes sense. If you're at the play centre five days a week . . .'

'Six actually,' she corrects him.

'Wow. Well, no wonder you want to refocus.'

Lou grins broadly; that's it exactly. She is refocusing. How did Johnny put it when he called her to wish her luck? *You're focusing on what's important, Lou. Yes, I know you might not want to work in a bar forever, but you're right – it could be the perfect solution for now. No, I don't think you're crazy. That's the last thing I'd ever think of you* . . . And she'd headed off to work as if on a cloud, feeling freer than she could ever remember.

'If you can cope with Let's Bounce,' Ben remarks, 'I'm sure you could deal with even the rowdiest Friday night crowd here.'

'I'm sure I could,' Lou says firmly, glimpsing the clock on the wall behind him, realising her lunch break should have finished ten minutes ago and that Dave will be asking Steph what on earth she – loyal, dependable Lou – is playing at.

As Ben tells her about the shift patterns and the others on his team, Lou knows he's going to offer her a job. She knows, too, that the first person she'll phone as she leaves the bar on this sunny Tuesday is Johnny, who's eagerly waiting for her call, and that she'll walk back, in no particular hurry, to Let's Bounce. There, she will pull that despised garment from her bag and hand it to Dave, who'll be amazed when she tells him she's leaving. She doesn't care that it's going to be tough, or that she might find herself stalking the orange sticker girl in the supermarket for a little longer.

Lou doesn't care because she is dizzy with excitement at the thought of Johnny arriving in London for Hannah's wedding – and she knows that she will never wear a brown tabard in her life again.

SEVENTY-TWO

Three days, Spike has been back. Three days of living with Charlie, and Charlie's brittle girlfriend Toni with her Pre-Raphaelite hair and silvery cat and inability to walk into a room without pausing to straighten something. On this drizzly Tuesday morning, Spike calculates that he has called Lou thirty-four times – sometimes landline, sometimes mobile, always getting her chirpy answerphone voice. He's even tried calling Let's Bounce and, to add insult to injury, got an answerphone message there too, telling him about opening hours.

Now, with Charlie and Toni at work, he is alone in their flat. Lou has forbidden him from turning up at home, grudgingly suggesting that he collects his stuff once his new bank cards arrive, his old ones having being lost along with his wallet. He must then post his key back through the letterbox, and all of this must take place while she's away at Hannah's wedding. So, although Charlie and Toni have saved Spike from homelessness, he knows that, at some point very soon, he'll have to find somewhere to live. He'll also have to find a way to pay Charlie back the £100 he's lent him to tide him over. All he has on him is the small rucksack he'd taken to Glasgow containing his toothbrush, razor and a spare set of clothes. A fuzz of anxiety starts to bear down on top of his head, and to distract himself he heads into town.

Sound Shack is busy for a weekday. Spike's guitar is still there, no longer in the window but on the wall, with a slight price reduction, he notices. In case Rick thinks he's still mourning the thing, and has come in on a kind of pilgrimage, he feigns interest in a hefty book of Leonard Cohen songs. The shop door opens, and as he looks up, Spike's breath catches in his throat. *Astrid.* No, not Astrid, but a girl who looks so uncannily like her his heart jolts alarmingly.

Spike stands, clutching the book, as she wanders over to look at the guitars on the wall. As she moves from one to the next, he focuses on her bottom; the most *exquisite* bottom he's seen in a long time, snugly encased in dark jeans. Spike feels a shiver of desire. A girl who looks like Astrid, but is also into music; he can barely imagine anything closer to perfection.

Conscious of not wanting to stare, he replaces the book in the rack, pulls out a collection of Bob Dylan songs and tries to appear fascinated by it. But his eyes keep flicking up again, and when he sees the girl studying *his* guitar, he can't stop himself.

It's a sign.

'That's a nice guitar,' he says casually.

She turns and looks at him, frowning slightly. 'Mmmm.'

Mmmm? Is that all she can say? 'Er, it used to be mine,' he adds with a self-deprecating laugh, conscious of Rick studying him intently from behind the counter.

'Really?' she says with mild interest.

Spike shrugs. 'Needed the cash.' Hell, why did he say that? Now he sounds like a loser. 'And I guess you can only play one guitar at a time,' he says, finishing with a ridiculous guffaw.

'Yeah, I suppose so.' She turns back to the instrument and bites her bottom lip.

Why is she making it so difficult for him? Then Spike realises. Of course – it's what happened sometimes during his brief period of being famous, in the days of eager girls in dressing rooms and George with the purring Merc. Sometimes, instead of fawning over Spike and asking him to sign various body parts, a girl would put on the aloof act – a sort of, 'Yeah, of course I know who you are, but I'm damned if I'm going to let on.' It worked too. Spike was always lured by the frosty ones. Well, Spike can play that game too. With a shrug, he mooches away and studies a keyboard whilst still keeping the girl in his vision. She's now making for the door. Spike frowns, realising he's still gripping the Bob Dylan book, and that he's bent the cover and will have to slip it back into the rack before Rick notices. The girl doesn't look back as she opens the door. He waits for her to turn round, to crack a smile and admit that she knew who he was all along. But she doesn't even acknowledge him as she leaves the shop.

Spike stands there, oblivious to Rick's concerned frown and a group of teenage boys who are clearly whispering something derogatory about him. He stares at the door, realising he has to stop this right now – this waiting for that girl to come back in, waiting for Lou to forgive him, waiting for his life to somehow, miraculously, fix itself. He needs to get away from all of this – to escape from a life of waiting and start *doing* something instead. With a start, he knows exactly what he must do.

He'll go back to Charlie and Toni's and collect the letter he wrote for Lou, and he'll creep round to the flat and post it through the door. Then he'll spend the rest of the money Charlie lent him on a return train ticket to Ayr, and he'll go the sheltered bungalow to spend time with his parents before it's too late. Then, as he walks with them on the blustery beach, he'll figure out what the hell to do with the rest of his life.

SEVENTY-THREE

'You kissed him? You kissed this . . . *Andrew*?'

Sadie nods mutely in the middle of their living room where her children are now playing beneath their activity arch. 'You got off your face and snogged someone?'

'Yes,' she whispers. 'At least that's what Hannah and Sadie said. I'm sorry, Barney. I had these cocktails, they went straight to my head. It's all fuzzy and I can't remember . . .'

'Did you do anything else?' he snaps.

'No! Of course not . . .' She tails off, realising this is the first time she's ever seen Barney this angry.

'I knew something had happened,' he mutters, his dark eyes boring into hers across the room. 'You've been different since you came back . . .'

'Look, I said I'm sorry, you can't imagine how much I wish it hadn't happened. But if it means anything, and I'm not trying to make excuses . . .' She glances down at their children, wishing with all her heart that a magic nanny would appear and whisk them out of the room. 'If it means anything,' she continues shakily, 'it was the first time I'd done anything on my own since having the boys and I think it went to my head.'

'It obviously did,' he says gruffly.

'I'm sorry, Barney.' Blinking away the tears that have started to form – she will *not* let the children see her cry – she pulls out the baby shoe from her pocket. 'I found this,' she adds in a whisper.

'Did you? Where?'

'In the woods . . .'

'The woods?' he repeats, eyebrows shooting upwards.

Sadie studies his face, then glances down to see Milo peering at his reflection in the dangling mirror. When she looks back at her husband she doesn't see caring Barney who tries to do the right thing, or even furious Barney, confronting her about kissing a man in a bar. He looks trapped and scared as she calmly asks, 'How did Dylan's shoe get in the woods?'

And now she's the one glaring as it all pours out: 'Met these girls . . . works in the café . . . fancied Pete . . . nothing happened, I promise . . . really uncomfortable . . . all Pete's idea . . .' She knows she should cut in and yell, 'Don't try and blame it all on Pete! You were aiding and abetting . . .' But as the words form in her mind, she almost laughs at how ridiculous they'd sound: *aiding and abetting?* Who has she turned into – the sodding police?

'I'm sorry, Sadie,' he says now, coming towards her and holding her tight, burying his face in her hair.

'God, I'm so sorry too,' she says as they kiss long and hard, unaware of the two pairs of large brown eyes fixed intently on them.

SEVENTY-FOUR

Early on the morning of Hannah and Ryan's wedding, Sadie and Barney take the boys for a walk round Hissingham Park. The wedding is at two, and they are leaving the babies with Barney's parents overnight. Both Sadie and Barney are feeling a little edgy about the prospect, despite Barney's mother reassuring them that their home is now fully baby-proofed with an impressive assortment of guards and gates.

They are so busy running through the list of things they mustn't forget to take that they don't notice Magda across the park. She is walking her dog and stops to watch them, never having seen them out together before. Magda knows, of course, that Barney is married because she sees his wife every Monday and Friday through the café windows, pushing the buggy in all weathers. She's served her coffee, offered to warm the boys' bottles and seen her gamely trying to breastfeed her babies on a park bench, making a mental note to perhaps delay becoming a mother herself for as long as humanly possible.

What is it with men? she reflects. Why the pretence of being a single dad? Magda hadn't told Barney that she'd met his wife, as she was interested to see if he'd mention her. And of course he didn't. Even when she praised him, jokingly, for coping all by himself, he didn't correct her then either. She chuckles to herself. It was pathetic really – although he doesn't strike her as some kind of would-be playboy, not like Pete, who has yet to realise that Amy's flirty texting will lead him precisely nowhere.

Barney and his wife are hugging now. Well, that's nice, Magda thinks, starting to walk again as her dog pulls on the leash. Perhaps it's not all over when you have kids. Magda checks her watch. She's due to meet her boyfriend – the twenty-year-old photography student who, it seems, cannot take enough pictures of her. Taking a big lungful of morning air and seeing him waiting for her at the gates, she smiles and waves, her dog straining so hard now he's pulling her along towards him.

*

'That's a really nice dress,' Daisy says, observing Hannah from the bedroom doorway.

'Thanks,' Hannah says. 'Come on in. You don't have to stand there at the door.'

'Where's Dad?' Daisy asks, glancing around furtively as if half-expecting something or someone to bounce out at her.

'He's upstairs, getting dressed.'

'What, in your studio?'

'Yes,' Hannah laughs. 'He's been banished to the attic. No, actually, he offered – said he'd give me some space to get ready. You know, the bride and groom aren't really supposed to spend the night before their wedding together.'

Daisy frowns. 'Why not?'

'I don't know really. Just superstition, I guess, like not getting married in a red dress.'

'What's wrong with a red dress?'

'Nothing,' she laughs. 'Anyway, I don't believe any of

that. I knew this was the dress for me as soon as I saw it – before I'd even tried it on.'

'It's a lot nicer than the other one,' Daisy agrees.

Hannah turns and gives her a quizzical look. 'Did you sneak a look at it in my wardrobe?'

Daisy nods, her cheeks flushing pink. 'Yeah.'

'I don't mind. It's pretty frumpy, isn't it?'

'Yeah, a bit.'

'It made me look like a fat nurse,' she sniggers, and Daisy laughs too.

'I don't think you're fat.'

'Thanks, Daisy,' Hannah says with a smile. 'I don't think so either. The dress just wasn't very flattering. Yours is lovely, though – d'you feel good in it?'

'I love it,' she declares, looking down and appraising the bold stripes.

'It really suits you. You look beautiful.'

'So do you, Han,' Lou says, wandering into the bedroom. 'You *both* look stunning.'

'Did you make Hannah's tiara?' Daisy asks.

'Yes, I did. D'you like it?' Lou perches on the edge of the bed near Daisy's printed-out story.

'I really do. D'you sell them in shops?'

'I used to,' Lou explains, 'and I'm going to start again. I was working on some new ideas last week and I'm going to make them up when I get home. I've even found a couple of shops to stock them, and I'm going to update my website.'

'That's great, Lou,' Hannah smiles.

'D'you think Dad would buy me one?' Daisy asks, fixing her gaze on Hannah.

'Oh, I'm sure we could sort out something, couldn't we, Lou? It's Daisy's birthday in three weeks' time.' She glances at Daisy. 'You haven't told us what you'd like yet.' Told *us*. She's said it, and it feels just right.

382

'Well, that's what I'd like,' Daisy says firmly. 'I don't mean a little girlie tiara like princesses wear . . .'

'No, you're too grown-up for that,' Lou agrees. 'That's not the kind of jewellery I make anyway.'

'I mean a proper tiara, just like Hannah's,' she says with a grin.

*

Johnny and Cal take a cab from Felix's flat, where they stayed last night, to Hackney Registry Office. Felix will meet them there after setting up at the bar, making sure everything is just so. Hannah, Daisy, Josh and Lou are travelling together in her boss Michael's bright orange vintage Saab; Ryan tried to persuade his kids to come with him and Jack, his old college friend and best man, but they wouldn't hear of it. 'Imagine having a driver,' Josh keeps saying. 'Wouldn't that be the best thing – being able to go anywhere you like?'

Having left their overnight bags in the hotel, Sadie and Barney climb into a black cab, while Hannah's parents have arrived at the registry office far too early and are wondering if that smart-looking couple might be Ryan's mum and dad, and whether they should go over and say hello. They are relieved when more people start arriving – first Ryan and the best man, then a group of Ryan's colleagues from the ad agency and a bunch of excitable women from Hannah's design company.

There's Sadie and Barney and some funny-looking blond man who could have got a haircut before the wedding, and now their daughter is here, looking stunningly beautiful as she steps out of an orange car and hurries over to hug them before mingling with the group. Rose, Hannah's mother, swallows hard and tries to steady her breath.

Ryan's children are chatting to Hannah now, both

looking very smart, and there's Lou, the one who makes jewellery, wearing a dazzling flowery frock. Rose vaguely remembers the tall man who looks like he's with her, and thinks he lived upstairs from the girls in Glasgow. She sees his son, who's the spitting image of him, march over and start talking to Daisy, who looks a little startled.

People keep coming, some with babies and toddlers, the adults all kissing and hugging each other before filing into the building. Once inside, Rose can focus on her daughter properly. She is so overawed by the sight of the beautiful bride in the stunning red dress that she is unable to speak. She sees Ryan glancing at Hannah, perhaps a little taken aback by how different she looks today – so radiant and self-assured. Hannah smiles at Ryan, a big, broad smile which says she's ready for this, and that it promises to be the best day of her life.

Hannah's mother is conscious of her husband squeezing her hand as she takes her seat at the front, but she can't look at him now; she knows it'll set her off if she does. Instead, she fixes her gaze upon the couple standing before her as the wedding begins.

Read on for Fiona's tips for a perfect girlie weekend away

Fiona's perfect girlie weekends away

The Great Escape was inspired by my love of a girlie weekend away. In the book, Hannah, Sadie and Lou have very different reasons for craving a bit of respite from everyday life, and I'm convinced that a couple of days with your best girlfriends can be a real sanity saver. Of course, escaping with your partner and family is wonderful too, and I cherish the two weeks each summer when the five of us go away together. But there's something about being with old friends – the ones who've known me for decades – that lifts the spirits in a different way.

Of course, there are different types of girlie weekend, and the key to making yours a success is matching the right kind of break to the right people. Here are some of my favourites.

The wild one: Throughout my twenties I worked on teenage and women's magazines, in offices staffed with lovely people who I still count as my closest friends now, twenty years on. Back then, we were all footloose (and, crucially, child-free) and would hop over to buzzy cities like Dublin, Florence, Paris and Berlin whenever funds allowed. I have to admit that these weren't exactly cultural trips. Once, on our ferry journey home from Amsterdam, a man marched over to where we were sitting, feeling a little fragile, and barked, 'Not so bloody lairy now, are you?'

'No,' we whimpered. It's safe to say that we hadn't seen the inside of any museums on that trip.

The restorative one: Ah, how times change. I might no longer be up for dancing all night but I still love getting together with my friend Jen, and wallowing in the bubbly rooftop pool of an Edinburgh spa. It's our once-a-year treat where we indulge in a bit of 'life planning', talking about where we're headed and what changes, if any, we'd like to make to our lives – all that life-coachy stuff you can pay a fortune for. It's a brilliant head clearer and puts a smile on my face for weeks afterwards.

The mums and kids one: As I write this, I've just come back from one of these weekends – complete chaos with three women and seven kids in a house we rented in Norfolk. There are always several small disasters – on one trip, unbeknown to us, one of the younger members of our party used the holiday house phone to call 118118 (120 times!) to ask 'the lady' to marry him. Quite reasonably, we were presented with the phone bill to pay a few weeks later. This time, one of my sons accidentally pierced a radiator in the games room with a dart, causing the dramatic spurting of water and frantic calls to a plumber. Luckily, there's been no bill for that one . . . yet.

The get-over-heartbreak one: After a big break-up I took myself off to Barcelona with a friend, which worked wonders to set me back on track. It's a bit like having a drastic haircut when a relationship ends – you just want things to look and feel a bit different. When I came back, the flat we'd once shared no longer seemed like a sad little place. Barcelona is one of those cities where you can kick up your heels if you want to, but also have a more mellow time exploring and browsing.

The just-because one: As you grow older, you often find that close friends are scattered all over the country. Even phonecalls are tricky these days – most of us work full time and have families, and even emailing falls by the wayside. When I lived in London, I'd get together with friends whenever I liked. Since we moved to Scotland thirteen years ago, it's taken a little more planning – which is where the 'just-because' girlie weekend comes in. It's a brilliant way to enjoy a big chunk of time together, and I love it all – from late nights spent chatting, to lazy breakfasts over a pot of coffee, to exploring during the day. It brings everyone together again and it's so much more satisfying than a speedy drink after work. In fact, I think I'll plan another one right now . . .

FIONA GIBSON · MUM ON THE RUN

The dreaded mums' race at school sports day – every mother's worst nightmare.

Laura Swan hopes to wriggle out of it – but her daughter's not taking 'no' for an answer. Racing against the super-fit mums is bad enough. What Laura hadn't bargained for was spotting her husband Jed, smirking on the sidelines with his delectable colleague Celeste . . .

Laura decides it's time for drastic action. She steals her son's trainers, drags herself around the local park – and gets a lot more than she bargained for when she finds herself a cute new running buddy in Danny . . .

Is Laura falling hopelessly in love? And is it normal for a mother of three to buy saucy lingerie in the supermarket? *Mum on the Run* will have you cheering Laura on as she desperately tries to rediscover her true self – and her pre-motherhood, wobble-free tum.

From the bestselling author of *Mummy Said the F-word* and *Lucky Girl*.

AVON

£6.99
ISBN: 978-1-84756-249-4